Owlfeather

Book 2 of the Blodeuedd Trilogy

Christiana Matthews

C M Matthews

Published by C. M. Matthews

Toowoomba Qld 4350 Australia

Cover design: Joolz and Jarling

Map and Dafona's Family Tree: Zenta Brice

Edited by: Emma's Edit

Proofread by: Maddy216@Fiverr

Publisher's note: This is a work of fiction. Names, characters, places and incidents, while based on the Welsh Mabinogion, are the product of the author's imagination. Welsh place names are used, but this is a mythic landscape and bears no relation to the actual places. Any resemblance to actual events or persons, living or dead, is entirely coincidental.

Owlfeather/Christiana Matthews – 1st ed

Paperback edition: ISBN: 978-0-6453369-8-6

Electronic edition: ISBN: 978-0-6453369-7-9

"The most powerful weapon on earth is the human soul on fire."

—*Ferdinand Foch*

Contents

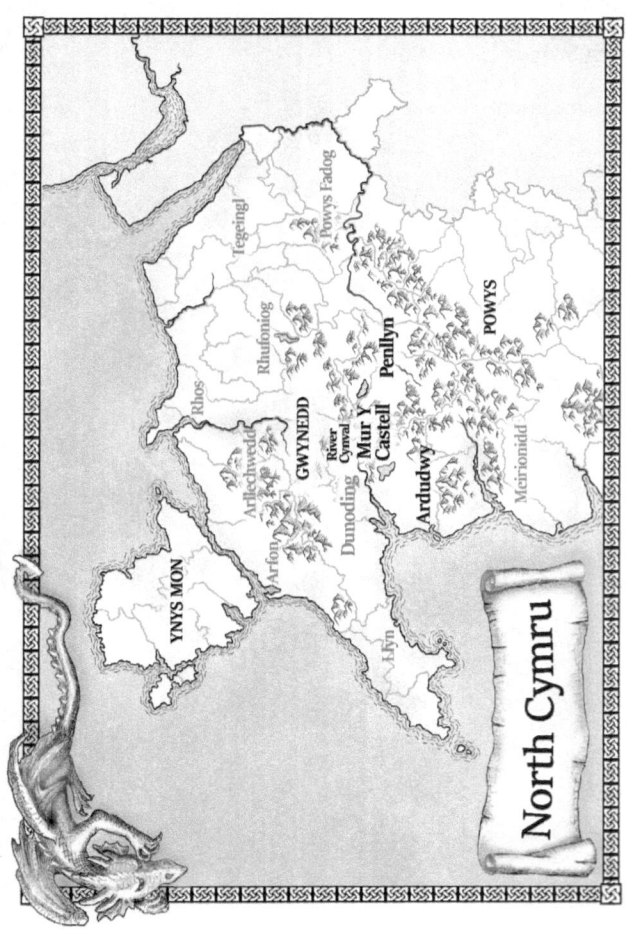

North Cymru

The Line of Dafona

PROLOGUE

Math ap Mathonwy, King of Gwynedd, climbed over the last boulder in his path and jumped down onto the beach. Grey clouds loomed overhead, and slate-dark breakers crashed upon the shore.

Impervious to the weather, Math set off along the sand. He had only a vague idea where to find that which he sought, but he knew it lay in one of the many caves lining the coast. Closing his eyes, he extended his magical senses, hoping the image he held in his mind would be enough of a link to its location.

The tomb of a dragon.

Excitement tingled across his broad, leather-clad shoulders and down his back. He'd only met two of the great beasts, and centuries had passed since then. He even came close to feeling grateful to his nephew, Gwydion ap Don, for making this trip necessary—almost.

Over a year ago, Gwydion, known as the Trickster, had stolen a drove of pigs from Pryderi, Prince of Dyfed. This had led to war between Dyfed and Gwynedd, at the start of which Pryderi had challenged Gwydion to a duel.

Scoundrel that he was, Gwydion had cheated, choosing to fight with a blade made from a dragon's claw. Deadly and nigh unbreakable, the sword had broken Pryderi's weapon and killed the prince. Disaster had then followed. Not only had the ensuing battle been bloody and bitter, resulting in far too many casualties on both sides, but Math had then discovered that an innocent woman—a woman he loved deeply—had been raped by his nephews.

As punishment, Math had transformed Gwydion and his brother Gilfaethwy into a pair of beasts and condemned them to remain in that form for a year. Not only that, but he'd made one male and the other female, and forced them to mate with each other—the most fitting penance he'd been able to think of. A bitter smile twisted his lips at the memory.

The problem of the dragon sword's existence he'd solved by first confiscating the thing, then giving it into the keeping of his brother-in-law, Beli of the Gates. That left the sword's source: the dragon itself. As soon as Gwydion regained human form and the use of his hands, he'd hasten back to the cave and replace the claw with another. Math would bet his wand and his crown on it.

That must not be allowed to happen. Math intended to remove the dragon's remains from the reach of Gwydion or anyone else who might seek them. When the dragons had departed Cymru—and elsewhere—for parts unknown, they'd hidden their tracks well. Gwydion had apparently stumbled across the cave by chance, and it had taken Math a full year of sifting through a lot of fishermen's sometimes highly embellished stories to find it. But the effort had proved worthwhile.

A frisson of heat prickled over his skin, a sign that he was close. Magic called to magic, and that of the dragon, imperceptible to humans and even some immortals, whispered throaty nothings to him in an ancient lover's voice.

A little higher up, above the high tide line, a dark fissure showed among the rocks. Sure-footed as a goat, Math clambered up and squeezed through the entrance. As caves went, it wasn't especially large, and the space was made suffocatingly cramped by a pile of huge bones. Most had scattered and fallen. Only the massive skull, the size of a large chariot, identified the creature they'd once belonged to. With teeth like stalactites and eye sockets as deep as the maw of Annwfyn, the dragon seemed to claim the cave as its own, warning interlopers to disturb its rest at their peril.

Math reached up to rest a hand on its smooth, age-polished cheekbone. "I'm sorry, Great One, but I'm afraid I must give you a fitting farewell. Knowing my nephew, he'll soon come back to desecrate your remains once more. How did you come to this pass, I wonder? Were you injured in a battle with another of your kind, or did age finally catch up with you?"

Dragons lived to a great age, but unlike Math and his kindred, they weren't immortal. There were very few of them left. Evidently, this one had crawled into the cave to die, but there was no way to tell how that death had come about. Dragons were more than monstrous, bat-winged, flame-eating, fire-breathing predators. Because they'd originated in the mortal, not the Otherworld, their magic was incompatible with Math's, and would resist any attempts to scry the dragon's past. No doubt he could achieve it, given time, but he had more important things to do than waste magic on such frivolities.

He uttered a prayer to the great ones of old and gathered his magics about him. Light swirled through the cave, lending the pale grey walls an opalescent sheen. Notes of music hummed through the dragon bones, brought to life by magic. When it swelled to a crescendo, the light rivalled the sun, burning along the bones in an ecstasy of god-fire.

The creature's size, combined with the echo of dragon-magic still clinging to its bones, made the process time-consuming. And even for a god of the Cymru, it took effort.

Outside the cave, the hidden sun sank below the mountains, and the sea changed from grey to black, silvered in fitful bursts by the moon when she broke through the clouds. Night fled and dawn came again before Math's magic ran its course, but at last nothing remained of the dragon bones but a pile of ivory dust.

Sweat sheened his brow, and his breath came in ragged gasps. He sank onto a rock and considered the pale dust coating his hands. What next? Should he sweep the remains out to sea? No, that seemed disrespectful. Better to let nature and the Great Goddess dispose of them in her own time.

To be certain no one else could find the dragon's tomb, Math pulled the surrounding boulders across the cave's entrance before he left. At last, satisfied that he'd made all secure, he turned and headed inland to his castle at Caer Dathyl and his beloved queen, Goewin of the raven hair.

1

FORTRESS

The summer months were long over in my domain of Ardudwy in Cymru, and restful autumn, too, was almost done. In the middle distance my newly expanded castle glowed softly golden in the sunlight, and the trees surrounding it blazed in hues of red, bronze, and orange. The end of the Ivy month was drawing near, with the festival of Calan Gaeaf, which marked the first day of winter, fast approaching.

I loved trees. They made me feel safe and secure. So, when the need arose to fortify my castle, Mur Y Castell, I sought to build a living barrier rather than erect walls made of stone.

The process had proved unexpectedly challenging. I'd expected problems when tackling the entire cantref, but one medium-sized castle and grounds ought not to have tested me so greatly. To weave a barrier from living plants without harming them wasn't easy, I discovered. An encircling hedge of briars would be ideal, but that would disrupt the natural landscape. My aim was to retain the trees in their places but make them grow thicker. Much thicker.

"Why do you need an inner ring of protection?" asked Cynar ap Garnoc, my newly appointed seneschal, on a crisp, clear autumn day. "If they can't get past the borders of Ardudwy, won't that be enough?"

I dragged my attention away from the ancient, gnarled yew in front of us. Part of a massive stand of trees encircling the outer walls of Mur Y Castell, this was the grandmother of them all. "We're talking about

Gwydion, Cynar. Nothing short of divine intervention will be enough to stop him."

Cynar grunted, dark brows drawing together. "Aye, Lady Blodeuedd, but we know that's not likely, seeing he's one of them."

By them, of course, he referred to the gods of Cymru. Gwydion was the son of Don, the great mother goddess, and her consort, Beli Mawr. He was also, in a sense, my father—or at least my progenitor, having made me out of flowers as a wife for his nephew Lleu. My creator...and my nemesis.

Several new trunks ringed the enormous yew, where its drooping branches had buried themselves in the earth and taken root. I stepped up to caress the parent tree, encouraging it to make more and more youngsters. I planned to ring my home with an impenetrable green barrier which would confound even a god.

Or possibly two of them. My husband Lleu was still recuperating in his great-uncle's Otherworldly castle, Caer Dathyl, after I'd turned him into an eagle and Gwydion had subsequently transformed him back into a man. He'd been languishing there for a while. I would have suspected him of malingering, but I could admit that several changes of form in a relatively short space of time might take some getting over. Not that I objected to his prolonged stay in Caer Dathyl, if it meant he stayed far away from me. I had no desire to see my ex-husband again. *Ever.*

For Lleu was the immortal Lord of Summer, King of the Oak, and I'd given my heart to his opposite number. The man who now ruled by my side was the mortal champion of winter, Goronwy Pebyr, the Holly King. My second husband.

Satisfied that I'd successfully imparted my desire to the yew, I turned back to Cynar. We had started early and had had no break since lunch time. "That will be enough for today, I think. I don't know about you, but I'm completely exhausted. Tomorrow I'll add different varieties—oak, alder, ash, and others—and later plant some flowers beneath them. I need that jolt of colour."

My seneschal nodded and bowed awkwardly. After being attacked by one of Gwydion's sons in his boar form, Cynar had suffered nerve damage, resulting in him losing the use of one arm. Consequently, he always wore a sling.

"Let me know how many labourers you need," he said. "I'll organise them for you. You'll have no shortage of volunteers. The young men especially are eager to serve you, to prove their devotion and loyalty."

I smiled. My second term as Lady of Ardudwy might have begun under circumstances less than ideal, but both Goronwy and I had proved equal to the challenge. For most, the resentment at having their lord replaced by his rival had quickly faded. For a few, the canker grew and spread, but none dared to challenge him. Not my wonderful Winter King.

Perhaps we should have followed my original intention in the wake of Lleu's spearing and subsequent transformation: to run. Go north, past the land of the wild Picts to Orknyar, the place of the ancients. But we had Goronwy's nephew Rhun and his extended family to think of, as well as Cynar and his pregnant wife, the pretty, red-headed Delith. Once my handmaiden, and now my most trusted friend. I'd known Delith almost all my life.

For the other young married women of my household that would be between twenty and twenty-five years, but although we looked of an age, Delith and her peers had lived a lot longer than me. Math and Gwydion had created me a mere six years ago. Consequently, I'd never had a childhood, and still experienced occasional gaps in my knowledge of the world. Gaps which Delith and my increasing circle of friends daily helped me to fill.

"How is your lady wife?" I asked.

Cynar groaned. "Tired, ravenous, cranky, and getting bigger by the day. At the moment she's fixated on blackberry pie, which is both good and bad. Good because the fruit's plentiful at this time of year; bad because it's my favourite too, and I lack her excuse for gaining weight."

I laughed and laid a hand on his bound arm. "Don't worry—I'll keep you so busy you'll work it all off in no time. But I too am fond of blackberry pie. Perhaps you'll share some with me?"

"Of course, my lady."

After cleaning the grime from my violet linen gown and my person, something I could achieve merely by thinking of it, I followed him to his new quarters. These were a luxurious suite of rooms in Mur Y Castell's most recently completed wing. My home was now as much a masterpiece as my garden, thanks to the young architect named Bryn I'd first met in Caer Dathyl, shortly after my creation. I'd invited him to work his magic on Mur Y Castell, remodelling and expanding it, when Goronwy and I had taken over as its lord and lady. I needed to expunge the memory of its previous lord—to make it indisputably mine.

Delith looked up as we entered, setting aside the tiny pot of lavender-scented unguent she'd been stirring. Cynar's cousin Modwenna, who'd also been one of my handmaids, took it from her. Gently, she set it and the accompanying dainty spoon on the carved oak cabinet against the wall.

Delith scowled at her companion. "I can get up and down by myself," she protested, rocking clumsily to her feet. "Why I ever contemplated doing this for a second time I really don't know."

Modwenna and Cynar exchanged a glance of shared laughter, but unfortunately Delith saw it.

"Wait until it's your turn," she muttered darkly. "Whoever described pregnant women as glowing either meant we were about to explode or were mealy-mouthed liars. I don't know why we can't simply lay eggs. I'd rather be a duck or a goose right now."

"I have heard of red-headed ducks," said Modwenna, bouncing Delith's year-old firstborn on her knee. "But I believe they're the males of the species, like little Garth here. The females are just dirty brown, like me. And the rest of their plumage is nowhere as fine as yours, Del. That colour suits you so well."

I tutted, sinking into the chair Cynar drew up for me. "Dirty brown! What sacrilege to describe your hair so. It's the colour of a tawny owl's feathers, soft and beautiful. You're right about the gown, though. I excelled myself with that batch of blue dye."

"The three of you look like a peacock, standing together," offered Cynar over his shoulder. "Blue, green and rich purple." He disappeared into the adjoining room, which would be allocated to the baby after it arrived, but in the meantime had devolved into a scrap room. I heard the sound of pottery clinking together, and he reappeared a few moments later carrying three plates of pie.

He was right about the clothes; I'd indeed had peacocks in mind when I selected the last batch of dyes. Thankfully, I'd added my own dye yards to the working areas of our castle. That had been one of the few accommodations Lleu had agreed to make for me in its planning. Everything else was arranged for his comfort, which Goronwy admittedly also appreciated. I smoothed my violet-blue skirts, admiring how well they complemented Delith's blue gown and Modwenna's green.

The dyers of Mur Y Castell had gained the reputation of being the best in Cymru, and beyond. I could use my touch as a mordant and coax colours from plants into cloth which no others could match. Few knew exactly how I was able to do so, and had I been asked to explain I probably couldn't have. However, dyers are canny folk with an eye on their balance sheets. Understanding my gift wasn't necessary to appreciate it, nor the profits it generated.

Cynar served up the pie, which was excellent. He hadn't exaggerated. Taking a seat, he pulled his wife onto his lap and put his good arm around her. She fed spoonfuls into his mouth, alternating with her own.

The rest of the afternoon passed in pleasantries. We discussed the new additions to the stables and their merits, the birth of several litters of puppies, a few betrothal announcements...and, of course, the preparations for the upcoming festival of Calan Gaeaf. Regretfully, as twilight descended, I refused a second helping of pie and prepared to descend to the Great Hall. I hadn't realised how hungry I was, or how physical the day's work had been, but I didn't want to ruin my appetite for dinner.

Modwenna's husband, Yestin, met us at the Hall's entrance. No longer the scrawny, shy youth I'd first met, Yestin had grown into a brawny, well-muscled man. A bull, as Goronwy had once named him. Behind him stood my love, my lord, Goronwy.

Delight fizzed through me, curving my lips, and filling my heart. Smiling dark eyes, curling dark hair, a tall and powerful frame. Men deferred to sandy Yestin and to handsome Cynar, but Goronwy's presence dominated the room. A stranger entering the hall would know at once who ruled here.

"How's the planting going?" he asked, training that slow smile on me.

"Slowly, but well." I slid into the seat he held out for me, savouring the delicious odour of leek soup wafting from the bowls set before us. "Enough to give me an appetite, certainly."

Goronwy nodded, dipping a large chunk of lavishly buttered dark grain bread into his soup. "It's an impressive wall of trees you've planted; the place looks like something out of myth...a secret glade enclosed by fey enchantments. I know you still need to add more, though. Do you have enough seedlings?"

"Once the current lot shoot, I will." I inhaled in pleasure as more food arrived: wild venison with a side dish of cow parsley and mushrooms.

"Aye, by witchcraft," muttered one of the junior bards sitting at the next table. "Dark times are coming."

I stiffened, Lotha's parting words echoing in my brain. The yawning pit of night eternal, the old toad had prophesied for me. Cursed by man and beast, he'd said, condemned forever as a harlot. But I didn't care how posterity remembered me, when I was surrounded by love in the here and now.

Others felt differently. Cynar surged to his feet, his good hand clenched in a fist. "What did you say?"

"Sit down, Cynar." Goronwy's voice remained calm, but his tight jaw and narrowed eyes proclaimed his displeasure. He crooked a finger. "You, young man, come here."

The boy—he was just a boy—blushed scarlet, rose shakily to his feet and approached, head hanging. "I... I beg pardon, my lord. I meant no offence."

"Yet you've caused it. You've insulted me, and worse, my lady. I could have you flogged, or turned away from Mur Y Castell, which would effectively end your career. No-one else would engage you. Do you want that to happen?"

"No, my lord. But..." He glanced back at his companions, none of whom seemed anxious to offer him support. "But that's what the others say. Gwydion is the poet's god, and we owe him honour. Besides, Lotha the Seer foretold it, didn't he? He said Gwydion will cast the betrayer into eternal night and restore Lleu, our rightful lord."

Cynar continued to scowl, and Goronwy's voice gained a bladed edge. "If Lotha's talents were so great, he'd have seen his own disgraceful end and taken steps to avoid it, don't you think? Instead, he died a traitor's death, like the rest of Gwydion's followers. Just as you are like to do, young man, if you continue sowing discord." He held the young bard's eye. "Will you apologise?"

The boy's eyes dropped to the floor. "Yes, my lord, my lady. I'm very sorry. I'll never mention it again."

Goronwy nodded. "Accepted. You're young yet and have doubtless been led astray by those who should know better. I'd advise you to form your own opinions in future, instead of parroting the views of others." He swivelled back to face me, smiling. "You were saying, *cariad*?"

I took my cue from him and continued as if there'd been no interruption. "Yes, the weather's been favourable, and even when it's not, I can coax my plants to grow."

The memory of Lotha's words kept intruding, but I shook them away and concentrated on the performance just begun by an older, wiser bard. The soil of Cymru grew songs and stories like weeds after rain, and this tale celebrated a local heroine—Dafona of the Birds. Not only were feathered creatures said to have been her constant companions, but she could communicate with them. Different versions of the story existed; in some, species was no barrier, while in others she was limited to birds native to Cymru, or, expanding a little, to the island of Prydain.

Like her descendant, Modwenna, Dafona had lived in Ardudwy. And according to legend, her gift had passed down her family line, daughter to daughter.

The song finished to enthusiastic applause, and rising from the table, Goronwy held his hand out to me. We departed arm in arm, still discussing my vision for the future. It would be the work of weeks, even months, to reinforce the borders of the entire cantref of Dunoding, but my helpers were legion. Together, we would implement my plan. And encircled by impenetrable forests, my domain would be as strong and secure as I could make it.

We were close to self-sufficient in Ardudwy, meaning I could afford to barricade our landward borders against the outside world. Our farmers, gamekeepers and fishermen could provide enough food, our weavers enough cloth, and our smiths the necessities of everyday life. And weapons—I had them make weapons, too. Every road in, every exit, I'd buttressed with layers of spells. Any forays into the outside world for necessary trade were always led by my trusted people, armed with prearranged signals alerting me when they wished to return. I'd disarm my spells briefly to allow them exit and re-entry, before replacing my magical wards. I'd begun to feel almost safe.

Only two other people knew the keywords: the path leading to the Otherworld I had to share with King Math, and the way to Penllyn, I'd entrusted to Goronwy.

I would have liked to enclose Penllyn as well, and indeed the whole of Dunoding, but two things stood in my way. Firstly, the lords of other cantrefs didn't relish being cut off from the outside world to benefit me in what they regarded as a purely private war. Secondly, it would have taken far too long. I had to be content with securing the borders of Ardudwy.

One potential entry remained unguarded—the heavens.

I glanced sideways at Modwenna, the last living descendant of the legendary Dafona in the direct female line. Because she and Cynar were cousins, he too could claim Dafona of the Birds as ancestress. But if any males of her family had possessed the ability to communicate with avian kind, there was no record of it. I'd asked Modwenna once if the gift had passed down to her, but she'd denied it.

However, I had an idea for an alternative. My erstwhile brother-in-law, Dylan Ail Don, could speak with all the sea creatures, including birds. Seagulls were endlessly inquisitive, and several ospreys made their nests along the cliffs. Perhaps he could recruit them for me. I'd work something out. If I couldn't yet cast nets of arcane power across all the skies of Ardudwy, at least I could safeguard the coast.

2

CONFRONTATION

Strange as it might seem for a woman made of flowers and with such a close affinity to the earth, I loved the sea. I swam often for pleasure and exercise, even as the seasons turned colder.

My forests grew as close as I could coax them to the water's edge, but swimming left me vulnerable. Normally I had Dylan's protection, but periodically he'd be called away on mysterious 'business' or feel impelled to spend time with his selkie lover, whose home lay to the north. In his absence, Goronwy insisted on accompanying me whenever I ventured onto the beach, but I thought it unlikely that Gwydion would seek me there. He wouldn't expect me to commune with seaweed and shells. As late autumn edged towards winter, I continued to swim in my free time.

It wasn't a great distance, and we could have easily walked down to the shore from the castle. But because Goronwy always wanted to return as quickly as possible, we rode, and let the horses graze while he fished and I swam or walked. Manon, the faerie steed Arianrhod had given me, became too easily bored, so I left her to entertain herself in the surrounds of Mur Y Castell. Instead, I rode the lovely bay mare, Taffy. Goronwy took her brother, Eilio.

With Calan Gaeaf only a few days away, the days grew shorter and colder, so my swims became shorter as well. One day, after quitting the icy water and taking a brisk walk along the beach to warm up, I was surprised by a cry for help from the rocky headland above. I looked around for Goronwy and saw him some distance away, hauling in a fish. Not wanting to disturb him, I climbed up to investigate alone.

The trees which kept all others at bay parted smoothly before me. Further along the trail, I found the source of the cry. A woman lay on her side, nursing one foot, with her skirts rucked up and her hose and shoes splattered with mud. Stranger still, I recognised her.

"Cara!" I exclaimed. "What are you doing here? And what's happened? You're hurt!"

Cara had once been a kitchen maid in Mur Y Castell. She'd left during the overlordship of Cynar's deceased brother, Emlyn, who'd been one of Gwydion's followers. I had never found out where Cara had gone. Truth to tell, I hadn't been that interested.

She threw out a hand, gesturing to the enveloping forest. "I was travelling back home to Ardudwy to visit my mam but couldn't get through. There are trees grown right across the track, did you know? I tried to go around, but the undergrowth's so thick it's like a jungle. Would've taken a sickle or knife, which I don't have. So I tried to climb over, got tangled and fell. Think I've twisted my ankle."

I frowned. This was why I'd posted guards until my magical barriers were complete—to sort those with legitimate business from unwelcome intruders. "Did you come here by boat? I didn't see any down by the shore."

"No. No, I've come south, from Arfon," she moaned, clutching her injury. "It's not that far if you know the ways, and I've lived here for most of my life. Seems to have changed a lot, though."

"So why didn't you come by the main road? My people would have alerted me, and I'd have allowed you through. You didn't need to try to plough through the forest."

"I had no time for that, my lady. Mam's ill—I wanted to get to her right away. I wasn't planning to go anywhere near Mur Y Castell. I wouldn't have bothered you or your new lord. I just want to see my mam."

Which still didn't explain why she'd thought trying to negotiate her way through a trackless thicket would be her best choice. I put those questions aside for later and focused on the immediate problem, going to my knees beside her to examine her foot. I'd seen many sprained ankles and broken bones when helping the healers, and this didn't appear to be either.

"I think you're right," I said, straightening. "It's just twisted—strained rather than sprained. Here, let me help you sit up, and I'll fetch my husband. He's down by the beach, not far away."

Putting my arm around her shoulders, I helped lever her into a sitting position. She rubbed her afflicted foot and gripped my arm. "Oh no, don't trouble him. It feels a bit better now. If you give me a lift, my lady, I think I can stand."

I did so, looking down at the muddy wicker basket which she clutched by her side. "What's in there?"

"Stuff for me mam. Vittles and suchlike, and a new rug I've made for her. She's getting on, you know, and feels the cold something cruel these days. See?" Leaning against me, she opened the corner of the basket to display a tawny woollen blanket.

I wondered idly what else she had in there, and why she seemed to want to keep it hidden. Stolen goods, perhaps? No; I had no reason to distrust her, apart from an instinctive dislike.

"That's sweet of you," I said, determined not to let my feelings show. "It certainly does look warm."

We pottered along for a while, Cara hobbling, and me matching my gait to hers. I spoke the spell needed to get us through the barrier to return to the beach track, and was startled by a repetitive, piping whistle from overhead. I looked up but saw nothing.

"Oof!" Cara stumbled, bumping against me. "Basket's getting heavy. Would you mind carrying it for me, my lady? My ankle's so sore."

"Of course." I halted, genuinely contrite. The way ahead was steep, too, and slippery with leaf mould. "I'm sorry, I should have thought of that."

"Not all you should have thought of," Cara muttered reprovingly.

My spurt of compassion faded. "What's that supposed to mean?"

She looked away. "Nothing really. It's just..." Her fleeting, sidelong glance held nothing of subservience. "Just that I was never so shocked in all my life as when I heard what happened to Lord Lleu. Some say you had a hand in that, you and your man. Of course, I'm happy for you both. Can't keep on grieving, can we? Even if it is a bit of a step down for you. I mean, who'd choose a mortal man over a god, given the choice?"

Heat rose in my cheeks. "Goronwy's worth ten of Lleu, and I'm perfectly happy with my choices. I married him because I love him, even if he is mortal. As for Lleu, he deserved his fate. He didn't care for me; he never has. He'd had a mistress for years, and only married me in the first place so he could be with her."

She sniffed. "Don't matter. We girls don't choose who we marry. Our parents do, because they're better able to judge. You were wed to Lord Lleu and should have honoured your marriage vows. At least, that's how I was taught. I s'pose things are different for the high-born. Meaning no disrespect, my lady."

"Honour them no matter what? Believe me, Lleu was guilty of far worse things than betraying me in the marriage bed. He's a killer, and he planned to kill Goronwy. Not out of jealousy, which I suppose you might condone, but to shore up his own power."

She looked frankly disbelieving. I knew I couldn't offer her an adequate explanation if she believed, as did Gwydion, that a wife must be bound to the husband chosen for her, having no say in her parents' choice. Nor would she accept my views that balance should be maintained between the Oak and the Holly Kings. No doubt she thought Lleu had the right to do whatever he pleased because he was a god. If she even knew he was a god.

"Do you understand Lleu's nature?" I asked, helping her down the slope. "Or Gwydion's? Do you know they're both Children of Don?"

Cara nodded, her expression adoring. "Aye, that I do. Gods, both of them, and worthy of worship." She laughed softly. "Who'd ever have thought I could tempt a god to my bed?"

What! Shock pulled me up short. Gwydion and Cara? No, it wasn't possible. Was it? The look on her face said it was, and on reflection, it aligned with all I knew about Gwydion. Seduce an easily impressed girl, and plant her as a spy in my household. Yes, it was entirely possible.

I snorted and started moving again. "You surprise me. I've always suspected Gwydion preferred men. Look at how obsessed he is with Lleu. Seems odd, don't you think?"

"Lord Lleu's his son!" she blurted out, horrified. "What you're suggesting is incest. My Gwydion would never do something like that, he wouldn't."

I laughed. "You don't know your Gwydion very well, but I suppose that can be forgiven. He is, after all, called the Lord of Lies. Callous, manipulative, cruel... I can't think of a single good thing to say about him, really."

Cara gasped, her face flaming. "That's not true! He's an upright, moral person, not like you and... and that usurper you got sitting in the Hall beside you at Ardudwy. I wonder how the men stand it, working for the likes of him. Taking the place of their rightful lord and all."

The irony was obviously lost on her. I didn't bother pointing it out. "Funnily enough, most like the change. They not only find Goronwy much easier to talk to and less prone to favouritism, but he takes a much keener interest in the affairs of the estate. Under him, Ardudwy is thriving as never before. And I am its lady, so I'll thank you to keep your seditious opinions to yourself from now on."

Brows drawn together, Cara seemed uncertain what to make of that. After a few minutes of silence, she shrugged and sniffed disdainfully. "That's as may be. But it ain't right, at all, it ain't."

By then we'd emerged from the trees and reached the trail which led to the beach. Cara kept glancing upward at the now visible sky. Looking for Gwydion? Given the trend of our conversation, that seemed likely. I suppressed the temptation to shove her away and leave her there in the forest to rot. She'd probably poison my trees.

From then on, I too scanned the heavens. No red kites marred the serenity yet, but our resident sea-eagle passed overhead. Once, then again, and again, back and forth. Swooping and circling in endless, conscientious patrol.

Even if I hadn't been watching for it, Cara's delighted gasp would have altered me to the red kite's appearance. He swept across from the northern horizon, smaller and sleeker than the eagle, and almost as swift. Not swift enough, though.

Still gripping my arm, Cara stopped in her tracks. I heard her indrawn breath of delight. "My lord!"

I believed her. This wasn't just any kite.

He dived, screaming, and the eagle flipped onto its back. A broad, muscular wing swept upward, batting the smaller bird away. Gwydion pivoted, shrieking shrilly, and planed up again, talons extended. He meshed his feet with the eagle's, and for a long, heart-stopping moment both plummeted to the earth.

Both birds twisted, upside down, wings spread and wicked, hooked claws entangled. Then the eagle bore skyward, screaming its defiance, with the kite dangling beneath. A heartbeat later they disengaged, and the red kite turned and fled.

Cara gasped, her face white. "No! No, that can't be. How can a mere bird defeat my lord Gwydion?"

I laughed. "He's not as all-powerful as you thought, is he?"

She drew another shaky breath, her nails digging into my flesh as if she too had talons. "You can't keep him away forever. Ardudwy belongs to Lord Lleu, and his uncle will take it back for him. You and your fancy man have no place here. It's wrong, so it is."

I detached her hand from my arm, noting that she remained steady. Her injury seemed to have miraculously healed. Tracking through the dense forest cover, we'd returned to the shore at a gentler angle than the one by which I'd ascended. My husband was now visible, standing among the rocks further along the beach with his rod in his hand. Fish heads and tails protruding from the wicker creel at his feet attested to his success.

"Goronwy!" I called. "Look who I found. Cara's decided to pay us a visit."

Confronting my husband obviously didn't fit into Cara's plan, whatever it had been. She dropped her basket, picked up her skirts, and ran.

Curious to see where she was headed, I let her go. Apart from avoiding Goronwy, who'd looked up at my hail and begun walking towards us, she apparently had no real goal. Head down, hair come loose from its bun and whipping around her face, she stumbled through the sand. I could hear her harsh breathing.

"Foolish girl," I muttered, loping after her. Goronwy also broke into a run, and Cara, glancing behind her, let out a strangled cry and collapsed on the beach.

"What were you trying to do?" I asked, coming level with her. "I know you weren't really injured. Did Gwydion send you back to Mur Y Castell to spy on me?"

"He didn't ask," she gasped, sitting back on her haunches and looking up at me with a kind of wild defiance. "Didn't need to. I offered. Thought he deserved to know what evil you and him were getting up to." She jerked her chin at Goronwy, then turned her head and spat, lips twisted and eyes glittering with malice. "Dark deeds, I'll bet."

"What in the Lady's name is she on about?" Goronwy had drawn close enough to hear her last comment.

"Foolishness. Nothing worth noting." I reached down to grab Cara's hair, twisting the loose strands around my fist. "But we might have to transform a room into a prison, at least for a while. Either that, or…" I stepped to one side and drew a finger across my throat with an accompanying hiss. I also winked.

Goronwy saw the wink, but Cara couldn't. She gasped. "You wouldn't!"

I smiled, tight-lipped. "Why not? I'm evil personified, remember? And trust me when I say I'll do whatever it takes to keep my lands safe from Gwydion, and from Lleu. But for now, I'll settle for locking you up for a while. Even if this was all your idea, I'd be surprised if he bothers to retrieve you. Gwydion's helpers are always expendable."

Goronwy raised his eyebrows at me.

"Tell you about it later," I said, answering his unspoken question. I reached for Cara's discarded basket. "Now, let's see what you have here."

The blanket proved to be the largest item: a square of woven wool in shades of old ivory, ochre, moss green and amber. Although large enough to cover a good-sized bed, it didn't account for all the basket's weight. An oiled packet of spiced sausages and several pottery jars of jams and relishes added more bulk. The lightest item was a small, soft cushion, embroidered with a floral design which felt as if it had been filled with down.

At the bottom, tucked beneath the blanket, I found half a dozen black-banded, rufous feathers, tied with a strip of red ribbon.

Holding them out to Goronwy, I said, "I'd like to break these up into tiny pieces, but if they've been bespelled, that might not be wise. However, I don't feel comfortable taking them with us."

"Bespelled!" Cara's eyes widened, her mouth pinched. "They're no such thing. That's a love-gift, a keepsake from my lord. Give it here!"

I swayed away from her, holding the feathers gingerly between the forefinger and thumb of my other hand. "All right, bitch, you wanted to return to Mur Y Castell. Let's go."

3

TRAINING

Cynar and his kin weren't my only supporters. I also had a god on my side—Math ap Mathonwy, the King of Gwynedd and brother of the mighty Don. Although I'd been unaware of it in the beginning, Math had been a constant presence in my life from the moment I'd stepped out of his silver cauldron. From the time he and Gwydion, between them, had first made me.

After Lleu and I had departed Math's castle for our own home at Mur Y Castell, Math had remained with us—in disguise. Owain, he'd called himself, posing as Lleu's Master of Horse. When I'd speared Lleu, he'd abandoned his masquerade and offered me his open support.

But even with Math's backing, the shadow of Gwydion still hung over us all. Like the rest of the Cymric lands, we lacked a prison system. Therefore, I'd detained Cara in an unoccupied guest room until I worked out what to do about her. All my guards were armed with bows or slingshots, and orders to shoot if any kites appeared, but so far none had.

Still, I remained uneasy. My first impulse after locking Cara up had been to find Math and ask his advice about those feathers, but he was nowhere to be found; nobody had seen him for several days. I put the matter aside temporarily and continued working on my green fortifications.

About to leave the compound early next morning, I was brought up short by a sudden blurring of the air, like a heat haze, just outside the gates. The smudge became a shadow, then solidified into the shape of a horse and female rider. A tall, confident woman astride a black mare with a silver mane and tail, bound with scarlet ribbons.

Gently smiling, the statuesque newcomer dismounted, patted the mare's neck, and looked around with an air of polite interest. She was impeccably groomed, smooth-skinned and elegant; each finger was tipped with a crimson nail, echoing the silk sheen of her dress. I had no need for an introduction. Arriving in that manner, confident of welcome, she could be none other than Math's wife—Queen Goewin of the raven hair.

Until this day, I'd never met her face to face. I didn't know that much about her. Math had talked about her constantly, but only in glowing inanities which revealed little. I understood her to be well-versed in magic, including that of my domain, the natural world, as well as excelling in divination and the power of words. Math said she retained a lingering fondness for Lleu, alongside a burning dislike of Gwydion and an abiding contempt for his brother. She loved horses, snakes, and the sea. Shades of red and purple delighted her, and she was partial to gems set in gold.

Other than that, I hadn't known what to expect—except that she was reputed to be beautiful. Stunningly, breathtakingly beautiful.

Gwydion had created me to be the helpmate of a god, a perfectly crafted jewel. Yet compared to Goewin I felt like a laundry maid. I'd heard bards extol her praises in every realm from Powys to Kurnow, from Lloegyr to Orkneyjar. Some compared her to the golden warmth of autumn or the vibrancy of springtime; others invoked the sparkling frost of winter or a bright and dazzling summer's day. She was all those things, and none of them. Words did not exist in any human tongue to do justice to the Otherworldly Queen of Gwynedd.

Gliding across to me—it seemed unutterably crass to describe Goewin as performing an activity so humdrum as walking—she spoke in a voice as rich and sweet and warm as sun-kissed berries.

"Blodeuedd!" Taking my hand in her cool grasp, she kissed me on the cheek. "How lovely to finally meet you. I apologise for the lack of warning, but I did mention to Math the last time we spoke that I might be popping by." She laughed. "From your expression, I gather the ill-mannered creature failed to pass the message on. He tells me you've agreed to magic lessons. Is that so?"

I nodded mutely, still bedazzled by her presence and her precipitate arrival.

"I'm sure you'll do well," continued Queen Goewin, patting my arm. "You were born of enchantment, after all, and Math describes you as a clever little thing. He likes that. My husband admires intelligent women."

From anyone else, such a comment might have sounded snide; from Goewin it was a simple statement of fact. I laughed. "Of whom you're a prime example, so the stories say."

Amusement gleamed in her eyes. Not dark brown or black, as I'd first thought, but a deep, pansy violet. "You should never put much faith in stories. They tend towards exaggeration. And you must call me Wynne, all my friends do. Let's go and find my thoughtless husband, shall we?"

She whistled, and the mare obediently trotted to her side. A fine-looking creature indeed, almost as striking as her mistress.

"Do you have urgent business with the king? I'm afraid he's not here at the moment." I fell into step beside her and retraced my steps back to the castle proper. Workers hurried to and fro in the yard, servants traipsing from one set of rooms to another, gardeners, dyers, weavers, cooks, and the healer's apprentices. A stable hand hurried up to see to the lady's horse.

Goewin—Wynne—handed the boy her reins with a smile and shook her head. "No, I've come to deliver a gift. Did you know it's his nameday tomorrow?"

I blinked. Somehow, I'd never considered Math having birthdays. Had he been born in the normal way, a squalling babe suckling at the breast of the greatest, eldest goddess? I'd always imagined him simply appearing in the world, much as his lady wife had just done on the path outside my home.

My expression must have broadcast my thoughts. Wynne shook her head, laughter dancing in her eyes, her lips curving into a perfect rosy bow. "Oh yes, Math and Don and all the rest were tiny godlings once, dancing through the skies on moonbeams in the dawning of the world. But of course, that event was so long ago, now he thinks it not worth celebrating. I disagree and like to give him a small memento every few decades or so."

So how old would she be? Snatches of a confusing conversation I'd had with Arianrhod several years ago teased my memory. I'd never fully understood exactly when Lleu had been born, but I knew Wynne had witnessed the event as an adult woman. And Lleu's lover Caron had first incarnated several centuries ago, before returning as Gwenavala, and later as Arlais. Which made Lleu at least several centuries old, and Wynne...

"Ah, there he is!" The object of my musings broke into an even broader smile and spread her arms wide.

Math had just entered through the main gate, wearing red and ochre battle leathers, a polished hazel wand dangling awkwardly from one hand. A pile of twigs cradled in both arms and pinned by his chin gave him the look of a well-dressed forester. He approached at a leisurely pace, dropped his burden, and swept his lady into his arms. Laughing delightedly, he swung her around in a circle, her crimson skirts fluttering like scattered rose petals.

"You're late." He set her down and kissed the tip of her nose.

Wynne widened her lovely eyes and fluttered her extravagant lashes. "Not at all. I'm a day early. Where have you been, and where are you off to with that thing?" She glanced down at the wand, which had slipped from the top of the pile to lie gleaming on the lawn. "And why are you carrying half the forest?"

"I've been collecting potential wands. I'd planned to get some practice in for Blodeuedd's training session before she returned from her planting, but I see you've waylaid her." He drew back, his arm around his wife's shoulders, and addressed me. "But seeing as she's here now...what about it, my lady? Are you ready for your first lessons in the finer application of magic?"

What? No, I wasn't ready. "Shouldn't the queen get settled in first?" I glanced back at her. "How long do you plan to stay? You're very welcome, of course, but I should summon servants to see to your..." My voice faltered. I'd almost said 'luggage', but she didn't appear to have any. Thinking back, I realised there'd been no saddlebags or anything else on her horse.

"My king will provide all I need," Wynne assured me airily. "And there's no need to delay proceedings on my account. Indeed, I'd love to watch. I might learn some new techniques too, and I'm always eager to expand my repertoire."

I shrugged and resigned myself to an audience. Turning left, I led the way to the courtyard by the postern gate where Cynar had taught me and my ladies the means to defend ourselves against attackers. But this time I was to be the sole pupil, and I had a sinking feeling that Math's lessons would be harder by far.

I was right.

Wynne helped her husband carry his twigs, and after laying them in a pile on the grass, settled beside them. She seemed unworried about the prospect of stains on her beautiful silk. I knew I could repair them for her, but did she? Perhaps, perhaps not. Maybe she could do that herself. Math had said she was proficient in plant lore. While I puzzled over this, she waved her hands, inviting her husband to begin.

Math obliged her. For the next couple of hours, he attacked, physically and psychically, while I tried unsuccessfully to defend myself. True, he was a lot larger than me, giving him an unfair advantage—but that wasn't the whole of it. Craft as well as brawn kept him out of reach of my flailing fists, and the magic sparking from his wand prevented me from draping him in ivy or sweeping the dead leaves from beneath his feet to throw him off balance.

Twice I rolled away from the gusts of frigid air he threw at me to lie flat on my back on the ground, hands outspread and breathing hard. Math stepped back, wand swinging, and prepared to send another trail of icy pinpricks across my exposed face and hands. In the few breaths he allowed me, I drew upon the power of the earth and uprooted clods of soil to throw at him, grass roots and all.

That trick didn't serve a second time. Math swayed aside, caught the loam in an arcane net, and tossed it right back at me.

"You have to react instinctively," he said. "You already do when communing with nature; you know what the plants need without thinking about it. Use your defensive magic the same way."

"Ugh," I groaned, sitting up and wiping sticky mud from my face. "Can we stop now? I need to visit the privy. Also, it must be well past noon, and I'd like some lunch."

Math laughed and agreed to a brief respite. With an effort, I hauled myself upright and escorted my guest and her husband past my castle's glistening new walls to the Great Hall. Even on an overcast day, the faded light warmed the stone from sand to pale gold, and the new gardens foaming around the foundations and slowly finding purchase on their pristine walls would be a pastel sea of pale colour come springtime. Deep blue violets and the blooms of the winter's darling, hellebore, subtle and rich by turns, provided a dark contrast to the sharp white snowdrops and pale lilac crocus.

I soon found myself back in the courtyard, sustained and energised by some leek soup and crusty herb bread.

"Keep your guard up." Math spun his wand in a circle and adopted a warrior's stance. "Gwydion won't hesitate to use every advantage, should you meet him again face to face. Whenever that might be."

I knew time behaved oddly in Math's home of Caer Dathyl, and although by my reckoning Gwydion had returned there with the injured Lleu many moons ago, it might not have seemed so to him. "How is Lleu?" I asked.

"Don't worry," said Wynne from the sidelines. "He's mending, but slowly. His body's fully healed, but I suspect his mind might take longer. It's Gwydion you need to worry about."

"Aye," agreed Math, flashing her a brief smile. "But Wynne's ruled Caer Dathyl for years in my stead, and she's a cunning lass. She'll delay his departure for as long as she can, by trickery and magic."

Although grateful to Lady Wynne, I heartily hoped she'd take her husband home with her when she left. I leaned against the castle wall, barely noticing the bitter cold emanating from the stone, massaging my aching wrist and rotating my stiff neck.

Attuned to every nuance, scent and texture of the plant kingdom from the instant of my creation, I'd thought I couldn't have much more to learn. Math soon disabused me of that notion. He said I had to delve deeper. I'd thought my ability to recognise every plant that grew in Cymric lands would be all the protection I'd need, but no; he expected me to tune in to those across the border in Alba, Eriu and Lloegyr, as well as what grew on the seabed!

"Bloody Gwydion. Can't you just lock him up?" I asked the queen, knowing my question was rhetorical. Gwydion had paid for the ill he'd done to Caer Dathyl's lady long ago, and nobody but me would fault him for trying to help Lleu. Whatever measures she planned to use against him, she'd have to accomplish by stealth, leaving the rest of her people unaware of them.

Math straightened and shook his head, performing ever more complicated movements with his twig of hazel. "Wynne's doing all she can. She knows well how to manipulate the flows of time and the pockets of space—I taught her. In many ways Gwydion's more powerful, but he has no grasp of subtle magic."

"Feminine magic," clarified his wife. "I'll also do my best to create uncertainty in his mind about Lleu's chances of recovery. Such tactics won't last forever, though. You must be ready to confront him." She selected a twig of willow from the stack at her side and handed it to me. "Now, pay attention, Blodeuedd."

The raw wood in my hand differed radically from the work of art Math held. His wand's gyrations were making me dizzy. "How does waving a stick of wood around help me refine my power?"

Math drew a series of sigils in the air with the hand holding the wand, and sketched a courtly bow with the other. "All magicians need wands. It's part of our mystique. But first, we need to decide which tree you're attuned to. I've always suspected the willow. Let's see if I'm right. Now, sit down."

I heaved an exaggerated sigh and sank onto the damp grass, laying the willow twig aside. "If I catch cold, I expect you to cure me."

My attempt at humour was not appreciated. My instructor pointed his wand at me and prodded it, like a weapon. "Hands flat on the ground, connect with the earth. Close your eyes and tell me what you see."

Huffing out a breath, I did as instructed.

At first, nothing: I was too tightly wound. Slowly I released the pressure, breathing deeply, in and out—reaching for that calm, peaceful centre we all carry within us but can seldom access. In and out. In. Out. Slowly. And more slowly still, until I found her—the Goddess within.

Time stilled, and the tension in my body drained away. Images swam before my closed eyelids, murky unformed shapes in grey and brown and green, the shifting light on water. A pulse of power shot into my fingertips, clutched my wrists like a vice and travelled up my arms to wind around my heart.

I gasped and jerked, but kept my eyes closed. "The willow! It is a willow, I see it."

My vision showed me shamrock-green leaves on arching branches, cascading to the water. Twisted, nigh-indestructible roots holding the riverbanks together. Beautiful, elegant, and strong. They were re-silient, too. Even when severely pruned, willow regrows stronger than ever. Men tell of willow staves being stabbed into the ground and taking root, even if set into the soil upside down.

The King of Gwynedd laughed. The sound, his voice, seemed to come from far away. "As I suspected. The tree of intuition, illusion, and enchantment. Meadow-green child of the morning, whose leaves are shining tears of the sun. According to the poets, anyway. Perfect for a goddess crafted from flowers." A disturbance ruffled the air as he sank to the ground beside me, eyes still closed. "You can dispense with the wand, too, if you like. I was just teasing about that."

"No." I drew a breath and opened my eyes, reconnecting with the outer world. The air zinged with clarity, as fresh and inviting as the day I'd been made. Lifting my willow wand, I waved it in an arc, just as he'd done with the hazel twig. "I think I'll keep it as a reminder of who and what I am. Willows also symbolise immortality, don't they? And renewal. And like me, they're invaluable to healers."

Although I'd been born with an instinctive understanding of plants and their properties, my dealings with the healers had expanded my knowledge. I'd often helped them make an infusion from the bitter bark as a remedy for colds, fevers, and rheumatism. Patients were advised to chew young willow twigs for pain relief.

"The dyers appreciate us both, too," I added. "Willow bark pro-duces a lovely reddish brown, and can even be used to make cloth."

Wynne clapped, and Math grinned. "If you do plan to use the wand, you'll need to develop a bit more finesse." He drew a lazy figure eight in the air, then flicked the hazel rod in a spiralling zigzag which left trails of light in its wake. "Can you do that—draw power down with it?"

I tried. The figure eight came easily enough, and after several at-tempts I perfected the zigzag motion, but while it may have looked impressive, I felt nothing. No flare of energy, no change. It was another exhausting few hours of practice until a trickle of something flowed through the wand.

I let out a squeal of excitement, and the trickle promptly dried up. My instructor—my tormentor—sighed and bade me try again. And again. And again, until a tiny prick of pale green light glowed at the willow's tip.

At last Math desisted. My wrist cracked with every movement, my shoulder blazed with stabbing pain, and the grit of exhaustion rubbed against my eyelids.

"Well," he said, "you have the refinement of a turnip, but I suppose it's a start."

If I hadn't been so tired and sore, I might have slapped him, Otherworldly king or not. Instead, I closed my eyes and went limp as both tension and newfound power drained away. I'd almost got used to the sensation. It felt as if someone had fastened their lips to my bones and sucked the marrow right out of them. Had Gwydion materialised in front of me, I couldn't have offered any resistance. I had to hope that once I'd absorbed everything Math was trying to teach me, that would change.

Completely drained by the unfamiliar use of magic, I sagged against the nearest wall.

Math smiled. "Ah, I've pushed you hard, but you've done well. I think we're done for now."

He lifted me into his arms and carried me up to my opulent new room, with its rich carpets and brass lanterns and carved, painted posts. Wynne followed, offering praise at my progress. Before they left, I invited them to a banquet the following night to celebrate Math's nameday.

4

ENFYS

In hindsight, my impetuous decision to offer to host a party for King Math's nameday was foolish. As if my life didn't contain enough challenges! The head cook nearly had apoplexy when I explained what the event was to celebrate.

"A meal special enough to impress the King of Gwynedd, and his queen?" he spluttered. "With a single day's notice! I hope you're volunteering to help."

His tone left no doubt that if I failed to offer, I could expect cold porridge and wilted vegetables at table for the foreseeable future.

"You'll have all the herbs and spices you need," I assured him, and went out to my kitchen garden to pick only the best.

Winter being hunting season, we had plenty of venison in the larder to provide for the feast. I'd ask Dylan to ensure a good catch of seafood—fish, crabs, lobsters and oysters, as well as sea lettuce and porphyry laver. I collected bay leaves, juniper berries, rosemary, sage, savory, and sweet marjoram for the deer meat, basil, dill, mint, and parsley for the fish. The cook might not need them all, but at least I'd given him a wide choice.

That done, I collected Cara's basket and went to visit her mother. Mabli ferch Elen, wheelwright's widow and onetime castle chambermaid, lived in a tiny roundhouse cottage just outside the southern wall. It didn't take me long to get there; negotiating my vastly extended castle took more time than the walk across the grounds. A thread of smoke from the apex of the roof told me Mabli was home, and after rapping loudly on the doorframe, I lifted the rush flap and walked in.

The widow sat huddled on a stool before the small central firepit, rocking back and forth and mumbling under her breath. Her clothes looked clean, if rumpled, and wisps of thin grey hair had escaped her loose bun to frame her pale, wrinkled face. Despite sitting directly in front of the door, she didn't look up or acknowledge my presence. I wondered if she'd begun to go blind as well as deaf.

"Mabli? Old mother, it's Lady Blodeuedd." Two steps took me to her side; the one-roomed house was tiny. I bent to bring us eye to eye. "May I talk to you about something?"

She started, looked up with watery eyes, and stumbled to her feet. "Of course, my lady. Please, you ought to sit down." She indicated a second stool on the opposite side of the fire. "And...and mebbe a hot drink? I...I think I have..." Her voice trailed away, and she looked around helplessly.

"No, no." I laid a comforting hand on her arm. "Don't trouble yourself. I just want to talk about Cara. She tells me you're unwell, and I'm sorry to hear it. Can I help in some way?"

Mabli made a noise like a disgruntled sow. "That girl! It's worry about her that ails me, naught else. Five boys I had, and a single daughter to look after me in my old age and give me grandchildren to dandle on my knee. And what does she do but run off after that... that... *rheibwyr*! That Blaise! Rot his immortal hide."

Blaise was the alias Gwydion had used while living in Mur Y Castell. Pleased with the turn the conversation had taken without prompting from me, I took the seat offered. "Magic workers are an untrustworthy lot, it's true. Did Cara consort with many of them? Is that what led her to become Blaise's follower—a previous interest in sorcery?"

The old lady snorted. "Pah! He didn't have to enchant the little fool. A few kisses and a pat on the arse was all it took. T'was the wand between his legs she lusted for, nothing to do with his magic. I warned her. I warned her away from him, but she wouldn't listen to me. Too handsome by half, I said. Never trust a man who's better-looking than you, I said. He'll always put himself first."

A somewhat simplistic view, but as it summed up my ex-husband and his uncle pretty well, I didn't feel qualified to refute it. I tried to word the next part of my message as delicately as I could. "I'm sorry to tell you that her association with Blaise has led to problems for Cara. You see, his true name is Gwydion, and he's more than a simple magician. Cara knows that, too. It caused... friction between us, with the result that I now have her detained."

Silence. Mabli folded her arms on her chest and studied her knees. Eventually she looked up at me from beneath untidy grey brows. "Whereabouts?"

"In a guest room in the castle. I can take you to visit her if you'd like."

"Upstairs or down? I can't get up stairs, milady. I got bad knees."

My turn to stay mum. I'd placed wards around Cara's room and had no intention of allowing her to leave it. If Mabli couldn't go up, and Cara couldn't come down, their reunion would have to wait until I'd rehoused her.

Mabli didn't press the issue. Instead, she nodded to the item beside me. "What you got there?"

"This?" I'd almost forgotten about the basket. "Some gifts from your daughter." I laid the contents out on the wall ledge beside me, as the hut didn't have any table. Mabli ignored the bottled goods, but her eyes lit up at the sight of the lovely autumn-toned blanket.

"Would you like to try this sausage?" I asked, wishing I'd had the foresight to bring bread to sample the jam. A flagon of mead might not have gone astray either, or some honey-cakes as a bribe.

The old lady shook her head. "No, just leave it all there and I'll set it in the larder later. You can keep the basket, though. I got no use for that."

I set the basket aside. "Tell me more about Cara."

Mabli started rocking again. "Ah, she were a sweet child. Hair like down and yellow as meadowsweet, and such pretty eyes. Like bluebells, her da used to say. A good girl, but her brothers spoilt her. Should have had more girls. I asked the Mother, but it weren't to be. I remember a time..."

She rambled for a while about Cara's childhood exploits and misdemeanours, which didn't interest me at all. By the time we'd reached the golden girl's entry to womanhood, Mabli's eyes were drifting closed and her words barely decipherable. With a defeated sigh, I guided her to her bed and tucked the blanket around her before returning to my rooms to prepare for the feast.

The cook excelled himself that night. The meal was superb, followed by individual blackberry pies topped with thick clotted cream. There were bards performing, of course—works of prose and song, as well as jugglers and the usual entertainment—but the most memorable show that night was provided by the Queen of Gwynedd herself.

She bided her time until the bards paused for breath and a long drink of cider, and the jugglers refreshed themselves likewise, then rang a small silver bell to get everybody's attention. When all eyes were on her, she slid from her chair to kneel before Math.

"My lord," she said, eyes downcast, one hand in her lap and the other behind her back, "I've a special gift for you. To begin with, I thought of giving you the beast emblematic of your birth month, but frogs are jittery creatures and don't make good companions. So I sourced one for *my* birthday instead, to symbolise the enduring link between us."

Bringing her hidden arm forward, she held it out. A thick-bodied snake coiled there, its jewel-bright scales glinting with every undulating movement.

"I've called her Enfys," said Wynne with a beaming smile, "for the rainbow. Isn't she the most beautiful thing you've ever seen?"

I gasped, along with several others. I had nothing against serpents, and only one Cymric species is venomous. But this creature had not originated in Cymru, or anywhere else on Prydain's Island. Constrictors such as the one Wynne held were found far from our shores, and to my mind were more dangerous than any shy little adder. Those things could hug huge deer to death.

Math, obviously, saw the matter differently. With a smile that outshone even Wynne's, he reached out to touch the tips of his fingers to hers. The snake undulated from her arm to his and transposed itself to his torso, wreathing him in satiny rainbows.

"You've excelled yourself, my queen, something I wasn't sure could be possible. A question, though. What does she eat?"

"Mice," replied Wynne promptly.

"But we have so many cats," demurred Math, laughter etched in every line of his face. "Are you sure they won't be jealous?"

Wynne's lips twitched. "If they are, I doubt they'd do anything about it. This species is very aggressive, normally. When not soothed by magic."

"In that case, I should take steps to ensure she doesn't feel challenged in any way. I'm sure everyone in Mur Y Castell would sleep better." He gestured, and the serpent unwound itself from his torso, shrank to the dimensions of an earthworm, and curled around his left wrist instead. "And now, my queen, will you dance with me?"

Thus prompted, the musicians struck up a lively tune, and Math and Wynne demonstrated synchronised grace to my household. They leapt and spun and twisted, gaining in speed as the flutes and lutes increased in tempo. Wynne's long black hair was a silken fan, her violet gown a streamer. Math's physical eloquence matched hers, his smooth, assured movements those of a warrior translated to the dance.

When the music slowed again, Math stepped back and invited others into the circle, myself and Goronwy included. The music changed again, first slow and stately, then brisk and lively before swelling to a fast, staccato beat. We skipped and hopped, kicked and jumped, boots stomping and gowns swirling until the pitch of the music slowed again and the dancers halted, panting.

"Your husband tells me you have a somewhat troublesome guest," said Queen Wynne, slipping silently into the seat beside me. Unlike the rest of the company, now holding their sides and laughing, sagging against pillars, or flopping onto the benches, she showed no sign of discomfort. Even Math appeared out of breath as he returned to his chair.

I sighed, reminded that I still hadn't found a chance to ask him about Cara. "In more ways than one. I don't know exactly what kind of mischief she intended and can't be entirely certain I've thwarted her. Also, she's in the way here, but I can't very well let her go, can I?"

Wynne tsked sympathetically. "Why don't you tell me exactly what happened?"

When she said 'exactly', she meant every fine detail. I had to backtrack over my narrative several times.

"Where did the eagle come from?" she asked at the end of my recital, head tilted and one knuckle supporting her chin. "Did Dylan send it? You said he was away, but he might still have orchestrated its appearance."

I blinked at her in confusion. "I...I don't know, and I haven't asked him. Do you really think he could have done that?"

"Absolutely. He and Math have appointed themselves your protectors, and having met you, I can see why. Now, let me see these feathers which unsettle you so much." She rose, her swirling skirts a bright flame lifting to the sky and crooked a finger at me. "Come along."

I made my excuses and led her up to my bedchamber, where Cara's precious bundle of feathers nestled inside a small onyx box on the mantle.

"Oh, yes," breathed the Queen of Gwynedd, running each shaft through her fingers. "As you thought, they're ensorcelled. Not Gwydion's doing, though—much too clumsy and, dare I say it, too petty for him. They carry an ill-wishing spell, meant to cause disharmony between you and your love." Her eyes flashed, and she shot me a small, satisfied smile. "Has there been any?"

I shook my head.

"As I thought. Not only is your love too strong to be swayed by whatever minor *gwarch* Cara paid to do this, but your... composition, shall we say, is too different." She stroked the feathers gently and laid them back in the box. "You could destroy them without mishap or find another use for them. I'll leave that up to you. Now I must collect my husband and use the night to remind him why he shouldn't stay away from me for too long."

Her laughter echoed after her as she glided down the hall to Math's bedchamber, black hair floating behind her in a silken cloud.

"How did she know where his room was?" asked Goronwy, when he followed me upstairs shortly afterwards and found me gazing blankly at Cara's love charm. A quartet of hounds trotted at his heels. Taran belonged to me; the other three were Goronwy's.

"The same way she could circumvent my wards to turn up here in the first place, I assume. Math must have sent her a message." I put the feathers back in their box. "You know, I have never understood how Gwydion chose the random slivers of information he passed on to me, or why. For instance, I know the Greek name for their 'place of chains' was the *desmoterion*, but not what it looked like, or how many people it housed."

The Romans had specialised in cruelty, locking those condemned to death or a life of slavery in cramped, damp underground cells. I knew these things, but not why Gwydion had implanted memories of them in my head.

"Perhaps he foresaw a future need," suggested Goronwy, sinking into a deep chair by the fire. The dogs padded across to lounge at his feet. "Although I doubt he imagined you'd want to imprison Cara."

I snorted. "Unlikely he envisaged me locking anyone up. Good wives don't do such things, unless ordered to by their husbands. No, I suspect it was just one of those strange, disordered facts he'd collected that slipped through his filters, along with methods of locating water in the desert, and the mating habits of peafowl."

Taran, leaning hard against my leg, looked up inquisitively at the last word. I laughed and rubbed her ear. "I wasn't talking to you—there's no bird hunting in the offing. We were just discussing the problem of what to do about Cara. We can't keep her in the guest room forever."

"Well, we're not receiving guests at the moment," said Goronwy. "Particularly as nobody can get in. But," he added, in response to my frown, "young Bryn's growing bored now that most of the building additions are done. Commission him to make a purpose-built prison. Start a new trend."

I shuddered. "Like the Romans? Winding tunnels and tiny cells far underground, with people tethered like animals? No, thank you. That's not the Cymric way. Nothing of the sort's ever been seen here, and I know that for a fact because everything Gwydion imparted to me about the history of these lands has been borne out as truth. Lleu's wife needed to know such things."

At the mention of Lleu's name, Taran huffed, and Cochach, one of the other dogs, sneezed. Dawelo didn't stir. Either he had no opinion to offer about Lleu, or he was too comfortable. I couldn't tell.

Goronwy reached down to pet them. "It needn't be cramped and unpleasant," he said. "Just a small roundhouse, with guard's quarters attached, as isolated as we can make it while still being within castle walls. Far away from the entrance."

In the shadow of the yews, perhaps, which now hung far over the northern wall and would lend any building situated there a gloomy aspect. The thought pleased me. Cara's current accommodations were too cheerful for my liking. Of course, I couldn't hold her indefinitely without trial, but would look for a more permanent solution in the coming weeks. Holding her on suspicion of being in league with Gwydion would satisfy the cantref's druids. None were admirers of his.

"Then tomorrow, you must talk to Bryn about building a prison." I rose, disturbing the grey cat which had settled onto my lap. Both the remaining chairs were occupied by a huddle of black-and-grey-striped tabbies. They yawned and stretched, but immediately settled back down again. "But now, I think we should emulate Wynne and Math."

He laughed, eyes twinkling, and lifted me off my feet. "Like this?" Sliding into the steps of the dance recently demonstrated by our guests, he twirled us around the room. "Shall we dance the night long, my love?"

"If that's what you want to call it." I started undoing the ties of his shirt. "The Paphian jig, it's known as, isn't it—cavorting between the sheets?"

He grinned and tossed me onto the bed. "Or on top of them." Shirt and breeches were disposed of and flung aside in an untidy heap on the floor. Catching my wrists and joining them above my head, he clasped them together with one hand and skilfully removed my gown with the other. It didn't take long. He'd had a lot of practice.

I couldn't say whether the royal couple enjoyed their night as much as we did, but when Wynne departed in a cloud of magic the next morning, it certainly looked like they had. Math seemed exhausted, but happy; his wife's expression was that of a cat who'd licked up every drop of cream and was well-pleased with her reflection at the bottom of the dish.

5

CAER DATHYL

A lthough not grand, my childhood home, Dôl Bebin in Arfon, had been considered a respectable dwelling in its day. In a later era, my father would have been called a gentleman farmer: a man of means and no little importance. He was also an ardent follower of Math ap Mathonwy, the mighty magician who was King of Gwynedd and brother of the Great Goddess Dôn. When Father heard that Math sought applicants for the position of Footholder in his household, he hastened to put my name forward.

Part masseuse, part royal secretary, the opening attracted a lot of applicants, but I had an additional edge; I'd always had a talent for magic. Father was unsurprised when I got the job, although he raised his eyebrows later when I told him Math had asked me to marry him. Naturally, he didn't object.

I liked the job, and I loved Math, but one of the greatest delights turned out to be my home. Nothing in all my twenty years of life up to then had prepared me for the glorious, shining enigma of Caer Dathyl.

Visitors were apt to call Math's castle strange, just because the rules of logic and permanence didn't apply. Although it allowed extensive views of the surrounding countryside, it had no true windows, and the doors and hallways wandered at will. I had spent centuries exploring Caer Dathyl and knew every trick and turn of it: every mood, every nuance, every shift of appearance. I wouldn't claim the ability to manipulate those moods without anyone noticing—my husband, for instance, was always attuned to his home. But Math was special, and others were more easily fooled. Could I count Gwydion among those others? I planned to find out.

Upon my return from Lleu's former holding of Mur Y Castell in Ardudwy, I retired to my vast and sadly empty bedroom and prepared. Sitting alone on a padded settle, I upended a small, fur-lined leather pouch onto the marble-topped table before me. The Dewi-stones scattered, some curvetting and spinning before coming to rest, others falling straight down to land with a clink. I'd already lit the candles, and perfumed smoke from a variety of sweet herbs wreathed around me.

The stones numbered twenty, each marked with the runic letters of a secret alphabet known only to magic-workers. Some called my people illiterate. They were wrong. We were simply better at retaining knowledge than those in the mortal world. Ours was an oral tradition which had no need for scratched marks on paper to recall information. Marks on stone, bone, or wood served a different purpose.

Math and I had found time to converse during that passionate night before I left Ardudwy, if only briefly. Somewhere between couch and cushioned bed, he'd delicately suggested that I should seek Gwydion out on my return to Caer Dathyl. I'd demurred as we descended to the carpeted floor. Math's insolent and cruel nephew was the last person with whom I desired speech.

But throughout the previous night, giving and withholding, urging, tormenting, delighting, Math wore down my defences. At last, tangled once more in silk sheets upon the wide, carved oak bed, I'd agreed to try to discover Gwydion's intentions, if I could do so without actually talking to him.

It shouldn't prove too difficult. Apart from a couple of trips to his Arfon properties and an occasional visit with his two eldest sons, Gwydion seemed to divide his time between Caer Dathyl's library, or spell depository, and waiting on Lleu. If I couldn't find a likely spy in the library, I might be able to set up an eavesdropping spell.

Absently rubbing the friction burns on my elbows, a souvenir of that rug, I thought I should have applied salve before casting the stones. However, I healed quickly, and although I'd gathered several such abrasions, the discomfort they caused was minor. Holding in my mind an image of the halls of Caer Dathyl, I closed my eyes, pressed my fingertips to my temples, and breathed in the writhing smoke.

Still buoyed by the memory of pleasure, my body relaxed and my mind pliant, I sank easily into the trance. Swirling colours enfolded me, cascading over my body from the top of my head to my toes; blue, orange, violet, turquoise, red, magenta, green and yellow, blending together to form a sphere of brilliant white light.

I breathed in the colours and exhaled the light. In the centre of that brightness a door appeared, solid black oak. Registering no actual movement, I passed through it. Time and space vanished. I floated somewhere outside reality, divorced even from Otherworld realms. Feelings bled into sound, noise became taste, and sight pricked and tickled over my skin.

For a time, I floated in a state of unbeing, allowing possibilities to unfold around me. It had taken a lot of effort, and many long years of practice, for me to even approach the level of magical skill Math and his family had been born with. They needed only to think about transformation to achieve it; I had to put in long hours of meditation, visualisation, chants, and sometimes painful rituals to get similar results.

Nevertheless, I'd found there were compensations. Those born with such gifts often took them for granted, but those like me who had to work hard at spellwork were forced to explore many avenues. I never contemplated or acknowledged failure. Every path I found, although it might not be the one I currently sought, would lead somewhere. I filed the information away until I found a chance to reuse it.

This was one such opportunity, a path discovered by accident some time ago. I'd forgotten what piece of arcane knowledge had led me to it. That no longer mattered. All that mattered was that it was now perfect for my needs.

Still divorced from the waking world, I opened my eyes and studied the design made by the Dewi-stones. In my altered sight, a fine web of silver lines appeared, joining the glyphs on each stone into a pattern. Each represented one of the winding ways of Caer Dathyl, and each was more fluid than normal—that was to say, this castle's version of normal. I had only to name the rune each glyph symbolised to bind it to my will, enabling me to realign them in whatever pattern I chose.

"*Morwyl.*" I picked up the corresponding Dewi-stone, holding it in my palm. A straight line etched its surface, with a shorter one branching from it. "*Beyel.*" This one resembled a stretched, flat ended star.

"*Rhaff.*" I selected the third stone, marked with three joined triangles. Six more followed. "F*odwy, einion* and *aradyr; cordyn*, *basged* and *fust.*"

Three times three, the sacred number of endings and beginnings. Perfect for my needs. My candles flickered, burnt to stumps, and the perfumed smoke slowly cleared. With a last, deep inhalation, I committed the stone's glyphs to memory, murmured the spells to close the channels I'd opened, and sat back.

Once I would have sallied forth immediately to implement my plan, but over the years I'd learned the folly of such an act. Traversing the rooms and corridors meant I was bound to run into people, and to do that safely, I needed to anchor myself back in reality. A half-turn of the hourglass should suffice. I relaxed and waited for the glow of enchantment to fade before setting out on my mission.

I'd barely reached the brass entrance doors before being accosted.

"Pleasant weather we're having, my lady," said a gravelly voice behind me as I contemplated my next addition. To Caer Dathyl's 'normal' elasticity I'd begun adding extra meandering passageways which led nowhere—little dead-end niches and circulating rooms.

I quirked an eyebrow and turned to confront Heilyn, my husband's master of arms. "That's hardly unusual, is it? Seasons are optional here."

Short, gruff, and spare of frame, Heilyn only paid mind to the weather when it affected one of his endless campaigns, which I had no interest in discussing.

"True." He stroked his neatly trimmed grey beard, pale umber eyes thoughtful.

Brown skin and eyes, grey hair and beard, clothes a mixture of both—those were Heilyn's signature colours. Incisive, insightful and a warrior to the bone as he was, I suspected he favoured drab raiment to fade into the background.

"Might be why Gwydion brought young Lleu back here," he continued after a pause. "Easier to recuperate somewhere like this than out there in Arfon, with its wild winter storms."

Ah, there it was. The crux of the matter, and the real reason Heilyn had sought me out. Gwydion. I raised my eyes ceilingward, entreating the greater gods to grant me patience. "What's he done now?"

Heilyn didn't pretend to misunderstand. He knew to whom I referred. "Hidden Lleu's sickroom." He folded his arms and planted his legs firmly apart. "Not wishing to speak out of turn, but if you ask me, Gwydion's always been a tad irrational where Lleu's concerned. Some say he sees Lleu as his heir, and they're not far wrong, I reckon."

I nodded in agreement. Although their gifts and their personalities were poles apart, a close bond existed between them. When Gwydion had returned Lleu to Caer Dathyl to recuperate under the care of the finest Otherworldly physicians, he'd been distraught—for which I was grateful. It kept him out of my way.

"I'll talk to him," I promised, all the while wondering how many more layers I could add to this section of the castle without attracting undue attention. Beyond a certain point, altered reality tended to collapse in on itself, and nobody wanted that.

Unfortunately, Heilyn wasn't yet done. "You do that, my lady. And maybe explain to the king that I did my best to watch over Lleu, as instructed, but was thwarted at every turn." He jerked his chin over his shoulder towards a group of green-robed figures who'd gathered in the corner of the room. "Come on over here and deliver your gripe, you lot."

They obeyed, eyes downcast. From their wrinkled faces and silver-threaded hair, I understood four of the six to be human, and at least as old as Heilyn. Those who'd dwelt in the Otherworld for years beyond the norm for our kind aged slowly, if at all. Some, like me, chose not to do so. Others, such as the warriors, administrators and artisans, paid no attention to appearances and let the years run as they would. Most healers felt the same.

The other two, smooth-skinned, fair-haired, and lithe as dancers, were the oldest of the group, even though they didn't look it. Not that they looked young, either. These were Math's relatives, descendants of the Great Goddess Don. Ageless and close to immortal, the latter especially being a handy trait for a healer, they'd travelled widely and studied under the best from a dozen different lands and cultures.

Ianaura, the tall blonde woman, glared at Heilyn but did as he asked. "Gwydion's gone to great lengths to hide Lleu's location," she said. "He magically blindfolded us before he'd even let us into the room, then laid a tynged upon us to prevent us discussing Lleu's condition with anyone. We're not to speak of it until he's completely recovered, or Gwydion's magic will blind us all. Permanently. No one should treat a healer so, even if he is the king's nephew."

Especially if he was the king's nephew. I sighed and assured them I'd speak to Gwydion, or better yet, to the king. Math, I explained, would be far more likely to listen to me than would Gwydion.

Mollified, they departed, and Heilyn watched them go with the wraith of a smile. "You handled that well," he said, sounding satisfied.

As if such an outcome was ever in doubt. I issued a chilly dismissal and returned to my task: doing everything in my power to detain Gwydion in Caer Dathyl and keep him from returning to the mortal world too quickly.

6

LLEU

G wydion's paranoia worked in my favour. If he hadn't felt compelled to stay by Lleu's side, intent on supervising his nephew's recovery and fretting about the outcome, I might not have succeeded as well as I did.

The memory of Gwydion's arrival with the wounded Lleu still made me shudder. While deploring the influence Gwydion had on him, I'd always had a soft spot for Lleu. Unfortunately, nobody else, his mother included, had ever supplanted Gwydion in his life. I understood Blodeuedd's desire to sever all ties with him. In her place, I'd have felt the same way.

I still saw traces of the sweet, sunny child he'd been when Gwydion had first brought him to Caer Dathyl. A child who resembled Dylan, his twin. I'd raised Dylan, along with Gwydion's other three boys, and regarded the four of them as my own adopted children.

Although not as brawny as Dylan, Leu had always been tall and well-formed, but the privations he'd endured while hunched as an eagle in that tree had sloughed every ounce of fat from him, and muscle as well. Not only that, but maggots had infested his rotting flesh. When they'd heard this, the healers expressed thankfulness. I understood why—the vile little creatures had cleaned the wound—but the image conjured had made bile rise in my throat.

Whole again, and human, when they'd arrived back at Caer Dathyl, Lleu had been barely recognisable as the bright avatar of the sun. His hair and skin were dull, his eyes shadowed, and his frame gaunt. Seeing that, I'd been prepared to dislike Blodeuedd until I heard her side of the story. No relationship breakdown was ever straightforward. I needed to find Lleu and talk to him.

Luckily, Gwydion hadn't extended his *tynged* to anyone except the healers, no doubt relying on his magic to hide Lleu's refuge. Perhaps he thought fear of him would deter people from looking. But I wasn't afraid of Gwydion, even though I avoided contact with him as much as possible—easy enough in an Otherworldly abode where the alignments changed from day to day, hour to hour.

I set out to find Lleu.

The sight of Caer Dathyl's lady endlessly traversing its corridors, adjusting panoramas, updating décor, or tweaking colour schemes caused no comment. I'd been doing so for centuries. At first, no obvious changes leapt out at me. I made another circuit, then two, until at last I found it: a faint vibrational dissonance on one of the far northern walls.

The image before me showed a vista of snow-capped mountains and foaming, dark grey clouds. A rugged, inhospitable landscape. However, the colours weren't those I or any of Math's craftsmen would ordinarily use. I tweaked reality aside, like a curtain, to view the other side of the wall, and beheld a sunlit glade carpeted with wildflowers and domed by soft blue skies. By hiding it behind such a harsh picture, Gwydion had obviously hoped to discourage visitors, and so far, he seemed to have succeeded. So far. Smiling, I stepped through.

The area contained no buildings, just a sleeping platform piled with furs beside a burbling brook. Warmth caressed my skin, and floral perfumes hung heavy in the air. No doubt this outdoor 'room' would be temperature-controlled and shielded from the elements. No rain would ever fall here, despite the green lawn beneath my feet. The spreading oaks, the towering pines and cypresses, like the flowers and the grass, were sustained by magic, not the natural elements.

"Lleu," I called into the stillness. "Are you there?"

No answer. I raised my voice. "It's Wynne, your Aunt Wynne, come to see how you're feeling. Will you come and sit with me a while?"

Silence blanketed the glade, so profound I could hear the hum of every bee and the trill of every tiny bird. A calming ambiance pervaded.

Not something I'd ever associate with Gwydion, and I wondered if this tiny sanctuary had been designed by someone else.

The magical shields around the dell bore his imprint, though. According to the men and women I'd set to watch him in both the Otherworld and mortal realms, Gwydion would disappear for long stretches—days or even weeks at a time. I suspected he'd barely left Lleu's side since he'd returned with his nephew to Caer Dathyl, several seasons ago. I'd have searched for and found Lleu long before, if he hadn't been constantly shadowed by his uncle.

Avoiding Gwydion had become second nature. Both he and his brother Gilfaethwy had long ago apologised for the injury they'd inflicted upon me, and Math had dealt out adequate punishment. But although I'd agreed to move on for the sake of family peace, I'd never forgiven them. Either of them. Hence my refusal to talk to him unless forced to.

Still no sound or movement disturbed the dreaming dell, apart from a few small forest creatures who paid me no attention. I sighed and looked around. A cluster of sun-warmed rocks by the edge of the water beckoned invitingly. Seating myself as comfortably as I could, I prepared to wait.

Inquisitive and unafraid, a cream-furred rabbit hopped from behind a tree and approached.

"Have you seen Lleu?" I asked.

The little creature cocked its head, regarding me solemnly with big dark eyes. We considered each other for a moment, before movement on the other side of the stream startled it into flight. A russet dogfox trotted up, explaining the rabbit's fear.

"Hello, Aunty Wynne," it said.

I jumped with a squeak of surprise.

Standing upright on its hind legs, surrounded by the telltale, pulsing glow of magic, it stretched and expanded into the shape of a man. Golden-haired and golden-skinned, he bore an ugly, twisted scar upon one naked shoulder. He filled out the dark blue leather trews nicely, though. He'd been nothing but skin and bone when I'd last seen him.

"Lleu!" I pressed a hand against my chest to still the agitated beating of my heart. "Don't tell me you've learned how to shapeshift?"

"Hardly. That was Gwydion's doing." Transformation complete, he settled on the rock beside me, long legs stretched out before him and feet crossed at the ankles. "He glamours me each morning before he leaves, in case someone finds their way in here by accident."

"But you can change back again by yourself? How?"

"It's an illusion spell, not a true shapeshift. If you were to touch me—not that you'd be quick enough to catch me—you'd feel skin and not fur. All I have to do is think the right words to reverse it. How did you know the key to get in, by the way?"

"I know all the hidden ways of Caer Dathyl. I trust your recuperation has progressed well, and you're no longer in pain? This is certainly a restful environment."

He waved my platitudes aside. "I'm fine. Have you seen Caron?"

That was unexpected. I pretended ignorance. "Who?"

"Caron, of the line of Dafona. Where is she, and why can't I see her?"

I'd been afraid of this. Our conversation promised to be difficult. "Gwydion didn't tell you?"

"Gwydion's trying to wrap me in featherdown and pack my ears with wax. Where is my Caron?"

A disturbing glow settled around him, sun-bright and hot. Trying not to flinch away from the raw anger in his voice, I lifted my head and assumed my sternest expression—the one that never failed to cow my daughter and send the servants scurrying. Only Math was immune to it.

And, apparently, Lleu. He regarded me stonily. "You must know where she is. Did Gwydion send you to distract me?"

"What?" I squeaked, then cleared my throat. I never squeaked, and he'd made me do it twice in the space of a few breaths. "No, that's…"

I stopped, belatedly considering that to accuse Lleu of insanity might not be a good idea, particularly because it was too close to the mark. I'd been warned he might be a little irrational. Or even more than a little. Having come so close to death, or at least as close as was possible for an immortal godling, I couldn't believe he was still obsessed with his mortal lover, Caron. His *dead* mortal lover, who—defying good sense and all the gods—had stupidly vowed to return to him in every incarnation.

Apparently, he was. He stood up, glowing and glowering, and the temperature rose by a few more degrees. "Where is she? I want her. *Now!*"

I backed away, sweat beading on my temples. Whatever controls Gwydion had put in place in his replica of the Blessed Isles couldn't cope with Lleu in a temper. "She's in the Moonlands," I said bluntly. "In Emania. I'm afraid you might have to wait a while before you can be reunited, if at all."

"What do you mean?" His scowl brought to mind a lightning-riven oak tree; his voice was building thunder. There was a good reason Beli Mawr and the elder gods had forbidden Lleu to interact directly with the source of his power. Manawydan ap Llŷr, Lord of the Sea, could become one with wind and wave, and rule the creatures of the deep ocean. While impressive, this ability rarely posed a danger to others. Someone who could merge with the fire of the sun, however, had the potential to unleash burning chaos.

That someone was Lleu Llaw Gyffes.

I tried to mollify him. "Dafona's line is thinning, you must know that. The only daughter left is Modwenna, and so far, she and Yestin have had no children."

Lleu's frown deepened. So did his voice, booming and echoing around the clearing and sending several small creatures scurrying for cover. "She's young yet. And even if she can't provide a vehicle for my Caron, Cynar can carry on the bloodline. True, Caron promised to reincarnate only in Dafona's female descendants, but there's nothing to say they might not skip a generation. She didn't specify direct lineage, from daughter to daughter. A granddaughter could fulfil her vow."

"What's your urgency?" I asked, with genuine puzzlement as well as a desire to soothe. "If you're quite certain the conditions didn't call for a direct bloodline, it doesn't really matter how many generations might pass. Her soul has probably progressed to Annwfyn by now. Once she's fulfilled her obligations to the gods and accepted her new life lessons, Arawn will release her for rebirth."

Privately, I wasn't sure that would be the case. Caron's vow had upset the order of things in the Moonlands and beyond, and I'd heard rumours that Arawn, Lord of the Dead, might throw some impediments in her path. Mortal souls were supposed to learn from life to life, eventually accumulating enough spiritual credit to ascend to higher realms.

Those places demigods only got to by confronting their hamartia. All immortals had them: a fatal flaw which could part them from life, although that seldom meant true death. They didn't reincarnate as mortals did, but passed into another form, one they'd utilised most frequently, or one indelibly associated with them. In Lleu's case, he'd been transformed into an eagle, because eagles were connected to the sun.

Caron, by pledging herself to Lleu throughout many of her lifetimes, had sought to bypass her life lessons. And some said that by aiding her, Lleu made it possible for his non-mortal wife to wound him with a bespelled bronze spear, and so bring about his hamartia.

His wife Blodeuedd, who was receiving succour and lessons in magic from my husband.

"I'd advise you to put aside your obsession," I said at length, "and forget about the mortal world for a while. Take your place here, in Caer Dathyl. Mankind will always worship the sun; they can't survive without it. And you, as its avatar, will always receive their honour. Let that be enough."

He shook his head, but at least some of my rationality must have penetrated his thick skull, because he visibly deflated. The dangerous heat dispersed, leaving the glade once more to emulate the gentle warmth of spring.

"I can't." He sank down to sit cross-legged in the grass. "I was made to give love, Aunt Wynne, and Caron was made to receive it."

I resumed my place on the rock, hoping he couldn't hear the pounding of my heart. "That sounds rather one-sided. Did Caron give none in her turn?"

"At first, yes. But...she changed, over the years, over the centuries. I could see it happening, and I know others judged her harshly for it. But I didn't. I couldn't. She and I belong together, throughout all her lives and all time." He closed his eyes, rubbing at his shoulder. "If I can't retrieve her, I don't know what to do. If I can't be with her, Gwydion should not have brought me back."

His version of the story smacked of high romance. I was inclined to view it as a tragedy. "Have you seen the boys?" I asked, seeking to defuse his wrath and turn the conversation into safer channels. "Hydd or Hych? I know Blei's away at the moment, but the other two will be around somewhere."

After an ill-advised battle with Math a few months ago, both were now confined to Caer Dathyl. Bleiddwn had disappeared afterwards, his current whereabouts unknown. Those three were Lleu's cousins, or according to some, his half-brothers. That was how his full brother, Dylan, viewed them.

I knew better than to ask Lleu if he'd been in touch with Dylan. Twins weren't always close, and those two had clashed from the day they'd first met, at eighteen. That they'd been raised apart in very different households might have had something to do with it. A lot to do with it, even.

Dylan and his brothers weren't to blame for the iniquities of their parents. I'd always been fond of Lleu, too, even though his upbringing had left a great deal to be desired. Lleu had been stolen from his mother Arianrhod by his father-uncle Gwydion shortly after he'd been born. Arianrhod harboured a grudge about it to that very day.

She and I had always got on well, partly because of our shared hatred of Gwydion, partly because we had quite a lot in common. I suspected she also approved of my steadying influence on Lleu.

"No," said Lleu. "Meghan's been here, though. I didn't speak to her, but she tried to make friends with the fox. Not sure whether she thought I was a real one."

"Meg!" I was startled. My daughter wasn't a great deal younger than Lleu but, having lived her whole life in Caer Dathyl or other sections of the Otherworld, had aged less. Not that Lleu looked old, even allowing for the stiff movement caused by his wounds. It was more a matter of outlook, of experience. He was a man of the world in many worlds; she was a sheltered darling unused to the ways of men.

I rose from my rock, looking around. It had taken me some time to locate Lleu's refuge, for Gwydion's illusions were impeccable and his wards strong. Only because I knew every inch of Caer Dathyl and possessed a detailed memory of its habit of morphing from one vista to another, had I been able to find the one spot which didn't quite fit. That view of the mountains. How could Meg have found her way in?

Walking slowly and deliberately from one end of the glade to the other, I tested it, every tree, rock and blade of grass. All were magically sealed against detection. I hadn't been wrong about Gwydion's wards. They were designed to keep any but the most magically talented out.

Meg might be the light of my soul, but I knew beyond doubt that she wasn't experienced enough or creative enough to have found this place on her own. She had to have had help. From whom? Perhaps Lleu would know.

"If you didn't wish to speak to her, I assume you didn't guide her in," I said.

He shook his head.

"Well then, do you have any idea who did?"

"None." He cocked his head to one side, studying me. "She looks like you, except for the red hair. Uncle Math's legacy, I suppose. It's been so long since I've seen her, I'd forgotten how fiery it is. Meg's much better-looking than her da, though. Nobody's ever called Math a beauty."

"Are you trying to flatter me?" I spoke without heat, or even much interest.

Given Lleu's fixation on his vanished Caron, I had no fear that he'd make any advances to Meg. Not that she'd be likely to welcome them if he did. Meg, like her Aunt Arianrhod, appeared to have a distinct preference for mermen. Of course, that might have been Dylan's influence. She might not have made much headway with her magical studies, but thanks to Dylan she was very much at home in the sea. Which, now that I thought of it, perhaps explained why she'd come looking for Lleu. She was extremely fond of Dylan; it made sense that she'd want to catch up with his twin. Even though Dylan didn't.

"What did she say to the fox?" I asked.

"Inanities. What a pretty creature I was, and how my fur and her hair were close to the same shade. Did I chase the bunnies, and if so, did I catch them and eat them. She didn't seem at all worried about them, just curious."

Eyes narrowed, I nodded in understanding. She'd wanted to test the rules governing life in Gwydion's enchanted bubble... for what reasons, I hated to guess. Time to have a chat with my daughter.

I rose and shook out my skirts. "I'd like to continue visiting, if I may. But for both our sakes, I'd suggest you say nothing to Gwydion."

Lleu agreed, his expression rueful, and kissed my cheek in farewell.

7

MEGHAN

I'd often heard it said that Meghan had inherited my looks, but while we might share a similar build and bone structure, I disagreed with Lleu's statement that she resembled me closely. We had very different colouring. Her hair was brilliant copper, not black, her skin had a tawny cast, and her eyes were tiercel gold instead of violet blue. She was unmistakably her father's daughter. She lacked long, mobile lips, however. I liked to think she had my mouth—plump lips which curved into a cupid's bow. Her delightful dimples she owed to neither of us; they were all her own.

Bottom lip outthrust, she stepped nimbly over a small marble statue of a Cymric dragon in one of Caer Dathyl's many gardens. A massive tabby cat reclining atop it hissed at her. After taking a swipe at her leg and missing, he departed in high dudgeon, fur on end and tail erect as a spear-staff. He dwarfed the carving by a considerable amount. Who needed dragons when descendants of the *Cath Palug* roamed free?

Sweet Meg looked less attractive when pouting. "Why should it matter who helped me? I wanted to see Cousin Lleu and wish him a speedy recovery. What's wrong with that?"

"Nothing at all, but you're avoiding my question. Who helped you get in? That little magical pocket's well hidden, and unless you've become very proficient in spellwork overnight, I'm sure you couldn't have found it unaided."

She tossed her head. "So I had assistance. What does it matter? I can't see why it matters to you."

I squinted at her, eyes narrowed and skin tingling with suspicion. "Whoever circumvented Gwydion's wards must be an accomplished enchanter. I *need* to know who it was. His name, please."

With a typically swift change of mood, she caught the white metal post of a gazebo and spun around it, bright hair swinging. "Gwri Goldenhair, the well-favoured one. True, his hair's brown, not blonde, but I think he's tolerably handsome."

"No such person has ever existed. That was an alias given to Prince Pryderi before Terynon finally named him. Tell me the name of your accomplice."

Meghan rocked back against the post and folded her arms. "I'm not a child, Mother. I don't have to confide everything to you."

"You do when it concerns the security of this castle. I'm in charge while your father's away, young madam, and don't you forget it." I grasped her arm and thrust her before me into the gazebo, plonking us both down on a polished wooden seat. A foaming sea of white roses formed the walls on three sides, their perfume sweet and delicate. "Out with it. Who've you been dallying with?"

Fingers entwined in her hair, she laughed and dropped the haughty tone. "*Dallying.* Oh, Mam, you're so quaint. He's an old friend, that's all. We were out walking a few days ago, watching the walls drift apart and reform, and he noticed an anomaly in the north. He didn't enter, but he pointed it out to me and told me how to disable the magical locks. I went back later, alone, looking for Lleu. I couldn't find him, though."

I studied her, looking for the teeth-teased lip and sideways glance that always accompanied her lies. Neither appeared. "What made you think Lleu would be there?"

Meghan stroked her thighs and lifted her eyes to the branching canes overhead. "Tch. Come on, Mam. I might not be your star pupil, but I'm not deficient in brains. Everyone knows Gwydion's got Lleu secreted away in a hidden room in the *caer*, so what else could it have been? But either he was elsewhere that day or has a well-concealed lair within the glade."

True enough. I plucked a white rose from the bower behind us, holding it to my nose and inhaling the musky, slightly spicy perfume. "I've spoken to Lleu, and so have you, although you failed to recognise him. Remember the fox?"

She blinked at me. "No, really? That's an unlikely glamour for him to choose, I'd have thought."

"He didn't choose it, Gwydion did. But he's invited me to return, and if you're a good girl and tell me what I want to know, I'll take you with me. Otherwise, I'll add my wards to Gwydion's to keep you out."

Meghan tried a pleading hangdog look, which was difficult to achieve with piercing yellow eyes. "Promise you won't be angry?"

I sighed. "A statement like that makes me suspect I have cause to be. Out with it. Who was it?"

She hitched her shoulders and began plaiting her hair. "Well...it was Blei."

Curses! An unseen burden settled on my shoulders, weighing me down. After joining ranks with their father and attacking Math, who'd raised them, the sons of Gilfaethwy and Gwydion had been hunted down by the king's loyal men and arrested. I'd been heartbroken when I'd heard about their betrayal. We were their parents, not Gwydion.

But Hydd and Hych, at least, had always shared his love of mischief, and perhaps their shared blood made them too susceptible to Gwydion's golden tongue. I'd put aside my hurt and tried to forgive them, as mothers always did.

Math was less forbearing. After the battle, they had been bundled back to Caer Dathyl, bound for sentencing and imprisonment. Unfortunately, Bleiddwn had somehow slipped his magical shackles one night, shifted into wolf form, and escaped. No one had heard from him since.

Having been held captive in their rooms for three months and served as labourers and kitchen drudges for another three, Hydd and Hych were now free to roam Caer Dathyl while still confined within its walls. But Blei would face harsher punishment—not only for evading the king's justice, but for re-entering Caer Dathyl unseen and unannounced.

"Where is he now?" I asked, rising. "Apart from skulking somewhere in my castle. He can't have returned to his own quarters, someone would have noticed and reported to me. Which means..."

"That someone else is shielding and hiding him," Meg finished for me, getting to her feet as well. "I realise that. And no, it's not me. You should talk to his brothers. Or his father."

Not bothering to dignify that with a reply, I signalled for her to leave first. She turned down a meandering path, which became a flight of steps beneath a covered colonnade before transforming into a hallway. Satisfied that Meg was on her way to her own room, I backtracked, folding the fabric of Caer Dathyl upon itself and muttering spells as I went. Not to the rooms of Gwydion's other two sons; as prisoners, they were under constant surveillance and would have no hope of concealing a fugitive. I continued past their quarters, deep into the Caer's labyrinthine heart.

Soon the door I sought stood before me, although an inexperienced eye wouldn't have recognised it as such. Nor would many seasoned magic users, either. This sanctum housed a master magician; this was Gwydion's chamber.

Another spell confirmed it to be occupied, but not by whom. I hesitated. I had no plan or desire to confront Gwydion, and should he be there, my use of magic would have already alerted him to my presence. Problematic, given that my spells were those used by humankind and relied on herbs and incense, glyphs and incantations, rather than the pure energy manipulation common to Math and his kind. If the room's resident was Gwydion, he'd immediately know exactly who was outside. Dare I risk it?

Fate, or the Elder Gods, took the decision out of my hands. A section of wall shimmered and vanished in a flamboyance of flamingo-pink light. I shrank against the far wall, all my usual aplomb deserting me. A sinewy, brown-haired man of middle height appeared in the gap, lent a ruddy cast by the glow of the fading doorway.

"Aunt Wynne," said Blei, slurring his words slightly. He shrugged away the remains of the disintegrating entryway and regarded me with lifted brows. "You looking for Da? He's not in. Hasn't been for a while; says he has other places to be right now. Luckily for me." He drew a deep breath and pressed the fingers of one hand against the knuckles of the other. I remembered the gesture. It meant he was nervous.

"No," I said, heartened by this display of unease. "I was looking for you. Will you invite me in?"

He stepped aside and waved a theatrical hand to unfold the door again. "You don't seem to have any manacles, so I suspect this isn't an official visit. I'll be delighted to play host, in that case. Would you care for a glass of wine? Father has some excellent vintages."

"Delighted," I lied.

Even knowing that his father was unaware of my trespass and there could be no danger, part of me still shrank from the idea of supping at Gwydion's table. Nevertheless, I followed Blei inside, looking around curiously. As one of the Children of Don, Gwydion still maintained a room in Caer Dathyl, even when living at his own home in Arfon. Because of the animosity between us, I'd never been here before.

It wasn't quite what I'd expected, but then I couldn't have said what I had expected. Something flashy, perhaps. Patterned carpets, heavy dark oak and rich, red velvet furnishings. Instead, the bare blonde wooden floorboards shone with polish and the stone walls were whitewashed. Latticework furniture, also crafted from a pale wood, like ash, beech or even possibly sycamore, comprised a low table, a green upholstered settle and several chairs in the Roman style. Each one sported a different coloured cushion, all of them jewel-toned.

To offset this neutral scheme, the far wall, opposite the door where it would catch and hold one's attention, crackled and dazzled with colour. Light from an unseen source played across its surface. In the central motif of the image, a mighty salmon leapt and spun in a whirling vortex of rainbows. In the background, wolves watched from the heights, while foxes, hares and otters mingled with small frogs and tiny bees in the foreground. A massive bear dominated the far right of the image, perched on a rocky crag some distance from the wolves.

Looking more closely, I discerned a range of other creatures hidden among the trees. Stags, hinds, cows, boar, and sheep dwelt in unlikely partnerships with cats and dogs, cranes and geese. Eagles, kites, blackbirds, robins, and ravens soared in the sky above. I couldn't see any owls, but that wasn't surprising on many counts, not least being that this was a daytime scene.

"How beautiful," I breathed, approaching with my hand outstretched. That smooth, shining façade invited touch. My finger trailed across it, seeking the channels joining each tiny fragment together, and finding none. It might well have been polished marble.

"Glass chips," said Blei. Halting by a recessed cupboard in the adjoining wall, he selected a pair of fine-stemmed pewter goblets and a heavy glass bottle filled with pale golden liquid. "And ceramic. Da apparently got the idea from an eastern mosay...mosay-ah-sh...Ah, bugger it." He shook his head as if to clear it, and finished by enunciating deliberately, "*Mosaic artist* when he was researching the design for Lleu's house."

Swaying only slightly, he selected a seat with a saffron-yellow cushion and collapsed into it. By some miracle he spilled none of the wine.

"It's...unexpected." I accepted a goblet and sat down opposite him on a spindly but surprisingly comfortable chair cushioned in brilliant blue silk. "Not the sort of décor I'd expect Gwydion to choose. The man appears to possess unforeseen depths, although an appreciation for beauty doesn't mitigate his faults. His many faults. Have you seen him lately?"

A wry smile tugged at the corners of Blei's wide mouth, and amusement lit his tawny brown eyes. "You know I must have. How else could I have got back in here? Poor Hydd and Hych can't move without their warders shadowing them." He took a mouthful of wine, savouring it before swallowing. "Gods, but that's good. I'd love to know where the old man gets it from."

I almost said something cutting about Gwydion's impressive ability to keep secrets, then remembered I'd just breached one. Which might make me equally crafty. I replied to his question instead. "Across the sea, in the Bretagne lands, I think." Taking a sip—it really was exquisite—I added, "Why did you return?"

Blei shook his head, slowly. "No, the question you should be asking is why I ran to begin with. Because that's what lies at the heart of my decision to throw myself on Uncle Math's mercy. And I'll tell it to no one else. Nobody. So you may regard this as nothing more than a pleasant little chat between kin."

Arrogant cub. He always had been, perhaps because he'd actually been born a wolf. That was why he could take that form whenever it suited him. I'd heard stories of tribes who'd forcibly change when the moon was full, their sinews, muscles and bones twisting and morphing painfully from human to lupine. I considered them no more than folktales. For one thing, the imbalance in weight between wolf and man made it difficult to imagine, unless they became enormous beasts.

Blei in his animal form blended in with other wolves, grey-furred and tawny-eyed. Wolf-Blei weighed a good deal less than Man-Blei, who at a little under six feet might not look as impressive as his brothers, but was taller and broader than a lot of human men. The same was true of Hych, who could become a boar at will. When he transformed, he looked no different from the others. The third brother, Hydd, had been born as a deer, whose mass was more commensurate with that of a hefty six-foot man. Nevertheless, the change was accomplished with magic, for which I was sure he was grateful. I couldn't imagine the headache he'd get, having antlers regularly burst from his skull.

I set my goblet down and tilted my head. "You must know I'm Math's surrogate and can dispense justice in his name until he returns. Tell me everything I need to know, and I might be lenient when passing sentence on you. Absconding from custody and striking one of the king's guardsmen ought to earn you at least twenty lashes. I could halve that. I will have to imprison you, of course, there's no way around it. But..."

"But nothin'." His words stumbled and ran together. "Do y're worst. Trust me, I've had worse trea'ment lately than a mere whi...whipping."

He drained the rest of his drink as if it were water—a truly sacrilegious act—and refilled the goblet to the brim. I eyed it with disapproval.

"I'll certainly deprive you of the means to get drunk. Have you been doing that a lot lately?"

Blei grunted. Taking another large swig, he leaned back in his seat, legs and arms spread. The goblet dangled precariously from his fingers.

"If you spill and waste that fine vintage, I shall be most upset." I got up, covered the short distance between us and gently detached it from his grasp.

He barely reacted, his eyes already drifting shut. Deprived of the goblet, his hand fell lax against the arm of the chair, fingers uncurling. His head nodded forward onto his chest, and the slight movement of head and shoulder was enough to shift the unlaced neck of his garment slightly to one side. A ragged scar, like a healed claw mark on the side of his neck, disappeared beneath his shirt.

Worse than a whipping, he'd said, and he'd suffered enough of those at his father's hands, so he ought to know. Could Gwydion have caused these injuries, though? I doubted it, or Blei wouldn't have accepted his offer of sanctuary. Motherly impulse made me want to peel the fabric away and inspect the damage, before attempting to soothe it with poultices and spells. But when startled, Blei was apt to transform without warning. I didn't feel up to dealing with an angry, frightened wolf.

Reluctantly, I left him there and, with a muttered curse, set the goblet safely down and turned to go.

One thing I could do for him. For us all. Before I departed I used magic to alter the entry wards and summon guards to watch the door. Until I made other arrangements, Gwydion's chamber would be his wolf-born son's prison.

As for Gwydion himself, I heard he seldom left the dell, dividing the rest of his time between Hych's room and Hydd's. By keeping track of his whereabouts, I could time my visits to Lleu to ensure we never met. That pattern would also help me keep him contained in Caer Dathyl. Math, Dylan and several others had been worried that as soon as Lleu recovered enough, Gwydion would fly back to Ardudwy in his kite form and attack Blodeuedd.

So I thought of a way to improve on Math's strategy. Rather than altering Gwydion's surroundings, which he'd be bound to find his way out of eventually, I'd also attempt to alter the flows of time, distorting the differences between our place and the mortal world. Even more than usual, that was.

Being so different from anything I'd done before, or indeed anything I'd even considered trying, it took me some time to refine the technique. But with time and perseverance, I succeeded. A mortal witch such as I couldn't send time rolling backwards, but I could make it stutter. Make it skip and jump and twirl in place, snarling the threads which anchored us to the flows of time in the mortal world. Thus time passed at a much faster rate in Ardudwy, Arfon and other kingdoms than in my Otherworldly castle. Whatever extra time my beloved needed I would do my best to give him.

I made seconds last for hours, and days pass by in seconds. Summer bled into autumn and winter followed spring. Most of the Caer's inhabitants failed even to notice, except for the cooks and the servants. The seneschal approached me to lodge a complaint—well, not a complaint so much as an expression of deep concern—and I assured him that all was well, and Math's imminent return would soon set things to rights. A passing tremor in the ether, I said, a hiccough in the magic. Nothing to worry about at all, really.

I lived in constant dread that either Gwydion or Lleu would notice what I'd been doing and call me to account, but neither did.

Once I'd regained access to Lleu, I began to feed him calming herbs, with perfect justification. I'd always understood his nature—always known exactly who and what he was. Birthed from the moon goddess and the trickster god, grandson of our world's chief deities, he was tightly tied to power. To awesome, destructive might. Once, he'd never have thought of loosing that chaos. His grandparents would not have allowed it, nor would the rest of his family.

But from the display of temper I'd witnessed, Lleu's control was in imminent danger of slipping. Drugs seemed a logical option, if they could keep that from happening. I'd received enough of a fright to shorten my lifespan by decades as it was.

8

GIFTS

C alan Gaeaf came and went. Math and I returned to my training, practising with willow wands, incantations, and the knowledge of plants. This went on for weeks, day in and day out, until my arms developed muscles I was sure few women possessed and my fingers could grip like steel vices. Who'd have thought that the practice of magic could be a physical workout?

At Math's suggestion, I extended my range of plant sympathies, and could identify and communicate with every kind of aquatic greenery with as much ease as I could their land brethren. Seaweed, seagrass, saltwort and liverwort, algae, eelgrass and samphire.

Lleu's twin brother, Dylan, was a great help in this. He knew them all, as a gardener knows his produce. With him by my side, I could dive deeper than anyone except Dylan himself and investigate not only sea plants but tiny creatures and fishes—even birds. And seals. I enjoyed making friends with the seals.

When he had leisure to spare, Goronwy would sit on the rocks, fishing, or sometimes even plunge into the water for a swim. Not often, though, for the midwinter temperatures made it uninviting and his free time was better spent at home to oversee the running of Ardudwy.

"Do you consider the aquatica delicacies?" I asked Dylan one morning after we'd returned to shore from a deep-water dive, skin tingling and hair tangled with salt. Pearl-grey skies lowered over darker grey, turbulent water, but below, along the seabed and the estuaries where the waving seagrasses grew, the water was calmer, if colder.

Dylan shook his head, his sun-bright mane cascading in twisted ropes down his back. Water droplets scattered from his beard. "No, but I'll eat them if I have to. I prefer my samphire pickled, beside a nice leg of roast lamb, and washed down with some of Ardudwy's finest honey mead." He retrieved a towel from beneath the rock he'd used to pin it down, rubbed himself dry, and began to dress.

Dylan disdained clothes when swimming, commenting, rightly, that they took too long to dry, especially in winter. I agreed, but although nakedness didn't normally bother me, Dylan looked too much like his twin for me to feel entirely comfortable going sky-clad beside him. Instead, I wore a skin-tight woollen garment of my own design which allowed me to move freely through the water. After courting grippe following the first few sessions, I discovered I could make it dry quickly, too. Cold and discomfort are excellent motivators.

"A glass of hot, spiced mead would be very welcome right now," I said, after I'd shrugged into my gown and wrapped my cloak securely around me.

Dylan, already dressed in his leathers and cloak of thick, pewter-grey sealskin, paused at the edge of the sand where the dunes met the scrubby grass to wait for me. Before us rose a thicket of holm oak, mountain ash and imported pine, all trees which will tolerate sea air. I spoke the required words of the spell, and the interwoven branches parted before us, opening into a winding, shadowy tunnel.

"Aye," he agreed, stepping onto the path. "But I've a training session with Cynar to go to, first."

I snapped my fingers, and the barrier closed in our wake. The tunnel still stretched ahead, winding over hill and vale to reach the sanctuary of Mur Y Castell. "Thank you for helping him. I really appreciate it, and I know he does too. He's never said so, but I suspect he feels the lack of his arm rather keenly."

"Never fear. By the time I'm done he'll be able to hold his own against most assailants. I know tricks they'll never see coming."

I nodded. "Can I come and watch?"

He grinned and gave a shrug, which set the surrounding shadows dancing. "I'm amenable, if it doesn't bother Cynar. And I don't see why it should; having two ladies of the court to cheer him on gives him added incentive to do well, I think."

"He's determined," I agreed.

Dylan chuckled. "He's stubborn—a good trait to have. His will burns strongly in him, else he'd not have survived that injury."

"Overcoming early trauma can have that effect," I said drily. "You never met his brother, Emlyn, did you?"

"No, and from what Cynar's told me—the beatings, the abuse—I'm almost thankful."

"Almost?" I peered up at him through the gloom. Even at midday the sun only penetrated this passageway fitfully, and that was still hours away. The smell of damp earth, pine needles, goldenrod, and the indefinable odour of twigs and tree-bark surrounded us.

"Well," said Dylan, laughter crinkling the corners of his bright blue eyes, "if we had met, I could've had the pleasure of thumping him into oblivion. 'Tis me nature to regret missed opportunities like that."

The image of barb-tongued Emlyn being pummelled by Dylan was an appealing one. True, his behaviour had been learned from their brutish father, but that didn't excuse it. In his other dealings, Emlyn's weapons of choice had been words, swords, or fire. Only on his defenceless baby brother had he used fists, rods, or whips.

I shook the hateful images away. "He'd have tried to talk you out of it, or appealed to his overlord, Gwydion, for aid."

Another shrug. "I'd not have listened. And I'd love to thrash Gwydion too, if the chance ever arises. Unfortunately, that sort of thing is frowned on without provocation. Us being related, an' all."

Ahead the light increased, beckoning, as the entrance to Mur Y Castell came into view. "Wait long enough and he's bound to offer it. That's what tricksters do." I paused and looked up as he followed me through the gates. "I need to change first. You're meeting Cynar in the yard by the postern gate, yes?"

Dylan nodded and bowed. "That's right. I'll see ye there."

It didn't take me long to shed my swimsuit, don a gown, several layers of petticoats, warm, fur-lined boots and gloves, and repair to the small courtyard now designated as the training ground. Cynar had taught me and my ladies there as well, over two years ago. I'd found the need to put his lessons into practice since and would be forever grateful for them. I owed him as much as he did me.

Delith and Modwenna sat on a rug-covered hay bale on the side-lines, offering support and encouragement. Hugging the edges of the yard, I circled around to take my place beside them.

"He's good, very good." Modwenna nodded to the blond whirl-wind ducking and spinning in the centre of the ground, demonstrating his fighting techniques.

"I've never seen anything like it," added Delith, her eyes round and her brows perfect half-moons.

"Hmmm." I folded my hands in my lap and tilted my head, studying the two combatants. I hadn't seen the moves Dylan demonstrated before, either, but I had a good idea of what to expect. Those who journeyed by sea were well travelled, and thanks to Gwydion and my own voracious research I was conversant with the fighting forms of other lands.

Dylan was, without doubt, an expert at one-handed combat.

"Keep your distance," he ordered, twisting away from Cynar's clenched fists. Perhaps in an automatic response, Cynar had bunched his useless left hand as well, the one held in the sling. He angled his injured side away from Dylan instead of facing him squarely. Also an instinctive move, I guessed.

"Good, that's good." Dylan bounced back and forth, always moving, never still. "Ye should hold your fist more loosely, though. Tighten it when ye need to jab but be equally prepared to deliver a slap to the face. Remember those facial nerves I pointed out. Damage those with a good strike and ye've won your fight. Saves wear and tear on the knuckles, too."

Obediently, Cynar opened his hand and struck out with three fingers held taut. Dylan swayed away from him, grinning. "Perfect! Strike the throat or the eyes. Always keep that hand lead. Maintain an arm's length space between ye and the other man, never give him an opening. Now, try to kick me."

Cynar twisted, pivoted, and struck out with his right foot. He wore soft leather shoes, but I still heard the impact on Dylan's shin. If he'd been wearing the heavy boots Dylan recommended, he could have broken a bone. Crossing his hands in the signal for 'stop', Dylan stepped back and nodded approvingly.

"That's it, ye've got the idea. Footwork's the key. Your legs are strong and well-coordinated, and I know a dozen more moves besides that one. Kicks that'll let ye outmanoeuvre your opponents."

Cynar grinned savagely and slashed out again with his foot. First one side, then the other, turning and twisting, balancing on heel or toes and never once faltering. They kept at it for hours, until at last Dylan called a halt. Reaching for a towel, he rubbed the perspiration from his face and his hair, motioning Cynar to do likewise.

"We need to work on strengthening that injured arm too, though. Tomorrow, my lad, ye're coming swimming with Blodeuedd and me."

Delith rolled her eyes and shook her head. "Not me, the water's too chilly. Come spring, I might join you."

Modwenna laughed. "I agree—you can have that to yourselves. We'll keep watch on the dunes, guard your clothes and your towels, and make sure the crabs don't run away with our lunch."

We parted ways soon afterwards, Dylan to rendezvous with Math, Cynar and the others to return to their quarters, and me to catch up with Goronwy. I found my love in the office above the stables with Yestin, going through the next year's breeding program. Someone had to keep the place running smoothly.

Despite being perfectly at home in it, Dylan didn't really seem to relish cold water. I'd often see him look south with longing in his eyes and wasn't surprised when one day he declared he needed to leave soon for warmer climes. Not permanently, he assured me, just for a while.

I begged him to wait until after midwinter, which this year would be a subdued affair compared to previous festivals. He agreed; partly, I suspected, because he wanted to witness the highlight of the holiday, the battle between the Summer and Winter Kings, which was scheduled for the following day.

The origins of that combat stretched back through the millennia into the mists of history. An annual ritual taking place as part of the twice-yearly solstice celebrations, it had once been a fight to the death—a tradition Lleu had recently tried to revive. Luckily, he'd failed. Goronwy and I had conspired to spear him, resulting first in his transformation into an eagle, then in his lengthy stay in Caer Dathyl.

Because of my interference, the mortal Winter King, Goronwy Pebyr, remained free and healthy. None of the priests had demanded the battle go ahead in Lleu's absence, so this year would follow earlier ones. The fights between combatants were only for display. I planned to ask the healers, bards, and other members of my court to keep it that way. That ancient tradition should never be revived.

"He's coming in too low with the dagger," said Goronwy the next day, leaning forward in his seat, fists on his knees and expression intent. "And oh, Great Mother, his footwork's pathetic! A trained bear could do better."

Dylan, seated on his other side, laughed. "You're jealous because ye wish it were ye out there. Fightin' me brother."

"Hush!" I leaned backwards to glare at him behind Goronwy's back. "Enough of that talk. The priests revised their plans last summer, and I hope they won't reinstate the custom."

With luck, Lleu would remain in Caer Dathyl for a while. All of Mur Y Castell had seen Summer's champion fly away from those same grounds in eagle form and understood now, if they hadn't before, what kind of creature Lleu was. Not just an adherent of the sun god, but his very embodiment.

Goronwy shot me a sideways look of indulgent amusement and continued to comment on the fight. Giving up on trying to bring him to his senses, I linked my arm with his. Fool man.

As always, food and drink abounded among the bonfires and dancing. The Winter King soundly defeated his opponent, despite being a stripling in his teen years pitted against a seasoned veteran fighter. As was to be expected, for the fight was purely symbolic, with neither party wishing harm to the other.

I watched him sway past in the arms of a maiden. Several other couples wound around and through the bonfires in time-honoured tradition, seeking to secure the god's favour for the coming year. Celebrating the death of the old year's sun, and the birth of the new one.

"Where will you go?" I asked my former brother-in-law over a full tankard of mead. Ardudwy's finest, naturally.

He smiled widely and spread his brawny arms, the sealskin cloak falling back from his shoulders. Gold gleamed at neck and wrists, and the leaping flames touched his wild hair to ruddy copper in the firelight. "South, where winter never visits, and the brown-skinned, blue-eyed maidens are the fairest in the world. Where the malkiha sing songs by the shore and giant pogarats haunt the sea caves."

I'd never heard of either of those. "And what might they be?"

"Mermaids with rainbow scales and feathered heads, reputedly," said Goronwy. "I'd always thought they were nothing but a legend."

Dylan snorted. "Legendary, maybe, but I assure you they're real. Charming lasses. The pogarats aren't so attractive—they look like a cross between a frog and a goblin. Huge beasties, but relatively harmless. Can't say that for the lisca, the giant squid."

Goronwy raised his brows. "They'd dare attack you?"

"Nah, they're not that silly, they tend to avoid the likes of me." He rumbled with laughter. "Most fey beasties do. They can sense my magic, you see, and it scares them."

My beloved grinned. "I'm not surprised, having seen you fight. Good luck with the merladies, though." He rose and held out his hand to me. "Will you dance with me, my violet?"

"Of course."

I followed him out to the cleared space beyond the castle courtyard where most of the fires had died. A few couples danced through the embers.

"Do you really wish you could have fought Lleu?" I asked as he whirled me around the one remaining full bonfire.

"No, because I wouldn't want to worry you. Otherwise, I might have been tempted. But Lleu's gone, and so's Gwydion. At least for now."

I let the matter rest, although one problem remained. Gwydion had only to change into kite form, and he could fly right over my defences. As yet I had only a vague, untested idea of how to stop him.

9

SCOUTS

According to tales of the Elder Gods, those lords of the outer darkness who lived beyond and between the stars, that realm experienced a cold even greater than the polar ice. I wondered, as I surfaced, took a breath and dived again through the bitter, churning water, if they'd ever swum in the seas around Ardudwy on a freezing winter's morning. Surely, they'd be perfectly at home there.

"Ye're lagging," chided Dylan, bobbing in the surf as calmly as if it had been a pleasant summer's day. He hadn't mentioned leaving again, but I knew he wouldn't stay much longer and was determined to mine every second of his instruction that I could.

"It's hard to follow instructions when your limbs are frozen solid." I nodded to Cynar and Modwenna, wrapped in layers of blankets and huddled around a roaring fire on the foreshore. Delith, whom the midwives said could expect to give birth any day, remained at home, and Goronwy was busy helping Yestin play matchmaker to livestock. "Why are they allowed to thaw out, but you deny me the pleasure?"

"Ye're god-born, they're not." Dylan disappeared momentarily beneath a surge of white foam, and I wondered if he'd be swept underwater. He'd be at no risk of drowning, and I could return to shore. A vain hope: seconds later, he resurfaced and grinned evilly at me. "Try once more, deeper this time. Don't try to cheat again, either; ye know I can see for fathoms."

I tried to sigh and failed—my deep inhale netted me cold salt spray instead of air. Once more, he'd said. Vowing to hold him to that promise, I dutifully ducked beneath the water and plunged toward the sea floor. Schools of tiny fish flickered past, racing towards an unknown destination, and a large bronze cod eyed me distrustfully before darting away. I paid them no heed. Dylan said the purpose of this exercise for me, as well as for Cynar, was just that—exercise. Battling freezing water was apparently supposed to strengthen the muscles and build resistance. To what, he had yet to explain.

Grains of sand from the seabed slid through my fingers, proof that I could go no deeper, and without waiting for permission I curled and speared up towards the surface before striking out for shore. Curious or simply following its own agenda, a juvenile silver-scaled salmon brushed past my leg.

A piercing shriek rang overhead. A susurration of air, and a feathered missile slapped into the water near my face. Startled, I batted at it, connecting with a feathered wing. Too late, I realised late that the assailant, a mighty sea eagle, had been aiming for the fish, not for me.

"Blodeuedd, no!" Dylan's voice blended with the eagle's harsh cry as it struggled to lift into the air. It failed.

I gasped in horror, fearful that I'd injured or even broken the poor creature's wing. I tried to grasp the creature, but it shied away from me, beating the water with its healthy wing, and piping its distress.

"Go. Get ashore and leave this to me." Dylan waved me aside, his expression grim. His voice echoed the chill emptiness his distant forefathers ruled. Clucking softly, he gathered the injured bird to him, laying its head against his own and gently stroking its damaged wing.

Unable to offer an excuse or apology, I did as he directed and made for the beach. Cynar and Modwenna had seen what happened; I supposed they could hardly have missed it. They met me as I emerged, dripping, from the sea, questioning and exclaiming, anxious to know if I'd been harmed.

I shook my head, scattering droplets of water. "I'm fine, but I'm terribly afraid I may have crippled the eagle. If it can't fly and hunt, it will die."

The eagle appeared almost unconscious when Dylan waded onto the beach and set it down beside me. I initially thought it lay too near the blue, edged-gold flames, then I noticed the way they curved and twisted away from the patient and deduced that Dylan must be responsible. It puzzled me for a moment—unlike his twin, he was attuned to the sea, not the sun. But of course, the sea and air are inextricably linked. Dylan must have been controlling its flow.

"It's calming, I think. Can you heal it, Lord Dylan?" Concern laced Modwenna's voice. Her grey eyes shone with tears. "The poor thing, it feels so...so confused."

Her certainty sent a rush of warmth through my veins, a wild, singing hope. Almost afraid to ask in case I was mistaken, I did anyway. "How do you know?"

She drew a shaky breath. "I...I can hear it, in my head. That's never happened so clearly before. It's just been feelings, vague impressions." As if in a trance, she sidled up beside Dylan and stretched out a hand to the osprey. "It trusts you, I think."

I'd been right; she had Dafona's gift. I waited for her to elaborate, but apart from that perfunctory enquiry after my health, her focus remained fixed on Dylan the way a sea leech attaches to a fish. The same wind which whipped the sea to froth bit through my soaking woollen vestments and threatened to freeze me where I stood.

"C-Cynar," I said through chattering teeth, "would you mind adding wood to the fire? I trust you've kept my clothes, boots, and blankets dry."

"Of course, my lady." With a reproving glance at Modwenna, he escorted me up to the levelled wooden stumps they'd been using as seating and built the fire up to a roaring beast. He then left me to get dressed and returned to the water's edge to wait with Modwenna for Dylan. I remained by the fire, assuming that everyone else would shortly join me; I needed to warm up. Quickly.

Modwenna sank to her knees beside them both, her gaze unfocused, pink lips slightly parted and lovely features soft with compassion. "It will be all right," she whispered, reaching out to stroke the damp head feathers. "We have you now, we'll help you heal."

No thanks to me. A shaft of shame stabbed through me, and I had to fight the impulse to cringe away and leave the rest of the company to handle the bird. I bit my lip and stiffened my spine. "What can I do? How can I help?"

"He doesn't blame you," Modwenna assured me, understanding alight in her eyes. "He's just annoyed that you cost him his dinner."

Dylan gave a puff of laughter. "I imagine the fish feels differently. She'd be grateful to ye, Blodeuedd."

"How do you know it was female?" I asked, momentarily distracted. "The size?"

He shook his head. "They're little different to look at. But I'm Dylan Ail Don, remember. I can always tell such things." Eyes narrowed, he bent a considering look on Modwenna. "Does your tender heart encompass nursing skills? Have ye ever looked after an injured bird?"

"Oh, yes, but..." She bit her lip and looked away, hands folded tightly in front of her. "But only little ones, my lord," she said in a rush. "Sparrows, robins, and the like. Great Mother, I've never been this close to such a magnificent creature!"

Dylan's eyes slid to me, holding questions and, possibly, answers. Or maybe suggestions. I suspected his thoughts tended in the same direction as mine.

"The brave lad's quiet now," he said, caressing the great bird's neck feathers. "If you can spare one of your blankets, I'll wrap him up and deliver him to the healers so they can set the wing. I can dull his senses enough that he won't object to being handled, but afterwards I'd ask you to be his carer, for I think he trusts you."

He trained on her the flashing smile and dancing eyes which had such a devastating effect on the maidens of Mur Y Castell. Modwenna succumbed to it, happily married woman or not.

"You're shameless," I told him with mock severity.

"Why are ye laughing, then?" Still crooning to the eagle, he swaddled it in the blanket and nestled it in the crook of one arm, clasping it to him with the other. "By the way, I've a proposition for ye, Blodeuedd, but we can discuss that tomorrow. For now, we need to see this lad comfortable with the healers, and make sure he's on the mend."

We set off along the track. The sea eagle endured the journey in silence, a beak-nosed, feathered child in Dylan's careful embrace. Occasionally a deep golden eye blinked at me, but he didn't ruffle a feather or utter a pip of protest.

Cynar left us when we entered the gates of Mur Y Castell, heading for Yestin's office above the stables to apprise his lord, my husband, of the latest turn of events. I tried to imagine Goronwy's reaction and failed.

Whatever Efrawg the healer thought of being presented with a huge bird of prey and commanded to heal it, he hid his reaction well. He and his comrades and apprentices were used to tending to livestock as well as humans. They suffered from similar ills and often responded to similar treatments. Under Dylan and Modwenna's watchful eyes, he splinted and bound the fractured wing, settled the patient in a wire cage more commonly used to hold lambs or piglets, and promised to tell both me and Dylan at once should there be any change in its condition.

When I related the day's adventures to Goronwy later that night, he took the news in his stride. I supposed that after a while one became inured to astonishment or disbelief.

"A proposition? Hmm." He bent to add another log to the fire. The weather hadn't improved, and with nightfall the temperature had dropped more dramatically still. "Shall I hazard a guess what that's about?"

"Modwenna," I said, and he nodded. "I'd like to talk to her first. I think the idea might be less alarming coming from me than from Dylan. Charming though he might be, I don't credit him with much tact. He's likely to hail her as a modern-day version of Dafona of the Birds without even asking if she shares her ancestress's gift."

"But you think she does." Goronwy climbed into bed and lifted the covers invitingly, a suggestive smile lifting his lips at the corners.

I slid in beside him. "Yes, I'm certain of it."

Thereafter, unimportant conversation ceased.

I didn't get the chance to corner Modwenna immediately, because on the first day of the Rowan Month, Delith was brought to bed of a second son. She and Cynar named him Pyrs, after her grandsire. Cynar declared the babe looked just like his mother, and the small family group who'd gathered around to offer congratulations agreed.

Garth kept cooing "Pup-pup!" but whether he thought his new baby brother was a puppy or was saying he'd prefer one, I was uncertain. Dylan appeared to agree, pronouncing the infant to be as adorable as a seal pup, which may have caused Garth's confusion.

Never having witnessed a seal's birth, I couldn't confirm or deny that, but to my eyes baby Pyrs looked exactly as Garth had when he was born; small, pink, bald, and wrinkled. Garth had grown into a sturdy, dark-eyed, red-haired child with traits from each of his parents, so doubtless Pyrs would too.

After presenting the proud mother with a string of glowing, milky pearls to commemorate the occasion, Dylan said his farewells.

The next morning, he travelled through the tunnels of my guardian trees and returned to the sea without making his proposition, seeking those warmer southern waters. I allowed myself to hope that what I'd learned from him and Math would keep us safe, and determined to arm myself against the trickster's return by strengthening my own magic. Ardudwy was my home and my responsibility.

I did all I could during the following weeks to make good on the promise I'd made to myself. Forests had always covered our lands. I needed them to grow thicker, taller, and stronger—wild enough to close the roads against any who didn't know the right charm. But magic wasn't limitless. Sometimes it needed a boost from mortal, mundane methods. So I conscripted the two young couples as apprentice gardeners, and put my maturing power to work.

Seedlings of tall firs, pines and cypress trees would thread through the existing trees to form an outer barrier, hugging the ascending hillsides. Within them, on the downward slope, I planted brambles of various kinds—blackberries, raspberries, dewberries, wild roses, and honeysuckle. Anything which, if left untended, would form a nigh impenetrable thicket. I twined invisible ropes of magic between them to alert me, should anyone try to hack their way in.

We toiled through the waning days of winter and into the first blush of spring, and as the weather warmed my plantations spread and thickened.

"This is bloody hard work," complained Yestin, wiping sweat from his brow. Pushing his cap back with a dirty, gloved hand, he leaned forward on his shovel. His discarded coat now lay draped across Cynar's good arm. "Besides, I don't think these plants are any good. They have little green things all over them."

Modwenna set down the basket she carried and smirked at her husband. "You'll find that's a common complaint. They're called leaves."

Yestin rolled his eyes. "Ha, ha."

"No." I knelt to investigate more closely. "That was well spotted. They're *llyslau*, pine lice, and they're not welcome. Here, help me get rid of them."

Fire would kill them but would also destroy my small pines. Fiery plants were the answer. Combining water pepper, spignel, and pepper dulse seaweed, mixed with soapwort, in water and sluicing it over the seedlings should end the threat, or at least mitigate it. I sent the girls off to refill the buckets from a nearby lake, wishing Dylan was still with us. The ability to call rain would have been useful to water my new plants, without dribbling it from the goatskin. Luckily, it was never too far away. In the green land of Cymry, rainfall was constant.

"Couldn't you magic this up the hill?" asked Delith when she and Modwenna returned, setting her bucket down and rotating her shoulders to loosen them. "Wish the water to flow from the lake, without needing buckets. Water's heavy."

If only magic were the panacea she thought. Being able to place a protective bubble around the cantref or move the whole of Ardudwy into a hidden Otherworldly hollow, would solve so many problems. Of course, if I possessed that kind of power there'd be no need for such tactics. I could defy not just Gwydion and Lleu, but the elder gods on their thrones.

"If wishes were fishes, everyone would cast nets." Palm down, I reached into the earth, seeking the signatures of the plants I needed. My range had extended considerably over the past few months, thanks to Math's tutelage. We were miles from the sea, but I could access the dulse's essence, as well as the other three plants I needed. I handed Modwenna the spade. "Stir the water well, then dip each plant in it before you pat them into the ground."

We set to work, and by mid-afternoon, as the shadows lengthened, the first stage of my defence was in place. The other four laughed and chatted as we trudged homeward, passing beneath the crowding trees and out into the cultivated lands, a patchwork of brown and green and ochre.

My barrier would keep out wingless intruders, but kites and ravens could fly right over the top. Our people needed farmland, though, so I couldn't condemn us all to live in forest-shrouded twilight. I needed another strategy...and Modwenna might be able to help me carry it out.

Looking back at my helpers as we wound our way homeward, I found my chance to separate her from the others and speak to her alone. Clad in working clothes—the men in trousers and shirts, the women in plain house gowns, bundled into thick woollen coats, caps and gloves against the spring chill—they seemed unlikely saviours. Yestin carried the shovels, Cynar the basket containing the now empty seed trays in his good hand, and each woman swung a bucket, skipping and singing as they went.

On the path outside the castle walls, I halted, bending to loosen my shoe. "Curses—a pebble's worked its way in there. You go ahead, I'll catch up. Oops!" I swayed, clutching Modwenna's arm for support.

"Oh, Blodeuedd," she chided, "don't be silly. You'll fall, wobbling around like that." She passed her bucket to Delith and smiled at her husband. "I'll see you soon. Save the bathwater for me if it's not too filthy."

I laughed. "It probably will be, we're all grubby. But thank you."

Draping an arm around her shoulders to steady me, I made a show of removing the non-existent pebble. When the others were out of earshot, I straightened.

"I wanted to ask you something in private. You're descended from Dafona, too. You're able to communicate with the sea eagle, aren't you? I'm sure Dylan wouldn't entrust you with its care otherwise. You healed that owl, too, the morning Arlais was injured. Do you have her gift? Can you talk to the birds?"

She hesitated, casting an uneasy glance toward the three who'd just disappeared inside the postern gate. She didn't want to admit to it. The corners of my lips lifted, despite my efforts to keep them straight.

"Yes," she said, unwinding from my embrace, "you guessed right. I have the so-called gift—although why anybody would call it that, I really don't know."

"Are you saying it's a curse?" I couldn't imagine why.

Modwenna sighed, turned, and ambled toward the castle gate. "More a distraction. An annoyance. Do you think birds contemplate philosophy? It's all about food, and the weather, and avoiding predators, and... and mating and breeding."

The laugh I'd swallowed burst forth. "Like cats! You don't want anybody to know, because you think they'll form expectations you can't deliver on. I understand—I tried it once with cats and insects, without success. As you say, their priorities differ from ours. But you might reach the feathered ones better than I could their furred brethren. I wondered if it might be possible for you to try something like that?"

We neared the postern gate in the castle wall. "To give you warning if Gwydion approaches in the form of a kite." Modwenna stopped beneath the naked cherry tree as we passed through, biting her lip. "Of course." Shoulders squared, she lifted her chin and stared me down. "That's all it would be, though—a warning. Most will have migrated south by now. Only a few of the small breeds stay behind in the winter, and they'd be no match for Gwydion. Besides, I doubt even another kite could stand against him, and I'd never ask them to try."

I nodded soberly, impressed by this show of defiance. "Would you demonstrate your gift for me one day, so I can fine-tune my plan? Perhaps with the eagle. Of all birds, he and his kind might be a match for the Trickster. You could even try to tame him, and others of his kind. Use them as an aerial guard."

She studied me silently for a moment, face expressionless. Then she said quietly, "No."

Off-guard, I blinked. "What? What do you mean—"

Modwenna exhaled, scanning the distant skyline. "Weren't you listening to me, Blodeuedd? This man, this god, destroyed a stone circle not too long ago. He threw the dolmens around as if they were pebbles, and ripped furrows in the earth they stood on. How can you expect me to send a bird—even the largest of the raptors—to fight against that?"

Perhaps she was right. It would be unfair, and cruel. But one must be prepared to make sacrifices when fighting among gods. I'd revisit the idea later if necessary. "Very well. I won't ask you to put him at risk. In the meantime, we'll rely on my fortress of trees, and your network of small, feathered sentinels."

Mollified, Modwenna agreed. "At this time of year, we won't even have to go far to find them. Lots of sparrows, finches, starlings, and cardinals hang around the castle, foraging for seeds among the bushes and throughout the garden. We can start with them. There might be crows or ravens around, too. They rarely move very far, unless they're looking for a new nest site, and that won't happen until later in the season."

The next day I contrived to draw her aside before the others set out for work, on the pretext of searching for specific herbs. Once we were out of earshot, Modwenna led me to a cluster of tiny sparrows foraging for seed amongst low growing brush. Occasionally a tit or a wren flittered among them, fighting for morsels, but the sparrows dominated, chirping, cheeping, and cheerfully singing.

Modwenna leaned against the rough bark of a naked elm and closed her eyes, concentrating. "They've seen nothing untoward lately," she reported, "but I've just had a thought. We need magpies."

"Why?"

"They're the most curious—more likely than others to investigate unusual sights or sounds. Haven't you noticed the way they haunt the courtyards of Mur Y Castell? They're fascinated by the splashing noises from the fountains, and they love coloured baubles, too. We could put toys out to attract them, and I could then try to train them to become useful sentries. They're also quite clever."

I shrugged. When envisioning my feathered army, I'd pictured something larger—eagles, falcons, and kites. Even owls. But until I could convince Modwenna that more aggressive action was needed, this would do for a start. Further thought convinced me that laying the groundwork in winter had an unexpected benefit. By practising on the small birds first, Modwenna could build up a rapport, and when the weather warmed and they bred, she'd already have half-imprinted their hatchlings. When the larger birds returned in spring we could add them to our arsenal. Some, like the sea eagles, went no further south than our lands. Birds could tell the difference between a true kite and a shapeshifter, and if they spotted the latter, Modwenna would know.

We agreed not to mention these added defences to anyone except Goronwy. I had faith in my people's discretion, but still couldn't afford to take any chance of information leaking out. And while I trusted Cynar and Delith with my life, I didn't want to burden them with more responsibilities.

I estimated that it would take about a month to build the rest of my barrier around all of Ardudwy, to shield us from the sight and the reach of my enemies in Caer Dathyl. It might be enough; it might not. But I'd do all I could to guard against the threat foretold by Lotha the Seer.

10

FEATHERS

"Clear vision's seldom granted to mortals," scoffed Math when I shared my forebodings about Lotha's prophecies. Bright winter sunlight filtered through the overhanging branches, casting runic patterns at my feet. Despite the day's golden glow, the message I read there depressed me.

I swung the willow wand in a lazy arc, relishing the uncanny weight of it. Magic possessed its own gravity, detectable only to its users.

Math nodded, arms folded and expression blank. Trampled, frost-cured grass lined the practice yard, testament to the many hours we'd spent there, incessantly going over the same boring actions. "Again."

"And again? How often must I practise this?" Frustration jittered along my arm and into the wand, creating a series of sparks.

"Until you get over *that*." He jerked his chin at the trail of glowing firefly embers, the visible evidence of my shortcomings.

I fought the impulse to scream, to stamp my foot, to tell him and the world at large how I felt about being abandoned to fight my creator alone. Only the knowledge that to do so would mark me as an ungrateful wretch stopped me. I wasn't alone. Goronwy, Cynar, Delith, Modwenna, Yestin and a host of others stood with me, and would offer whatever support they could. But they were mortal, and Gwydion wasn't. I wanted—I needed—more powerful allies.

Math's stern expression softened. "Relying on the gifts we gave you at your creation won't be enough to defeat Gwydion. You need to expand your repertoire, Blodeuedd. Which means practice, practice, and more practice."

So I was to lose him as well as Dylan. We'd still had no word to say when my brother-in-law would return.

"Must you go?" I gripped the wand in stiff fingers and tried to blanket my disappointment. The sparks fizzled and died, but flickers of sensation still twined around my hand.

Math pocketed his own wand and stepped close, putting a comforting arm around my shoulders.

"I have to return to Caer Dathyl; I've been away for too long," he said as we walked back to my quarters. He hadn't needed to carry me for the past several weeks. "I know you still doubt your abilities, but you've absorbed my lessons well, and I'm confident you can hold your own until help arrives. Remember the plan we discussed and implement it."

"You can't leave straight away," I protested. "I'll need at least a week to organise your farewell feast. My cook will resign if I spring another last-minute one on him."

He sighed heavily, but agreed to wait that long, and to attend the dinner I arranged in his honour.

The meal and the entertainment were worth the wait, though the latter lacked the drama of last time. Math almost made up for it, appearing resplendent in royal purple and clanking with jewellery. He even wore his cloak of raven feathers, something I gathered was reserved for very special occasions.

At the end of a long night, when the last glimmer of moonlight had faded and the first streaks of a pale winter sun slanted through the hall windows, the court and the servants departed, leaving me alone with my king.

"You'll be fine," he said, wiping a tear from my cheek with his thumb. "And if you need my help, call me."

I nodded, blinking rapidly. "How?"

"With this." He waved his hand over his wrist, the one with the snake on it, and a bright and glittery strip peeled away. "Even miniature pythons shed their skin, and you can use this to alert Enfys of your need. She, in turn, will summon me."

He hugged me then, an unprecedented move, and flung out his arms. Multi-coloured lights eddied around him, teasing echoes of blue, green, and purple from the surface of his raven-feather cloak. He spun his wrists in a twisting motion, flung back his head, and amid a bright dazzle of colour, was gone.

Math's departure coincided with the completion of Cara's new prison. It was not quite what I'd had in mind.

A small roundhouse, I'd said, with guards' accommodation attached. The roundhouse comprising the prison was basic enough, but in addition to the main room, the guards' section included a kitchen, a washroom and sleeping quarters. The structure resembled a Roman fort, except it was round instead of square. A covered walkway led to stalls for their horses and, beyond that, a private latrine. Of course, it was built of Bryn's favourite pale golden sandstone. The effect was whimsical rather than forbidding.

"I warned you," said Cynar, smirking, as we watched a pair of brawny youths march Cara downstairs from the guest room on the way to her new abode. "Never give an architect free rein with a building when he's enamoured of his craft."

"No, you didn't," I protested. "You warned Goronwy, who said he'd talk to Bryn. I took that to mean firmly. Obviously, I was wrong. I'm disappointed in both of you."

Cynar grinned. "Why doesn't Bryn attract any censure?"

"As you said, he's in love with his designs. He has an excuse." I hesitated a moment. "You go and see her installed; I'll meet you there soon. I've offered to take her mother to visit her as soon as she's moved."

He didn't question me, but nodded and followed in the wake of the guards and their captive. I returned to my own chamber to collect a new woollen shawl and a box of provisions for Mabli. Motivated by sympathy, mingled with guilt, I'd taken to visiting her regularly to ensure she had all she needed.

Mabli loved preserved fruit, which she considered a luxury. That morning, the kitchen staff had delivered a box to my room, plus a large jar of honey and a bottle of fine mead. These they'd placed on the mantle, where the dogs couldn't reach them. As I collected them in my basket—smaller than Cara's, which Modwenna now used to hold spades and other gardening implements—my eyes fell on the onyx box containing Cara's precious feathers. An idea occurred to me. I added them to the basket and set out for Mabli's house.

As usual, I found her on her stool by the fire, but this time she was engaged in mending a pair of woollen stockings. I set my gifts on the shelf as I always did and showed her the feathers. "These were in Cara's basket as well, but unlike the rest of its contents, they weren't intended for you. I have it on excellent authority that they have an evil spell on them, but it wasn't Gwydion's—that is, Blaise's—doing. Who else would Cara know who could do such a thing?"

I was curious about Cara's hedge-witch. Although as far as I knew she'd never dabbled in magic, her attachment to her 'love-charm' seemed more intense than I'd expect from a purchased object. Could she have attempted to set the spell on it herself, imbuing it with her own essence?

Mabli eyed the bundle with distaste and shuddered dramatically. "They're from him, ain't they? Shouldn't have truck with someone who can turn himself into a bird, either. It ain't natural, not at all." She shook her head, tucking a vagrant strand of hair behind one ear. "She didn't keep that kind of company while she lived with me, my lady, but I fear she fell in with a bad crowd after she left. There are plenty of *gwarches* out there who'd prey on a young, innocent girl."

Her assessment of Cara seemed a bit inconsistent, but I supposed mothers often held opposing views of their offspring. She seemed unaware of any involvement with spellwork, at any rate. I changed the subject. "I have good news for you. Cara's been moved out of the castle, and at last you can visit her without climbing stairs. Would you like to see her now?"

We'd discussed this before, but Mabli's recollections were shaky. Sometimes she'd remember what I told her and seem eager to call on her daughter, at others she expressed no interest at all. Today was the latter case. She shook her head, stabbed her thumb with the needle, and let out a lurid and highly original curse.

She thrust the stockings aside and creaked upright, or as close as she could. "Now look what you made me do. Have to soak them now, to get the blood out. Blood stains bad, you know."

I smiled. "I can fix that for you; I've a rare way with stains. Give them here."

She looked mistrustful but complied. It was a simple matter to tease the blood from the fibres, running the stockings through my fingers until it flaked away and fell to the floor.

"Here you are." I handed them back to Mabli, who held them in shaking hands, her eyes wide.

"Keep forgetting you're a *gwarch* yourself," she muttered, hunching away from me. "Not that you're like that Blaise, of course. I'd never say that. But still, mebbe you oughta keep these. Wouldn't feel right, I wouldn't, wearing 'em now."

I sighed, my hopes of learning anything useful from her dissipating on a wave of superstition. "Of course," I said, rising. "I'm sure I can find someone who'd be grateful for a warm pair of stockings. Thank you for the gift, and I'll take you to Cara some other time."

I left her mumbling to herself and went to see Cara, alone. None of our previous interviews had proved fruitful, but I hoped her change of circumstances might loosen her tongue. When Cynar met me at the prison door, I explained that Mabli had declined my invitation. Upon receiving his assurances that Cara was now secure, and two guardsmen installed in the tower, I gave him leave to go.

I nodded to the guards and lingered for a moment outside the door, contemplating those feathers. *Find another use for them,* Wynne had said. Although I hadn't destroyed them, until this moment I hadn't thought of any alternative uses, either; but now an idea took shape. Mabli's description of her daughter as an only girl, indulged by her five older brothers, suggested that she might not have developed a talent for subterfuge. She'd have lacked the need or the desire. Perhaps I could convince her that the spell set on them was working and that Goronwy and I were experiencing difficulties. By tempting her to gloat, I might convince her to drop a hint or two regarding the origins of the *gwarch* responsible.

Still thinking, I unlocked the door, knocked once, and walked in.

Cara sat on the bed, huddled in rugs. Under Cynar's instruction the guards had lit a fire, but it had yet to warm the room. A bitter chill lingered in the air.

"I'm cold," she complained, without any greeting.

"So you keep telling me. Be grateful I allow you blankets, as well as a fire. Generous of me to allow you one, I thought. Unnecessary, even. After all, you have your memories of Gwydion to keep you warm."

Cara spat on the floor: a thick, phlegmy globule which sat slimily quivering. I said nothing. Every visit followed the same pattern, punctuated by displays of contempt and outbursts of temper. How had I ever considered her a sweet, pliant young thing?

Apart from the narrow bed, the room contained only one item of furniture—a hard three-legged stool. The bed itself, although far from luxurious, was cushioned with a deep feather mattress and down pillows. I placed a cushion carefully on the stool and sat down.

Cara glared at me. "I don't know why you keep coming. I'd tell you nothing, even if there was aught to tell. And why won't you let me mam come to see me? Poor old dear must be worried sick."

"Funny, that's not how she tells it." One arm folded across the other, I tapped one finger against my lips. "I offered to bring her with me today, and she flat-out refused. That was after I showed her your feathers. They seemed to disturb her. Why would that be, I wonder?"

Storm clouds gathered in Cara's blue eyes, turning them grey. Fascinating. I retrieved the feathers from my cloak pocket, watching what effect they had. Her eyes lit up, and she quivered slightly, as if longing to reach for them. I smiled and deliberately moved them away from her.

"I got the impression she dislikes Gwydion, and disapproves of your relationship. I have to say, I like your mam a lot more than I do you." Twirling one dark feather—from his tail, most likely—I shaved a few downy barbs from the bottom of the shaft.

Cara gasped, then winced, as if the action hurt her.

As if they connected her to Gwydion, somehow. They were still in pristine condition. What would be the effect if I altered that? A few singe marks, for instance, along the edges... Slowly, nonchalantly, I moved across to the fireplace, and bending, touched a flame to the feathers' edge.

Cara screamed. Not a yell of protest, but an actual cry of pain.

My resolution almost failed me; I made myself recall what she'd tried to do to me and Goronwy, and who she was in league with. I snuffed out the flame, wrinkling my nose against the aroma of burnt feathers.

"Will the threat of burning them to ash loosen your tongue?" I asked quietly. "Tell me who bespelled them, and I'll promise to leave them intact."

The girl before me resembled a trapped animal now rather than a defiant rebel. Or perhaps they were the same thing. Perhaps Gwydion held her in thrall, even if she wouldn't acknowledge it.

Cara swallowed, and said in a shaking voice, "If you ruin them, you'll set the spell and 'twill never be lifted."

Not the reaction I'd hoped for. But gradually escalating threats to destroy them might earn me the information I needed: Gwydion's plans for retaking Ardudwy, and what part Lleu played in his schemes.

11

REUNION

Having been married to Math ap Mathonwy for eons—or what sometimes felt like it—I knew the man's moods. When he returned from Mur Y Castell after an extended absence, he seemed pleased with himself. Some wives might take that at face value, thinking he was merely happy to return home to his wife. I knew better. He exuded satisfaction, meaning he thought he'd achieved something great.

The portal he'd created to return to Caer Dathyl disintegrated in a shower of sparks. The two retainers who, like me, had been alerted by Math to its imminent appearance, bowed low. There was nobody else around, and the echoing vastness of the Great Hall magnified the hiss of the portal's closure. At this advanced hour, most of the castle was either fast asleep or otherwise occupied in pleasant nightly pursuits.

"Welcome home, my liege," said Teilo, the elder of the pair. He affected long grey hair, a lined and leathery face, and watery blue eyes in an attempt to underscore his great age, although his physique belonged to someone much younger. I supposed there were limits beyond which vanity triumphed. He waved his hands with a flourish, an expansive gesture, including me and his companion. "The place has seemed empty and hollow without your mighty presence. We've all missed you sorely."

Teilo was a bard—a good one, when he wasn't indulging in histrionics. Mighty presence, indeed!

"I've alerted the kitchens to prepare a feast to mark the occasion," said Emyr, a dark-haired, smooth-faced version of his father. He cleared his throat and caught my eye with a conspiratorial wink, before turning back to Math. "But I'm sure you and Lady Wynne have much to discuss, so we'll leave you alone for a while. Come on, Da."

His father frowned. "But we need to advise King Math of the latest security problem, and…"

Emyr shook his head. "Later. Our king's been absent for several years in the other realm; I feel certain he'd appreciate some time alone with his wife. We can talk about that tomorrow."

He grabbed his father by the arm and pushed him towards the massive carved doors of the chamber, to which Teilo acceded with ill-disguised reluctance.

"What was that all about?" asked my husband, undoing the gold knotwork brooch at his throat and letting his raven-feather cloak fall over one arm. He tossed it aside onto a carved onyx bench, before reaching out to draw me into his arms.

I melded against him, warm and buzzing with delight, and raised my hands to his shoulders. "Nothing too important. As Emyr said, it can wait. Tell me about Blodeuedd. Are you absolutely certain it's safe to leave her alone?"

"Yes, I think so." Math stroked a thumb along the bottom edge of my jaw, smiling down at me. The gold circlet confining his long silver hair followed the cloak. "Father Beli, I hate wearing that thing. If I were mortal and susceptible to such problems, I swear I'd have a headache by now."

I lifted a hand to run my fingers through his hair. So fine, so soft, so thick for a man many centuries old. "You know you didn't have to dress up just to impress me."

"Blodeuedd insisted on a formal leave-taking, all pomp and ceremony. Hence the titivations." He stretched with a click on his shoulders and rubbed his temple.

"Perhaps you need to have your coronet adjusted. It shouldn't cause any discomfort if it fits properly."

"Perhaps I just don't like wearing it." He began edging us both backwards as he spoke.

"Ah, the trials of being royal." I sat down as a bench pressed against the back of my calf, and Math settled beside me, still caressing my face. His touch felt strange, for some reason.

"Of which there are many," he agreed, gliding both hands through my hair and removing the pins, one by one. I turned my head as he pulled a strand over my shoulder, my lips seeking his fingers. At the contact, I pinpointed the difference that had disturbed me.

The easy smile I knew of old, the strong, fit body, the piercing hawk-yellow eyes. But his hands... I caught one, turned it palm up, and held it before me. Calluses. It took a lot of work—hard, heavy work—to coarsen Math's skin, and it would heal very quickly. Therefore, he must have been doing something strenuous recently. Something he'd either found enjoyable, or which he considered would benefit him in some way.

"What have you done to Blodeuedd?" I asked, circling my fingertips over each roughened pad.

He twirled the fingers of his other hand around my hair, twisting it into a coil. "My dearest love, my beautiful wife, my footholder supreme, what makes you think I've done anything to her?"

I continued stroking his palm. "You didn't get these calluses by simply offering her advice. Which was, if memory serves me, your stated reason for staying away for so long."

"Unavoidable. So you did miss me?" He bent to kiss the lobe of my ear.

Tingles of pleasure coursed through me. I stretched my neck and arched my back. "No. No more than breathing. Tell me what you did. Without obfuscation or riddles, or you can sleep alone tonight."

His lips danced from the nape of my neck down my spine to my shoulder blades, and I squirmed. Mother Don, but I'd missed him.

"I completed her training." Between kisses, he ran through the highlights, his voice muffled by the folds of my gown. "You don't need this, my queen." A tearing sound followed, and my shoulders were suddenly bare.

"That was tussah silk, you realise," I protested half-heartedly.

Math grinned and very deliberately ripped the rest of the fabric down the middle, all the way to the floor. "What? No undergarments?"

"I've never worn undergarments." I turned sideways, stretched out along the settle, and opened my legs. "If you've forgotten that, you *will* be sleeping alone."

The doors to the audience chamber slammed shut, followed by the sound of locks snicking into place. "True," he growled. "Because I don't plan for either of us to do any sleeping at all."

I'd have foregone sleep for a week, for a month, to experience the joy his presence brought me. *My king. My own beloved.*

"Is Enfys content?" I asked several delightful hours later, running an exploratory finger along the iridescent scales of his enchanted bracelet. Snakes slept a lot, I knew. I'd done my research. "Or do you let her regain her true form now and then? I think it would be too cruel not to."

"Don't worry, your serpent suffers no ill-effects. Now that I'm home she can have the run of the place, but I couldn't let her loose in Ardudwy. It would have upset the natives and disturbed my training sessions with Blodeuedd."

"What sort of training?" I asked, trying to restore my ruined gown—at least enough to exit the chamber without causing a stir. "I don't suppose you could conjure me a new gown?"

"What do you think I am, a magician?" He lifted a foot to his lips—he was now sitting at the end of the settle—and sucked gently on my littlest toe. "Actually," trailing kisses over the arch of my foot to reach my ankle, "I taught her to properly use her innate magic. You were there; you saw how well she took to the willow wand. And there's more to plant life than most realise, including Blodeuedd herself. Did you know they can sing?"

"Now you're just making stuff up." I twisted my foot in a circle, joining both feet together. Math brought them up to either side of his face, kissing the soles.

I melted into the depths of delight. Nobody ever understood the benefits of being a royal footholder who hadn't occupied the position.

Feet were packed with nerve endings, a gateway to pleasure through which few bothered to pass. And of course, both parties participated. History might know me as Math's footholder, but the truth was that he performed the same office for me.

"I'm not. Let me tell you a few more interesting facts. They can communicate through their roots—something Blodeuedd worked out long ago; they cohabitate, cooperate, and help each other out to a remarkable degree. Humans could learn a great deal from trees."

"I'll wager Gwydion didn't know that when he decided to make Blodeuedd from herbage. Did you?"

"Hmm." Math sat up and pulled me onto his knee. "I didn't, but I should have. There's a lesson for all magic wielders there. And speaking of Gwydion, how is he?"

I took a moment to respond. Having to deal with Gwydion, living in the same castle even if we didn't interact very often, was trying. If I hadn't adored Math and felt a lingering fondness for Lleu, I'd have banished him from my presence, as I had done his brother Gilfaethwy.

At last, I said, "Haughty, rude, ill-tempered... the same as he's always been, really. Oh, you meant how is he coping with Lleu's troubles? Not well. Gwydion expects things to happen simply because he desires it and rejects the idea that Lleu might have suffered a trauma strong enough to affect even a god."

"What about Lleu? Have you spoken to him since Gwydion brought him home?"

"A few times. He never speaks about what happened with Blodeuedd, about being struck by the spear; he's completely focused on reuniting with Caron. But even though neither he nor Gwydion will discuss it, that event has to have affected them both. Lleu met his hamartia, which for most would be the end. Gwydion doesn't consider that Lleu might have difficulty reconnecting with his previous life, even though his hurts are now healed."

Math sighed and kissed my brow. "I can't thank you enough for all you've done to keep him here. I know you dislike being around him still. But until Blodeuedd had all her defences in place and learned full control of her magic, I couldn't risk leaving him to his own devices. Did he notice what you were doing?"

There it was—the well-hidden doubt nestled beneath the bonhomie. I pushed that thought aside and laughed, rather harshly. "If he had, he'd have torn down your castle in his efforts to escape. No; I suspect Gwydion's mind, most of the time, has been as befuddled as Lleu's."

Blodeuedd wasn't the only one who'd needed to study in order to overcome the threat posed by Gwydion. Since that long-ago day when he'd aided his brother to rape me, I'd trodden many arcane pathways in pursuit of power. Magical power, to ensure nothing of the sort ever happened to me again. I'd long ago ceased to be a maiden. I'd passed through motherhood and was now on the cusp of becoming a crone: the wisest of all women.

"He hasn't realised you've been altering reality around him?" Math tilted my face up to meet his, worry in his eyes.

"To tell you the truth, I doubt he's even noticed any difference. He's totally absorbed with Lleu, and Lleu at the moment shies from even looking at the mortal realm. Every other realm, in fact. He appears reluctant to venture out of this Otherworld, or even away from Caer Dathyl. I think perhaps his memories are simply too painful."

"His own fault. He made them that way." Math spoke dismissively, then stood and gestured.

We both regained all our clothing, but while his was whole, mine now resembled a cloak. I hastily wound it around me, and in one smooth motion he lifted me into his arms. Although I was not a dainty creature, he managed it easily.

"Show-off," I murmured into his beard.

He smiled down at me, moving towards the outer doors. "That's my line."

"Meaning?"

"The impressive job you've done in fencing Caer Dathyl off from the rest of reality. I almost couldn't find my way back here."

We reached the entrance, and the massive carved oaken doors swung open without so much as a blink from the master magician.

"If it's a contest," I said, "you'd best put me down. I'll need the use of my arms."

"Which means I've already won. I don't need mine." He shifted one hand slightly, the one cradling my arse, and snapped his fingers.

"Do you want to hear about our other problems now?" I asked as we arrived in a brilliant, icy glow in our chamber.

He dropped me in the middle of the bed, amid bright quilts and piled cushions. "Later. Much later." A gesture, and our clothes quit our bodies to reappear in an untidy heap on the floor. "After breakfast, perhaps," continued Math, sliding in beside me and trailing one calloused hand between my breasts. "Or even after that. Lunchtime, say."

With a twist, I landed on top of him. "Better make that dinner. You've been away a long time, and I've a lengthy stretch of abstinence to make up for. One brief night in Mur Y Castell doesn't count."

"After dinner it is." Another snap of his fingers, and the cushions landed on the other side of the floor.

I pouted. "You could have done that with my gown, instead of ruining it."

He stretched his arms above his head, grinning at me. "I could have, but sometimes a hint of violence adds piquancy."

"Or perhaps more than a hint." I ran my nails down the curling hair of his chest.

"Tigress." He surged up to bite my shoulder, chuckling as I rolled away from him.

Unfortunately, I rolled a little too far, and still laughing, we fell off the edge of the bed.

12

BLEIDDWN

"We have to talk about Meghan, to start with," I said over breakfast.

Emyr had organised a magnificent spread to be delivered to our room: ham, eggs, mushrooms, and the luscious red love-apples from the other side of the mortal world. A highly prized delicacy. These were followed by thick, buttered *bara brith,* dark bread and steaming hot peppermint tea, also sourced from far to the east of Cymru.

"What's that daughter of yours been up to now?" asked my husband around a mouthful of ham. "Is it a magic problem?"

"*Our* daughter," I corrected. "And I suppose you could say magic's involved, in a roundabout way."

Everyday life in Caer Dathyl was touched by enchantment, and that held doubly true for Meg. Not only was she Math ap Mathonwy's daughter, claiming immortality as her birthright, but she, like Lleu and so many others before her, had been born and raised in Caer Dathyl. She'd breathed enchantment daily, soaking it into her pores. Her failure to detect Lleu's current dwelling place by herself evidently rankled, particularly when she'd discovered I'd locked Blei up and allowed him no visitors. Including her.

Math began attacking his eggs. "And?"

"She's found out where Gwydion's hidden Lleu and has tried to visit him. He didn't want to talk to her, though."

This news failed to upset Math. "Her spellwork's improving, then. I knew it would eventually. She worked out how to shapeshift all by herself. I can't see why that would concern Teilo and Emyr, though. What else is going on?"

I piled my plate high with buttered mushrooms. "You're right, there's a little more to it. Meghan didn't decipher the wards by herself. She had help."

Eggs already demolished, Math buttered a hunk of thick, crusty bread. "From?"

I'd mentally rehearsed and discarded several ways to break this news to my husband. Now, face to face with him, none seemed appropriate. I sighed. "Bleiddwn."

His good mood evaporated. Brows knotted and eyes narrowed, Math pushed his plate away and surged to his feet. His displeasure filled the room, a palpable, crackling presence.

"Well, that leads to another question, doesn't it?" He set his hands on the edge of the table and leaned forward. "Who in Beli's name let him into my castle? I don't believe for a moment that it was you."

I shook my head, and Math's next word exploded from him. "Gwydion!"

"It must have been. Nobody else admits to having seen Blei at all. And no, I haven't approached Gwydion about it. We don't speak, if possible. You know that. Gwydion spends all his time with Lleu, so I've locked Blei in his father's room. I've tried to persuade him to tell me everything that happened after he eluded your men. But he's being foolishly stubborn and says he'll explain only to you."

Unexpectedly, Math relaxed and sat down again, laughing. "I'll say this for him—he's consistent. And predictable. That's what comes of sticking to noble ideals, I suppose."

Frowning, I reached across the table to relieve him of his uneaten toast. "What do you mean? I can't see anything gallant about Blei's behaviour, and whatever happened to him would seem to have been violent. I didn't get a good look, but he had new wounds on his neck, extending down to his shoulder."

"It won't appear in the official reports, but when his brothers were questioned, they had a lot to say about Blei's strange beliefs. Apparently, they had to bribe him to accompany them when they attacked me and Blodeuedd. And afterwards..." He broke off, regarding his empty plate with dismay. "Hold on, you stole my breakfast."

"I thought you weren't going to eat it, and I dislike waste, no matter how well stocked our larders." I clicked my fingers, and a bell by the door chimed to summon the servants. "We have plenty of bread. I'll order some more. Tell me about Blei."

Math selected an apple and bit into it. "Apparently he feels called to the old gods," he said, his voice slightly muffled and juice running freely down his chin. I reached across to wipe it away. He licked my fingers, grinning at me. "So when Artio showed up at the end of our little battle, he took it as a sign from beyond. Decided to track her down and offer to enter her service. I don't know the rest of the story, but at a guess, she refused him. Bears aren't generally fond of wolves."

I winced. A solid refusal, if the scar I'd seen was anything to go by. "He wouldn't tell me anything, and I've asked a couple of times since confining him. Perhaps if we visit him together, he'll be more forthcoming."

"Very well, lead the way." Math downed the rest of his tea, snatched up a couple of slices of *bara brith*, and gestured for me to precede him. With an apologetic smile at the servants who'd just turned up with more bread, I bade them deliver it to those breaking their fast in the Great Hall instead.

I swept past my husband, touching his bristly cheek on the way. "You need a shave, my love, I'm not really a great admirer of beards. As for Blei, I've talked to his brothers, but they're being uncharacteristically close-mouthed as well. I suppose your men's interrogation methods were more heavy-handed than mine."

Math nodded. "Even so, the accounts I've had so far were second-hand and garbled, and strong-arm tactics have never worked well with Gwydion or his sons. Gil would be a different matter, but he's removed himself from the affairs of the world for a while. I wouldn't be surprised if he's influenced Blei. They've always been closer than Blei and Gwydion."

From Roman-style columns to vibrant frescoes, from delicate eastern watercolours to vivid, realistic landscapes, the ever-fluid halls of Caer Dathyl never remained the same for long. "It must be odd," I said, as we passed a landscape sparkling with crystal snow, "to acknowledge a man as your mother."

"Odder still for Gilfaethwy." Math's voice was expressionless, as it always was when he spoke of the circumstances leading up to Blei's begetting. He'd acted in anger, in blind, crushing rage when he'd bespelled Gil and Gwydion to walk as hind and hart, then boar and sow, and finally as a she-wolf and her mate. Each time, young had resulted from their pairing—Hyddwn the fawn, Hychdwn the piglet and Bleiddwn the wolf cub.

Guilt pinched me sometimes, for it had been outrage on my behalf that had prompted Math's spell—retaliation for my rape. Guilt towards the children, that is. I had little sympathy for their parents. A harsh punishment, yes, but fully deserved.

The thought of each of them enduring childbirth had helped me come close to forgiveness, however. I thought I could truthfully claim to have forgiven Gil, for the experience had radically changed his outlook on life. He'd retired from court afterwards and set up a series of hospices aimed at helping indigent women.

Gwydion was another story. Gil had been the instigator of the plan to attack me, so Math had changed him into a female beast twice. Gwydion, who'd only once had to take on female form, had emerged from his ordeal more misogynistic than ever.

We reached the invisible door of Gwydion's camouflaged chamber. Math waited until I'd disabled my own wards before slicing through Gwydion's. Soft, ambient light spilled into the corridor from the glow of many candles.

Blei turned, his glance sliding off me to land on my husband. His king. He sank to the floor, head bowed. "My liege, I must beg your forgiveness. What I did was...was..."

He halted, apparently unable to find the right words.

"Unforgivable?" suggested Math drily. "Possibly, but you're here now, which goes a small way to mending the breach, I suppose. Are you going to fill me in?"

Lifting only his head, Blei looked up. "I'd prefer to do so in private, my lord."

Fair enough. I turned to go, but Math stopped me. "No, Bleiddwn. Your offence also affected my queen; she deserves to hear your motivations and excuses too." He settled on a long couch, upholstered in dark blue leather, and motioned for me to sit beside him before nodding to Blei. "You may rise."

He did so with a stiffness that hadn't been evident in our previous encounters. Perhaps the marks on his neck weren't the only souvenirs Artio had left him. Math noticed it, too. "What happened to you?"

"Not what, who." Blei levered himself into a matching chair, wincing. "Great Artio, the Bear Goddess."

Math snorted with laughter. "Her loving too much for you, was it?"

"No," replied Blei, not meeting his eyes. "We fought. I lost."

I tsked. She'd routed him completely, judging from the runnels I'd seen carved on his neck. "Have you had someone look at your wounds? Bear's claws can cause infection, especially with deep gouges like those."

He stiffened in offence. "How do you know how deep they are? Have you been spying on me?"

"No need," I told him. "I have eyes, and even from here I can see the marks she left. Besides, you were always quite nimble, and right now you move like an ancient a few centuries old. Now be a good lad and take off your shirt so I can inspect the damage properly." I looked at Math. "Gwydion spared no expense in the healers he engaged to treat Lleu; I've spoken to some of them. Ianaura was one, and Alaun another. I'm sure if you raised the matter with him, he'd agree to have them look at Blei while they're here."

As expected, Blei started to protest, but Math overruled him. "You'll do as you're told and be happy about it. Hasn't it occurred to you that although you can heal effortlessly from wounds inflicted by a normal bear, Artio might be something else again? Otherworldly wounds require Otherworldly healing."

"At least it wasn't an afanc's tooth," muttered Blei with ill grace. "Hych tried to stick me with one of those once. He only managed to graze me, but even that hurt like blue blazes."

"Not as bad as a dragon's claw." Math's face clouded with the memory of that disastrous long-ago battle, which had taken place before Blei or his brothers were born.

"Afanc, bear goddess, neither are good for the health," I said, losing patience. "Your shirt, please."

Face expressionless, eyes hard and flat, Blei dragged the fine linen garment over his head. Long practice kept my gaze and my breath steady, but my hands gripped the chair arms so tightly that I felt its carvings imprint on my palms.

Artio hadn't intended Blei to live. The marks on his neck were scratches compared to the deep network of gouges criss-crossing his torso. Pink and raw, they appeared to be only semi-healed. At least they weren't leaking pus or blood, nor were there any striations denoting infection.

He must have survived only because he was the son of Gwydion and Gilfaethwy: twice over Great Don's grandson and, like Lleu, a godling possessed of hamartia. All the godborn had one, a single sure means of ending their life and ushering them on to another phase of existence. Attack by a divine bear, no matter how vicious, was obviously not destined to be Blei's.

I managed a shaky laugh. "You look like a *tafl* board. Perhaps Artio had mislaid hers and wanted a game."

"You and Lleu are a good pair," grunted Math, signalling me with a look. "Wynne will fetch Ianaura, and you'll tell me exactly what went on between you and the Bear Queen." Then, as I rose to leave, "Wait. Do you know where to find the healers?"

I nodded. Gwydion might have hidden the healers' quarters as well, but he didn't prevent them from attending meals each night with the rest of our household.

It was now close to dinner time. I slipped out quietly and made my way down to the hall. When Ianaura looked up and saw me beckon to her from the doorway, she quietly slipped away from her seat among the rest of her colleagues. She listened gravely as I explained my request and nodded.

"Physical healing might be the least of your nephew's concerns," she warned as we left the hall and entered the subtly shifting ways, surrounded by leaf glitter and birdsong. Shafts of golden light flowed over her face, her robes and the leather bag she carried. I made a mental note to adjust my time slippage by at least a full twenty-four hours, so day didn't bleed into night.

Before we'd taken half a dozen steps, another healer came racing down the corridor, her dark hair flying and green robes awry. I recognised her as one of those who'd sat beside her at the table. "Ianaura! Mistress, wait."

With an apologetic smile to me, Ianaura held up a cautioning hand. "Mind your manners, Aisbel. I'm speaking with the queen."

The woman flushed carmine and dipped into a curtsy. "My apologies, Your Grace. But this warning is for you." She heaved a sobbing breath and pushed an errant lock of hair out of her eyes. "He's coming!"

My pulse danced a little jig. "Who is? Coming where?"

The answer confirmed my quickening fear. "Lord Gwydion. He must have seen you two leave together—he appeared before us out of nowhere. He said to tell you even the highest-ranking healers aren't free to trespass in his rooms, and..." She broke off with a squeak as a red kite swept past her head, outstretched claws missing her by less than half an inch.

Summoning my reserves, I thrust Ianaura behind me. "Thank you, Aisbel, you've done well. Now run! Get back to the hall, quickly!"

She stumbled away, hugging the wall, and I turned to the now transformed kite. "What do you want, Gwydion?"

He came close, too close, and stood glaring down at me. "Answers. Did you think I wouldn't notice somebody adding extra wards to my own quarters? You have a nerve."

Ianaura gasped in outrage. I held up a hand to silence her and trotted out the official line that I'd given to everyone else. "You weren't using them, apparently, and I needed somewhere to incarcerate your son. He attacked the king's men, which carries a heavy penalty. He really needs a healer, though. If you care about his welfare, you'll allow me to take Ianaura to him."

Gwydion leaned closer still, and despite myself, I cringed away from him. He growled, "I've paid the fines for myself and the three boys. An exorbitant sum it was, too."

I took several steps back, hating that I felt the need. Hating that he could outface me. "No," I said coldly, "you paid the commensurate sum for attacking your king, as well as Blodeuedd and her people that day in Ardudwy. In many other countries they'd call such an action treason and have you all executed for it. You should be grateful that we seldom use capital punishment. I'm talking about Blei's attack on Math's guardsmen, when he escaped from them while they were attempting to escort him home to face his king."

A slow smile spread across Gwydion's too-handsome features, so far removed from mirth it could have been cast in marble. "Capital punishment!" he scoffed. "You wouldn't know how to kill me. I'm not stupid enough to divulge the spells needed to induce my hamartia to anyone."

I laughed, regaining my composure. "The way Lleu did to Blodeuedd? You're calling him a fool?"

Gwydion didn't grace that with an answer. He scowled and snapped his fingers. "Let's take a shortcut, shall we?"

The surrounding air wavered, and when it steadied Ianaura and I found ourselves outside his apartment. "Disable your wards," he ordered, "unless you want me to do it for you."

Should I call his bluff? Wards, like spells, could only be undone by the one who'd set them, but Gwydion was a lot more powerful than me. He could, potentially, simply destroy the wall and part of the room behind it—including those who sheltered inside. Tight-lipped, I did as he asked.

Gwydion waved a hand. "Come in, come in, make yourselves welcome. I'm sure Blei will be glad of the company, as will Uncle Math."

Two heads whipped towards us. Math was already on his feet; Blei, still bare-chested, struggled groggily to sit up. He looked as if my husband had already dosed him with something, preparatory to having the healer perform surgery.

At the sight of his wounds, Gwydion let out a sharp hiss. "You told me you weren't badly hurt."

Blei shrugged. "I needed somewhere to stay and thought if you considered me an inconvenience you might rescind the invitation."

"So you've been playing the martyr all these weeks, until our lady queen finally found you." Gwydion circled the room as he spoke, drawing sigils in the air and drawing sparks from my wards. "Nice spellwork. You will, of course, take them all down at your earliest convenience." He glanced at my fuming husband. "Settle down, uncle; you look as if you'd like to throttle me, but we both know you won't endanger your wife or my son. Has he confessed the details of his liaison with the bear goddess to you? He wouldn't tell me the whole of it."

"We've been over it." Math nodded to Ianaura, who'd been stealthily edging closer to Blei. "Look after your patient, healer. You need fear nothing from Gwydion."

She shot him a look of gratitude, settled down beside Blei and opened her healer's bag. "You already look nice and dopey," she murmured. "Let's make doubly sure you don't feel the next part, shall we?"

Blei sighed and took the vial she held out, before falling back onto the bed. Ianaura began applying cleaners and salves.

"Blei said you found him close by the screaming pit in Arfon," said Math, referring to a notorious feature of Ardudwy's landscape which the locals believed to be haunted. I thought the weird moans and whispered screams were more likely caused by the wind. "I presume you'd been to visit one of your castles?" He settled onto a green-covered bench and gestured for me to join him.

Gwydion nodded, still standing. "Once I knew Lleu was out of danger, I made a couple of quick trips back to keep an eye on things. I know my servants wouldn't dare defraud me, but they're not above making errors." The corners of his lips hooked upwards. "Caught up with young Cara while I was there. You remember Cara, don't you, Uncle?"

"Her feather charm failed to work," I cut in, to see his reaction.

He laughed. "I'm glad you said hers and not mine. That would give too much credit to the hedge witch who made it. If I'd cast such a spell, Blodeuedd and her disgusting human lover would have strangled each other in the bedchamber in love-play gone awry. Shame I didn't think of it, really. But I have something more fitting in mind."

Before anyone could react, he shifted into his kite form and vanished in a cloud of crimson-tinged grey smoke.

13

BETRAYAL

Math's form also blurred, but stopped before the change was complete. "Damn," he said, solidifying into man-shape again. "Heilyn's calling me." He took my hand and nodded to Ianaura. "Stay with him—there's a bed made up in the guest alcove. We'll check in again later."

One of the peculiarities of Caer Dathyl enabled Math to move from one corner to another simply by thinking about it. He transported us both back to the Great Hall to see what had caused Heilyn to summon him. It was, unsurprisingly, connected to Gwydion.

"Those two have been busy," he said. "Gwydion was looking for you, and now I can't find Lleu. I suspect he's headed back to Ardudwy."

I was not fond of irony, least of all when I was its subject. I couldn't fail to see it at work, however, when my own subterfuge not only worked against me, but rebounded in spectacular fashion.

I repaired the timeflows as soon as I heard the news, but that was the risk of messing with time. When a month in mortal realms translated to mere days in the Otherworld, misfortune could be measured in heartbeats. No sooner had I realigned night and day, an undertaking of an hour or more, than Lleu reappeared. Always dramatic, he arrived in the middle of the Great Hall in a broad beam of sunlight.

"Have you harmed her?" Math demanded, stalking up to him and poking him in the chest.

Lleu looked at him blankly. "Harmed who?"

That didn't sound as if he had. I relaxed. "Blodeuedd," I said. "Your ex-wife."

Lleu scowled, but shook his head and, when Math gestured to him, meekly followed his uncle.

Thanks to his usual foresight, Heilyn had not been caught unprepared. He'd gathered a force of seasoned, armed warriors, who were prepared to answer any challenge Gwydion might make. They now greeted the returnee, a force at least fifty strong. Led by Math and backed by Heilyn, they escorted Lleu to the king's audience chamber. Lleu treated them as an honour guard, and for all I knew he saw them that way. Nevertheless, their presence reassured me.

I didn't get the full story from Arianrhod until much later, but even if I'd known that Lleu's first goal upon leaving Caer Dathyl had been to visit Ari's castle rather than his own, it would have made no difference. He was spoiling for a fight, and the only thing that could have stopped him, no one could provide: his Caron.

"Don't be foolish," I said, exasperated. "Caron's soul is in between lives, she can't return to you so soon. You know this."

Lleu's lips thinned, his eyes glittering. "Gwydion says otherwise. He tells me the stars are perfectly aligned for Caron's return."

"What would he know about it? The fate of human's souls is far outside his purview."

I voiced every sensible objection, but he refused to listen. I considered threatening to ban Lleu from Caer Dathyl if he attempted to return with an abducted child. Unfortunately, that would likely send him straight to Gwydion's demesnes in Arfon.

"It's rank cruelty. Think about the baby's poor mother," I pleaded, gliding across to Lleu and laying a hand on his arm.

He'd thrown himself onto a bench by the door as soon as he entered the hall, radiating anticipation and displeasure in equal amounts. Heilyn and his men fanned out around the perimeter, lamplight shining on jewelled or twisted metal sword hilts and bronze spearheads alike. Lleu paid them no attention.

"I prefer to think about the poor baby and spare her everything Arlais went through." He stroked his knees, eyes fixed on the rafters but seeing the Mother only knew what. Endless futures with his beloved at his side, I supposed.

I tried the voice of reason. "But she'll be so very lonely. It was different here when you were young; you had Hych and the others to play with. A little girl, all alone..."

Lleu smiled. "She won't be alone. She'll have me." He glanced over his shoulder, watching my husband cede his place to Heilyn and back out of the massive oak entrance door. "Where's Uncle Math off to in such an almighty hurry?"

"Attending to his duties as king," I said with asperity. "You're not the centre of everyone's interest, much as you like to think so. Tell me more about your plans for little Caron. How will you house her, entertain her, see to her daily needs? You'll need a wet-nurse in the beginning. Have you considered that?"

Flattery and lies, all of it. I had no intention of allowing him to carry out his intentions, but I had to keep him talking, not let him focus on Math.

Happily, my ruse worked. Lleu leaned forward, elbows on the board before him, and gave me a detailed outline of his plans for Caron's new life. Yes, they'd begin in Caer Dathyl, where both his and Gwydion's magic was strongest, enabling them both to fight off any other family members who might be tempted to interfere. As for the wet-nurse, there'd be countless mortal women he could entice into service in the Otherworld, with all the benefits that entailed.

Feigning a half-hearted interest—he'd be suspicious if I appeared too easily won over, too soon—I drew him out, asking how he'd deal with every childhood problem I could think of, from teething to tantrums, nightmares to nutrition and the sundry other issues which would manifest as she grew.

We'd gathered an audience by now, half-horrified, half-fascinated, and all noticeably shocked.

"You can't actually mean to raise her as Caron," protested one of the older healers. A venerable silver-haired gentleman with the dark skin and eyes of the southlands, his nose was strong and beaked. "That kind of knowledge could invoke deep trauma in a young child. It's... it's unconscionable."

"But she'll already *be* Caron, don't you see?" Lleu sat up and spread his hands in entreaty, the light of missionary zeal in his eyes. "Whenever we've been reunited, she's always recognised me instantly. Recognised, and loved. And this way will give us more time, more years together. Many more, if she's raised here in the Otherworld." He glanced at me, eyes narrowing. "After all, it worked that way for you, didn't it, Aunt Wynne?"

Perhaps, but I hadn't been hamstrung by a goddess's curse. As I hesitated, seeking a diplomatic reply, another healer forestalled me. He'd been a redhead once; now his flaming mop had faded to the greyed russet of a brittle autumn leaf. "She'll look upon you as her father. Have you considered that? Will you still seek to bed her, then?"

A wave of apprehension fluttered through the room. Lleu's face tightened, while the healer's did the opposite, slackening into remorse. As if, an instant too late, he'd recalled Lleu's antecedents, and his power, and wished to retract his words.

Lleu growled deep in his throat, but before he could react further, a brilliant violet glow sprang to life in the centre of the room.

I'd been waiting for this. From the look on Lleu's face, he guessed what was happening: Math's grand re-entrance. Not as his indulgent Uncle Math, but as Mathonwy, King of Gwynedd, in all his splendour. An appearance calculated to stop all argument.

The fist-sized ball of light swelled and expanded until the entire Great Hall was bathed in red-purple iridescent mist. Every face, whatever its natural pigmentation, assumed a rosy hue. The sea of onlookers parted, awed but not alarmed by the sheer amount of magical energy such a feat required.

A harsh, ripping sound followed, accompanied by bells and drums and the deep, vibrating blare of the carnyx. A song which normally called armed men to war. It stirred the blood and juddered through the bones. In the centre of the violet haze an oblong shape appeared, a little over six feet high, and as the battle song increased in tempo, the outline firmed to form a man.

The mist dissipated to reveal my husband, robed in porphyry silk banded with gold, more gold gleaming at his neck and his wrists and binding his long silver hair. The same colours slid in wavering bands across the surface of his raven feather cloak. Aware he'd planned this entrance, calculated to milk the moment for every drop of drama, I still felt a swell of pride and admiration at the sight of him.

Lleu growled deep in his throat, but before he spoke, Math cut across him. "I've just been to Caer Sidi to confer with your mother and brother. Gwydion lied to you, Lleu."

Lleu's radiance dimmed for an instant. "Why would he do that?"

"Why?" Math strode up to his nephew, feathered cloak swirling behind him and the sapphires in his torc glittering. "Because he's slipperier than the serpent I wear on my wrist, or the sea wrack out in the bay. Gwydion's incapable of telling the truth; you ought to know that by now."

"Not to me." Arms folded, Lleu again began to glow. "He never speaks falsehood to me."

"If you believe that, you're more of a fool than I thought. Caron won't return to you. I've also been to see Arawn and told him what you said. He was most displeased, and vows he won't release that poor, fragile woman to fulfil her foolish vow another time."

Math paused, as horrified understanding drained Lleu's face of colour. "Arlais killed herself. Such an action points to a deeply troubled soul—one which requires an extended stay in Annwfyn to rediscover its balance. She negated the binding of her own promise by ending her own life."

Silence descended on the hall, fraught with tension. Lleu shook his head, hands extended as if trying to shield himself from unwelcome truths but his uncle continued, relentlessly. "Face it, Lleu. She's not coming back."

14

THE AFANC'S SPUR

G wydion kept his kite form until he reached his largest Other-worldly castle in Arfon, where he changed back into a man and selected a faerie steed from his stables. From there, he transferred to the mortal world and headed south to Ardudwy, covering the ground at much greater speeds than could be accomplished by mortal mounts. It had been some time since he'd entered that realm; hard to tell exactly how long, thanks to Goewin's meddling. Bloody gwarch. He still couldn't believe his Uncle Math had married her.

The encounter with Blei had upset him as well, at first. It would serve the fool right if he got turned into a goat, the symbol of stubbornness. Or better yet, maybe a bear. That would teach him to offer obeisance to Artio, the bear goddess, when she'd shown herself no friend to Blei's own father. The boy deserved those wounds.

They'd reminded Gwydion of a smaller, older scar along the edge of Blei's ribs: one that had been delivered by Hych wielding an afanc's tooth when the two of them were children. The sight had given him an idea and greatly improved his mood.

The Children of Don had always been fractious, squabbling among themselves. Great Don and Beli of the Gates had long ago put constraints in place to stop them from killing each other. Thus, outright war was forbidden, but not even the forces of nature those two controlled could prevent the occasional skirmish. Or fights involving dangerous beasts... like afancs.

Such a creature would be a welcome addition to Gwydion's arsenal. He knew exactly where to find one, and whom he planned to use it on.

Of all his sons, Gwydion loved Lleu the most. He felt a mild, off-hand affection for Hych and Hydd, with Blei coming a distant fourth. Dylan didn't rate even a mention. The animosity between the twins harked back to their childhood, and had been fostered from the beginning by Arianrhod. Gwydion had no compunction about injuring either of the last two.

A little over an hour later, he reached his destination. The veined network of small streams, rivers and waterfalls that snaked endlessly through the landscape of Ardudwy cantref made it an ideal home for an afanc. Some called the lake-dwelling monsters demons, but Gwydion didn't believe that. They were merely beasts... albeit vicious, ugly ones. An adult female—always larger than the males—stood approximately as high as a man when on land, with yellow-green scales and long, pointed, bristled snouts. Their teeth had a certain beauty to them, though. Long, white, curved, and sharp—oh, so very sharp.

The creatures were fast, too. Gwydion had seen them slide from the riverbank to wrestle their unsuspecting prey beneath the water in the time it took a man to blink. They'd still be no match for him, and what's more, cold weather made them sluggish. Cold-blooded, he suspected, and introduced from warmer climes. That they'd survived at all, he put down to Lleu's influence. Perhaps they could somehow tap into his magical energy to replace the sun they'd need elsewhere.

Tethering his horse some distance away, Gwydion uncoiled the rope from around his waist and cursed, yet again, the limitations of his magic. It had taken time and effort to learn to cast clothing and anything else he wore into the void and retrieve it, unchanged, when he resumed human form. The first time his uncle Math had transformed him into a beast, without his consent, he'd been made to strip naked in front of the entire court. Humiliation and rage still burned in him at the memory. Not anymore. Now he always reappeared in his human seeming fully clothed.

He held no grudges on that count. No experience, no lesson was ever wasted. He'd determined long ago to learn from good and bad alike and work out how to turn both to his advantage. The sons he and

Gil had made together retained the ability to transform back into the beasts they'd been born as. Math probably hadn't intended that when he'd cast his spell. But it had happened. And what the sons could do effortlessly, so could their father.

Neither stag, boar nor wolf would serve him now. This task required the dexterity afforded by human hands.

Unfortunately, unlike the despised Blodeuedd, he couldn't use the plentiful plants to fashion nets. Trials had proved that trying to transport one fashioned from rope over long distances resulted in a tangled mess. A coil of rope was easy, though, and it took him very little time to weave it into the net he needed and reinforce it with magic.

He draped it carefully over a nearby rock, morphed into bird form, and planed upwards, mapping the area. Always lush, always green between the grey boulders, a wide variety of trees sloped down to the river, where they gave way to small shrubs and ferns. The surface of the river below sparkled in the wan sunshine, but Gwydion was in no mood to appreciate bucolic beauty. He sought prey.

Although unsure how often the afancs needed to eat, he was confident they'd attack if another animal invaded their territory. As a kite, he could easily carry a rabbit. He plucked one from the ground, and, swooping low over the riverbank, dropped it into the shallows. Stunned by the shock and the fall, it lay unmoving for a heartbeat, until a scaled, bristled form surged from the depths to claim it.

The rabbit didn't even have time to scream before it disappeared into the afanc's gaping maw. Gwydion heard the crunch of bones.

Before the creature could slide back into the river's depths, he swung the net. He'd made each hole small, only a thumbwidth wide, and far too tiny for the beast to get its paws through. Claws and teeth would fit, right enough, but charmed to the toughness of steel wire, the net would withstand the afanc's frantic attack.

Gwydion wound yet more magical bonds around it and hauled it back to his horse. A mortal horse would have bolted as soon as it caught the afanc's distinctive scent. It wouldn't have handled having a large, writhing, scaled creature lumped on its hindquarters, either. With a word of praise to the steed for waiting so patiently and remaining so calm, Gwydion attached the bound afanc to the back of his saddle. Ignoring its hisses and deep-throated snarls, he set off for the coast.

Winding down the track towards the northern coast where his quarry often congregated, he went over his plan one more time.

He hadn't foreseen the close friendship that had evolved between Dylan and Blodeuedd, Lleu's wicked slut of a wife. But perhaps he should have. Both were the antithesis of his beloved Lleu, the son of his heart. And both were allies of his sister Arianrhod, whom he abhorred most of all.

It stood to reason that if—when—he finally caught up with the deceitful Blodeuedd, both Dylan and Math would attempt to aid her and stand in his way. His logical next step was to eliminate Dylan, which was why he needed the afanc.

The ban against war meant he couldn't cause Dylan any permanent harm. He also didn't know how to bring about this son's hamartia; this meant he couldn't transform him into another form and cast him out of his human skin, as Blodeuedd had done to Lleu. Nor did he want to risk facing censure if he unleashed the afanc on Dylan, resulting in injury—but he could threaten others whom Dylan held dear. And Dylan was with the selkie clan now; he'd checked that before seeking the afanc.

The sound of roaring surf broke into these pleasant reflections. He'd reached his destination, a long curving stretch of pale golden sand ringed by misty blue mountains. Unloading the afanc from the faerie steed's back, he set her loose among the tough coastal grasses and bade her wait for him. He then called upon kite sight and scanned the rocky area at the other end of the bay. Yes, there they were: a cluster of dark brown and black heads on blubbery brown and grey bodies. A colony of seals warming themselves in the pale spring sunshine.

Thanks to a long-standing habit of keeping track of all his sons' movements to ensure he remained a step ahead of them all, Gwydion knew Oonagh Nic Aillie by sight.

He needed to approach unawares. Both the rumbling growls coming from the afanc and its distinctive scent—some might say stench—would alert the seals to its presence too quickly. If he released it into the water among them, there was no guarantee it would attack Oonagh. Gwydion needed it to strike her. Dylan would rush to the aid of any whom the beast threatened, but he'd risk more for his woman.

Gwydion sighed and growled back at the frothing afanc. Strands of foaming saliva dribbled into its beard with each snarl, increasing its fusty body odour and malodorous breath.

"There's nothing else for it," he said to it. "I can't haul you out there without being noticed, and I can't carry you that far in normal kite form, either. God form it will have to be."

Unfortunate, because appearing as a man-sized bird with a netted monster in his claws would remove any doubt about who was responsible. The selkies might complain to the Mother Goddess about him, but they owed allegiance to Manawydan, chieftain of the rival clan of Llyr. To call Don and Llyr antagonists would put too kind a gloss on it. Those two loathed each other.

The Children of Llyr were more at home in the water than on land, and Gwydion had heard some wonder if Manawydan, or one of his merfolk, had fathered Dylan. Gwydion knew that was impossible, given the close resemblance between the twins. He'd proven Lleu was his. But it gave him yet another reason to despise Dylan Ail Don, son of the waves.

He shifted his shape, scooped the still struggling afanc into his claws, and swept out to sea, moving at his top speed, which was even faster than a normal kite. From high above, he could see the ripple of unease his sudden appearance caused, and the subsequent attempted flight into the water. But selkies in their seal skins were slow-moving on land, and it also took time for them to shed those skins and take on human form. He reached the woman called Oonagh long before she reached the open sea and safety.

A quick snip with his beak, and the strands of the net parted, sending the snarling, terrified beast plummeting into the shallows. To ensure the fall didn't kill it before it could ravage the selkie woman, Gwydion sent a stream of air, buoyed by magic, to soften its landing.

His aim was perfect. The snapping, screaming animal landed squarely on top of Dylan's woman, hissing and spitting, much like a feral cat. Her screams vied with the afanc's as a swipe from its paw delivered a long red gash to her back, near her tail. A neighbouring selkie, thinking to help, batted at the beast with his flipper. It careened into another rock, instead of into deeper water and freedom.

Gwydion shrank to normal kite size and hovered above, sliding from air current to air current. Watching and waiting for a familiar bright yellow head…

He was not disappointed. Summoned by the woman's cries of distress, Dylan leapt from the water. In an arcing spray of foam, he landed by her side, his bright hair dulled to bronze by seawater and salt. The afanc reared up onto its hind legs, leaned back, and balancing on its broad tail kicked out with both back feet. The right hind leg, as Gwydion was well aware, was equipped with a poisoned spur. It could kill a child, and while not usually lethal to adults, it often caused agonising, potentially crippling pain. Gwydion was interested to see what effect it might have on one of Don's grandsons.

Lithe as a fish, Dylan twisted, bending sideways so the spur, instead of raking through clothing into flesh, caught in the snarls of his hair. Thwarted, the afanc exploded in a fizzing ball of fear-fuelled fury, rocking forward to sink those powerful fangs deep into Dylan's thigh.

The selkies shifted. Around them, grey and brown fur sealskin coats lay abandoned, draped across the rocks and sand like so much flotsam from the ocean. A host of naked men and women, brown-skinned, black-haired, and solidly built, converged around the embattled trio, armed with rocks, sticks, and what weapons they could find.

"Stop! Don't hurt the beastie—can't ye see he's as frightened as any of ye?" Dylan waved the others back, ignoring the blood pouring down his wounded leg to paint his trews and boots scarlet. Rapidly dancing and weaving, he avoided the raking claws.

"Aha! Got you, my laddie." Balancing on the creature's tail, he wrapped strong arms around its flailing front legs and pinned them to its side. "There, there, now, settle down. You and I will just take a little swim, and you can make your way back to the river mouth. Then you head upstream and return to your nest. Alrighty?"

Gwydion couldn't believe it. The bloody fish-spawn had actually calmed the creature. Not a lot, but enough to defang the threat to the selkie clan. And the wound he'd taken, although it looked serious, didn't appear to worry him overmuch.

Whistling curses, Gwydion turned and flew inland, following the fleeing afanc. His plan might have gone awry, but no matter. He could still reach his next goal well before Dylan finished attending to his own and Oonagh's injuries. All was not yet lost.

15

DAUGHTERS

Dylan reappeared unexpectedly on the fifth day of the Alder month, as spring nudged winter aside—the day after my birthday.

Bleak-faced and brittle-tempered, he sported a black eye, an assortment of cuts and bruises and a long gash on the back of his hand. Those were the visible injuries; from the way he walked, slow and limping, I deduced he'd also sustained at least one to his leg.

"What happened to you?" I demanded, chivvying him into the healer's rooms. He resisted at first, but harassed by three women as well as Cynar and Goronwy, he eventually gave in.

"It's nothing," he insisted, looking and sounding grim. The lack of his usual cheerfulness emphasised his height and his breadth, forcing one to look at his powerful frame instead of his laughing face and dancing eyes. He remained impassive when one of the older healers requested he peel off his clothes, revealing a deep wound on his thigh. "I always heal rapidly, and I promise it's not as bad as it looks."

I found that hard to credit, but he submitted to the healers' ministrations with good grace, and by the time we left an hour later his limp had noticeably improved.

"Because you're godborn," I said.

"That, and it only scratched me with its claws—I avoided the spur. It was an afanc," he added, as I prepared to deliver a lecture on the evils of avoiding questions. "Set on us by Gwydion."

"An afanc!" I exclaimed. Like many other creatures Dylan regarded as commonplace, I'd thought those beasts existed only in legends. "What was it like?"

"Scarier than a jungle full of tigers. On a par with a sky full of dragons." He shook his head. "But others fared worse. Selkies need the sea to heal, so I sent them to Manawydan's palace undersea. That's why I came back here, to work with Cynar. He needs to regain as much strength in that arm as possible—and fast."

If his return owed as much or more to hatred of his father than to support for my cause, I would not protest. All three stood to benefit—I gained strengthened defences, Cynar received physical therapy, and Dylan himself found an outlet for his frustration and rage.

The days continued to lengthen, and Dylan unbent as the weeks passed, regaining flashes of his signature humour. The Alder month retreated, and we entered the time of the Willow. Unlike some years, we had a few bright, sunny days, which at Dylan's urging were always spent by or in the sea. Training, of course.

So, Cynar continued his swimming lessons. His wife, however, rarely ventured too far from their quarters with a new baby to look after. Modwenna took her place, training with the eagles. She'd graduated from sparrows and starlings, working her way upwards through ravens and small hawks to large birds of prey. The one with the broken wing, which had healed perfectly, had become a regular visitor. Yestin came down to the beach as well—to ensure his beloved's safety, I assumed.

Sometimes I almost forgot the urgency of our situation, watching the eagles soar above. Majestic, fierce, and patient, they were unchallenged as lords of the air. Gliding aloft on the air currents, they circled, endlessly searching the water for signs of food until, spying it, they swooped and dived, wings beating and talons extended. Birds of prey didn't flock like other birds, but when hunting, groups would gather in the same area. Some had perfected their fishing technique; others sought other means.

"Will you look at that," Dylan said one day as he allowed Cynar and me a brief respite. He pointed upward, laughing. "If you fail at hunting, fall back on theft. Cheeky sod."

I followed his gaze. A smaller bird, either a male or a juvenile, had successfully snatched a fish, only to lose it to a larger and presumably hungrier female. Dinner clutched in her claws, she rose flapping into the air and flew to a rocky outcrop at the head of the bay. The other bird dived again and, rising with its prey securely clutched in its talons, fluttered across to land beside Dylan.

"Oho," he said, affectionately chiding, "you think I'll act as your doorkeeper, do you?"

Busy feasting, the eagle made no response except to fluff its feathers. It pinned the fish, a sizeable cod, with both sets of talons, tearing off chunks of flesh, which it then swallowed whole, bones and all. Seated on a rock beside me, Modwenna watched with fascination.

"What's he thinking about now?" I asked.

Her answer was dry. "Guess."

Dylan's guffaw echoed around the cove, startling the eagle. Hunger prevailed, however, and after a moment, it returned to the business of eating. I laughed with everyone else, but quietly.

At a nod from Dylan, the female, whose maw was bigger and whose fish had been unhappily smaller, took wing and drifted down to alight on his shoulder. "When our boy's eaten his fill, we'll do some more work with the two of them together, with Modwenna as handler. It's not much different from the techniques falconers use." He nodded to her. "In fact, you might have an advantage. They raise the birds from chicks but can't communicate with them the way you do."

She smiled. "They make the gift feel like an honour, even when they're focused on fish. Hunting fish or small game is more exciting than chasing insects or looking for berries or grain."

As if in response, the female bird hopped down to the ground, waddled across to Modwenna and laid her head against the girl's leg.

Her eyes wide, Modwenna looked first at me, then at Dylan, and I heard her breath hitch. She remained still for a moment, before slowly, gently, reaching out a hand to stroke the proud head.

"He's...he's her mate," she said, her voice breathless with awe. "Her forever mate, the father of her future chicks."

Dylan nodded and pointed to the male bird, now perched on a rock on the headland. "Sea eagles mate for life, unlike humans or gods."

"Pfft." Still stroking the raptor at her knee, Modwenna tossed her head in denial. "Speak for yourself. Yestin and I are lifelong partners, as are Cynar and Delith and Blodeuedd and Goronwy. We're bonded by true love, you see. You will be too, one day. You haven't met the right woman yet."

"Lleu and I might not have been a great example," I agreed. "Not all gods are destined for solitude. Look at Mother Don and Beli Mawr, or Wynne and Math."

Dylan didn't respond, staring out to sea, where a sleek round shape could be seen idly bobbing about in the water. It looked like a head.

In fact, it was the head of a dark-furred seal—part of a colony which inhabited this coastline, no doubt. Dylan continued to watch it as it came closer to shore, but the tension in him drained away.

I expected the creature to avoid the group on the beach, for although seals would sometimes frolic with humans in the water, they were too wary to do so on land. In the ocean, their own element, they had the advantage. On land, that was reversed. This seal, however, seemed intent on joining us.

At about ten feet away, it submerged and disappeared from view. I revised my initial assessment. A slow smile spread across Dylan's face, and he leapt to his feet as the seal rose from the ocean, streaming water. It—no, she—no longer wore the shape of a seal. A collective gasp ran round the assembly, barring Dylan. He was the only one familiar with selkies.

As he strode down to the water and she emerged from it, it became blazingly clear that he was very familiar with this one. They came together like a wave meeting the shore. An instant of violence, then easy withdrawal, accompanied by soft sucking sounds as his arms enfolded her and their lips met. Then the wave crashed over them both once again, of longing, of passion, of joy.

With a whoop of delight, Dylan ripped off his clothing and flung it away, and both plunged naked into the sea.

"See?" said Modwenna after a minute's stunned silence. "Sea gods aren't immune to love either. Do you think he'll introduce us?"

"Her name's Oonagh," I said. "I can tell you that much. Arianrhod's mentioned her once or twice, and apparently, she's reputed to have the sight. She and Dylan have known each other for a very long time."

"I'm pleased. He deserves happiness after all he's been through." Modwenna cast an uncertain eye at the eagle beside her. "I hope he's not gone long, though. I'm not sure I want to try the manoeuvres he'd planned for today without his support."

"Perhaps it will be enough to cement your relationship with them," I suggested. "Fine-tune the way the link between you and them works."

"That might be a good idea." Modwenna returned to stroking the eagle and gasped suddenly, her free hand flying to cover her mouth. "Oh, Great Mother."

"What? What is it, are you all right?" Yestin was at her side in an instant, and the rest of the group had shot to our feet.

A blush stained Modwenna's cheeks as she smiled up at her husband. "I'm fine. Couldn't be better, in fact. She just asked when my chick's due to hatch."

Yestin spluttered. "Women! Even the birds love to gossip. How in Annwyfn did she know?"

Dafona's many times great-granddaughter knew the answer to that. "An eagle's hearing is almost as acute as its eyesight. I wouldn't accuse her of spying, but she has been observing us. On Dylan's orders, I expect."

"Hmmph." Yestin seemed taken aback. "I thought we'd agreed to wait a while longer before making that announcement?"

"We did," agreed his wife. "But a child whose coming is announced by a queen of the air deserves to be acknowledged in her presence, don't you think?"

"That's wonderful news! Congratulations to you both." I sank onto the rock beside her and wrapped her in my arms, simultaneously laughing and crying. "Does Delith know yet?"

"No. And don't you dare tell her before I have the chance. She'd never speak to me again."

I laughed again and kissed her cheek. "Of course, I'll do no such thing. But you must let me organise a celebratory feast soon."

Both Cynar and Goronwy hugged Yestin, to his obvious discomfiture. He'd changed a lot from the awkward, socially inept young man I'd first met, but not that much. He still appeared embarrassed by public displays of emotion.

"Be thankful Dylan's not here to hear it," said Cynar. "He'd probably crush you to his hairy chest and squash you." He nodded seaward. "And here he comes now."

Two heads appeared among the rocks, sluicing through the sea foam. The closest, sleek and black, looked little different from the seals visible further out. The other, its golden brilliance deepened to rich amber by the water, belonged to Dylan.

"What are you all jumping around and exclaiming about?" he asked, shaking himself like a dog as he came level with us and spraying everybody with salt water. Yestin appeared to be struck dumb, which amused Modwenna so much she couldn't speak for giggling, so Cynar told him.

"Blessings be upon you," said the woman who'd exited the water in Dylan's wake. About my height, she looked to be more solidly built, with short, sleek black hair curving in at chin-level. A glistening umber-grey cloak swung from her shoulders; a curvaceous figure could be glimpsed beneath it, brown-skinned and limber. Her ears were small, their pointed, furred tips showing through the sweep of her hair, and her eyes were lustrous dark pools. Much as I'd imagined a selkie to look.

Her voice, however, was a surprise. I hadn't exactly expected her to bark, but the golden voice of Oonagh Nic Aillie belonged to a songbird, not a child of the deep.

Dylan smiled at her, eyes crinkling at the corners, white teeth on full display. "You've recovered well," he said. "I'm glad."

I gathered that Oonagh had been one of those attacked by the afanc. She showed no evidence of it; Manawadyn's healers must be highly skilled.

She turned to me. "I've a message for you, Blodeuedd ferch Math."

I, too, was rendered speechless. Although technically correct, nobody had ever addressed me thus before—as the daughter of Math. I decided I didn't mind. But let no one dare to call me Blodeuedd ferch Gwydion!

"What message, and from whom?" I asked.

"The Lady Arianrhod desires your presence as soon as you can. She has news of some import to impart." Her dark gaze swung back to Modwenna. "The eagles say they wish to spend more time with you. Do you know how to swim?"

"Of course, but I prefer warmer water. That sea's likely to freeze my extremities off."

Cynar grinned. "Is that why I can't tempt Yestin—he's worried about being able to produce more offspring? It's not been a problem for me. Ask Delith."

Modwenna raised her eyebrows. "I will when I see her."

Ignoring this byplay, Oonagh glided up to me and laid a hand on my arm. "Never fear the water," she said, "or the skies. Earth is not your only home. My grandmother saw your coming, long ago. She saw dark times ahead, and so do I. But you can prevail, with effort. Look to the future, always, and strive towards the day. If you close yourself off and wallow in your hurt, you'll be forever lost to darkness. Let your friends in, and your family. Accept their help. Know that you are not alone."

Every hair on my body lifted, every pore grew gooseflesh, and shivers raced down my spine and up again. How could a voice so lovely sound so melancholy?

Silence descended. Even the normally jovial Dylan seemed to find nothing to say. At last, the sea eagle broke away from Modwenna and, flapping wildly, lifted into the air as her mate coasted down to join her. Together they flew off, the clamour of their cries finally breaking the selkie's spell.

The following day brought another invitation, but while the first had piqued my curiosity, the second fuelled my nightmares.

It dawned like any other: a crisp, clear day in summer. Nothing to suggest that my life was about to be uprooted, crushed, and changed beyond recognition. Goronwy opened one eye, stretched, massaged the back of his neck and said, again, "No. It's out of the question."

I fluttered my eyelashes. "Please?"

"Why would you want to visit your mother-in-law after all this time, on Dylan's lady-love's say-so? Our lives are so peaceful without her—with none of that family. I'd like it to stay that way."

I lifted my arms above my head and spread my hair in a glitter of gold over the pillows. This threw my breasts into prominence and seldom failed to achieve the desired outcome.

He grinned, tweaked a nipple, and climbed out of bed.

"Aren't you even slightly curious?" I sat up. "We owe her a lot, Goronwy. She persuaded Math to support us, even though he'd never admit it. He followed us to Ynys Môn for his own reasons, then announced his intention of leaving. I didn't expect to see him again, did you?"

A shake of his head.

I went on, "But he stayed. He came home with us and smoothed the way for us after spending time with his sister. Even if you don't, I want to know why. And we don't have to travel far; we can go through the standing stones now that Math has repaired them."

"We? The invitation was for you alone. Part of the reason for my objection." He finished dressing and sat down on the bed. Running his hand up my naked torso, over stomach and midriff, he teased my nipples between finger and thumb.

I squirmed with pleasure beneath his touch. "Perhaps it involves secrets that aren't for men's ears. Goddess lore, women's magic. Arianrhod's never harmed me, and I see no cause for nervousness." I laughed. "I almost said I see no reason to fear her. Which is untrue—sometimes she terrifies me. But I know she won't harm me. She called me daughter once. Did I ever tell you that?"

"You did." He pulled me close and nuzzled my neck. "Very well, you go, but I fear I can't come with you. I've another meeting to attend at Penllyn. The king of Dyfed arrives this morning with some trade agreements, and Rhun needs to look over them, too. Can we defer this delightful encounter?"

I delivered a kiss to his palm. "Very well. I forgive you for leaving, as long as you don't forget where we were up to."

"Such a forbearing soul you are, sweet violet."

His eyes followed me as I pulled garments from the chest under the window and slipped into them. A new fashion from overseas, and one I found attractive as well as practical: instead of long, sweeping sleeves, their voluminous length was gathered and tied at wrist and elbow, over which I wore a linen waistcoat displaying a great deal of cleavage. A wide, matching belt in similar vivid colours encircled my waist. Naturalistic designs in red, orange, pink, blue and yellow swirled and twisted across the coat's black background, and the full, sweeping blue linen skirt left plenty of room for movement. It was even possible to ride astride in this outfit. I liked it a lot.

Last, I slipped a small gold locket over my head, containing the rolled-up skin shed by Enfys.

"Why don't you come with me first?" asked Goronwy. "Your claim to Ardudwy is better than mine."

"I suppose I should," I said, "but I'm not sure the other kings relish being lectured by a female."

Goronwy grinned. "You don't lecture. You suggest."

"Well, they don't relish suggestions from a woman, either. I used to think Lleu and Gwydion had the monopoly on such short-sightedness, but it seems to be a common masculine failing. Feminine too, sometimes," I added.

"Oh," he said. "You mean Arlais. But she was a special case."

"I meant Cara. Who's still taking up space in my castle, and who I really want to get rid of as soon as possible. Goewin—Wynne—said there'd be no harm in destroying the feathers, but I can't bring myself to do that. Perhaps I can use them to wrest some information from her. So far I've had no luck though."

Goronwy nodded. "But the fact that Gwydion hasn't come for her, or for her love charm, must mean the queen's plan is working and he's still in Caer Dathyl. Plus, you now have a willing network of birds to warn us if he comes near."

"Yes, but Gwydion doesn't give up. He may have been thwarted for now, but I know this respite won't last."

Goronwy drew me into his arms, stroking my hair and looking deep into my eyes. "Whatever happens, we'll face it together. We've planned for this eventuality, trained for it. You're as much a warrior now as me or any of my men."

"I know. You really don't deserve me." I yielded against him for a moment before the sound of a cleared throat made me pull away.

Cynar stood in the open doorway. He wouldn't interrupt us for anything of little importance; he must have come to claim Goronwy for his meeting.

"Yes, Cynar?" I said, smiling. "What is it?"

Cynar adjusted his sling and delivered the news I expected. King Auryn of Dyfed had just arrived and awaited an audience with the Lord of Penllyn.

Goronwy ruffled my hair. "Are you sure you won't come?"

"No. Much as I'd relish discomfiting Auryn and the nobles, I've something important to discuss with Arianrhod, apart from whatever her message is. Something I've wondered about for some time, and I don't want to delay it. I feel it may end up being important."

"Ah," he said. "About owls?"

I nodded, and he kissed me and left. I followed him out the door, pausing to speak to Cynar. "How's your shoulder? Is the new treatment helping?"

He smiled. "It is, thanks to you. I have more movement, and the pain's barely noticeable now."

"I'm sorry the healers and I couldn't mend it completely."

"Don't be. A seneschal has no need of a sword arm, and I've learned to become pretty proficient with my left hand by now. Having Yestin around helps, too. He learned a lot from Owain. I mean, Math. Do you need an escort to the stone circle? Sorry, I couldn't help overhearing."

Unsurprising. He and Delith now occupied Arlais's old room across the hallway. I accepted his offer with thanks and followed him down to the stables.

There I waited, stroking my fairy steed Manon's nose, while Cynar struggled onto Gyso's back using the specially made mounting block Goronwy had commissioned for him. In a way, his injury had done as much to make Cynar the calm, decisive and competent man he'd become as his relationship with Delith. Fatherhood might have helped, too. He was the soul of patience with his sons, this former angst-ridden firebrand.

We rode to the standing stones in companionable silence, the mark of old friends between whom speech was unnecessary. The dogs, Taran and Glas, trotted alongside. I rode nowhere without Taran. The thicket parted before us; I continued to change my spells regularly to keep intruders out. Although I missed the green vista of rolling hills which the crowding forest obscured, the trees didn't oppress me as they did some of my subjects.

Once inside the sanctuary of the stone circle, I slid to the ground and helped Cynar down. Then we turned together and led our horses through the veil, the two dogs at our heels.

As the mists parted, the shifting colours of Arianrhod's northern palace appeared, sliding down the sky like glazes on a newly
thrown pot. Only the sky showed colour; the snow-covered landscape
stretched white from horizon to horizon.

I handed Manon's reins to Cynar. "Will you come in?"

He shook his head and settled onto a rough-hewn bench beside a
stunted birch tree against the wall of the palace. The dogs jumped up
beside him, while Manon and Gyso waited a short distance away. "I
might be her devoted servant, but I've no desire to confront Arianrhod
after all this time. I enjoy my quiet life and have a mind to hoard all
the peaceful moments I can against the storm I fear is approaching."
He rubbed his hands along his thighs. "She knows we're here, though,
and will look after us. Can't you feel the air warming already?"

I could. He and the hounds were in no danger of freezing, even
outdoors. I nodded. "You heard what I said about Gwydion."

"Yes, and about the owls. Whatever it means, Arianrhod's the goddess you need. She's your ally, as well as everything else. Don't forget
that."

"I won't. And thanks for your support and encouragement." With
a final smile, I left them, and made my way down the path to the
entrance of Caer Sidi.

16

REVELATION

Voices drew me to a door on the right of the hallway. When I entered it, Lleu's face loomed before me.

I let out a yelp of dismay and backed up, hands cupping my face. When my heart stopped jigging, I recognized the bristling beard and pale skin.

"Dylan! Lady Mother, for a moment I mistook you for Lleu. How did you get here so quickly?"

"I swam, of course."

Without further explanation, he offered me a drink, then guided me to a gilded chair upholstered in white leather. Carved snakes twined around the arms and legs, and two brooding owls formed the back. The larger one, white and alive, clutched the carved one beneath her with shining talons and mantled as I sat in front of her.

I glanced at her over my shoulder. "Hello, Gwenhwyfar."

She danced a little at the sound of her name, folded her wings, and sat still—guarding or watching me, I could never be sure.

I looked around, seeking Arianrhod. Another figure stood in front of the mantle with his back to me. Tall and broad-shouldered, his long white hair flowed over his raven-feather blue cloak to blend seamlessly with the intricate silver embroidery. Nervous tension rippled through me. Only Math ap Mathonwy wore a cloak fashioned from the plumage of ravens.

"Welcome, daughter."

My mother-in-law, approaching silently from behind, made me jump.

"Hello, Mother. Are you going to tell me why you invited me here?"

"It's about Lleu."

"Lleu's here, too?" My voice dropped too low, making me sound like a frog. I cleared my throat and tried again. "This can't be an attempt at reconciliation, surely? Our marriage is most emphatically over."

"But you're both still alive and are man and woman again." Eschewing the delicate furniture, Dylan sat cross-legged beside the wide fireplace. "There are twists still to come in this story."

"What...what do you mean?"

Beside him, Math turned to face me. He sported a white beard to rival Dylan's blonde one and wore a robe of rich royal purple beneath the cloak, collared with ermine. A gold torc peeped through the fur, its ends fashioned as snake heads with sapphires for its eyes.

"Drink up," he advised, nodding to the untouched glass of wine in my hand. "You're probably going to need it. We need to tell you about Arlais."

I glanced at him uncertainly and took a tentative sip of the rich, ruby wine. "Why should I care about Arlais? She's dead."

Arianrhod settled neatly beside me. "Her body may be gone, but her soul endures, and that soul is bound to Lleu. Caron swore before the gods that she'd return within her mother's female bloodline, and he in turn promised he'd always find her."

I frowned. "I know that. But doesn't it take time? The druids say that souls have lessons to learn and tests to pass before they reincarnate."

Dylan cut in. "Ordinarily, yes, but Lleu is getting impatient. He doesn't want to wait centuries to be reunited with his love."

I shrugged. "I can't help that."

"No, but your friend Modwenna can." Seeing my blank expression, Math came to stand beside his niece and took over the explanation. "The child born to Yestin and Modwenna will be a daughter. As a child of Dafona's bloodline, she'll be a suitable host for the soul of Arlais. You need to warn her parents, because this child is bound to Lleu."

"Stop mincing words." Dylan leaned back on his hands and studied the painted stars on the ceiling. "Lleu's been lingering in Caer Dathyl, where time flows like treacle. I suspect he's been loath to venture back into mortal realms until now because they hold too many memories of Arlais. But he's now fully recovered, and all our efforts to delay him are falling apart."

"That's an understatement," Math said dryly. "He's been terrorising my court, demanding that somebody tell him where his Caron is, or at least where her soul is. I assured him Arawn won't allow her rebirth, but I'm not sure he believed me. Gwydion told him it's possible because a woman of Dafona's line is with child, and he's so fixated on the idea I'm afraid he'll go back to Ardudwy and try to abduct the baby anyway." He paused, glancing at me with something like apology. "If I understand Lleu's reasoning correctly—although reason doesn't come into it—he plans to immure her in Caer Dathyl until such time as Caron can be reborn. However long that might take."

I frowned. "But won't Arianrhod's curse still take effect, even in the Otherworld? Otherwise, why didn't they try that before?"

Math shook his head. "Lleu has no romantic interest in Modwenna's daughter as yet; he sees her only as a potential vehicle for Caron, with himself in the role of foster-father. As you may have noticed is the case with Wynne, life in the Otherworld greatly extends the life of mortals."

Dylan cut in. "That's why we've called you here, Blodeuedd. To warn you and Goronwy to leave. Because when he returns, Lleu will want to retake Ardudwy, too. He'll challenge Goronwy for the lordship, and I can't see Goronwy refusing. Can you?"

I stared, horror-stricken. "Goronwy can't fight Lleu! That's insane! He'd be slaughtered."

Math said dryly, "That would be Lleu's intention."

"But that's the outcome I've tried to avoid—the reason I persuaded Goronwy to make the accursed spear and hurl it at Lleu! Now you tell me that everything we went through, the harm we caused, was for *nothing*? That this outcome is foreordained? No!" I threw my hands out in protest, sending the half-full wine glass flying. Ruby droplets splattered over Math's robes, our gowns, and the pale leather upholstery. Like spots of blood.

"I'm... I'm sorry." Unsteadily, I rose to my feet. "I have to go. To warn him." I spun around, sinking to my knees before Arianrhod. "Oh, Mother, what if he won't listen? What if he won't leave?"

Arianrhod looked at Math, and an unspoken message passed between them. Terror gripped me, stark and howling. They'd read more than the birth of Modwenna's daughter in the stars.

"What is it?" I demanded, still on my knees before the goddess.

"My dearest daughter," she said, tears forming in her lovely eyes. Tenderness, again. I'd almost got used to the notion that she could feel it. "Lleu's not the only danger. Gwydion's left Caer Dathyl and we fear he's coming after you, intent on retribution. He won't rest until he finds you. I'd help you if I could, we all would, but..."

I sat back on my heels. "But what?"

"We can't interfere. It's forbidden for the Children of Don to make war on one another."

"Pah! Gwydion fought Math eagerly enough, with no repercussions, that day in the forest. And his sons alongside him."

Dylan laughed ruefully. "That was only a skirmish. We bicker and squabble and fight amongst ourselves, and we take up arms without hesitation against the Children of Llyr, but we don't intentionally inflict serious harm on each other." He shrugged apologetically. "We can't—not intentionally."

"I see." I pushed away and got slowly to my feet. "But rape and forced shape-changing is acceptable. You needn't see me out. I remember the way. Goodbye."

I left them wearing various expressions of dismay and ran down the hall, my cheeks wet with tears.

Cynar saw and no doubt heard me coming but said nothing until I offered to help him mount.

"No," he said. "I can manage. I think." With a grimace, he removed his arm from the sling and uncurled half his fingers.

"What happened?" he asked as our pace increased to a canter, and we passed back through the stones into the pale light of early evening.

I told him, beginning with Gwydion and Lleu's plans for Modwenna's daughter. Arlais had been his sister; Modwenna was his cousin. He deserved to know.

Cynar gripped his one-handed reins tighter, staring into the cloudy distance. Against the darkening sky, the ring of mountains loomed shadow-black, covered by the thickets of my trees.

Eventually he tore his attention away from them and focused on me. "I won't allow it," he said at last. "I'll fight Lleu myself if I must."

"Idiot," I said mildly, without venom or condemnation. How could I expect him to react any other way? "We've established that your sword-fighting days are behind you, and even if they weren't you'd have no chance against Lleu."

He shook his head, eyes clouded. "It's too harsh a fate, especially if Caron follows through with her threat. We must protect that child."

"Of course. If Caron, with Lleu and Gwydion's connivance, transfers her memories into Modwenna's daughter in infancy, she'll never experience life for herself. She'll be forever caught in the snares of another life's love. Trapped by the machinations of mad gods and magic."

"As happened to my sister. Looking back, I think Caron's invasion began from the instant she first met Lleu. There were so many tiny clues that I missed, that I put down to the flush of 'first love'. Things she said, or did, that were so unlike Arlais."

"That's not all." I took a steadying breath and revealed the rest—Lleu's intention to challenge Goronwy, and Gwydion's planned retribution.

Cynar's solution was simple. "Don't tell him. Persuade him we have to protect Modwenna and her baby and flee. You had the routes mapped out last time. Follow them. Bypass Ynys Mon and head north, to Orknyar, beyond the reach of Don's Children."

Because other gods ruled in the north. That was also true of other lands. "Gwydion might expect that. No, I plan to go east, through Armorica and Gaul to Scythia or Illyria. Somewhere very far away."

We lapsed into silence. I spent the rest of the journey home fine-tuning my plan to pry Goronwy away from Ardudwy before Lleu came seeking his blood. Yestin and Modwenna wouldn't need convincing to leave once they knew Lleu had designs on their daughter. I knew I had Cynar's support. He was Goronwy's loyal servant, and mine.

On impulse, I asked, "Did you ever find it difficult, maintaining the fiction that Lleu was a mortal man? I understand his motives—he wanted a normal life with Arlais—but it also meant you and Emlyn were living a lie."

Cynar laughed bitterly. "So were Owain and Blaise, although I didn't know that then. I don't suppose it bothered them much; they must have been used to it. It caused friction occasionally between me and Emlyn. He accused me of not being careful enough, and when I pointed out that he was equally indiscreet, he'd smirk and say he was composing a ballad. People assumed any slips he made were fiction. Then we'd fight, bringing Lleu's wrath down on us both. He could barely tolerate mild brotherly bickering. The all-out battles Emlyn and I indulged in really tried his patience."

I frowned. "But he wouldn't discipline Emlyn the time that he shot you."

"Arlais forbade him to interfere. She always stood up for her little brother in the beginning, but by then she'd started favouring Emlyn."

"Because of Caron's influence."

"Yes. I didn't understand what was happening. I was confused, angry, and hurting. You know where that led me. I decided that if everyone thought I should imitate Emlyn, I would."

I shook my head. "You're nothing like Emlyn, Cynar. You never could be."

We'd reached the gates of my castle by this time, so I sent him to apprise Delith of my news and warn her to get ready to run. I'd speak to Modwenna after I'd persuaded Goronwy of the urgency of leaving. Cynar left to do my bidding, and I continued up the rise to the Great Hall, only to be met by a disquieting sight.

Three unknown horses stood tethered outside. Where had they come from? *How* had they come? They shouldn't have been able to get past my wards!

17

INVITATION

Warily, I entered the Great Hall. At the sight of the small group gathered there, my heart juddered against my ribs. Two men, approaching middle age, wore green robes belted with violet, and their heads were tonsured. The third, sporting a full head of flowing silver hair and a waist-long beard, wore white. All white, with no leavening of colour. He didn't need the moonstone-inlaid oak staff to proclaim his rank; authority pulsed from him as notes flow from a harp. A druid-priest, and the highest of his order.

"My lord." I performed the proper obeisance and straightened. "I bid you welcome, but confess I'm surprised to see you. How...?"

"They came with me." Goronwy spoke from behind me. "Unable to enter Ardudwy, they sought me instead at Penllyn." Eyes bright and wide, cheeks hectic with colour, he strode across to the visitors and bowed even lower than I had done, his chest and forehead almost touching the floor. "My lords, I formally welcome you to my home. May the moon ever light your way. I am your servant—yours and the goddess's."

He'd let them past my defences, just because they were druids. I resisted the urge to snap at him and gestured to a seat, but the white-robed druid shook his head and remained standing. His companions folded their arms, holding themselves erect and tense.

"My name is Newlyn and these are my ovates. We come in response to a complaint that has been issued against you. Who or what has given you the right to conduct trials, my lady?"

What? Oh, no, he must mean my detention of Cara. How could the druids have found out about her? Hands folded demurely in front of me, I studied my linked thumbs. "You must have been misled, your honour. I've never done so."

Behind me, Goronwy cleared his throat. "I assume you're referring to Cara ferch Mabli. She assaulted my wife, your lordship, and has proved to be exceedingly violent. We locked her up for her own safety, as well as that of others, but have never sat in judgement upon her." He harrumphed again. "May I ask who laid the complaint?"

"Mabli ferch Elen. Her message was delivered through a smith who'd been granted access to your lands to deliver metals. Perhaps we could speak with her?"

The old hag! She hadn't acted out of concern for Cara, I'd warrant, else why had she waited so long? This was a fear-based reaction. I should never have performed spellcraft in front of her. She must have been fretting over it for a while.

"Better yet, why don't I take you to see Cara? You can judge for yourselves whether I acted with cause."

All three heads nodded solemnly, and my tension eased.

I gestured to the nearest padded bench and signalled a passing servant. "But I've been remiss. Please, allow us to offer you food and something to drink."

"Thank you, my lady, we'd be honoured." Newlyn inclined his head, regally, and moved to take the seat offered. "Oh, there was one other thing."

My foreboding returned. "Yes?"

"We have an invitation for your husband."

Smiling, he turned to Goronwy, who looked as though he'd been granted a glimpse of the Moonlands or the Blessed Isles. I wanted to grab him by the ear, haul him upstairs and tie him to the bed, then eject those bloody priests and slam the door behind them. His adoration pleased them, that was obvious. All three had broken into smiles, their stiff formality easing.

"An invitation to what?" My heart beat erratically; my pulse thrummed. Great Mother, let it be something other than what I feared. A game of football, a round of drinks. Anything, anything but...

"We have chosen you, Goronwy Pebyr, Lord of Ardudwy, to be the Winter King, the Holly King, to defend the honour of our goddess and do battle with the Summer Lord. To uphold the ancient ways."

Goronwy expelled a long, slow breath and closed his eyes, gripping the back of a chair as if for support. I clamped my teeth together to suppress the moan crying in my throat for release, willing him to decline. But he wouldn't. Of course he wouldn't. For years, he'd dreamed of being chosen, and of completing the challenge.

"Who," I began, in a voice like an owl's hoot. I cleared my throat and tried again. "Who represents the Oak King?" Surely it couldn't be Lleu. Surely, they couldn't accept him as champion, knowing his true nature.

The blood pounding in my ears reached a crescendo, drowning out the priest's next words. I caught the name Berlak ap something, then a string of titles, a confused jumble of sound. Praise the mother and the father both, he wouldn't have to fight Lleu. Not yet.

"When does the contest take place?" My voice rose, high-pitched and breathy.

The white-haired elder raised his brows. "At midsummer, as always. Several weeks hence, so you have time to prepare."

Curse him to a lifetime of loose bowels and itchy balls. How was I to convince Goronwy to leave with me *now*, with that prospect in the offing? I fixed a smile on my face and made desultory conversation through the light repast of sweetmeats and wine the servants brought.

Afterwards, trailing after my husband and the priests, I couldn't even summon enthusiasm when Cara snarled and cursed throughout their interrogation, amply proving my point.

"It seems the girl is at fault, not you," said Newlyn, inclining his regal head. "I hereby give you leave to imprison her and punish her as you see fit. The same does not apply to her mother; you may take no action against her. Mabli was motivated by concern, not ill-will."

"Agreed," I said, nodding, even though I didn't. Mabli had acted from fear, edged with spite, but I could overlook that. She'd get no further treats from me, though—that was certain.

Satisfied, the priests prepared to leave. For a brief, seductive moment I considered refusing to open the barriers for them. But not only would that be unworthy, it would inflict them on me indefinitely.

We rode with them as far as the boundary, gathering a crowd as we went. They smiled and nodded to the throng, amid cheers and a hail of flower petals, before exiting through the main gates and along the dusty road. The entire population of the castle had recognised them, and word of their invitation had already circulated. That made my task doubly difficult.

As my wall of trees closed behind them, I gripped my husband's arm and said urgently, "I've bad news for you. Come upstairs."

He patted my hand, his smile beatific. "Don't fret, my violet. I'll win, you'll see. As the priest said, Berlak's a gifted fighter, but so am I. The Oak King's won for generations. Now it's my turn."

I all but dragged him up to our chamber, the words spilling out as we climbed the stair. "What if you lose, though? What becomes of me then?"

He stopped at the head of the staircase, at the start of the long, sun-dappled corridor which led to our room. Bryn had outdone himself. Narrow arched windows fitted with sheets of fine horn projected golden light across the richly coloured carpet, and brass lanterns swung from the beams overhead. A soft, woody scent drifted from the lanterns, and a faint hint of smoke. Designed to produce tranquillity in all who beheld it, today it failed dismally.

"The thought of leaving you almost destroys me, my violet, but it must happen, one day. And isn't it better to go to the Moonlands with a high heart and a sword in hand than wither away from old age and sickness? To lie rotting in bed?"

I wanted to cling to him, sobbing, there in the hallway, but preserved my composure until we reached our room. Most of my composure. A few tears escaped.

I shut the door and leaned against it, saying without preamble, "Do you remember Caron's vow?"

He frowned and brushed his thumb across my cheek, wiping away tears. "Is that a trick question? I'm unlikely to ever forget."

"It puts Modwenna's child in danger." I relayed everything I'd learned, watching the emotions chase each other across his face; shock, outrage, anger. That might be enough. "If you care for our friends," I finished, "you'll lead them away, to safety."

Strong arms drew me to him, holding me close. "And go where?"

"Across the sea to Armorica, then keep heading east to the Mountains of the Moon. The forests shrouding those peaks are close to impenetrable. I could make them doubly so. Weave a cocoon around us that nobody, gods or men, could penetrate."

"Such a journey takes months. Gwydion would find us before we left the shores of Cymru."

I shook my head. "I have allies, remember? Arianrhod and Dylan, even Math and Wynne. Perhaps they can't fight Gwydion, but they can try to mislead him, and muddy the trail behind us. Together, we'll find a path. Will you come?"

Silence, long and aching. "I think it's a long shot, but worth trying—for you and the others. I can't forfeit this challenge and keep any shred of honour."

Bloody honour. I thought about bees, and vines, and potions. Could I drug him and carry him, unconscious, halfway across the world?

One step at a time. I snuggled against him and lifted my lips to his. Breathing in his scent, the taste and the feel of him, committing those precious moments to memory. At last, I pushed away from him, and stood. "I need to talk to the others. They'll be in bed, and asleep, but I don't think this can wait. Perhaps a few more hours won't matter, but we are dealing with Gwydion. Wait here, I'll be back soon."

I slipped down the hall to Yestin and Modwenna's door and rapped sharply.

A few seconds later, it opened. Yestin stood there in his nightshirt, holding a lit candle in its stand. I hadn't interrupted his sleep. A chorus of delicate snores issued from within the room, where Modwenna lay on her side, her glossy hair fanned across the pillow.

I pulled Yestin into the hall and along to my chamber, where Goronwy waited. "I need to talk to you. It's important."

He followed without protest, a slight frown corrugating his forehead. I gestured him to a chair, sat on the bed and launched into my story, or at least the part that concerned him. A long silence ensued.

Yestin sucked in a breath, ran his hand through his hair, and huffed it out again. "That's... horrifying. I'll never allow Lleu to take my child. How soon can we leave?"

Goronwy spoke for the first time. "Blodeuedd has a plan. Go with her, all of you, and I'll join you later. We'll only need a day to set everything in motion. So, the day after tomorrow. Be ready."

Later. How much later? Long enough to meet his challenger and fight a duel to the death? I swallowed bile, fighting tears.

Yestin nodded and left.

Trying desperately not to burst into sobs, I sank onto the bed and patted the cover in invitation. After a moment's brooding silence, Goronwy tugged off his boots, shed the rest of his clothes and joined me.

I trailed my nails along his thigh and over his hip, marvelling yet again at the perfect symmetry of him. Sleek, solid muscles arranged around long, strong bones set off by sun-touched, scarred and roughened skin. So tough, and yet so fragile. I imagined a sword piercing that skin and shuddered.

He ran a hand over my hair, pressed his lips to my shoulder. "Don't fret, love. I'll win, I promise. And once that's done, I'll follow you to the ends of the earth, and beyond."

I nestled against him, breathing in his scent. "If it were Lleu you faced, instead of this other man, would you still insist on fighting him? Is honour worth certain death?"

"Yes."

No! On this we would never agree. Time to change tactics. How could I invoke the threat of Gwydion, without mentioning Lleu and the battle between the Summer and Winter Kings?

"Gwydion's overcome Lady Wynne's enchantments and has left Caer Dathyl," I said at last. "He's coming here, to kill me for what I did to Lleu."

Because my head lay on his chest, I heard his breathing change tempo.

I sat up. "If you won't run from this Berlak, will you do so from Gwydion?"

He was silent, as taut as a wound spring. The air quivered with tension, interleaved with dread, guilt, and something else. Longing? Regret?

"I'll do whatever I must to keep you safe, but...I've been chosen by the goddess herself. I can't run and hide."

Tears flowed unheeded down my cheeks. My lips trembled. "She doesn't care about that! I told you, it's a ploy of the priests to keep the people in line and hold onto power. The year's wheel will still turn, the seasons still ebb and flow without a blood sacrifice. Come with me, far away. We'll find a land free of these barbaric customs, free of gods. Somewhere governed by men's rules, or better yet, women's. Somewhere no one will condemn you."

"But *I* will. And men are judged in the afterlife by their actions in this one. I'd fear for my soul, Blodeuedd, if I were to flee, like a coward. I fear being detained in the Moonlands and not allowed entry to Annwfyn. Would you have me dwell in darkness forever?"

I'd never studied theology. As with so much of my knowledge, my only understanding of the subject came from Gwydion, who had no interest in the ultimate fate of the human soul. I had no reassurance to offer. I couldn't even form a theory. Defeated, I shook my head and clung to him, sobbing.

For a long while after he'd drifted to sleep, I lay watching him. Committing his features to memory. The way his dark hair curled across his forehead, the shadows cast by those thick, straight lashes, the stubble darkening his jaw. The planes and angles of his face. If he were to fight and die at the solstice, his soul would return, one day. Just as Caron's had. But, unbound by selfish, foolish vows, it could find a home anywhere in the boundless world. Would I be able to find him again? Perhaps Arianrhod could tell me.

Eventually I drifted to sleep, and once again fell into the dream.

Owls. Always owls. Some snowy, some tawny; small, large, short-eared and long, they glided nightly through my dreams on silent wings. Their mournful cries echoed through my head, gaining in frequency and volume. Louder they sounded, and louder, until a doleful 'Arrr-ooo' just outside my window jerked me awake.

Why were they haunting me? I believed it was a message from my mother-in-law, but I didn't know what. Her other news had shocked me so much I hadn't remembered to ask.

I swore I'd do so without fail, when next we met. Tomorrow, perhaps. Yes, I'd see her tomorrow. Satisfied, I rolled over and went back to sleep.

18

RETREAT

Arianrhod and I never did chat about nocturnal birds. The dream's urgency faded come morning, and all thoughts of owls were superseded. I had to organise our departure.

I hated the thought of leaving Mur Y Castell and Ardudwy, perhaps forever. I might be an Otherworldly being, but this corner of the human realm was the only home I'd ever known. The only one I'd ever wanted, among people I had grown to love. Tears threatened; I swallowed heavily, sniffed, and surreptitiously wiped my eyes. But regrets were pointless. Ever since the day Goronwy had returned with Emlyn's severed head and laid claim to Ardudwy, I'd known this day would come.

Trying to calm myself with industry, I gave the keys of the house into my chatelaine Una's keeping. To the gardeners I passed on my collection of seeds and seedlings, with special instructions on the care of my precious exotics. I then visited the healers' rooms and delivered a cache of salves and recipes, written in the foreign Roman script. Sadness tinged their delight, for as much as they appreciated the gifts, they'd prefer to retain my personal skills. But we all knew that couldn't be. Next, I did the same with the dyers, although this gift would be more ephemeral. I was the living mordant, and all others, no matter how good, would still be inferior.

They all knew why these steps were necessary; I'd set the groundwork in place long ago. Many refused to accept that this might be the last time the saw me but clutched my hand and insisted that we would meet again, one day. Others, who knew Gwydion better, looked at me with pity, and wished me a safe journey.

All these preparations went smoothly to begin with; the first thing to go awry was Goronwy himself, or his actions. Initially, he'd proposed installing his brother Rhun at Mur Y Castell. I talked him out of that, arguing that Rhun would be safer remaining at Penllyn. I'd have felt better if he and everybody close to us were to flee as well, but others thought me overcautious.

Now, he insisted on conducting one final item of business before we fled.

I frowned. "What business? What could be so urgent?"

"I'm taking King Auryn back to Penllyn this morning. The grain deals are done; next we sort out the livestock. Rhun's eager to trade horses and cattle." He pulled on his boots and ran a comb through his hair. "With less backing from Mur Y Castell, Penllyn needs to become more self-sufficient. Now I'd best be off, or I'll be late. Mustn't offend our neighbouring princes!"

My mouth fell open. After everything I'd told him, all the drama of the night before, he was thinking of trade? I tried to keep the edge of hysteria from my voice. "You don't think Gwydion might strike at us through others, as Emlyn did? Perhaps Rhun should come with us."

He kissed me, slow and sweet. "I'll be back before nightfall, my honeybee. Rhun and the others will be fine, I'm sure. Gwydion's a snake, but he's not as low as Emlyn."

I balled my fists, dearly wanting to punch something. Or someone. Emlyn had been Gwydion's servant, had taken his cues from the Trickster. If anything, Gwydion had to be worse. Far worse.

Once all that was done, later in the afternoon, I went to help Delith and Modwenna pack. They, too, had spent the morning distributing most of their belongings among family and friends. We'd need to travel fast, and light. Only a compact leather saddlebag each to hold changes of clothes and the small necessities of life. I knew what was needed; I'd done this before. One final time I ran through the list with them, making sure we'd forgotten nothing vital. This would be my second-last task before leaving forever.

Cynar and Yestin were similarly engaged, allocating duties to those who'd served under them. Idrys ap Meredith, whom Goronwy had grown to know and trust, was named as overseer of the estates. Others, equally dependable, would take charge of the stables, the granaries, the kennels and other roles vital to the running of Cantref Ardudwy. Cai ap Caradoc agreed to return from Penllyn to take up the post of Master of Horse.

"I'm sure Goronwy's right," Delith said, keeping a weather eye on the two small boys play-fighting with wooden swords in the garden outside her rooms. "No harm will come to Rhun and his family. Gwydion's not that vindictive, I don't think."

I sighed. Delusional, all of them. "That's what we thought about Emlyn, remember? You're all coming with me—if not now, then as soon as possible."

"I suppose it is best to be careful." Modwenna ran a hand across her stomach, as yet still relatively flat.

I eyed her curves with fascination. There, beneath her skin, curled the small being who would one day become Lleu's new lover, if I didn't prevent it. Caron, Gwenavala, Arlais reborn.

"We'll name her Yseult," she said, catching the direction of my gaze. "After Yestin's mother. We'd planned to use Llevelys for a boy, but if the Lady Arianrhod's right, it seems Yestin will have to wait a while longer for his son and heir."

I hated that phrase. It reminded me of Gwydion and Lleu... which brought to mind my final chore.

"We're all set, then." I drew a deep breath, steeling myself for the coming encounter. "I'll see you both in the morning."

I moved towards the door, then halted at Modwenna's startled gasp. Puzzled, I looked back at her, then I heard it too. The sharp, piercing cry of a distraught sea eagle. Within moments they crowded the sky; birds of all descriptions, wheeling, calling, sounding Modwenna's alarm.

Gwydion! I snatched up Cara's feathers and ran. Through the halls, across the yard and through the grounds to her prison. Wind whipped my hair into my eyes and tangled my gown around my legs, almost tripping me up. Feet pounded behind me, but I didn't look back to see who it was.

"Did you alert him somehow?" I demanded, wrenching the door open. A swirl of cool air raised goosebumps on my arms.

A slow smile spread across Cara's face. She didn't ask who I meant. She didn't have to, the traitorous wretch.

"How?" I grasped her by the neck of her gown and shoved her hard against the wall. "How did you contact Gwydion?"

"He has magic, remember?" Her smile deepened and her eyes lost focus, as if she recalled her lover's breath upon her skin, his face, his touch. "He comes to me at night, sometimes, singing."

"Horsefeathers!" snapped Modwenna, rushing through the door in my wake. Of course, she'd be to one to follow me; Delith had to stay with her sons. She half-turned and stabbed a finger into the air. "It was them. He's subverted other kites, and a few hawks and seagulls, too, apparently. They've been reporting your movements to him."

Cara giggled. I glared from her to Modwenna. "But he still can't get through my barriers. What good will that—?"

Thunk! A dead raven plummeted from the sky, landing near Modwenna's feet. Two more followed, black feathers drifted lazily in the slackening breeze.

Distraction. This was all a distraction. Suddenly I couldn't focus. The scene before me wavered, as if obscured by plumes of heat haze. I gasped, swayed, and clasped both hands to my chest, seeking my locket.

"Blodeuedd? Lady Blodeuedd, what's the matter?" Modwenna's voice came from far away. I was dimly aware of another figure in the background, who could only have been Cara. She slipped past us and disappeared through the open doorway.

Heat. Heat plucked at my skin and stole my breath, and in my head I heard a thousand voices screaming. Oak and ash and elm. Alder, beech, sycamore, birch, and all the others. Fruit trees, scrubs, and sedges—all, all were set alight. They cried out, one to another, and I could hear them all. Pain! Burning, fiery agony surged through the forest and found an echo in my flesh. Torment travelled, spitting and hissing, along my limbs and turned all my organs to jelly.

I screamed and screamed again. Pain ate at me, gnawed my entrails and threw me writhing to the ground.

After that, everything went fuzzy for a while. I curled into a ball, whimpering, remembering. Fire, destruction, and death. A death I'd caused. This time I wasn't in a forest, nor were there any bees. But the agony was worse.

Finally, with an effort, I lifted my head, seeking the source of it. Jagged spears of lightning made a mosaic of the clear sky to the west, splintered forks of white and violet against an azure background.

Goronwy and Delith had been wrong. Gwydion was crueller than Emlyn. Emlyn had relied on flints and fire arrows to set my trees alight; Gwydion had at his disposal the tinderbox of the gods.

Deep in the recesses of my mind, untouched by searing flames, a shadowy terror reared its ugly head. No. Oh, no, this couldn't be how my time here ended! Not before Goronwy and I could say out final goodbyes. I'd planned to spend tonight using every wile I knew to persuade him to change his mind, and if that failed, to savour every last moment we had together. To breathe in the scent of him, to commit every inch to memory so that I might never forget the sight, the sound, the loving warmth of him.

This morning's farewell kiss, delightful though it had been, must not be our last. This could not be the end of our story, of our love. I had to find a way to save him. I had to.

Modwenna put her hand on my shoulder, trying to help me up. I batted her away. Every touch was agony.

"Goronwy!" I wheezed. "Rhun!" That vivid, crazed display danced and crackled in the skies above Penllyn. "Fetch... fetch Cynar and Yestin," I gasped, making a prodigious effort and heaving to my feet. "And warn all the others. Gwydion's coming, and you must all leave straight away." I shook my head, trying to clear my blurred vision. Little sparks danced behind my eyelids. "I have to find Goronwy. I have to go to Penllyn."

"Then we're coming with you," Delith said firmly. Where had she come from? How long had I been balled up on the floor like a terrified animal? Long enough for Modwenna to summon help.

Footsteps sounded, and Cynar appeared in the doorway. At his heels came Yestin, followed by a troop of anxious, frightened dogs. More people gathered, alerted by my screams as well as the crackling spectacle in the heavens. I thrust down the wrenching fear about Goronwy and tried to focus on the here and now. I would find a way to save him, but it would have to wait.

"You...you can't help," I ground out. "Stay here and finish packing. Plans have changed."

My fumbling fingers finally flipped the locket open and rubbed a thumb against the tiny serpent's scales. "Math," I thought, unsure if it would work but willing to try anything. Using seabirds to summon Dylan was out of the question. The sky resembled a battlefield.

"Is it working?" Delith asked anxiously. "How will you know if it does?"

"He'll arrive in a blaze of light, I suppose, as he always does." I tried to smile, but the pain dragging at my jaw would only permit a rictus grin. I pressed my lips firmly together, trying to stifle the moans.

"We can't afford to wait for him. We have to go now, and you'll need help to get on the horse." Cynar nodded to Yestin. His second-in-command swept me into his arms and headed toward the stables, apologising profusely every time I groaned in pain. The dogs trailed behind, whining, circling and yapping in distress.

The stable door banged open and Modwenna struggled through, laden with provisions crammed into a series of baskets. Delith followed, festooned with woollen rugs.

"We won't need all that!" An ominous crack of thunder drowned my protest. The light inside the stable dimmed as the sky outside darkened. From bright blue, it became steel-grey and heavy. Snarling lightning flashes stood out in eye-searing relief.

Yestin ignored me. He issued instructions to the stable boys, sending them scurrying to prepare several mounts, and when Manon was ready, hoisted me into the saddle. Cynar mounted the warhorse Gyso and the two women and children readied themselves as well. More stablehands filled saddlebags with the women's contributions.

Cynar wheeled Gyso about and plunged out into the gathering storm. "Cai, tie the dogs up so they don't panic and get lost in the storm. We ride to Penllyn."

Thank the Mother, and Arianrhod, for the gift of my faerie steed. Manon absorbed my pain, sluicing it from my flesh to send it through her body to her flashing silver hooves, dispersing it in the air or the earth. She also protected me a little from the pelting rain, which began as sparse but heavy droplets and increased to a deluge. The path ahead turned to squelching, sucking mud and water dripped from our horse's manes.

However, it put out the fires. Ahead and around us, the flames sputtered and died, leaving a trail of soggy ash and the acrid smell of charcoal and stale smoke. My brethren's torment continued to rack me, but I could function and to think clearly again. Math's words haunted me, playing again and again in my mind. Lleu would take Berlak's place to challenge Goronwy, and my lover would accept. He'd go knowingly to his death for no better reason than to uphold his male honour.

The unknown Berlak would have been infinitely preferable.

We crossed the Cynval without mishap before a mist descended, thick and white and eerie, slowing our progress. Rain and biting wind worked against me, increasing my anxiety with every small delay. Every insidious rustling in the grass, each ominous creak and mournful whisper, added to my dread: a sensation I remembered all too well. Common sense argued they were caused by the wind, but I couldn't shake the fear.

Around mid-afternoon, a twig cracked behind me, louder than the rest. I twisted in the saddle, scanning the muddy trail, certain I heard plodding hooves. "What was that? Is somebody tailing us?"

"If they are, I'll deal with them," Cynar said reassuringly. "Keep moving. We don't have time to waste."

He didn't venture to guess who that someone might be, but the name hung in the air. Cara. She'd escaped in the hubbub and vanished like a wraith. It would be like her to shadow us, hoping to hinder us and aid Gwydion. The troops left behind to protect my people had saddled their mounts in readiness; Cara could have stolen one of those horses in all the confusion. I nodded, plodding miserably onwards.

Soon we left the rolling downs and climbed through the hills toward the mountains proper. Mud and wet leaf litter made the narrow, rock-strewn trail treacherous, so we dismounted and went on foot for a while. Earthy, melancholy scents rose from the path, reminding me of the first time I'd ridden to a hunt, so long ago. The horses had been the same then, too. Gyso, the warhorse Math had introduced me to, Taffy, who'd been carrying Delith, and Garth, as well as Rhosyn and Cant, all came from Math's—now Yestin's—stable. A link to my lost past.

Yestin carried Pyrs, and Delith led Garth by the hand. The little boy stumbled over a loose stone and fell, with a cry more of surprise than of pain.

Behind us, a feminine voice squealed, as if someone else had also slipped on the treacherous path.

I pulled up short and turned, scanning the track. A piece of soggy brown drapery, like a woman's skirts, peeped from behind a roadside shrub.

"I know you're there, bitch. Come out." Despite my best efforts, my voice shook. "Whatever you're planning won't work. In case you hadn't noticed, you're slightly outnumbered."

The fabric twitched, then disappeared for an instant as if swept back by a hand, and Cara sidled into view. Her damp fair hair hung lankly around her face, and her cheeks and nose were red-raw. She held a horse's reins in one hand, and something clenched tightly in the other. Those damn feathers!

"I'm cold," she whined, "and wet and hungry. Got any food?"

What? She had the nerve to expect me to feed her? "We barely have enough for ourselves," I said, stepping back. "You've obviously foraged well until now. I suggest you do so a while longer."

"Or she could starve," muttered Modwenna, absently stroking Rhosyn's neck. Both Delith and my mount, Manon, snorted in agreement. I almost laughed. Even the horses saw through Cara.

Her eyes slid from one to the other before fastening on the ground. "Please? I'm faint with 'unger, so I am. You wouldn't see me dead, would you, milady?"

So, I was back to being her lady now. I grimaced. "I won't dance on your grave, but I've no desire to cover it with flowers, either. Yestin, bind her hands, and Delith or Modwenna can feed her when next we halt for a meal."

Yestin untied the cord from the waist of his tunic and advanced towards her, but Cara dropped the horse's reins, twisted away and darted back into the trees. A white form, so pale she all but glowed in the dim light, danced across to cut her off.

"Good girl, Manon," I said with approval. The faerie steed snuffled in answer, blue eyes fixed on her target.

If Gwydion's stables included faerie steeds, he probably didn't allow mortal women to ride them. The sight of a horse with glowing sapphirine eyes seemed to unnerve Cara. With a squawk of terror, she spun and ran again, straight into Cynar's solid chest. He wrenched the feathers out of her grasp and looked a question at me. Cara gasped and made a grab for them, but Manon slid between them and pushed her away.

Anger burned through me. "Drop them and grind them under your heel."

A howl of grief or despair burst from Cara, and as Yestin wound the cord around her wrists she sagged against him, sobbing. "No, please, no. I need them. I need him."

Did she, indeed? "Manon," I said, "your turn."

A shudder passed through Cara, and she doubled over, clutching her stomach and panting. "No," she moaned. "You can't destroy them all, it hurts. It hurts too much. I beg you. Please, please stop."

"She hasn't even touched them yet. Which makes me wonder if the histrionics are just for show. Let's find out, shall we?" I signalled Manon. Lifting one elegant leg, she bought her hoof down hard, then again, and again, until nothing remained of the feathers but a few barbs, glued together by mud.

Cara gave a final wail of supposed anguish, before straightening and glaring at me.

"See?" I said. "You're more resilient than you knew. Let's go."

Dropping her eyes to the ground again, she demanded sullenly, "What if I have to pee?"

My lips twisted. "Keep still and spread your legs wide. A position I'm sure you're quite used to."

Her jaw dropped, mouth open wide as if about to refute this, but the condemnation on all the surrounding faces seemed to stop her. She whined and subsided, pouting. Her quick recovery raised my suspicions, but I didn't complain. If we had to drag the bitch with us, I'd prefer not to listen to her continual moaning.

Gradually the mist lifted, although it rained intermittently. Between showers I studied the cloud-dappled heavens, searching for ospreys, but saw none. Something must have happened to Dylan; I didn't believe he'd abandoned me. Even without the eagles' warning, he must have seen the smoke from the fires if he was anywhere near our coast. But the skies remained empty of bird life save for the occasional kite.

Clever, but I'd always known Gwydion was no fool. Sometimes, the most effective means of hiding something was to leave it in plain sight. He might be one of those up there, and he might not. We could only keep going and hope the tree canopy would provide enough cover. And if it didn't? Turn and fight, I supposed, with my men at my side, and persuade the women to flee with the little ones.

I touched my locket again, but the rainbow skin remained inert. Great Mother, had Gwydion been able to hobble Math, too? The Trickster wasn't just clever, but cunning, ruthless, and cruel. A cloud of despair enveloped me. Had I doomed all my friends and supporters as well, by subjecting them to Gwydion's wrath? Math and Dylan could look after themselves, surely. I was less certain about Cynar and Yestin, but all my appeals had failed. They were determined to escort me. Please, let me reach Goronwy in time...

As the sun sank toward the horizon, another fog descended, which in turn became yet more drifting rain. We forged onward, looking for somewhere to shelter overnight. In high summer we could have kept going and reached Penllyn before full dark, but the trails we travelled were too treacherous to negotiate in the shorter, wet nights of spring.

Ranks of oak, birch, alder, and sycamore climbed the hillside to one side, while the sounds of rushing water meant a river lay to the other. Lichen and moss grew everywhere, cloaking the rocks and the tree trunks. This forest rarely saw sun.

To my surprise Cara kept pace with us willingly, although she too scanned the skies. Unlike mine, her expression was hopeful. Some sense warned me that her master was close. We both felt his looming presence, setting our nerves on edge.

At a bend in the track, an almighty crack sounded ahead. I caught my breath, and Cynar pulled Gyso up short. The rest of our train also stopped.

Cara jerked around, and her lips lifted in a simpering smile. Face flushed, eyes sparkling, she bent in an exaggerated curtsy.

"My lord," she breathed. "You've come at last. I knew you would."

Of course he had. I'd been a fool to think I could ever outrun him. My maker and my nemesis.

Gwydion.

19

PUNISHMENT

The curtain of the rain parted to reveal Gwydion ap Don. Sparks issued from his fingertips and crackled in his long dark hair, as they'd done the first morning I'd met him. He lifted his hands and flung them wide, strewing flowers and leaves across the path. I glanced down at them, then into his eyes. His cold and calculating blue, blue eyes. My stomach tied itself in knots, twisting and squirming like a snake; my heart tried to break my ribs, and my lungs screamed for lack of air.

I recognized those plants.

The nine herbs of my making.

"Gwydion." It came out in a whisper. I cleared my throat and spoke again. "Gwydion, what are you doing?"

Preparing to remake me, by the look of it. Or...unmake me altogether. Could he do that? Oh, Mother Don, perhaps he could. I couldn't die yet! I loved life too much. More, I loved Goronwy and had to save him, whatever it took.

"I'm... I'm sorry about what happened to Lleu that night by the Cynval. I didn't mean to cause him pain. I didn't realise... That is, I thought he'd only transform. When I heard the spear strike, heard those awful screams..."

The rest of our company appeared to be struck silent, Cara included.

Gwydion's accusing glare scalded me. "You couldn't have heard the spear strike him. You weren't close enough. But I was."

Memories of that fateful night played again in my head. "I...I did. I heard..."

"Nothing. A blade entering flesh doesn't make much noise. He doubled over from the pain, did you notice? I suppose not. I saw you there, kneeling, shielded from the sight of your betrayal by a dozen other bodies, pretending shock and sorrow. But it was all pretence, wasn't it? You felt nothing but triumph. You'd wanted Lleu out of your life for years, and finally you achieved it."

That stung. I found my voice. "How dare you say that to me! Things might have been different if Lleu had ever truly wanted me. All he needed was a... a sex toy, a means of negating the curse. Lleu took all his cues from you, and because you never saw me as a woman, as a person, neither did he. Not even as—"

I froze. All the hints dropped by Arianrhod, Artio, Dylan and Math crystallised into a stunning new mural. Everything they'd tried to say without words.

"Not even as... a goddess," I whispered. I'd always known I was more than mortal, but until that moment I hadn't fully grasped that I'd grown to be the equal of the Children of Don. Perhaps not as powerful in some ways, but no less important.

"A goddess? You?" He snorted. "You're no goddess. You're a conniving whore."

"No." I lifted my head, proudly defiant. How dare he insult me! "I am the Maid of Spring and the Lady of Autumn. Consort to the kings of both summer and winter. Both will die, but both will rise again."

Gwydion smiled cruelly. "But the winter king is mortal. He always takes a mortal form, and when he returns you won't know him. You can scour all the lands, but he'll be sacrificed again before you find him. You should have cast your lot with the summer king, Blodeuedd; then you'd still have a god to warm your bed instead of a man who's doomed to die. And that right soon. Because I've cured Lleu, did you hear? Now he wants retribution. Lleu's on his way to Penllyn right now to issue a challenge, one I'm sure your cursed lover will accept. He's a proud man, isn't he? Every winter king is."

"That's murder!" gasped Delith.

Gwydion glared at her. "Shut up!"

"Yes," echoed Cara, sidling towards Delith and bumping against her with bound arms. "Shut your stupid mouth."

The whining wind, the hissing rain, and the thunder of the river almost drowned her words, but we all saw her intent. I screamed as Modwenna leapt towards them, but she couldn't reach around Cara to yank Delith back. Caught in the middle, Cara twisted, flailing at Modwenna. All three slid sideways towards the edge of the cliff.

Towards the foaming, roaring river far below.

Delith gasped, "Cynar!" shoved Cara aside, and tried to propel Garth out of the way. She might have succeeded if the damp, mossy ground hadn't parted beneath her feet. She and her son slipped from my sight.

Cara shrieked, "Master, help!"

Gwydion didn't even spare her a glance. Before my horrified gaze, she and Modwenna also vanished down the gully into the white-flecked water.

Before I realized his intent, Cynar gave a gagging shriek and threw himself over. Yestin jerked as if to follow, but he held Cynar's infant son in his arms; the need to protect was greater.

A harsh shriek rent the air, more kite's cry than laughter. Sparks again flew from Gwydion and lifted Yestin with Pyrs. They plummeted over the edge. "Go. Join your wife and misbegotten offspring!"

"No! No, no no!" I rushed forward, searching desperately for a means to save them. Greenery abounded, but how could I attach it? I reached for a vine and threw it down the bank, screaming for somebody to grasp it, to no avail. Although I made it thicker and stronger, I couldn't control its movement over the rain-slick rocks. It slid back and forth ineffectually, and dragged limply through the water while the rushing current swept their bodies away. I prepared to dive, and further downstream saw a flash of gold and pearl-white as another figure dived into the river and struck out toward the struggling bodies.

"No, you don't." The air solidified around me, holding me immobile at the edge of the cliff. I struggled against invisible bonds which tightened with every movement. Eventually I stopped, fearful that if I continued, I'd no longer be able to breathe.

"More deaths to be laid at your door," said Gwydion from behind me.

I tried to turn, tried to speak, but could do nothing but grunt ineffectually.

Gwydion stepped forward, peered over the edge and smirked. "Ah, they've gone. Looks like Dylan was too late. You can get up now."

The despicable piece of offal! As my bonds fell away, I stumbled to my feet and turned to face him, shaking with anger and grief. "You killed them. You pushed them in! You murdering son of a pox-ridden goat!"

"Your perfidy brought them out here. You're a wicked, wicked woman, Blodeuedd."

Me, wicked? He'd tried to kill eight people, including innocent children—one of whom might have one day provided a new body for Arlais. Was that why he'd done it? To ensure Arlais couldn't return?

"What about Cara? She loved you! Did you feel nothing for her?"

He smirked. "She was useful, that's all. And her usefulness is now ended."

Cold-blooded snake. No, that would be an insult to Enfys. He had no more heart than the afanc he'd mentioned. I glanced down at the nine herbs ground into the mud. "And me? Are you going to kill me, or just unmake me? Turn me back into flowers? You told me once you couldn't do that."

My tormentor grunted. "If only that were possible. But you were created as the mate of an immortal being, to be immortal also." He glanced down at the pathetic remains of the greenery. "I brought those with me as a reminder: of who you are, of who you were always meant to be. Lleu's bride. The Flowerbride."

He thrust back his dark cloak and withdrew a wand from his belt, more elaborately carved than Math's from a dark, reddish wood. "I can't kill you, but I can do to you what your lover's poison did to Lleu." A wicked grin curved his lips. "Turn you into a bird."

My stomach lurched as cold, sick horror gripped me. He wouldn't! He couldn't! Could he?

I searched frantically for the horses—all fled. My wand lay tucked in Gyso's saddlebag. Why hadn't I put it in my own? Manon was the only steed who remained, though even she was kept at bay by Gwydion's magic.

"And," continued Gwdion, "because of the dishonour you brought upon my nephew, I condemn you to live always in the dark, shunned by other birds and living forever in fear of them. Henceforth you will be not Blodeuedd, but Blodeuwedd."

A prickle of foreboding crept over my skin. I'd heard that name before somewhere. But where?

Gwydion gestured with his wand.

All the air left my lungs, dragging pain in its wake. So much pain! Agony ripped through me, worse even than the torment caused by the fire. Needles pierced my flesh as my skin warped and shrank—needles tipped with the sharp quills of feathers. I groaned, gasped and tried to scream, but all that emerged was a squawk.

My nails grew into talons, sharp, hooked, and cruel. My pert and dainty nose shed its skin and curved out and down, becoming hard and black with a vicious, scissor edge. My vision distorted; my bones became frail and light.

Shock threatened to smother me. Great Lady, I was drowning! Again. Memories of salt water, of panic, of a small drowning bear. Baby animals... Kittens...

I remembered. I remembered where I'd heard that name. Goronwy had used it years ago in my rooftop garden, the first time we'd met.

Goronwy. I hooted once, stretched my dappled wings, and flew as fast as I could for Penllyn.

Rhun came into view first, seated on a blackened log in the midst of a charred and smoking forest. His brother knelt beside him, lathering salve onto his badly burned hands before gently binding them. Soot smeared the faces of both men, and blisters had begun to form on the exposed skin of their necks and arms. There was nobody else in sight.

At first.

Hoofbeats sounded, and a tall chestnut horse hove into view, bearing an equally tall rider. Golden-haired and golden-skinned, with eyes of periwinkle blue. He pulled up beside Goronwy and Rhun, and a red kite swept past them both. Lleu dismounted and Gwydion transformed, standing side by side to face the man they'd come to kill.

Goronwy knew. I saw it in his eyes, in the set of his jaw, in the way he braced himself to stand, foursquare, before them. I dived at him, piping in fright and distress. Gwydion reached out to bat me away; his dark and awful magic bound me. It pinned my wings and my feet and stole what little voice I could command.

"So," said Goronwy, an edge of mockery in his voice. "You've come to challenge me."

Lleu nodded. "I have."

The mockery slid into laughter. "I don't suppose I could pay you off. A little gold, some jewels? Or horses, cattle? We still have a few left. The main house and holdings were untouched; the fire seems to have been concentrated here near the border of Dunoding."

Affront tightened Lleu's face. "You jest!"

"I do." Goronwy gestured with a bandaged hand.

Lleu hesitated then, but his uncle forged ahead. "Should any of your warband, your foster-brothers or your brothers wish to stand for the blow in your place, that would be quite acceptable, my lord."

Curse him. Rot his flesh and his soul. He could see what state Rhun was in, and knew Bryant lived too far away. I struggled ineffectually, pinned to the ground behind Gwydion, but nobody even noticed I was there. Eventually I managed to dislodge a single tawny feather. It wavered through the air and floated across to rest against Lleu's foot.

Rhun made a convulsive movement. Goronwy shook his head, moving to stand in front of his injured brother.

"I have no foster-brothers living and Rhun's in no condition to hold a weapon. Nor is Cynar, and Yestin is untrained. Those who might have offered—Geraint, Drustan, Ivar and their companions—are dead, killed by your men. Another four died today in these fires, along with a great many livestock and wild animals. I acknowledge I wronged you, Lleu Llaw Gyffes, but I think your revenge is overblown." He shrugged. "Nevertheless, I accept your challenge. Strike at me if you must."

Lleu laughed grimly. He'd never been able to recognise sarcasm. "Oh, be sure I will. Meet me tomorrow at sunset by the Cynval, in the same place you struck me."

I expended every ounce of effort to protest, to cry out to him, to make them all see reason. I may as well have been invisible. Perhaps I was, thanks to Gwydion's magic. I watched, panting, fluttering and squeaking, as Rhun and Goronwy trudged back to Penllyn castle. Their horses were either dead or long fled. When they'd gone,

Gwydion released me; both he and Lleu retreated, one on horseback, the other on the wing.

I wanted to savage him with beak and talons, to rub my hatred into his wounds like salt. But that would have to wait. Now I had a more urgent mission.

Goronwy! Taking to the air, I trailed after him, wanting to cry out to him, to communicate somehow. I squawked, I piped, I hooted, but although both he and Rhun looked up, they didn't slow their pace. Why should they? The sight of a lone owl flying in daylight might be unusual, but not enough to immediately signal magic. Nevertheless, I kept them in sight for all of their journey, swooping from branch to branch, trying to project my need, to persuade him of his folly.

Useless. Without speech, I couldn't reach him.

If I'd retained my human form, I might have been able to argue him out of meeting Lleu, although being well acquainted with his stubbornness, that might have been a foolish and vain hope. Even my power over plants might have availed me nothing with Gwydion acting as Second. I'd witnessed his power over lightning. Being able to control plants would be of little use if they were ripped apart by fire.

No, there was only one ploy left to me, and I made it.

Lleu and Gwydion were gods, but I was also a goddess. Nor was I the only one. We were the holy feminine, and our memory was long. I set my inner compass to Arianrhod's bleak fortress at the far edge of the world, winging my way northwards, deep stroke by steady stroke.

20

THE DRAGON'S BONES

Another tremor shook the ground, and a line of dolmens on the horizon tilted alarmingly. Gwydion swore and uttered a brief calming spell to settle his horse. Flying to his destination after leaving Caer Dathyl would have been preferable, but that would have made carrying the saddlebags he had lashed behind him rather awkward. Assuming his kite form in god mode wouldn't have served, either. Someone would have been bound to notice something that size flying above, and he wanted to avoid attention at all costs.

The earth vibrated again. That happened rarely in the Otherworld, although it wasn't unknown in mortal realms. Indeed, several years ago he'd been obliged to destroy a stone circle in Ardudwy, causing similar, if less violent, tremors. A shame, but he'd deemed it necessary to teach the woman Blodeuwedd a lesson. Her name had been slightly different then—Blodeuedd. The original had meant Flowerface; her current name translated as Owl.

Gwydion snorted. How appropriate that he'd been able to unname her by simply changing the syllables. If only unmaking her had been as simple. The amount of power that spell required had in fact, severely drained him, causing him to leave the field of battle at Caer Dathyl to Lleu.

No matter. He was sure his nephew-son could handle anything Math ap Mathonwy threw at him. Even Arawn, Lord of Shadows, would be no match for Lleu's increasing power. He'd have liked to stay and add his arm to Lleu's, but it had been clear that Lleu needed no help, and Gwydion recognised an opportunity when confronted with it.

The unsteadiness in the landscape caused by Lleu's violence at Caer Dathyl was likely to reach all the way to the coast. Sitting atop his horse on a ridge close to the Caer, Gwydion saw it had. Such disturbances might unblock the cave his Uncle Math had sealed away from him centuries before. He'd tried to wheedle the dragon blade out of his mother's consort, Beli, with no luck. And of course, he'd returned to the cave as soon as he'd regained human form, hoping to retrieve and reforge a second claw, or even a tooth. That would have required more time and effort to shape into a blade, but the thought turned out to be academic. Math had foreseen that move and taken steps to prevent it.

Now was his chance. Even Arawn would stand no hope against such a blade, and the notoriety attendant on killing the Lord of the Afterworld was something he found very attractive. He continued to the coast, and as Math had done years before, clambered over the rocks and onto the beach. There was no hesitation in Gwydion's steps. He remembered where he needed to go.

His breath caught as he neared the cave's entrance. As he'd suspected, the recent shocks had undone Math's barrier, something Gwydion's magic had been unable to achieve. For earthquakes, even minor ones, came under the governance of Gwydion's mother Don, the earth goddess, even when they were caused by another godling, like Lleu.

Grinning delightedly, Gwydion approached the cave—only to reel back in shock at what he saw through the narrow entrance. The dragon bones were gone! Totally and completely gone!

He ventured closer, looking around wildly. Water lapped at his feet, as high as his ankles, and the rocks were damp to the height of his waist. Slowly, he pieced together what must have happened. The tremors which loosened the boulders had also caused massive, destructive tides. That would lead to a lot of heartache in the small communities along this coast. Not that he cared.

His only concern was the fate of those bones. Could the tide have lifted and carried them out to sea? No. Surely some would have snagged on the rocks; they wouldn't have vanished so utterly. Math, curse him for a sea slug's entrails, must have destroyed them before he'd entombed them. But in that case, why bother with the seal at all?

A pale gleam high on the walls, close to the cave's roof, caught his eye. He shifted into kite form and flew up for a closer look. It proved to be dust: fine ivory dust, the very colour of the dead dragon's bones. The likely sequence of events fell into place. Math had pulverised the bones and left them there in the cave. Why, Gwydion couldn't imagine. Some warped gesture of acknowledgement, perhaps, of respect. Math put stock in such idiocies.

That put a crimp in his own plans, for certain. He changed shape again and sat on a handy rock, thinking. The power inherent in a dragon's claws and teeth was legendary, but he'd seen no mention of their bones. Their hide was nigh impenetrable, their teeth and claws indestructible, and the reason they'd become close to extinct was a mystery. Those that remained had quit Cymru and its Otherworld counterpart long ago and were reputed to dwell only in the far north of the world.

He untied his shirt and shrugged it off. Then, rolling a few flat-topped rocks against the wall, he stacked them like stairs and climbed up to the place he'd noticed the dust. On closer inspection, he found that a large section of the upper wall was coated with it. Effective though Math's barrier had been, sea water had seeped between the rocks, and king tides had redistributed the dragon's remains. Working delicately, Gwydion scooped as much as possible into the makeshift bag of his shirt and descended again.

With each passing minute, his power was recharging. Certainly enough to reassemble the scattered boulders over the entrance to ensure no chance passer-by disturbed him. That done, he sank cross-legged to the wet ground. With his back to the rock wall of the cave, he poured a small quantity of dragon dust into his cupped hands. He focused all his thoughts, all his intention onto that which he held, and probed the essence of the bones.

At last—when his back and shoulders ached, his eyelids felt as if they were lined with sandpaper, and the echo of the surf outside the cave echoed a thousand times louder in his skull—he felt it. A morsel, a smidgeon, a memory of the magic the great beast had once owned. Would it be enough for his needs?

It would. It would have to be. He would make it be enough.

Calling on the dregs of his waning power and emptying himself of it completely, he used the sand to fashion a small glass container. Carefully guarding every mote, he filled it with his store of precious dust. That done, he curled up on a high flat rock, still damp but not soaking wet, and composed himself for sleep. It might take some time to recover fully, but there was no rush.

Blodeuwedd no longer posed a threat, nor would the rest soon, particularly the two brats.

He smiled to himself, contemplating the future. He was confident of Lleu's ability to defeat those who'd gathered in Caer Dathyl—Math, his queen, and their people—without causing any permanent damage, and thus courting censure by the Great Goddess Don. Then, once Lleu was reunited with his Caron, he'd wait for Gwydion to join him. They'd proclaim themselves kings of all Cymru, and together they would rule the world.

Gwydion had no doubt his mother wouldn't approve of that plan, either, but as long as he didn't actively flout her arbitrary 'rules' he thought he'd be reasonably safe. His smile deepened. Even if he wasn't, he'd always considered the path of safety unutterably boring. Danger sang to him, as intoxicating as the harsh, wild call of the carnyx, as alluring as the gliding notes of a harp.

His gaze rested on the precious vial by his side. How much and what kind of magic did dragon bones hold? A savage grin split Gwydion's face.

Time to find out.

21

TRANSFORMED

Night fell long before I reached my goal, but that mattered little to an owl. I swept through the dark on silent wings at a much faster pace than I could have achieved on horseback. I didn't tire; whether that was a condition common to owls or exclusive to me, I didn't know. But horses were limited to roads and trails, whereas the dark skies above the treeline offered no obstacles. And despite never having flown this way before, I could easily navigate by the stars.

The pale colours of dawn's harbinger painted the northern sky as I approached Arianrhod's palace, and for once the sky was clear. Unaccountably, I found the wide doors standing open. I swept through them and glided unchallenged along the corridor until I found the room I sought: the little sitting room the goddess seemed to favour.

Voices—loud voices—attested to its occupation. Dylan stood in front of the fireplace. Arianrhod reclined on the settle with the white owl, Gwenhwyfar, on her shoulder and the ubiquitous pair of wolves sprawled at her feet.

I floated soundlessly to the back of one of the upholstered chairs and piped. Piped again, louder. Then fluffed my feathers and looked around the room, twisting my head in a circle. A difficulty I hadn't considered. How was I to communicate?

"Hello, Blodeuedd," said Arianrhod, speaking in my head as she'd done on Ynys Môn.

"That's not her name anymore." Lleu stepped forward from a spot beside the door, and I froze in shock. I'd come prepared to confront his mother; seeing him as well drove all my prepared speeches from my head. Fear and incandescent anger combined to rob me not just of thought, but of movement.

He crossed his arms on his chest, a scowl twisting his features. "She's Blodeuwedd, now."

Dylan's expression was equally thunderous.

I piped again, then squawked, and finally managed a hoot, long, drawn-out and distressed.

"Just think the words," said their mother in a soothing voice. "I promise we'll hear you."

Was that how the legendary Dafona used to communicate with feathered kind? I tried it.

"What is he doing here?" Hard to convey enough outrage, but perhaps that would come with practice.

"I invited him," said the goddess. "This is a family enclave, and it's fitting you've joined us."

Lleu snorted. "Invited! Commanded would be more like it. I was dragged here by my brother against my will, and I don't plan to stay long."

He sounded miffed, but that was nothing new. I considered, briefly, irritating him further by landing on his head and leaving a deposit. My human memories told me that owl shit stank, which summed up my feelings perfectly.

"Shut up," said Dylan. "Just shut up and listen." He jerked his beard towards me. "Did you know Gwydion was going to do this? Turn Blodeuedd into an owl, on top of everything else? I'm telling you, he betrayed you. Our father..."

"Our uncle!" Lleu's face was red.

"All right, let's stick with fucking Gwydion. Gwydion pushed Arlais to kill herself, and he almost drowned several people, including two innocent children. Three, if you count Modwenna's unborn baby. And Gwydion's lover. I pulled everybody from the river..."

Cooing with relief, I sagged against the upholstery and all but toppled from the chair. *"Oh, thank the Mother! I thought...I thought everyone was dead."*

Compassion shadowed Dylan's face. "Your friends are alive, but while most of the others have recovered, the shock of the fall was too much for Cara. I couldn't save her. What kind of man watches a woman who loves him drown without so much as blinking? He certainly shed no tears, from what I've heard."

Lleu's face reflected the incomprehension I knew of old. "Cara was only a kitchen maid. Why should she matter to anyone?"

Dylan made a choking sound, as if the words he sought were too jagged to speak without harm. "What is wrong with you? Fine, if you won't bat an eyelash about Cara, at least consider how callous Gwydion acted toward a mother and her innocent child. He knew Modwenna was important to you, but he just doesn't care."

Lleu shrugged. "Well, I admit he did seem to get a bit carried away, but he's reassured me that Caron's new vessel doesn't have to be a descendant of Dafona. We two are bound together, for all time. Arawn can't hold Caron's soul hostage forever, and when he releases her, she'll find her way back to me. Being able to incarnate in a descendant of Dafona makes it easier to find each other, but if that's not possible, we'll still find a way."

I stared at him, open beaked. Dylan looked equally dumbfounded. "Even if you wrest Caron's soul away from Arawn," he said, "it might end up anywhere in her next incarnation. On the opposite side of the planet, for instance. You could search for a whole human lifetime and still be unable to find her, or by the time you did, she could be an old woman."

This logic made no impression on Lleu. "I may be a little annoyed at Gwydion, but I know he didn't betray me. Everything he's ever done has been in my best interest, because he's the only person who's every cared about me. I'm sure Modwenna will recover, and to ensure she does, I'll take her to Caer Dathyl. There her life will be greatly extended, and together we'll await Caron's return."

"You're insane," I squawked. *"You can't make the baby live soulless until then. Do you expect her to just..."*

I stopped, remembering what had happened to Arlais, Caron's last incarnation. Caron had, at first by small degrees, later by large ones, ousted Arlais's soul and personality and replaced them with her own.

"So," said Dylan, his voice dripping contempt, "you're fine with using possession to assuage your desire, and now murder as well. Delith told me Gwydion's action was quite deliberate. Is that right, Blodeuedd?"

I shrieked, torn by the memory of Gwydion's cruelty, then remembered to project my response by thought. *"Yes, he did. He pushed all of them into the river. Are you saying he didn't know about Arawn's decree, and didn't want Arlais to return to Lleu?"*

Dylan snorted. "Gwydion wants Lleu to himself. He always has. Everything he's done, every tortuous plot and plan, has been toward that end. He planned Lleu's conception and his birth; I was an accident. He'd never considered the possibility of twins—that's why he made no objection when Uncle Math claimed me. He only wanted one son. One acolyte, one heir."

He glared at his brother. "He viewed your passion for Caron as mere infatuation and was prepared to indulge it, even creating Blodeuedd for you as a cover. But the scheme worked too well—much better than he'd bargained for. Blodeuedd's sentience was a factor he hadn't counted on, either. He saw you and Arlais growing closer and Blodeuedd slipping out of his control, so when Goronwy's spear transformed you, he saw his opportunity. He convinced Arlais you were gone for good, and the only way she could find you again was to look for you in Annwfyn."

Goronwy! If I could prevent Lleu from leaving, he'd forfeit the challenge by not turning up on time, and Goronwy would live and...and then what? How could we be together while I remained in feathered form? I turned to Arianrhod in desperation.

"Mother, I need your help. You have to turn me back into a woman!"

She shook her head sadly. "A spell can only be undone by the one who cast it. Look at the lengths Gwydion had to go to, to counteract my tynged on Lleu."

Lleu cast us both a look of contempt and strode towards the door.

"No!" Bating wildly, I dove at him, claws outstretched to rake red furrows down his flesh.

He ducked away, throwing his arm up to protect his face. I landed on his shoulder, piercing muscle and bone with strong, serrated claws, and gouged my beak across his neck. Lleu yelled and swore. Somebody else uttered a high-pitched, ululating scream. Arianrhod? I'd never heard her make a noise like that. I wouldn't have believed she could.

Something pierced my back, and agony ripped through me. Shocked, I let go of Lleu. Pitiless talons gripped me, dragging me into the air. Huge, snowy wings lifted me to the lofty ceiling. I shrieked; the claws holding me let go, and I plummeted to the ground. Gwenhwyfar loomed above me, her much larger form and wicked beak interposed between me and Lleu.

Clutching his injured shoulder, Lleu spat a vile oath at me, his mother and his brother, turned on his heel and swept out of the door. Seconds later I heard him running down the hall, no doubt to collect his chariot and fly south to keep his assignation by the Cynval. I had to follow him! To stop him!

Frantic, I launched into the air. The white owl glided above me and drifted down to pin me to the floor, like a mother bird containing a nestling. I cried, I hooted, I chortled, all to no avail. Even if Gwenhwyfar hadn't been a familiar, a creature of magic, I couldn't have dislodged her. She was too big. I sagged and went limp.

Gwenhwyfar didn't move but settled above me. Clucking softly, I tucked myself into a ball and shot forward from beneath her feathered breast. She stretched out her wings, extended a single talon and batted me to the floor again, resulting in a flapping, painful dance, and the loss of many feathers.

"Let him go," said Dylan, smiling.

Let him go? I squawked my disagreement, but the large body pinning mine didn't budge. How dare they order my life with no regard for my feelings? For my needs! Baffled and outraged, I bent my head and bit Gwenhwyfar's foot. She retaliated by plucking out several of my neck feathers, needling me with pain.

A mass of rumpled plumage, I subsided, smarting.

"Uncle Math's conceived a plan," continued Dylan. "A way for the two of you to stay together and reward the Winter King for his championing of the goddess."

I stared at him, torn between frustration and red rage.

"This isn't a game of tafl, and we are not your pieces! I can't conceive how the gracious Mother came to have such putrid children. You're arrogant, capricious, selfish, vain, and forever needlessly interfering. The entire clan of you. And you don't even try to rein in Gwydion's excesses—you let him get away with everything. He's won. He's destroyed my life and Goronwy's, and Lleu's as tied to him as ever!"

I went on in this vein for some time. Arianrhod listened impassively, Dylan with a wry smile.

"You're wrong," he said, when I paused for a mental breath. "Lleu doesn't want to believe it, but he knows what I told him is true. Gwydion intentionally tried to kill Modwenna and her baby to prevent Arlais from returning. He didn't know Arawn's forbidden it, anyway."

"*For now.*" I uttered a squawk for emphasis.

"Forever," said Arianrhod. "Or at least for a very long time. Caron's stupid vow horrified Arawn, and he blames himself for not stopping her sooner. The problem was that there was no precedent. Arawn's a stickler for the rules, and when somebody sidesteps but doesn't actually break those rules he doesn't know how to respond. Arlais's suicide changed that. The law governing the taking of a person's own life is very clear. They need counselling, healing, and that can't be accomplished quickly."

I bobbed my head instead of shaking it. *"Do you think Lleu will ever accept that?"*

Dylan shrugged. "He'll have to. Caron's gone, and he needs to move on. But simply knowing that Gwydion was prepared to kill Modwenna and her daughter might be enough to sow the seeds of doubt in his mind. Over time, the wedge between him and our father will widen. We can't harm Gwydion physically, but trust me, losing Lleu will cause him to suffer."

"And when that happens," added his mother, "perhaps Lleu and I will have a chance. All I ever wanted was to get to know my son. I hope Dylan, Lleu and I can become much closer. A true family at last."

Unable to express my thoughts any other way, I hooted. I could accept Dylan as family, but not Lleu. Not ever. I'd gleaned enough about relationships to know that mothers could be fiercely partisan toward their children, but even so, Arianrhod was too forgiving. He was a monster. A tyrant. A killer. He and his uncle-father both.

Muttering to myself internally, I changed the subject. *"What about the others? Dylan said he saved them, but not what happened next. Are they safely home again? Did Penllyn and Mur Y Castell survive Gwydion's fire? Are the rest of my people all right?"*

Arianrhod smiled at me. "Yes, yes, and yes. What's more, Math's offered to have some of his own physicians attend to Modwenna, to give her the very best chance of recovery. There are no guarantees, of course, but I believe she will heal, given time."

It was something, I supposed. Not nearly enough, but at least something. The goddess lifted an eyebrow and looked at me quizzically, apparently able to read my expression, if owls can have expressions, or to catch the tenor of my thoughts.

"Is there something else, Blodeuwedd?"

"Yes." At least I no longer needed to ask why I'd been dreaming of owls. I outlined my other demands. *"If Math's so dead keen on transforming everything in sight, I want him to do it for Taran, as well as Goronwy's three dogs. I want Math to turn them into wolves and make them part of Chynwyrn and Sipsi's pack."*

Arianrhod looked down at the wolves at her feet. "Well, my children, what do you think?"

Such a request would have been unthinkable for a normal wolf pack, but these were sentient beings, almost demi-gods themselves. Chynwyrn whined and flopped his tail; Sipsi merely yawned.

The goddess smiled. "They accept."

"What about Manon? Will she simply return to wherever she came from in the Otherworld?"

Arianrhod waved an airy hand. "She already has. Now, my sweet daughter, follow me. I have something important to show you."

Gwenhwyfar released me. I shot from beneath her and through every door towards freedom. A whoosh of air behind me announced the white owl's pursuit, but Arianrhod called her back.

"Let her go," she said solemnly. "She needs to do this."

I needed to stop Lleu and save Goronwy. Somehow. I had to find a way, I had to. Desperation squirled along my veins and made my pulse quicken. Throat tight, eyes burning with unshed tears, I burst out into the frosty air, and looked up.

No! No, no, no, it couldn't be. Even this far north, as the days lengthened into summer, night had fallen. The day which dawned as I arrived had vanished in the stolen hours of my imprisonment in Arianrhod's castle. 'Meet me at dusk, tomorrow,' Lleu had said. It was already tomorrow, and dusk was long past.

Curse Arianrhod. Curse them all! It should not have been this way. Even if my efforts to save him had failed, I could have at least said goodbye. If death was his fate, I should have been at his side. He couldn't die alone, so far away from me. Alone and helpless, at the mercy of an insane god.

They'd let Lleu get away and kept me pinned and helpless, when I could have been... doing what? My magic centred around plants, which I could no longer access. I wasn't certain how to negotiate a stone circle either, in owl form.

Panic flared. I swept into the air, wings pumping wildly, and an unfamiliar voice spoke in my head. *"You'll wear yourself out, doing that. If you insist on undertaking a long-distance flight, use the air currents and glide."*

A shadow loomed above me, a sweep of wings twice the width of mine. Gwenhwyfar. I sent a thought back. *"I have to find Goronwy. I have to stop Lleu."*

"Foolish little owl. You know it's too late for that."

Her shadow disappeared, but without expending energy on turning, I couldn't tell if she'd turned around or simply dropped back. With an aching heart, I followed her advice and let the currents bear me forward, above the dark, silent forests and south to Ardudwy.

The place Lleu had designated as their meeting ground would be forever burned into my memory. I never went there; images of the spear striking Lleu, and his subsequent transformation, tormented me with grief and guilt still. And now, from a place of ill-omen, it had become the tomb of hope.

Driven by desperation to the edge of exhaustion, I tumbled from the sky, landing beside a man-high stone with a round hole in the centre. Gaining my feet, I looked around, searching against all hope, all logic, for any sign of life. But the riverbank was deserted.

A brief stab of hope sputtered and flared to life. Perhaps, after all, he'd seen sense at last and fled? Or perhaps Lleu hadn't killed him, and his brother had taken him home to recover?

Perhaps the sun, when it rose again, would do so in the west. Both were equally impossible. Still, that spurt of hope refused to die. Until I saw his body, or...

Some instinct drew my gaze back to the stone which stood, dark and ominous, on the bank of the river. A glistening dark stain ringed the hole at its centre. Blood.

Goronwy's blood.

I hooted, a screech of raw unending pain, and a shadow dropped from the heavens to enfold me in the great white wings of Arianrhod.

22

FURNACE

Several of Heilyn's warriors tried to follow Gwydion from Caer Dathyl's Great Hall, and found Lleu blocking the exit. He had only to stand there; his appearance kept our dauntless warriors pinned in place. When dwelling in Caer Dathyl all those years ago, he'd always appeared to be bathed in sunshine, a warm, caressing radiance. Even in mortal Ardudwy he'd brought light into a room. Now, as his temper grew, he resembled a furnace.

"Where is Arawn?" he demanded in a voice that could have cut glass. "I won't be dictated to by him. No matter what my uncle says, I want my Caron back, and I will not be denied. Let Arawn come here and face me!"

Scarlet, blue and orange flames twisted and danced within an elongated ball of golden light. His hair crackled with the force of his passion, throwing off sparks. He exuded hatred and thwarted desire. I shrank away from him, my heart hammering against my ribs. My pulse beat in my throat in a rhythm which threatened to choke me.

Hairline cracks appeared in Caer Dathyl's walls. The painted columns tilted. I did choke then, gasping for breath. Lleu's heat drew all moisture from the air, searing my lungs and making my eyes water.

"Wynne, stay close to me." Math drew me to him and threw a cloak over us both, trying to create a breathing space with enough oxygen. "If you want to fight the lord of the underworld, Lleu, I suggest you go there and confront him. I won't allow either of you to wreck Caer Dathyl."

I coughed and drew my robe across my mouth, struggling for air. A horrifying vision rose before me of the destruction visited on Ardudwy by this out-of-control Lleu. Forests alight; people and animals fleeing or dying. Charred ground and ruined homes, polluted streams and new-made orphans.

Lleu leapt onto the table before him and his voice lowered to a hiss, little louder than a whisper. "You don't understand. None of you understand." His volume rose again, like slowly building thunder. "I love her, and she loves me. We belong together, and I won't allow you to take her from me. None of you know what it is to truly love!"

The timber beneath Lleu's feet smouldered, adding wisps of smoke to the mayhem.

Behind him, the door banged open, and Blei erupted into the room. "Idiot," he snarled, planting himself squarely in front of his brother. "Are you trying to burn the place down? The glow from in here's visible all over the castle. Horses and dogs are panicking, our people are fleeing. You'll bring Grandmother down on us next!"

A light step sounded at the door, which Blei had left ajar, and a light, well-modulated feminine voice cut through his diatribe.

"Cousin Lleu," said Meghan, advancing several steps into the room, wreathed in blue-grey smoke. "Blei's right. Behave yourself. You can't flout the rule of law established by the elder gods. If Annwfyn's lord says Caron's soul can't be released into life so soon, what right have you to challenge him? If you truly loved the woman, you'd want to do what's best for her. You're being stupid, and incredibly selfish."

Lleu flicked her a single, contemptuous sideways glance, but didn't answer. I sucked in a startled breath, threw the cloak aside and rushed towards her, with Math right behind me. She must have been eavesdropping, somehow. "Meg, no!" I gasped. "You have to leave. Quickly."

"You little fool!" Blei reached her in two swift strides and gripped her by the elbow. "You'll get yourself killed, barging in here. He won't listen to reason. Look at him!"

Not even a blind person could miss the inferno that was now Lleu. He radiated heat and noise as well as a furnace glow. Flames licked at his feet as the table burned through and collapsed with a roar. Lleu remained unaffected, hovering in the same place above the burning board.

"But—" Meg protested.

A screaming red kite sailed through the still open door and speared towards Lleu. I hugged my daughter close, my heart beating like a terrified bird. Math muttered a spell to throw a shield around us. At the same time, Blei dropped Meg's arm and stepped back towards the door, wrenching it fully open.

With a muttered imprecation, Math split his focus, reaching out to halt the kite while battling Lleu's fire.

Still shrieking, the bird landed beside Lleu. Framed in red-gold fury, the bird blurred and shifted to become a grim-visaged Gwydion, shrouded in shadows and a swirling dark cloak. He hovered for a moment beside Lleu, before alighting on the floor.

The ground shifted beneath him—beneath everyone, as the flagstones buckled. Despite Math's protective bubble, perspiration sheened my skin and dripped into my eyes.

Gwydion said nothing, but extended his hands, palms out, towards Math. Violet flames speared upward, then lanced across the space between them.

At a nod from Math, Heilyn shepherded his men from the room through the now open door. This was now a battle between mage-born kin.

With a deep-throated roar, Blei rose up and up, to twice man-size, becoming not a wolf, but a bear. "Desist, brother! Leave Meghan out of this!"

"You think tricks learned from Artio will intimidate me?" scoffed Lleu. "You'll have to try harder than that." He drew back his arm and threw a fireball at his brother.

Blei caught the full force of it. He dropped to all fours, screaming in agony. The stench of burning flesh and singed fur filled the air.

Chaos erupted. Blei collapsed to the ground in an untidy heap. Meg clung to me, sobbing. Math whipped around and threw a blast of sweet, cool air to quench the flames tormenting Blei. As he slid into unconsciousness, Math scooped him up, deposited him next to me, and extended the bubble around us all.

That moment's break was all the opening Lleu needed. With an eldritch howl of triumph, he spun, faster and faster, and the flames peeled away from him to set alight every flammable surface.

Flames leapt and snarled, curling up columns, tables and benches and crackling through the floor rushes.

Meg and I crouched beside Blei, muttering prayers and half-forgotten healing spells. I'd never studied healcraft. I'd never needed to, and nor had Meg. At least she could channel cool air through her hands, whereas my magic required herbs and salves and other tools, as well as time—none of which I had, especially the latter.

"How can this happen?" Tears slid down my Meghan's cheeks; her voice and her hands shook. "How can Caer Dathyl burn?"

"Normally it couldn't." It took an effort to sound calm, to hold the gibbering horror at bay. "Lleu's fire is Otherworldly. He can evade our magical defences."

Shaking violently beneath our touch, Blei's screams abated to a series of shuddering moans. I stroked his furry head.

"Why hasn't he changed back?" asked Meg. "Why is he still in bear form?"

Lleu's doing, or Blei's own decision? I leaned forward and whispered, "Transform, Blei. Become a man so we can better help you heal."

He stilled beneath my touch but didn't change.

Beyond us, the battle between Gwydion, Math, and Lleu continued to rage. A spark of fire zinged against the barrier, then another, and another. Groaning and creaking, it slowly buckled inwards. I'd once seen a Syrian glassblower at work, part of a travelling troupe. Math's magic barrier acted much as the molten glass had done; pliable as treacle, but with the potential to shatter.

Meg squealed and shuffled away from the edge of the melting dome. Finally, with a sigh rather than the expected roar, it disintegrated into splinters. Unable to move, Blei couldn't avoid it, and before my horrified gaze several shards of magic speared towards his prone body. All my plans were useless now. I muttered yet another timing spell.

"Meg, grab his legs—we have to move him."

Time emulated the glass, twisting and warping. I gripped Blei's shoulders, Meg took his calves, and together we heaved him onto his side as the fractured dome pierced the floor. Nerves shrieking and breath faltering, I concentrated on maintaining the spell for just a little longer. If I could halt the progress of the burns until we could get him to a healer, he'd stand a better chance of recovery. I didn't think his wounds could kill him—godlings weren't easily dispatched. But as they'd been caused by a close relative, he might be disfigured. I'd mitigate that, if I could. The screech and crackle of the battle in the background provided a bizarre accompaniment, but I had no time to see what was happening.

Meg eyed the broken barrier and edged gingerly toward it.

"No! Meg, stop!" My protest came out more harshly than I intended. By way of apology, I flashed her a reassuring smile. "You need to stay here, and if you want to be useful, sing to him. Something soothing. Something healing."

Her face cleared, and she nodded. Meg had a lovely, well-trained voice, and knew all the tunes the healers used to relax both muscles and a troubled mind. It worked on me, too. I allowed the gentle rise and fall of sound to wash over me, weaving a peaceful cocoon of music around Blei to keep him safe until the healers could aid him.

The odour of wet wood increased. In the periphery of my vision, as the background sizzle of the flames lessened, Gwydion unstopped a small glass bottle and tossed its contents over Math. My husband halted mid-movement, as if he'd encountered an invisible barrier.

"What is that?" he rasped, his voice lower pitched than normal. He sounded as if speech was an effort.

Gwydion grinned, before turning to me. "Dragon dust. Want some, Aunt Wynne?"

Dragon dust? What in Arawn's name was that? It might look like powder, but it didn't float through the air as normal motes would. Instead it snapped onto Math, clinging to him as iron filings will to a lodestone.

I twisted away as a trail of fine ivory powder arced toward me, and hastily threw up a time-slowing spell, hoping to avoid it. Contrarily, the dust gained speed. It settled over my face, my gown, my hands, in a spray fine as mist, anchoring me in place. None touched Meg or Blei.

Math remained stationary. So did the unconscious Blei. Meg started towards me, and Gwydion blew the last remaining grains of dragon dust into her face. It seemed he could direct their flow. To my horror, her form blurred and changed as she too became a bear. With a sigh, she collapsed at my feet, while outside our shield the flames devoured Caer Dathyl.

Internally, I screamed in distress, in aborted warning, but all that escaped my lips was a strangled gasp. I sank to the ground, reaching toward my fur-shrouded daughter, whimpering in raw disbelief. I couldn't reach her or Blei. Time seized and thickened around me, and the space between us wavered as if with a heat haze.

Before the world dissolved into mist, I looked up to see Gwydion and Lleu transform into their winged forms and depart, leaving devastation behind them.

23

EMANIA

Soft silver moonlight bathed the landscape of rolling downs, backed by a circle of immense, jagged mountains. Tiny flowers starred the ground at my feet, and stars blossomed in the sky above like clover flowers in summer.

Peace flooded over me, nearly dampening my sense of urgency. But I couldn't give in and accept it. I had to go... somewhere. Where, though? I couldn't recall.

With a sigh, I lay back on the comforting, cushioned ground of the Plains of Forgetting, and watched the pair of bears gambolling not far away. The large, healthy brown male bared his teeth in a smile; the smaller, russet-furred female returned it. She swiped at him; he ducked and evaded, then they wrestled and rolled. Again, and again, and again.

Bleiddwn and Meghan. Those names, together with Math ap Mathonwy, I would never forget. Meg was my daughter, the light of my life, Blei my husband's kin and my foster-son. I'd raised him from a cub, but he hadn't been a bear. Fragmented memories showed me a tiny wolf cub.

I frowned, trying to puzzle it out. Things simply didn't add up. Perhaps Math could explain what was happening. But where on Earth was he? On Earth... but I wasn't on Earth at all. This was... this was...

This was serenity, stillness, and an absence of care. I sighed again, and a wave of blissful sleep overcame me.

Time unfolded before and behind me, rippling down the years. I beheld a pair of deer, hart and hind, with a young fawn standing between them. Math waved his hazel wand, transforming the hart into Gwydion and the hind into his younger brother Gilfaethwy. The fawn became a young child, less than a year old, whom Math named Hyddwn.

He was a sweet child, far more biddable than the two who came after him: Hychdwn the baby boar and Bleiddwn the wolf cub. Of the three, Hych always retained more beastly attributes. He caused the roughest fights, the fiercest arguments, the most mischief. Perhaps it was simply because boars are destructive and aggressive by nature, or maybe because he'd been birthed by Gwydion, when he was transformed by Math into a sow.

Gilfaethwy made a better mother, when he'd run first as the hind and later as the she-wolf. Whatever the reason, Blei had always been my favourite of the three brothers. A serious, intelligent little boy, he sometimes showed unexpected flashes of levity, and a sly, wicked wit. An incisiveness which sharpened as he grew.

His cubhood lay many years in the past, now. Blei was a man, independent and clever. He'd always been less easily influenced by Gwydion than the other two, and certainly far less than Lleu.

I frowned. The thought of Lleu stirred violent, disagreeable images. Fire, extreme heat, and pain...

Memories of Lleu's unforgettable entry into the world bubbled through the ether, and Drama entered in their wake. She wore her long dark hair unbound, as always, with veils of silver light and shadows circling around her. Cold white stars glimmered overhead, outlining the tall masts of a ship. I couldn't see its name clearly; it remained an outline silhouetted against clouds. But I had the feeling I should know it—if the fog would clear from my brain.

I knew who the woman was, though. Arianrhod of the Silver Wheel, who never missed an opportunity to make a grand entrance. Despite my current state of uncertainty and tension, I smiled as she swept towards me. Arianrhod always had that effect. On me, at least.

"Hello, Ari," I said, turning to face her.

She inclined her head. "This isn't the right place for you, Wynne. What are you doing in the Moonlands?"

Ah. That explained the mystery of my current whereabouts. I glanced up at her ship again, and the elusive memory surfaced. The Oarwheel of the Stars. The vessel which transferred the souls of heroes to Emania and thence to Annwfyn. So, I'd somehow arrived in the Moonlands of Emania. But I wasn't dead. Was I? No, or Ari wouldn't have questioned my presence.

"What about my children?" I asked. "Have I followed them here? Are they..." I choked on the words. I could barely form the thought, much less speak those dreadful words.

Ari moved her head slightly in negation. "No, their presence is as much a mystery as yours."

"Then this—whatever in the Mother's name this is—must be your brother's doing." I caught her blue gaze and held it. "He's gone too far this time. I plan to call him to account, destroy his plans and all his power."

Her laughter resembled the trilling of birds. "I'm delighted to hear it. I'd have killed him myself years ago, if only it didn't break all the rules. But of course, you're not one of Don's tribe, so you're not bound by them. Why didn't we think of that sooner?"

I shook my head, feeling silken strands of hair brush against my bare skin. When had it come unpinned without my noticing? I must be more disordered than I'd realised. "Well, I'd say the rules have been thoroughly shattered now, but although I'm sure a reckoning will follow, it doesn't appear to be imminent. And being a sane, sensible woman, I don't plan to share it. Being bound to Math, I can't flaunt the rules with impunity. However, Gwydion himself has given us a weapon. Her name is Blodeuedd—his own creation."

Understanding brought a glow to Ari's fair face, and she laughed again, a wild note in her glee. "A triumvirate of women; goddess, flower-bride, and witch. Brilliant."

I smiled back tightly. Many had drawn parallels between the wrongs Gwydion had done to his sister and to me, but the similarities were superficial. Our reactions differed, too. Ari's undimmed anger was as explosive as her youngest son's. Mine had hardened over the centuries. My disdain and hatred for Gwydion lay deep in the core of my being, as cold and unyielding as granite.

"Don't get too excited," I warned her. "I have to make him change those two back, first. But once that's done, I'll be happy to help you rip Gwydion apart, limb from limb and feather from pinion."

"I'll help," said a deep, warm voice behind me. I turned and turned again, into my husband's arms.

One does not nurture a centuries-long relationship without becoming intimately aware of each other's more complex needs. Math knew without asking when I wanted gentleness or violence, poetry or crudeness. Saying nothing more, he held me close and waited until my sobs subsided.

"You'd fight Gwydion for me?" I rubbed the damp patch on the shoulder of his tunic, taking comfort from the warmth beneath. So strong, so solid. So enduring was my king.

He laughed softly, his breath stirring my hair. "It wouldn't be the first time, and I doubt it will be the last. But Gwydion, as you may have noticed, is very hard to kill, even if I were allowed to try. His hamartia is a closely guarded secret. You won't be able to trick him the way Blodeuedd did Lleu."

"Those rules are ridiculous and wrong. You should be able to restore Meg and Blei, instead of leaving their fates in Gwydion's hands just because he cast the spell."

"That's the nature of magic, my darling, as you surely ought to know. How would you feel if someone else could alter your enchantments? It would be insulting, for one thing, not to mention dangerous. So many possible disasters lying in wait."

I pushed away from him and looked around for the bears. Both had vanished, and so had Ari and her ship. The landscape had changed, too. The silvery shadows had dissipated, dispelled by shafts of sunlight, and the air was thick, heavy and damp. Awareness pulled at me, dragging me forward through the mist. I opened my eyes and scanned my surroundings, thoroughly disorientated. Even more so than I had been before.

Math, however, remained. Strong and comforting and solid.

"So, how do I break the enchantment?" I asked.

"You persuade Gwydion to do so. Which means you'll have to delay his dismemberment a little while, I'm afraid."

It all felt too overwhelming, of a sudden. "Where do I start? Where is he, and where's Blodeuedd? How do I reach either of them?"

"I can't answer your first question, but Blodeuedd is here." He lifted a hand and whistled, and a tawny owl swept out of the mist to alight on his shoulder.

"Where's Goronwy?" she demanded mentally.

I reeled back in shock. I'd conversed with the great white Gwen-hwyfar occasionally, but never one of her smaller kindred. I dismissed the notion that Ari might be training another familiar.

"Blodeuedd?" I asked, incredulous. "How did you..."

"*Well, Math isn't responsible,*" she snapped, with beak as well as mind. "*And how many other shapeshifting mongrel tricksters do you know?*"

Math raised a hand to stroke her feathers, ignoring the wicked talons which curled into him in her distress. They failed to draw blood, but on a mortal man they probably would have.

She hooted, long and low, then flexed her claws and bobbed upon my husband's shoulder. "*It's not Blodeuedd either, apparently. They call me Blodeuwedd now. One altered syllable, and I'm changed from the flower-bride into an owl.*"

Venom coated her words, and hatred burned in her eyes.

"Gwydion must have done more than change your name," I protested. "It took him some time to change Meg and Blei into bears; surely transforming you into owl form would have been no different."

Feathers ruffled, Blodeuwedd hunched, snaked her head up and called again. Nothing in this world sounds as mournful as an owl, especially one with a grievance. "*I don't know how long it took. It seemed to go on forever. It was... Great Mother Don, I can't describe it to you. I remember my first birth, and this was nothing like it. This was pain, and trauma, and heartache.*" Her tone softened, became pleading. "*Please, Lady Wynne, you have to help me find Goronwy. Math promised he'd be here, and that I could see him again.*"

"You know this is highly irregular, Math." A new speaker appeared out of nowhere, like a spectre. His voice sounded ghostly, deep, and sepulchral. Nevertheless, it sounded friendly, not frightening. The embodiment of journey's end, welcoming the weary traveller home.

The God of Death.

I shivered at his appearance, his overwhelmingly large presence. One never got used to coming face to face with Arawn, lord of the un-derworld realm of Annwfyn. Black robes blended with his crow-black hair and equally dark skin. His eyes were glittering portals into the abyss.

Math bowed low, and I sank into a hasty curtsy. I'd have suggested Blodeuedd do so as well, except that I wasn't sure how owls made obeisance. From the accusing look in her golden eyes, I suspected she'd have refused, anyway.

"I know," returned Math, straightening. "But this entire sequence of events has passed beyond unorthodoxy into the realms of the unparalleled. We're now in the opening pages of a new story, a tale to be told down the ages. Its prologue, if you will."

Arawn's dark gaze didn't soften, although the stern line of his mouth relaxed. "Some might say the mortal deserved his fate, dallying with the Summer King's wife. Should any of Don's children let such an insult pass?"

Math snorted. "I won't dignify that with a response. You know very well why Goronwy behaved as he did, and why Blodeuedd forsook Lleu for him. His death was a pure sacrifice, and he deserves high honour and recompense."

"I can't return a man to life too soon after his death," rumbled Arawn. "It leaves his soul unprepared."

The tawny owl that was now Blodeuwedd swooped too close to his head. He didn't duck but tensed slightly. "*It didn't seem to bother you when Caron did it,*" she screeched, verbally and mentally. "*You can't use that as an excuse to deny us our reunion.*"

Arawn's voice deepened further, if such a thing were possible. "To my shame. I cannot and will not allow such a travesty to happen again. But," he put up a warding hand as Blodeuwedd made another dive at his head, "but I will allow your lover to return to you. After a suitable time has elapsed here in the Moonlands, and in Annwfyn. If he so desires, of course. Thus far, I've heard only your wishes, your demands."

It's difficult to interpret any expression on an owl's face, but I would have sworn that Blodeuwedd's conveyed shock. "*You think he'd reject me? No. No, no, no. He would never do that. You have to let me see him, please. Please?*"

A second, much larger, owl swooped low, her snowy form blending with moonlight. Behind her came her mistress, now also wearing white—filmy, flowing white robes spangled with starlight and trimmed with owl feathers.

"You're back," I said, stating the obvious.

Ari ignored me and addressed the newcomer. "Don't tease the child, Arawn."

Blodeuwedd hooted in protest. Whether she objected to being called a child or wished to add her censure to Ari's, I couldn't tell. "Why don't we put the question to the warrior himself," Ari continued. "Welcome to Emania, Goronwy Pebyr!"

She turned and gestured—dramatically—to the man who approached, surrounded by starshine and moonbeams. Something seemed subtly different about him, compared to the man who'd ruled Ardudwy. He appeared both older and younger, with a lightness to his step and a brightness to his eye.

He wore warrior's leathers, dyed burnt umber and aubergine, and studded with close-set rivets of bronze. Bronze also were his belt buckles, and his belt knife, but his sword was formed of gleaming silver-grey iron, with a cruciform bronze and ivory hilt. As he got closer, I identified the other differences. The lines on his face had been smoothed away, and no grey salted his hair. This was a man in the first flush of manhood, strong, proud, and youthful.

His hazel eyes showed more green than brown, which I later learned betokened happiness. They darkened to brown in times of anger, sorrow, or distress.

"Blodeuedd! Cariad, I've been waiting for you." He didn't seem confused to find himself talking to a bird. But of course, he'd see her as he remembered her, not in the form she currently wore.

Arawn nodded, as if in approval, and Goronwy's vision became real.

I was well acquainted with shapeshifting, and this wasn't much different. Her form wavered, became a column of moonlight, then solidified into a woman-shaped mass. Finally, her features became visible, the Goddess of Nature in the flesh. Saffron-haired, green-eyed and gorgeous, laughing aloud in her joy.

"Goronwy! You came for me. I knew you would. I've been waiting for you, as well. Did you..." She hesitated, then went on in a rush. *"Did you see what happened to Lleu? Has he retaken Mur Y Castell? Are our people all right? If he harms them, I'll... I'll..."* She broke off, biting her lip. *"There's nothing I can do, is there?"*

I shook my head. "Unfortunately not. You..."

"You won't need to," Ari assured her, interrupting. "Lleu and Gwydion haven't yet returned to Ardudwy. They're currently holed up in Gwydion's castle in Arfon." She glanced over at Arawn. "I suspect their next target will be Annwfyn itself. Having revenged himself on you, Goronwy, Lleu's determined to find and reunite with his Caron, and he's not about to let anything stand in his way."

Arawn's growl shook the willows and reverberated through the mist. "Let him come! I've a few surprises in store for the sunlord. He's broken too many rules and wreaked too much destruction. I won't allow him to lay waste to Annwfyn as well."

Blodeuwedd paled. *"He's that insane? He'd actually try to attack the realm of the dead to recapture Caron by force?"*

The Underworld god laughed, a sound to strike fear into even the Lord of Summer, or his despicable trickster uncle. "I can deal with Lleu and Gwydion, don't worry about me. But now, we have a re-birthing ceremony to attend to. Before my lord Pebyr can move on to his next post on the wheel, he must revisit his past lives. Come, you must all be witnesses."

He turned and walked away, with Ari, Blodeuwedd and her lover in his wake. Math nodded to me, and after a moment's vacillation, I placed my hand in his and followed the rest.

24

CHAMPION

I 'd witnessed similar rites in Caer Dathyl, but never one in the Moonlands of Emania.

After a period of meditation, Goronwy's spirit appeared to stand on a beach, with towering white cliffs behind him and a semi-circular sun rising above the horizon in front. A pair of rainbows ringed the scene. Prisms of colour streamed from them, fanning across the water like a pathway to end at Lord Goronwy's feet.

A dark speck appeared against the face of the sun, drifting through the water as if following that rainbow road. As it came closer, it resolved into a figure crouched in the bottom of a crystalline boat, his body and face hidden in the dark folds of his cloak. The tiny vessel ground to a halt in front, and the man it had come for climbed in, without once looking back.

A whoosh of air above me, and Blodeuwedd, in owl form, launched herself upward to follow the boat.

Those left on the beach watched the craft and its occupants draw closer to the sun. This was the deity Lleu was ordained to and which his recent actions had disgraced. The second man, beside Goronwy, stood suddenly and flung wide his arms. Knowing what came next, I had the sense to cover my ears. Even so, the sound of the word of power he spoke rang through me like a baton meeting the drum.

It rocked Blodeuedd, too. She tumbled through the air, barely righting herself before she cleaved the water in a dive.

Together with Math and Arawn, I watched the boat and the men it carried disappear into the sun. The ringing in my ears subsided as the word of enchantment faded.

"That's not supposed to happen," said the Lord of Annwfyn, folding his arms across his chest and narrowing his eyes.

"As I said, we're in uncharted territory here," replied Math. "Let's wait and see what unfolds, shall we?"

"I suppose so." Arawn sank to his knees, folded his long legs beneath him and sat comfortably on the beach. He waved a hand towards us. "You set up the next stage of our young lord's journey; I'll wait here for the two of them to return. This should be interesting."

Math nodded and turned away, but instead of setting out on a journey as I'd expected, the scene shifted around us. From standing on the beach beside Arawn, I found myself in company with Math and Ari, transported inland and following the banks of a stream.

"Will Goronwy be all right, do you think?" I asked. "I've followed the path of the sun in meditations many a time, but I've never seen anybody do it physically before."

"Not physically," said Math. "That was Goronwy's spirit."

Ari laughed. "Well, of course. He's been incorporeal ever since he came here, for all that he looks solid enough."

I wasn't sure I wanted to explore this subject, but having started, we seemed bound to continue. "What about Blodeuedd? Blodeuewedd, I mean. I have to keep reminding myself to call her that now. She looked solid to me too, in both of her bodies."

Ari shrugged. "She's a goddess, and the likes of us don't have a spirit the way mortals do."

Finally we arrived at another temple, smaller than that of the sun but no less impressive.

Where are we?" I asked. The temperature steadily increased the further we ventured into the temple. Perhaps it was a feature intended for worshippers' comfort, but for me it had the opposite effect. I wiped beads of sweat from my brow and Ari did the same. Only Math seemed unaffected.

"The Temple of the Serpents," said Math. "Wherein lies the Hall of Memory. You gave me the key, remember?"

He held up his left wrist, and the glittering multi-coloured bracelet uncoiled. It slithered down his arm to his elbow, then dropped into the inky water, a sliver of bright colour against the still darkness. It slipped through the water to the right-hand door, the one containing the keyhole. The humming stopped and silence fell.

Twisting itself into a knot reminiscent of those used by sailors, the serpent slithered head-first into the keyhole. Its body disappeared, leaving its tail waving behind. It looked like a gesture of welcome.

Slowly, noiselessly, the doors swung inward, revealing a large, circular space floored with the same black grainy substance. I counted twelve marble pillars, also black. A circular pool occupied the centre of the room, ringed with white marble and crowded with waterlilies.

"I suppose," said Ari, fanning her face, "you could call this a storage space. Not for material things, for thoughts and memories. The minutiae that make up a life, and the actions, speech and even feelings held from birth to death, by which it is judged."

"Judged? By whom?" I was unfamiliar with this doctrine. As far as my studies had revealed, it was only the moment of death which mattered. Thus the masculine desire to fall in battle, to be named a hero by their peers and lauded by future generations. As I assumed Goronwy Pebyr had wished to do. Being felled by Lleu surely would have fulfilled his ambition, but from the sound of this he might have had the whole thing wrong. So might a great many others.

"Shouldn't it be the dead person, or their spirit, who goes rummaging around in here?" I added. "I don't feel very comfortable about eavesdropping on somebody's life like that."

"He's given me permission," said Ari, continuing her stately passage across the gleaming floor. She wiped a bead of perspiration from her brow with a little huff of annoyance. As a dweller in the frozen north, it made sense in one way that the heat would bother her, although as a goddess I'd imagined her immune. Perhaps within the temples, the gods suffered the same as mortals?

As she passed the pool, Ari dipped her hands into the water and brushed them over her face. "As a general rule, the dead pass through here to Annwfyn, consider their life lessons, make their future plans, and are reborn decades or even centuries later. Goronwy's impatient, for obvious reasons."

"How long did Lleu's Caron wait between lives?" I asked. A golden glow suffused the room, replacing the shifting silver moon and starlight. The perspiration had become a flood, running in rivulets down my face, dripping from my chin and sliding down my neck. Even Math looked somewhat glossy.

Approaching the niches, Ari stretched, face scrunched in concentration, and withdrew a tightly curled scroll, written on pale ivory parchment and bound with fine silver thread. "Ah, got it!" Her hands, like mine, were damp with sweat, and she wiped them on her robes before handling the documents. "Now we just have to get back to the Temple of Rebirth in the Sun Temple precincts and wait for Goronwy to return."

Cruel, wicked laughter echoed through the sacred space. "You think so? Hate to disappoint you, Mother, but you're not going anywhere. Nor is the soul of that cuckolding swine I killed recently."

Lleu strolled into the room, which explained the furnace glow and the increasing temperature. He looked as if he was on fire.

He was fire. The god of fire, lord of the eternal sun.

Unable to withstand the heat pouring from Lleu, the black sand floor melted beneath his feet to become a shining sheet of glass.

"I'll ask you again," he said, head thrown back and eyes flashing blue fire, "where is that mongrel, Arawn?"

I could no longer bear to look at him, and I wasn't alone. Math bowed his head next to mine beneath his raven-feather cloak, magicked to repel all harm and impervious to any weapons. Ari turned away, taking refuge in her own star-protected cloak. It no longer glittered with starshine but reflected brilliant gold.

Heat pulsed and stuttered with every syllable. My face, my throat, every inch of skin felt as if it was on fire and glancing at my arms I expected to see them blister. But no, my skin remained smooth, unblemished. So did Math's and Ari's. How?

"You stand within the Temple of the Moon," said Ari, unintentionally answering my question. "Your power's dampened here. Nor am I the only one who can call forth the shadow realms." She flung out her arms, and the image of a great snowy owl appeared to hover behind her, its wingspan equal to the distance between her outspread fingers.

Having known Ari for centuries, I was used to that. I was, however, completely unprepared for what came next.

Or to be more accurate, who. He arrived with heart-stopping suddenness, a presence to awe even the gods. Heralded by green light which stabbed through the purple mist and painted every face with ghoulish decay, and a blast from a war horn which rattled the rafters, the underworld king of Annwfyn stepped in our midst.

"I've had enough of your flagrant disobedience, Lleu," said Arawn, ignoring my gasp of horror and striding up to Math's nephew. "How many times do we have to tell you? Caron's not coming back to you. Not now, not for several centuries, if at all."

Lleu glared at him, golden day confronting the dark depths of night. Not all the candles in the room nor Lleu's affronted glow could strike the dimmest light from Arawn's dark hair or warm the pallor of his skin. His face was all planes and hard angles, his eyes pools of shadowed infinity.

My thoughts and my stomach were in turmoil. I glanced up at Math, trying to catch his eye, and met measured composure. He'd known about this. He and Ari had probably planned it together.

"You will release her," Lleu grated, rising from his seat, and clenching both his jaw and his fists. "Restore her to me or face the consequences."

Cold, bladed laughter whipped through the room. "You think to threaten me?" Arawn's voice was harsh, his expression blankly incredulous.

Lleu's voice also gained a cutting edge. "How will any of your precious souls fare, if I come down and burn your underworld hall to the ground?" He cocked an eyebrow, smirking mirthlessly. "Or the ocean floor or the outer rim of nothingness—wherever Annwfyn actually dwells."

He held out a hand, palm up, and a tower of flame leapt from it.

The underworld lord countered by extending a long, silver-nailed finger. The flame whimpered and died. A scream of frustrated outrage tore from Lleu, and his figure, glowing like an ironsmith's furnace, swelled to twice its normal size.

Arawn did the same, shadows coiling and snaking around him, wisping across the floor. They subsumed both the green light and the purple, sucking away all colour and joy. I whimpered; Math clasped me to his side, murmuring reassurances, which I had trouble believing. This was bound to end badly. Beyond a startled gasp, Ari said nothing. Perhaps she hadn't anticipated Arawn's appearance, after all.

"I want her back," boomed Lleu, his amplified voice bouncing from stone wall to carven pillar, from east to west and north to south. It filled the room, threatening tempests to come.

Instead of responding in kind, Arawn remained silent, but his very stillness became a palpable force. As Lleu's anger swelled and echoed, Arawn lifted his arms above his head. The sound died, muffled by nothingness. But the calm which blanketed the room held nothing of peace. Rather, it was a grim and solemn weight, in contrast to Lleu's volatility.

I could see Lleu struggling to combat that force, to shrug it away and unleash his power. His frame shook with the effort, sweat running in rivulets down his fair, handsome face to drip from his chin and pool in the hollow of his neck. Sinews and muscles corded with effort, he finally threw back his head and erupted.

25

ULTIMATUM

Not just an outburst of temper—hard words accompanied by violence. This was a volcano, spewing gouts of flame in wildly arcing ribbons through the air. Math and Arawn moved as one, snuffing them out before they could set the parchment scrolls and other artworks alight.

I shrank back against the wall beside Ari, unwilling to run but unsure how I could help. I might be a competent witch, but the power being thrown around here was as far beyond my meagre talents as a dragon's might was above a puny earthworm. If nothing else, I could work on ways to summon water and other means of fighting house fires.

Normally time would be an issue, for such spells are worked in stages, not all at once, but I'd had some practice at affecting time lately. Perhaps I could do so again. I thought about the relentless progression of the sun and moon across the heavens and reached out to halt their ever-turning wheels and make them spin backwards, however briefly. Ari saw what I meant to do and shook her head.

"You will bring her back to me, Arawn," screamed Lleu, oblivious to my efforts. Golden light ran over his skin. His hair was a writhing tangle of fire. "You will!"

He spread his palms, thrusting them towards his adversary and shooting more flame from his fingertips. Arawn responded with cold, damp darkness, but he couldn't extinguish Lleu. Fuelled by passion, the sun's avatar refused to be dimmed.

The background sizzle of the flames lessened, and the odour of wet wood from the wall cabinets increased. In the periphery of my vision, Arawn's shadowy hand reached out to grasp Lleu around the neck. Lleu twisted aside. Was he, as the lord of the afterlife, constrained by the same rules against harming Don's children as the rest of them?

Were my puny efforts making any impression? It was hard to tell. Math stood statue-still, eyes narrowed, hands raised, lending aid to Arawn.

"Enough!" Arawn's voice was the antithesis of Lleu's sun: the deep, empty cold of the space between stars.

Lleu expanded, doubling in size. Between the flaring light and swirling shadows, I couldn't see exactly what happened next, but Arawn snatched his hand smartly away, as if burned. He stumbled back, then bent double, reaching down beneath the earth, and gathering his power. Reaching far beyond the earth, past all otherworld and mortal realms to the vast emptiness which lay beyond. Shadows swelled, and darkness smothered every shaft of light.

Lleu no longer embodied sunlight, but the coals of a dying fire. Flickering crimson embers chased each other over his skin, before fading away. Arawn was in a similar condition; that last, desperate effort must have cost him dearly. Both combatants collapsed, drained of their power.

The entire world went grey. I staggered, and Math moved to my side, gathering me into his arms. Ari looked on, wide-eyed, with one hand pressed against her breastbone.

"Math!" Lleu tried to struggle upright, but the hunched figure of Arawn didn't move. "How could you side with him against your own kin? You prate on about the importance of family but are selective about who you favour!"

"Lleu, I'm afraid you've become dangerously unstable," said my husband gravely. He touched my cheek, looking down at me. "Are you all right, cariad?" I nodded and he let me go, moving sedately toward the two huddled on the ground. "I did what was necessary, Lleu, understand that."

"Oh, I understand too well." Lleu rose stiffly, his face set and cold. His gaze moved to me. "As for you, Queen of Gwynedd, I know what you've been doing, to me and to Gwydion." Cold hatred and red rage blended to create a palpable presence. "A neat trick, to play with the flows of time and separate us from the Flowerbride now in power in Ardudwy. But two can play at that game."

"Lleu, stop it, please." Ari moved slowly, deliberately, towards him, her voice catching on a sob. "I know what Gwydion did to Blodeuedd. I know you killed Goronwy Pebyr. Isn't that enough? Must you try to punish everyone, even those who still love you?"

Lleu's fiery gaze took in the parchment in her hand. The increasing brilliance around his head made it difficult to see his features, much less read them, but I saw delighted understanding on his face. Bile rose in my throat, and a shudder of fear rippled across my skin. An answering rumble of anger reverberated through Math.

"So," purred Lleu, "you're scrabbling through the records of a puny mortal's lives. It can only be that goat's turd Pebyr. You'd better give that to me."

"No." Arawn uncoiled like a column of smoke, and darkness, blacker than a moonless night, covered the entire temple. A rush of cold air heralded movement. Then grey moonlight filtered into the room, and Ari's hands were empty. Arawn had vanished completely.

"Fuck!" Lleu threw a smouldering ember into the pool and followed the expletive with several more. "Arawn thinks he can get away from me and return Pebyr to life, doesn't he? Not happening. Thanks, Mother. You've been a great help."

He turned to go, spraying filaments of flame throughout the building. I sank to the floor.

Together, Math and Ari dived towards Lleu, trying to reach him and hold him down. They failed. He spun away, still shedding flame, and a whirring disc of light descended from the sky above. As it floated gently to the floor, it resolved into a horseless vehicle, covered with swirling patterns in copper and gold. Lleu jumped aboard, lifted it into the air, and blinked out of existence.

Ari swore loudly and inventively. Math followed Lleu's example and said simply, "Fuck."

I couldn't speak at all. My mouth couldn't summon enough moisture. Feebly, I tried to stand, and failed.

"Wynne!" Math was at my side in an instant, worry etched in his face and audible in his voice. "It's all right, cariad, I've got you." He held a hand to my forehead before lifting me into his arms. "Great Beli, you're so hot. I'm going to lower you into the pool. I hope Lleu hasn't heated it too."

"He shouldn't have been able to," said Ari, kneeling beside it and trailing a testing hand through the water. "It's moonwater. And no, it's slightly warm, that's all. Should feel quite pleasant, I think. You two wait here. I have to go!"

So saying, she dived into the water between the crowding lilies, and disappeared as well.

I nestled against Math as he waded into the pool, still shaking with the aftershocks of fright. The cooling water lapping between my toes and around my legs soon calmed me. How much of that was due to the lower temperature, and how much to the spiritual nature of the pool, I wasn't sure.

"Where'd he go?" I asked when I could speak. "And how did he just...vanish? Ari, I presume, followed the moonpath through the water?"

"Yes." Math waited until I'd ceased to shiver and helped me climb out before magically dispelling the dampness from my clothes. His remained dry. "Lleu's sun chariot can do something similar, although it usually requires daylight. But moonlight's only reflected sunshine. Because he's in such a temper, wrapped himself in so much fire, he might have been able to use even that to power it. As for where, he'll be on his way to confront Arawn at the Temple of Rebirth."

I straightened, grateful to find that strength had returned to my limbs. "Then we have to follow."

My husband nodded. "Arawn followed the Underworld ways, which are easily accessed from here. Although I suppose he can find them without difficulty from anywhere at all."

With that, he became a mighty peregrine, the fastest bird in all the skies. Like Gwydion and Arianrhod, his bird form wasn't limited to mimicking those in the wild. He could reach a size large enough to transport a human woman in his claws. I curled myself into a ball, and Math extended a foot. His outsized talons hooked around me, caging me protectively within. Despite having travelled this way a few times before, I never got used to it.

Head against my knees and arms wrapped firmly around them, I closed my eyes and counted. I did not enjoy flight—I endured it. Humans were not meant to fly!

Up we rose, into the filmy clouds beneath a harvest moon. Cold air stung my face, so tight and shocking it dispelled even the memory of Lleu's fire. Fifty heartbeats; a hundred. At last, when I'd lost count twice, started again and reached a hundred and twenty, my stomach lurched, and warm air rose to greet me. I opened my eyes.

The concentric circular gardens of the Sun Temple lay spread directly below me, zooming up at me at a disturbingly fast pace. I shuddered and squeezed my eyes shut again, and the awful movement suddenly ceased. We'd landed. I peeled my lids open and looked around.

A crackle of heat, a ball of light, and a chorus of screams announced Lleu's location. Wisps of smoke drifted from the sun chariot, which lay on its side, wheels rotating at an awkward angle. A smattering of small fires smouldered around it, and the smell of wet charcoal permeated the air. Arawn and Lleu were facing off against each other, one expelling cold and darkness, the other light and heat. Embers from Lleu's outflung hands caught in shrubs and winter grasses, setting them alight.

It was a repeat of his first tantrum in Caer Dathyl, on a much larger scale. I looked around for Blodeuedd or Goronwy Pebyr but couldn't see either of them.

"Get inside," Math said urgently. "You're too vulnerable here, and I need to know you're safe. Praise all the Elder Gods that Gwydion hasn't shown, too. I wonder where the demon-spawn is?"

"I hate to think, but at the moment I'll just be grateful for his absence and try to help Ari," I said, scanning the surrounding chaos. "Ah, there she is."

Ari had never been a fool. Lleu's power derived from the sun, which even on a moonlit night offered a pallid shadow of itself for his use. And while it would be more than a moon goddess's life was worth to remove that light completely, she could attempt to change its face. Time, as I'd recently discovered, was more malleable than anyone realised.

A full moon had shone on the temple when we arrived. Under Ari's skilful manipulation, that same moon's phases were now being reversed.

She was, I could tell, aiming for a new moon, when Lleu's powers might be at their greatest ebb but when Arawn's were also strongest. Of course, it didn't matter to Arianrhod. Every face the moon turned to the earth pledged fealty to its lady. Should I try to add my puny strength to hers? Dare I?

A flaming ember sailed past me to set fire to a rosemary bush, throwing off a shower of sparks which almost burned my hair. Yes, I decided, I really had no choice. I scuttled to a sheltered alcove well out of sight of the two combatants and tried to sink into a trance.

I failed.

I could not calm my mind. Couldn't reach and keep that still, calm place at the centre of my being, at the centre of the universal flow. Flames danced behind my closed lids, and the burning sun fell from the sky. I imagined the fields of Ardudwy smoking under Lleu's wrath, and the same devastation leaping north towards Arfon. I had been born in Arfon, and my people still lived there.

Grief and horror embedded themselves in my soul, and I couldn't dispel them.

I threw back my head and screamed, needing to voice it. Needing to vent. Very well; if I couldn't help Ari produce a dark moon, I'd find another way to block out the light. A way more in keeping with my current mood. I sidled out of my hiding place and slipped furtively down to the shore, although the precaution was probably unnecessary. Nobody paid any attention to me.

The Lord of the Underworld, swathed in shifting, night-dark shadows, stood stock still in the temple's lee, legs astride and hands outstretched. Lleu Llaw Gyffes, child of the sun and the eternal King of Summer, held a similar position, bathed in light. They no longer threw taunts and insults at each other, but a grunt escaped one or the other now and then. Perhaps they'd exhausted their vocabularies.

But no more. I reached the sea, found a rock pool hidden behind a convenient boulder, and set to work summoning storm clouds.

26

MEMORIES

The ringing knell of the Word spoken by Goronwy's afterlife guide caught me unawares. So did the pupil-shaped rent splitting the sun in front of me. True, I hadn't known what to expect when I'd followed them both out across the water, but I'd been confident of my ability to remain aloft. Being thrown tail-over-head through the gap in the sun and hitting the water beak-first came as a shock.

Owls could swim, I discovered.

My first instinct, which was to immediately fly off again, was thwarted by the weight of my water-logged wings. Driving laboriously through the waves in an awkward breaststroke which would have drawn censure from Dylan, I finally gained the shore. Still unable to fly, I decided that lingering on the beach waiting to dry seemed a poor plan. I waddled inland, wings held out to each side to facilitate their drying.

I seemed to be on an island. Glistening, golden grains of sand rose in dunes leading back from the shoreline, beneath a bright cerulean-blue sky. Feather-fronded ferns and short, striated palms with showy fan-shaped leaves grew along the banks of a meandering creek. Reasoning that even in the Otherworld, most life-forms required water to live and would therefore build any dwellings or temples close to it, I followed the stream.

If I hadn't been saturated with salt water and anxious about Goronwy's fate and whereabouts, I might not have minded the time it took my feathers to dry. But being forced to proceed at a pace that would have frustrated a tortoise gave me too much time to think, and to worry.

My surroundings were admittedly beautiful. Tiny birds darted through the trees, their voices high and musical, their colours jewel-bright. They circled my head, singing, before disappearing in a flash of scarlet, turquoise, saffron, and emerald. Outcrops of white rocks formed a natural border on one side of the creek. The surfaces glittered with opaline brilliance, as if they'd been dusted with peacock feathers.

That thought reminded me of my dye yards. Of my ladies, Modwenna and Delith, as well as their children and spouses. How were they faring? Had Lleu harmed them? Mother, I needed to find Goronwy and get out of there. I needed to return to Ardudwy and make sure my people were safe.

A flap of my wings confirmed they were still a long way from dry. I hooted softly, annoyed. The sun seemed warm enough; why was it taking so long? Owl feathers shared few characteristics with ducks, obviously.

Finally, the narrow path I'd been following widened out to reveal a broad, sunlit plain undulating with feathery golden heads of wheat. A bare-chested, brown-skinned man in coarse linen trousers and canvas boots moved through the field with a thresher. He wore a chequered scarf tied around fair hair and he sang as he worked.

Goronwy. Although this man looked nothing like my lover, I recognised his eternal spirit. His soul.

I finally understood the nature of this place, and of the ceremony I'd witnessed. Many rituals and secret sacraments were associated with the Temple of the Sun, and this was one of them. These were the Plains of Memory in Emania, where the departed souls came to access memories of their previous lives, before departing for Annwfyn. There, they'd dissect and sort those memories, before deciding whether they'd successfully learned the lessons of their previous life journey. Otherwise, they'd have to revisit that path and go through it all again.

The lucky ones would deem the lessons learned and begin new ones. Others would not. They'd repeat the same experiences, sometimes painfully, until their conscious selves became attuned to the cries of their souls and heeded their advice.

And Caron, who'd overturned all the protocols? I didn't know what would become of her.

I tried again to fluff my feathers. Still too wet. Nothing for it but to huddle where I was and watch.

The scene before me shifted, the wheatfield gaining small, undulating hills and hollows, ringed by trees. These were also cultivated fields, but the crops grew in a varicoloured patchwork pattern—russet, gold, brown and many shades of green. Now the farmer was a woman, dark-haired and brown-skinned, shuffling along the rows on her knees as she planted each new seedling. I felt a kinship with her.

Would I ever feel that thrill again, that oneness with the earth? Perhaps not. Gwydion had said I was now doomed to flight and darkness, unwelcome in the day, and scorned by all other birds. I enjoyed the experience of flight, but that thought depressed me.

Worse, I'd never again feel Goronwy's arms around me, smell his scent, run my fingers through his hair, or listen to his beating heart. My own heart clenched in agony. In anger, loss and heartbreak. I hoped that whatever lay in store for Goronwy would be less bleak than the future facing me.

Slowly, achingly slowly, my wings dried. The images melted into one another, from farms and settlements to temples and fortresses, from swift, elegant longships to clumsy, slow rivercraft. The character at the centre of it all was sometimes a farmer, at others a warrior; druid or priestess, man or woman.

The fields below had now become thick forests, enmeshed by ferns and vines, much like Mur Y Castell had been the last time I'd seen it with human eyes. A narrow path wound through the trees, and along it moved a group of armoured men. One was shorter than the rest, with a weathered face and bright red hair, and of all of them, he drew me to him. This, then, was another body Goronwy had worn, in another life. Not so very long ago, either, judging by his style of dress.

I didn't see him die, but when the scene faded, no other took its place. This must have been Goronwy's last life before the one in which I'd known and loved him. From the half-recalled lore I'd gleaned from Gwydion, I understood I was merely a spectator here. Such as I weren't privy to beginnings, endings, or the web of thoughts, emotions and memories attendant on each individual life. That was for Goronwy alone to know, and to learn from.

Tentatively, I flipped a wing, and to my unending delight felt the air ruffle through my feathers and slide along my skin. I stretched on my long, ungainly legs, pushed back my wings, and rose gratefully into the sky. It was glorious! Surely no one who'd ever experienced it could deny the sheer joy of flight. If only I could retain my connection to the green world as well. I'd count myself quite content then, despite Gwydion's dire predictions.

Providing, of course, that I could reunite with Goronwy. I swooped down toward the red-haired man and saw him change as I approached. The man whose shoulder I landed on wore the face I knew and loved.

"Blodeuedd! You shouldn't be here." He ran a hand along my feathered head, his lips lifting into a smile. "Arawn must be having conniptions with so many rules being broken."

"I don't know. Everything happened too fast, and I couldn't hear or see anything once I passed through the sungate. What happens now? How do we both get back?"

His smile faded—literally. His beloved face became transparent, and the shoulder I sat upon dissolved into mist. "I must continue to Annwfyn, and you... you must retrace your steps. Find Arawn, offer him apologies, and wait for me in the world of men. I'm sorry I can't stay. So, so very sorry. But if the gods are willing, we'll be together again soon. Goodbye, my love. My Lady Violet..."

Deprived of my perch, I had to beat my wings frantically to stay aloft. *"No! Wait!"* I cried. *"Please, wait. I can't..."*

I can't face a single lifetime, much less eternity, without you.

"I know." His voice was the merest thread of sound, a whisper on the breeze. "I will find you again, I promise. Whatever it takes, and however long."

A heartbeat later, he had gone.

In that moment I understood, at last, the anguish which had driven Lleu and Caron. To think that I would never see, hear, touch or be with him again was more than I could bear. Was my plea to Arawn really all that different to the vow Caron had made? True, Goronwy's sacrifice had earned the god's favour, but if that hadn't happened, I'd have had no compunction in seeking another way. Even if it did break a few rules.

I hunkered on the ground for a long while, staring at the empty space where my lover's form had vanished. Around me, the landscape also faded to become a morass of shifting shadows, threaded with slivers of moonlight.

Steeling myself to face Arawn's likely wrath, I rose above the Memory Plains of Emania and headed out to sea.

To my surprise, I found the way easily. Perhaps because none other had ever dared to trespass in that sacred space without invitation, there were no wards set to hinder my return.

The scene that greeted me on the beach, fronting the Temple of the Sun, was one of utter chaos. Spot fires burned throughout the once-green grounds, now patched with dirty brown and charcoal grey. The barefoot, soot-smirched priests and priestesses hauled water from the lake to combat them by whatever means they could. Alarm flooded through me, followed by guilt-shaded relief. At least the Lord of the Afterworld might overlook my transgressions.

Plastered ramrod straight against a pillar was Arianrhod. Head thrown back, hands lifted to the sky and her eyes tightly shut, she threw out string upon string of incantations. With each spoken word, the moon retreated a little more, from less than quarter full to crescent, before decreasing to a sliver of silver.

Arawn, Math and Lleu formed a stationary tableau, barely moving, although even as an owl I could clearly see the flows of power flowing and knotting between them. Or perhaps my new night vision helped me see more clearly, for the shadows cloaking Arawn were darker than any night. Just as the fire that surrounded Lleu was brighter than the day. Strange, how the glory of the sun could instil such menace.

I looked around for Wynne and spied her crouched down among the rocks on the foreshore, gazing intently into a shallow pool of seawater. From clear water reflecting a blue sky, it seemed to blend with the shadows cast by the Lord of the Afterworld, turning first grey, then black. A cold breeze ruffled the feathers of my neck, and a bank of similarly coloured clouds advanced from the west.

As the roiling mass rolled closer, the sky darkened to a dense and inky black, covering the stars and obliterating the light of the moon. Darkness was Arawn's domain, but anathema to Lleu's fire.

Wynne's ploy worked. The shadows gather into a cohesive mass and leap at Lleu like a pack of deadly, silent wolves. He threw up his hands to ward them off, and as he did so Arawn gave vent to an ear-shattering scream.

At the same time, Math pounced.

Lleu crashed to his knees, his godly fire dimmed, and Math threw his raven feather coat over his nephew's shoulders to extinguish it completely. I drifted towards them both on silent wings, alighting on the roof eaves of the nearest temple building.

"Do you yield?" Arawn's voice might have issued from the bottom of an endless, echoing well.

Lleu shuddered, his face ashen. "Never."

"A shame, because I claim victory nonetheless." He approached, circling around Lleu and glancing sideways at him with contempt etched in every line. "I will not return the woman you call Caron to you, and furthermore I'll call her by her true name: Arlais."

"She is Caron," spat Lleu, droplets flying from his lips. "My Caron, and she always will be."

"That's where you're wrong." Arawn halted, transforming into a giant carrion bird, larger even than Arianrhod's owl or Lleu's eagle. "She trapped herself in that persona to please you. It was wrong, I knew that, and I should have stepped in sooner. I didn't, because I thought she'd come to her senses and repudiate you without my interference. I misjudged, to my eternal sorrow, and now that poor woman pays the price."

Lleu growled, reminding me of a large golden cat as he faced Arawn's wolves, unafraid and defiant. "What price? There is none. There is no cost to love, and ours is eternal. Even if the link with Dafona's line is broken, I'll find her again. No matter where you try to send her, you cannot hide her from me. She's mine, now and forever."

To my surprise, Arawn glanced up at me. I ducked my head and shuffled sideways, made uncomfortable by his dark regard. "Are you sure you're not thinking of your wife, the one Math and Gwydion made especially for you? You had your chance at forever, and you threw it away. I plan to give Arlais a normal chance at growth, and to ensure you don't find her and disrupt her efforts, I plan to remove you from the equation."

His voice echoed with the weight of judgement. Everyone in earshot froze, except for Lleu.

He reared up, shadows licking around him, caressing him like a lover. But even the mist of the Afterworld couldn't entirely extinguish his light. He still shed a glow, paltry but defiant.

"I'm not going anywhere."

And you can't make me. I heard the retort of a petulant child behind his words, although he didn't utter it aloud.

Perhaps Arawn had the same impression. A cruel smile lifted his lips, revealing too-sharp teeth. Had they always been that white and pointed?

"You are," he said. "You're coming with me, my lad, down to Annwfyn for a while."

"Would you plunge the entire world into darkness out of petty spite?" Lleu struggled to his feet and stood, swaying.

Math moved to Lleu's side, presumably to block any attempt at escape. "There are other sun-gods," he said solemnly. "Lugh Lamfada, for one; Helios, Apollo, Ra. Goddesses, too. Great Northern Sol and to the east, Arinna and Surya. The skies over Cymru might darken for a time, but not forever. They'll bide, till you return."

Lleu tried to remove the raven cloak but was thwarted by a gesture from Math. It could apparently act as a restraint if he so willed it.

Arawn saw the motion and smiled nastily. "This is the benefit of teamwork, Lleu, which you've never understood. We've worn you down, three godborn and a mortal witch. We've sapped your strength to the point where I could, if I so desired, separate you permanently from the light of the sun. Make you live in darkness all your days."

Lleu drew a long, shuddering breath. "No. No, not that. I couldn't stand that."

Because he'd had a taste of it when perched in the tree in the shadow of Yr Wyddfa, trapped in his eagle form. Guilt dragged at me...until a breeze ruffled my feathers, reminding me that he and Gwydion had visited a more than adequate revenge upon me.

They'd condemned me to a form of darkness: to haunt the night and shun the day. My earlier spasm of contrition wavered. Lleu had killed my lover, and Gwydion had razed my home. I might feel sympathy for Caron, but Lleu had made it very hard for me to do the same for him.

27

JUDGEMENT

The raven-feather cloak twitched around Lleu's shoulders, and flared outwards in a swirl of inky, iridescent colour—like a coal seam seen through water and silvered with rainbows. It lifted him into the air, an outré, golden-haired, black-feathered bird.

Math swore.

He hastily retrieved his cloak as it slid from the back of Lleu's winged form. It seemed that one form of magic cancelled out the other—the cloak would hold him fast when he wore the form of a man, but not that of an eagle.

The area became a blur of shifting shapes and colours as every god present took on their bird form. Arianrhod became an owl, Math a falcon, Arawn a raven.

And Lleu, cunning Lleu, who'd not been taught by Gwydion for nothing, soared aloft. When all three others launched themselves into the air after him, he turned and dived, straight for Queen Wynne.

Math hit the ground with a thump and a blistering curse. He landed a fraction too far away from his lady to protect her. I could see Lleu would reach her first.

"No!" I swooped between them, a tiny wren in comparison to Lleu's mighty eagle. I still had claws, though, and a beak. Before he reached her, I angled upward to land squarely on his back. Lleu tried to shake me off but found himself also attacked by Wynne.

Her magic would be useless against him, and she almost certainly knew it. Instead, she bent, grabbed a handful of the glittering black sand and throwing it at his head. Despite having additional eyelids for protection, Lleu retained a man's reflexes as well as those of the raptor. He ducked his head and swerved away, giving us the opportunity we needed.

Wynne scrambled backwards, into Math's waiting arms. I dug my talons into Lleu's flesh and followed up with my beak.

In the white flush of my anger, I'd forgotten about Lleu's major power. He reminded me. Instead of an outsized eagle, I found myself astride a bird of living flame. Searing heat wrapped around my feet, my legs, my wings, and burnt a path straight down my gullet. Tawny owls didn't often screech, but when they did, said the wise men, it foretold death. I screeched, long and loud, afraid the death portended was my own.

Unable to breathe or think, much less fly, I plummeted earthward. The ground rose to meet me with alarming swiftness, a blur of light and sliding shadows. Then the world went dark.

I tucked my head beneath my wing and waited for nothingness to claim me. Would I, too, find myself in Annwfyn, the Afterworld of mortals? Or did a different fate await me? What became of failed goddesses? Would I see Goronwy again?

Gradually, reason sifted back into my consciousness. If I could pose questions, I must still be alive, even if no answers were forthcoming. I relaxed and lifted my head. The darkness remained, but it was no longer all-encompassing. I discerned shapes here and there, and sounds began to filter through. Voices. They sounded comforting, concerned.

All but one. "Oh, in the Mother's name, woman, will you snap out of it? You're not burned—you're not even singed. Lleu's in worse shape than you right now."

Arianrhod's voice. What had happened to 'my sweet daughter?' Now I was just some anonymous 'woman', apparently, and a whiny one at that.

I turned my head. Not to its full rotation, but well past one hundred and eighty degrees. I still couldn't see clearly, but a wavy, silvery woman-shaped outline intersected the shadows to my right.

"Where is he?" My mental voice sounded normal to me, but I had no way of knowing if that held true for her.

"Right in front of you, awaiting his sentence. Arawn declined to pronounce it until you'd recovered enough to hear it."

I winced. *"Nice of him. What happened?"*

Math answered, his voice faintly muffled. "You wounded him, Blodeuedd, enough that he couldn't maintain his godform for long. We all applaud your courage. When also attacked by the white owl and the raven, he transformed back into the eagle, gave up and dived for the ground, to find Wynne and me waiting for him."

"We united against him," said Wynne. I'd recognise that musical voice anywhere.

Light bled into the darkness, and Arawn's shadows withdrew. A dull bronze ball of resentment kneeling at the feet of the Lord of the Shadowlands proved to be Lleu. Math and Wynne stood to one side of them, his arm around her shoulders and both of hers twined around his waist. Arianrhod loomed above me, her arms crossed and impatience surrounding her in a halo.

"You say I can't remove Arlais from your orbit," Arawn said coldly, glaring at the man at his feet. "But I can remove you from hers. For the crime of what you did to Caron, for setting fire to Caer Dathyl, mangling Wynne's spells and separating her from her children, for destroying Ardudwy and cheating in the duel between the Oak and Holly Kings, I sentence you to rejoin the source of your power. You, Lleu Llaw Gyffes, shall become one with the sun for a time."

Arianrhod let out a strangled sob. A moment ago, she'd been briskly impatient, but I'd grown to understand her well enough to realise that had been a mask. Arawn's judgement had cracked her hard veneer.

Lleu laughed, lifted his hand, and threw a fireball at Arawn. It ripped a hole in the Underworld Lord's shielding shadows and set fire to his night-black hair.

"Enough!" Dark veins stood out on Arawn's noble forehead, and more pulsed in his throat. Hands clenched behind his back, he dispensed shade to douse the flames and faultlessly repair the damage. More shadows writhed, thickening into ropes to wrap around Lleu's arms and pin them to his side, giving Math the opportunity to throw his cloak around Lleu once again.

"Do you think to mock me, Summer King?" Arawn thundered. "Do you suppose my domain is subject to yours? Not so. Men live small, separate lives in the daylight, one after the other as the years turn, but their souls belong to me. My realm stretches beyond the sun, beyond the stars, into the everlasting void. I can command you. I can judge you, and I do. A thousand years of exile, before you can return to earth."

I gasped, a tiny hoot escaping. A thousand lonely, love-forsaken years. Even I thought that judgement harsh. I could tell it devastated my mother-in-law.

A tiny silence followed, broken at last by Arianrhod's quiet sobbing. Lleu didn't speak but rocked back on his heels and rose to his feet. The golden colour had ebbed from his face, now still, and hard as stone. He lifted his chin and spat at Arawn's feet.

More shadows rushed over and around him, swathing him in darkness. But Lleu had recovered enough to push back a little. More flames erupted from him, battling the gloom and singeing the feathers. He threw himself at Arawn as the bindings around him unravelled, knocking the Underworld Lord to the ground. Back and forth they rolled, grappling, wrestling, and a kaleidoscope of light and shade spun and twisted through the temple. Math's cloak was now in tatters.

"Defy me, will you!" Arawn brought his knee up in a move I'd used more than once. Lleu grunted, jerked, and rolled away, giving Arawn the opening he needed. In an instant, he summoned more darkness, and both he and the Summer King vanished.

Arianrhod sank to her knees, her entire body shuddering with grief.

"Oh, Ari! Ari, love, I'm so, so sorry." Wynne swept up to the goddess and enveloped her in a hug. I could only burble in sympathy, nodding my head up and down in an effort to convey understanding.

Arianrhod dabbed at her eyes, although tears still stained her cheeks. "Thank you," she said at last, her voice trembling. "But I can't condemn Arawn. Lleu tried to kill both him and Math, and that's the one transgression for which there is no forgiveness. No matter what holds true in other courts, the Children of Don and their kindred do not make war upon our own. Lleu will return to me one day, and in the meantime all I can do is wait."

Those few words brought home to me the gulf that lay between us. I might be godborn, but I'd experienced fewer years in the world than most mortals I knew. I wasn't capable of taking such a long view. Arianrhod was. She'd seen millennia pass, and while another one without her son might be hard, even agonising, she could endure it.

"The battle may not be over yet," Math said, frowning. "Those two are too evenly matched."

Arianrhod laughed, unsteadily, and rose to her feet. "Now there's a conundrum. Who do I hope should win? Arawn, who I know is in the right, or my son, for no better reason than a mother's love? These are the kinds of problems which beset mortals... and with which I've never sympathised, until now. A lesson in humility, I suppose."

Among Lleu's relatives, silence reigned. Math and Wynne had settled on one of the few wooden benches Lleu hadn't reduced to ash, hand in hand. Arianrhod leaned against a pillar, as still and grave as one of the broken statues littering the grounds.

After a time, she wiped away the last trace of her tears and addressed Math and Wynne, her face serene once more.

"Come," she said, crooking a finger, "we three have work to do. Despite all the drama, I haven't forgotten why we came here. Blodeuwedd, your lover deserves a reward for his sacrifice, and I plan to give it to him. He deserves it now more than ever."

She explained her plan and waited expectantly for my agreement. As if I would refuse! But...

"Is Goronwy willing?" Hope surged in an almost suffocating wave, but while this might be my deepest desire, I had to know he shared it.

"Eager would better describe it. The process will take some time, however. I'll take you home to Ardudwy—where you, I fear, will have to twiddle your talons and wait."

28

HUNTERS

The clutch contained three egg; laid, as far as I could tell, on or close to my birthday, the Spring Equinox. Did birds celebrate the anniversary of their birth, and if they did, was it calculated from when they were laid, or when they hatched? I suspected the latter, but my experience was too limited to say with confidence.

As the spring days lengthened and the Alder Month gave way to that of the Willow, two of the three showed signs of hatching. I perched on a branch some distance away from the jagged oblong hollow in the oak opposite and waited, hopping from foot to agitated foot in feverish anticipation. Would I know him? Would he know me? And the most pressing question of all, had the spell worked?

Because I lacked the right kind of magical skill, I hadn't been party to it. Arianrhod had returned me to the forest outside Mur Y Castell before leaving to join her uncle and his wife. Together, they'd perform the needed incantations.

All I could do, meanwhile, was wait, for weeks or even months. And fret. And fume. The night to which Gwydion had condemned me seemed a bright, warm summer's day compared to the darkness in my soul. Owls were gifted with superb sight and faultless hearing, allied to sweeping, soundless flight. They were predators. Killers, not creators.

I had been born of flowers, kin to the trees, the mosses, the sedges, the blossoms, all the living green world. My element was earth, not air. Taloned feet could not test the loam, couldn't feel it filter through them, as could human fingers. Never again would I set seedlings into the ground and watch them grow and flourish.

I'd never again experience the embrace of the sea. Who would have thought I'd miss that? But huddled on my tree limb in that Ardudwy forest, images of the glistening sand, the crashing waves and the white seafoam taunted me with memories of a vanished life. Yes, owls could swim. We derived no pleasure from it.

Owls couldn't appreciate scent, either. The perfumes that had delighted me, and which I could once select at whim, were lost to me. So were the vivid, vibrant colours of my gardens. An owl's sight might be acute, but their colour range was limited. I now saw life in barely tinted shades of grey.

I missed my world. I missed my friends. And most of all, I missed my husband. Every night I yearned for his voice, his touch, his arms around me. The time we'd spent together in Emania, while blissful, had also been too brief, and held the seeds of pain. If the spell failed...

If we couldn't be reunited, how was I to survive? Arlais's solution wasn't viable—if Gwydion couldn't kill me, neither could I kill myself. I'd be doomed to an eternal bleak existence without hope, or light, or love. Perhaps I'd fall victim to Lleu's malady, and I too would go insane. I almost felt sorry for him then, until I recalled, again, that he and Gwydion between them were the cause of all my woes.

Those weeks of waiting were the darkest I'd ever endured. I paced up and down my tree limb and waited, and in between bouts of hunting, fretted and fumed. Prayed for those owlets to break through the shells confining them and make their joyous entrance into the world.

Because the nesting pair of tawny owls were highly territorial, I dared not get too close. But being still a goddess, I retained better-than-average sight and hearing, and average for an owl is very good indeed. Unfortunately, I couldn't see around the edges of the hollow and the anxiously hovering parents filled most of the entrance, but when I heard the female's satisfied purring coo I knew at least one egg had hatched.

Finally, both left to hunt, and I flew to a higher branch to see if I could angle my vision downward. And there they were on the floor of the hollow; a pair of tiny, black-speckled white fluffballs. The third egg showed cracks, but as yet hadn't released its owlet.

I launched a hopeful thought. *"Goronwy? Are you there?"*

And received the longed-for, needed answer. *"Blodeuedd. My love."*

Relief, so forceful I almost lost my footing, and delight so strong it caused the universe to sing. Trickster gods could sometimes be too clever. In his determination to punish me, Gwydion had discounted both his sister and his uncle. He'd forgotten, or hadn't cared, that the Lady of the Silver Wheel was, among other things, the Goddess of Death and of Rebirth. With Arawn's blessing, she'd caught Goronwy's immortal soul upon her oar wheel and reincarnated him into an owl. And thanks to Math ap Mathonwy, he too would be immortal.

Tawny owls fledged at around five weeks of age and relied on their parents for food for almost twice as long again. Thanks to Math and Arianrhod's magic, I had only half that long to wait. What were a few months compared to eternity?

Perhaps his parents were astonished to see their eldest chick grow at double the pace of his siblings, but they cared for all three equally. As soon as he was able, my love forsook their nest and joined me. We became a mated pair, bound not just for life, but forever.

All my other concerns, all my regrets, fell away. Unlike Math and his kin, I had no experience of shapeshifting. I hadn't known—could not imagine—what pleasure beasts knew with each other, but perhaps joy for each species took a different form. Snuggling together, cooing, purring, and preening resulted in a deep, abiding closeness. The sensation of his claws on my back, his beak touching mine, chittering against me, raking through my neck feathers, were as intimate as any human moment.

And more than that, we could now join minds as well as bodies.

"Do you love me?" I'd ask, sure of the answer.

"Always," he replied. *"Do you love me?"*

And I showed him—laying bare my thoughts, my memories, my desires, every soaring hope and crushing fear. There was no greater act of trust, no stronger declaration of love and faith than to open oneself in that fashion. Yes, we loved each other. Neither would ever doubt each other's commitment or desire any other. We were one, a single entity, for as long as our lives endured.

We nuzzled together in the hollow of the tree we'd selected as our own, and when he was confident on the wing, I joined him. Together, we explored the skies above Cymru.

Life for my people had returned to a semblance of normality. Cynar now presided over Mur Y Castell as its lord. His children grew and thrived, as did the rest of Ardudwy's inhabitants—all except Yestin, Modwenna and their infant daughter, Yseult. Their current whereabouts were a closely guarded secret and would remain so until Lleu was no longer a threat.

We often visited Cynar and his family, and although in Modwenna's absence it wasn't possible to communicate, Dylan sometimes translated for me. He'd assured everyone of my safety, that I hadn't been murdered by Gwydion, and conveyed the glad news of my reunion with Goronwy. I'd always valued the gift of his friendship, but never as much as in those early days of my owldom.

At other times, Goronwy and I ranged far beyond Ardudwy. Owl instinct shouted that we should seek our own territory and defend it, but our human curiosity and need to explore overrode it. Why limit oneself to one section of woodland when one could fly anywhere one chose?

As time wore on, the pull of the forest floor lessened. I changed from a child of earth to a winged herald of the air.

Flight! Smooth, effortless, and joyous. Cool air rushing by me as I floated on silent wings. The caress of gentle breezes, the fury of storm-driven winds, the cold kiss of falling snow. The shining snakes of winding rivers, the glitter of smaller streams seen from high above. Patterned patchwork of farmed fields, stands of ancient oaks, steadily dwindling forests and burgeoning cities. I avoided the latter, preferring the lofty crags of Cymry's mountains and her endless rolling downs. And far below, curled in their nests or burrows, scuttling along the ground or flitting through the air: my prey.

Tiny mice, voles, frogs, insects, or earthworms; none could escape me. Even blanketed by snow, I heard their movement and would glide down, talons extended. A flip, a crunch of bone, and their tiny life was extinguished. I'd lift and rise again into the night. Seeking, always seeking the greatest prey of all.

Gwydion.

Goronwy thought I was crazy. Moon-touched, or worse.

"We're free of him now! Why go looking for trouble?" he asked, nestled in our tree-trunk. In avian terms we were now old enough to be accounted a breeding pair, but there was a downside to our immortality—Goronwy and I would have no children.

"A pre-emptive move," I replied. *"He's lost Lleu, his darling son. Do you really think he won't blame me for my part in that, and come after me again?"*

" We don't know what happened to Lleu, though." Math's forays into the Underworld had yielded no answers. Nobody had seen Arawn or Lleu since they'd disappeared from the Sun Temple, and that had been several months ago. Goronwy fluffed his wings and uttered the tremulous 'twoo' that signified unease. I shuffled closer, cooing, and rubbed my head against his.

"All right." I offered a compromise. *"If I find him, I promise not to dive in with talons outstretched. But I still plan to contact our allies and ask for their help. Will that do?"*

He preened his beak down my neck, sending delicious sensations through me. Love and concern flowed through our link. *"You mean Math and Lady Wynne?"*

I cooed again. *"Or Arianrhod, or Dylan. We're not alone in this, I promise you. Gwydion's broken too many rules and offended too many of his kindred this time. One more misstep, and he'll suffer the same judgement as Lleu. And an attack on me would be such a misstep. Gwydion's days of freedom are numbered."*

My love agreed, albeit reluctantly. The next day we flew to the standing stones in Ardudwy and ventured through them to confront Arianrhod in her far northern palace. It was a long journey for an owl, one our wild brethren would never have considered. Tawny owls were highly territorial and didn't venture far from their home trees, and they avoided travelling over water. If any were to accidentally fly into a portal, I suspected they'd perish from shock.

As I almost did, for entirely different reasons. I had been unprepared for how alien the landscape looked when we arrived in Arianrhod's domain. While I'd adjusted to the differences in my vision—the increased acuity, the extra eyelid, the inability to roll my eyes in dismay or disgust or for any reason at all—I'd never got used to the comparative lack of colour. The glorious hues I remembered draping Arianrhod's skies now appeared as shades of violet-grey.

Chynwyn, Sipsi and Gwenhwyfar greeted us on our arrival. There was no sign of Taran and the others; I presumed they were outside, exploring their new kingdom. Escorted by the two wolves and great white owl, we approached Caer Sidi, the crystal palace, and—presumably having been announced—entered unimpeded. I knew the way of old, and it took no time to traverse those hallways as an owl. I'd always been struck by their width; now the puzzle pieces fitted together. They'd been designed to accommodate Gwenhwyfar's five-foot wingspan.

"What's wrong, Blodeuwedd?" asked the goddess when Goronwy and I fluttered into her presence.

"Twoo," I said. "*Is it that obvious?*"

Amusement crinkled her eyes and curved her lips in a smile. "I've lived with Gwynhyfar for centuries, and I fly as an owl. I can read their moods. You seem somewhat despondent."

I dipped my head, shifting from one foot to the other. "*I miss colour. I didn't realise how much until I viewed your skies.*"

"Ah," she said. "Don't fret, that's easily fixed. Come here to me, both of you."

I glided to her outstretched arm and tried not to flinch away when she put out both hands to grip my head between them. My vision shifted; a quiet clunking sounded in my head. I blinked all three eyelids rapidly, and the face of the goddess before me came back into focus. In vibrant, glorious colour.

"*How did you do that?*" I asked, chortling in pleasure. "*That is truly amazing!*"

"I adjusted your eyes a little. The part that lets you experience colour. Now you, my little feathered lord."

"*Can you give me back my sense of smell, too?*" I asked as she worked the same magic on Goronwy. He positively purred with delight when she was done.

"No, and you wouldn't want me to. Owls hunt by sight and sound; it would be distracting if they could scent their prey." Gwynhyfar hooted derisively, and her mistress chuckled. "Very true. Some also smell unpleasant."

I looked around the room, twisting my head. A multitude of scented oils and unguents lined the many shelves on the far wall, among pottery vases, glass bowls, small sculptures, and other items of mundane and esoteric natures. *"Is that also true of you when you take owl form?"* I asked, greatly daring. *"I see you still enjoy perfumes as a woman."*

Her smile lingered. "Quite so. I shed that characteristic when I return to this form. But I'm sure you didn't come all this way to discuss sight and scent, however fascinating those subjects are. How else can I help you, daughter?"

Would I ever get used to being addressed thus by her? Possibly not. I laid out the arguments I'd marshalled for Goronwy, and his responses. To my astonishment, Arianrhod dismissed my fears.

"As far as Gwydion's concerned, you've been punished," she said. "He holds owls in the utmost contempt, and having turned you into one, he thinks you're now a quivering mess. I, after all, take the form of an owl. He can't think of anything worse than making you resemble me. Owls represent darkness, intuition, inner wisdom, and silence—none of which Gwydion values."

"What about you, then?" I asked. *"Or the others?"*

She shrugged. "Gwydion and I have been in conflict since we were children. This is just another day in our ongoing war. As for the others, Wynne and Math are searching for Blei and Meghan, who were last seen in Emania before Lleu tried to set fire to it. Arawn can take care of himself, and if he's retreated to the Underworld, Gwydion won't venture there."

"If that's where Arawn and Lleu actually are," Goronwy objected, rotating his head to take in as much of the room as he could.

I turned mine too, equally astounded by the glory of it, by the array of hue and textures. Silver, white, green, and blue dominated the décor, emulating the glory of the northern skies. The furniture was an eclectic mixture, no doubt collected from the far corners of the world.

"And Dylan?" I asked, wrenching my attention away from those mesmerising colours. It felt so good to be able to appreciate them fully.

She sighed. "He's already struck at Dylan. I don't think he'll do so again. What purpose would that serve? Gwydion always has an agenda, even if it makes little sense to anyone else. No, whatever retribution he plans will be aimed at King Math next, because not only is he the greatest threat, but he was the first to insult Lleu. Gwydion's unlikely to forget that, or forgive it."

Convinced Math could take care of himself, I didn't pursue that any further. *"But what about..."* I hesitated, then continued in a rush. *"Will my friends be safe from him? Cynar and the others? And if Arawn can't contain Lleu in the Underworld, will he follow through with his threat against Modwenna's daughter? I couldn't bear to see that happen."*

Arianrhod stroked a finger over my head and down my back, smoothing my feathers. I preened, relishing the sensation. This must be what cats felt like when petted—why they always demanded more of it. "Don't worry, daughter," she said. "Math, Wynne, and I have that worked out."

Did I trust her? Dare I? I believed that she intended to help, but Arianrhod's view of the world and how it worked usually differed from mine. So did Math's, and possibly Wynne's. Whether because Math had unintentionally added too much compassion when he made me, or because I'd grown up among humankind, their motivations made more sense to me than those of Don's Children. I resolved to leave nothing to chance and keep an eye on Modwenna myself.

29

CAER SIDI

Time. Even as a mortal girl I'd never felt constrained by it and had therefore taken the peculiarities of Otherworld flows in my stride. Sometimes it tripped others up, though. Stories abounded of people who'd strayed into the Otherworld for an unforgettable day—or night—to find a century or more had passed in their world when they returned. I'd never experienced anything that dramatic, but found the correlation always remained a little out of kilter. Time passed more quickly in the mortal world than in Caer Dathyl, Annwfyn, or elsewhere in Otherworld realms.

After Arawn and Lleu disappeared, still locked together in battle, neither Math nor I felt any great need to hurry. We needed to consult with Arianrhod but could afford to wait until she'd returned Blodeuedd to Ardudwy.

Unable to alter the outcome for Lleu, we journeyed through the Otherworldly ways to her home at Caer Sidi to wait for her. To reach such a place from the mortal world it was customary to use a stone circle, or another artefact constructed for a similar purpose. From the Otherworld, it was a lot easier.

We didn't have to traverse miles of snow and glittering ice but arrived without fanfare in the portico of Arianrhod's crystal palace to be met by the resident snowy owl, Gwynhyfar. I was grateful for that; although Math had conjured me a fur cloak over fine woollen robes, the cold still seeped through. For a mortal to survive long in this place, in the far north of the world, many layers would be necessary. I rapped on a brass knocker, shaped like a ship's anchor. The glittering white carved doors swung open to reveal a pair of wolves, one silver-grey, one dark as charcoal.

Math nodded to them as he would any other servants. "Chynwyn, Sipsi, has your mistress not returned yet?"

The wolves, as far as I knew, weren't equipped for speech. They turned around and trotted silently down the hall, pausing outside an open door about halfway along to look back as if in invitation. Math waved me forward. "After you."

As always, the contrast between this, Ari's favourite sitting room, and the grandeur of the rest of the palace struck a jarring note. Why did she need so many chairs, and why, oh why, couldn't she have chosen at least two that matched? I selected one of the sturdiest, and Math sat down on the settle—really little more than an upholstered bench. The space between was cluttered with a miscellany of small tables; tall, short, square, round, or octagonal. Threads of quartz crystal, fine as lace, festooned the too-high ceiling. At least the temperature was agreeable, and the air pleasantly scented.

"Should we help ourselves to food and drink, or wait for our hostess?" I asked, unsure of the appropriate protocol. Math might have visited before in his niece's absence, but I never had.

Apparently all one had to do was to ask. No sooner had the words left my lips than a servant in blue and silver livery appeared, bearing a tray of flatbread rolls filled with smoked fish and pickled cabbage, accompanied by soft cheese and tiny honey cakes slathered with cream. Setting the tray on the nearest table, she approached the haphazardly spaced squares of an open cabinet against the far wall and handed us silver forks before silently filling a pair of twisted pewter goblets with mead. We accepted them gratefully, and she bowed her way out the door. She spoke not a word, and her footsteps made nary a sound.

"Do you suppose Ari employs ghosts?" I asked, swirling my pale golden drink. "Maybe they can hear thoughts and appear and disappear as needed. Come to think of it, I've never seen many people around on any of my other visits, either."

Math stretched his long legs and took a sip of his mead. "Why don't you ask her? I heard the door close a moment ago." He smacked his lips. "Ah, but that's a fine drop."

I cocked my head, and sure enough, caught the faint whisper of footsteps approaching.

"It ought to be good—it cost enough." Arianrhod swept through the door, went straight to the wall shelf, and poured mead for herself as well. She lifted the goblet. "Iechyd da!"

Math and I echoed the salutation.

"Cost in magic or coin?" I asked, and, unable to help myself, followed it up with a yawn.

"Magic, of course. I don't deal in money." Ari's pretended shock changed to laughter. "Poor mortal witch; I suppose you need a rest before we essay more magical work. Not a bad idea—even I feel a little depleted. When you're ready, follow me."

She waited until we'd finished our repast, then led us up a seemingly unending spiral staircase to a vast bedroom filled with colour and light. Both the walls and the ceiling appeared to be composed entirely of glass. A bed carved of black oak, or possibly ebony, dominated the centre of the room, topped by a downy white quilt and many white lace-covered pillows. Fur rugs coated the floor, also white, with an edging of pearl-grey here and there. It worked, because anything else would have fought with the display overhead. Colours bled through the sky above and around us, merging one into another in a ceaseless panorama.

"You do your guests proud," I said.

She grinned. "Only those I'm especially fond of. Now rest, and when you're ready call me. Math knows how."

Math apparently did know. He woke me several hours later to perform the work we'd gone there to do: namely, performing a spell to bind the soul of Goronwy Pebyr to the body of an owl. Animals were seldom bound to the wheel of life, death, and rebirth. They were not as distanced from the primal goddess as humans had become. They lived by instinct, and when their time on earth was done, however long or brief it might be, they returned to the bosom of the greatest goddess, she who'd birthed both Math ap Mathonwy and mighty Dôn.

This, however, was a special case. When Gwydion had transformed Blodeuedd into owl form, he'd intended her to live alone forever. Neither Math nor Dôn approved of such wanton cruelty, and while neither had been able to reverse Gwydion's spell, both had agreed with Arianrhod when she suggested this solution.

By no means a simple process, the enchantment involved hours of chanting, meditation and various other esoteric practices. Apart from brief respites for sustenance and other needs, we worked all through the night and most of the following day. Ari permitted us to relax afterwards, or at least she and Math did. It would be more accurate to say that I collapsed. I didn't know how long I slept for, because eternal night ruled in winter in the far north of the world. After a while, however, ravening hunger woke me. Magic working of that magnitude took a toll on mere human women, even those gifted with extraordinary lifespans.

We feasted on fish, venison, and seaweed, washed down with crisp white wine from lands far to the east. The pair of wolves lay at our feet, and Gwenhwyfar perched on Ari's chairback. It felt so very... normal compared to Caer Dathyl. I experienced a brief pang of homesickness. In some ways, Caer Sidi reminded me of Blodeuwedd's castle. Not in the icy brilliance of its crystal façade, but in the permanence of its structure. Looking at the same views all the time must be terribly boring.

We couldn't return home yet though. We needed to find Meg and Blei, as well as Gwydion, and force him to return them to their natural forms. But first, we had to ensure the safety of Modwenna's daughter Yseult. Without knowing whether Arawn had confined Lleu in Annwfyn, we had to consider him still a threat to the unborn baby.

Like the rest of Don's children, both Gwydion and Lleu were bound tightly by habit. The same sun which shone on Cymru circled the rest of the planet, but Lleu never ventured far beyond the borders of his own lands. He drew power down from the sun and spread it across his fields. That was enough, in his eyes. Just as Gwydion, whether he sallied forth as a man, beast, or bird, endlessly patrolled the same countryside.

Therefore, Math, Ari and I reasoned when conferring the following morning, Modwenna, Yestin and their unborn daughter needed to be temporarily removed from Cymru.

"What about Oonagh's home, Alba?" I asked, as a manservant, wearing the same colours as the woman we'd encountered before, set a bowl of fragrant porridge in front of me. This time we ate at a proper table in a spacious dining room, and although none of these chairs matched either, at least they all had sturdy backs and padded seats. The table could easily have seated twenty, so we'd grouped together at one end. "Surely her people would help. The selkies have no love for Gwydion, especially after that debacle with the afanc."

"Too obvious." Ari heaped small, bright red berries into her bowl and slathered thick cream on top. "Thank you, Nudd, that will be all for now." She nodded to the servant, who bowed and departed. "The same objection applies to my steading on Ynys Mon, or even here at Caer Sidi. Goronwy had family spread across the lands of Prydain who might welcome them, but there's a chance Gwydion and Lleu will remember that, too."

"We don't want somewhere completely unfamiliar, though," added Math. "Bad enough to uproot them from everything and everyone they know and love, without asking them to learn a foreign language and customs. Which leaves a group rarely mentioned or even considered by many people, including Lleu or Gwydion." He paused, watching us both expectantly.

We waited while a teasing smile tugged at the corners of Math's lips. I gave in. "You've built enough tension, now tell us."

"I propose we hide them with...wait for it...the rest of our family." He leaned back in his chair, a satisfied smile playing around his mouth. The man did love theatre. I had to admit, though, it was a satisfactory solution. More than satisfactory.

"Yes! Gofannon or Amatheon would welcome them." Arianrhod beamed at him.

Those two were among the nicest of her brothers. She had a lot of them, even more than me, but only three sisters that I knew of. Perhaps that accounted for her combative nature.

Math set his spoon down and pushed the bowl away. "Gofannon talks too much, and Amatheon too little. Van would be too likely to let something slip to someone he shouldn't, and Theon would make them feel as if they're in solitary confinement and abandoned by the rest of the world." He stroked his beard and thought for a moment. "How about Euyd? He's always been my favourite among your brothers. Resembles his da."

By which he meant the least prone to drama and violence. I liked Van and Theon but agreed with Math's assessment of them. Apart from Euyd and Gilfaethwy, the rest of their clan hadn't bothered to keep in contact with Ari and would be disinclined to put themselves out for an anonymous human. And I still bore a grudge against Gil, even though he'd changed his ways and become a model citizen in the human world.

"Euyd sounds ideal," I said. "He lives in Rheged now, doesn't he? That's not too far from Ardudwy, and the language isn't much different to Cymric. I believe Modwenna knows some Prydani as well."

So, it was settled. Math and I would escort the family north to Rheged, which lay on the western coast of Prydain's Isle. Euyd and Dylan between them would guard over our refugees until Llau Llaw Gyffes was finally dealt with.

Ari nodded agreement. I pushed my chair back and rose from the table. "Very well, you can contact Euyd and set it all up, while we go to Mur Y Castell and convince Yestin and Modwenna. Time to leave, husband."

After bidding farewell to Ari, we did so, this time taking the route used by mortals, as it required Math to expend less power.

"I wish we could have saved Lleu, too," I murmured as we approached the stone circle which led back to Ardudwy cantref, not far from Blodeuedd's old home at Mur Y Castell.

"You did your best for him." Math rubbed the back of my neck. "But Lleu is Gwydion's son, whether or not they acknowledge the relationship. Like calls to like."

I leaned back into his touch, wishing the pain in my heart could be as easily massaged away. "He might have turned out differently if Gwydion hadn't raised him. We should have intervened. We should have stopped Gwydion from taking him and insisted Ari raise them both."

My husband put his arm around and rocked me gently, side to side. "Ah, my love, you know what a state Ari was in that day. She rejected her twins outright, and it was only later when she'd calmed down that

she asked what had become of Lleu. By then it was too late, because
Gwydion had him well hidden."

Poor Ari. I hated and despised that brother as much on her behalf
as I did on my own. Would his atrocities never end? I contemplated
his latest.

"How do we find Meg and Blei?" I asked, running a finger along the
rough surface of the nearest dolmen. I wanted to rush off immediately
after we arrived back in Ardudwy but knew saving Yseult had to take
precedence. Besides, it would be pointless without some sort of plan.
Math needed to recoup his energy. We both did. That battle and the
subsequent spellwork had exhausted us both.

"Start with where we last saw them, in the Moonlands." Math
stepped into the circle, waiting for me to follow him around its winding paths.

Conversation ceased as the vortex whirled around us. The pathway
through every circle was a little different to the others, depending on
the points of origin and exit. Nor did everybody experience them the
same way. For me, the route to and from Ari's lands felt cold, although
not unpleasant. A fresh, sharp tingling that dispelled all lingering
traces of tiredness and left me alert and refreshed.

Interworld journeying ate time, as well. For every circuit we travelled, days or weeks passed in the realm of men. By the time we reached
Blodeuwedd's castle, she and Goronwy would have been reunited.

"My guess," Math continued, once we'd reached our destination,
"is that Meg and Blei are trapped somewhere in the Otherworld, if not
in Emania. Gwydion wouldn't risk taking them with him on any of
his recent ventures, so he has to have them stashed somewhere." He
yawned. Ari's circle didn't seem to have the same effect on him as it
did on me. "But that will have to wait a while. I promised Blodeuedd
before we left the Sun Temple that I'd check on Cynar and the others,
now that they've been able to return home. Once Modwenna's on
her way to safety, I'll take to the air in raven form and search for our
children. But first I need some sleep, my love, and so do you."

He paused and looked around. Little evidence remained of the
conflagration Lleu and Gwydion had unleashed, even though no more
than three months had now passed in the mortal realm. Rain fell daily
in Cymric lands in springtime, and thanks to Blodeuwedd's lingering
influence the trees and grasses had regenerated quickly.

I'd anticipated having to walk to the castle, but even before we turned onto the path leading there, I heard hoofbeats approaching at a steady pace. Math smiled and lifted a hand in greeting as two riders came into view, each one leading an extra horse. Cynar and Yestin.

"How did you know we'd be here?" I asked gratefully, as Math helped me into the saddle. He then mounted himself.

"The Lady Arianrhod sent a message," Yestin replied. "Apparently owls can be trained to act as carrier pigeons. Can you imagine?"

I smiled. Some might think Ari uncaring, but I knew better. She was always considerate of her friends' comfort—when it occurred to her.

When we reached Mur Y Castell, they offered us food, which I declined, and a warm, soft bed, which I accepted with heartfelt thanks. Snuggled against Math, I fell immediately into a deep, dreamless sleep.

30

DEVAU

"**W**hy can't you tell me where you're taking us?" asked Modwenna the next morning, surveying her packed bags with a hint of nervousness. As well as two sturdy leather cases, her luggage included a plain wicker basket stocked with foodstuffs. "Is all the secrecy really that necessary? I'm certain nobody here would confide in Lleu, even if he dared show his face. He's become really unpopular, you know, after everything that's happened."

"They've never encountered Lleu at the height of his powers," I explained patiently. "And if that weren't enough to cow them into submission, remember that Gwydion can change others' appearances as well as his own. Lleu could appear as a travelling bard, a merchant, a cobbler, or a humble fisherman, and easily persuade some unsuspecting soul to say more than they should."

"I suppose so." She rubbed her belly, now noticeably rounded, and sighed. "It's just that I've never been that far away from home, and the prospect scares me a little. But if I was prepared to do it for Blodeuedd, I can't refuse for my daughter, can I? Very well, Lady Goewin. Yestin and I will follow wherever you lead."

Few stone circles existed in Euyd's lands, lying at the northern end of the Penwynion Hills, and some of the Old Ones advised against taking a pregnant woman through the portals in any case. Which made me wonder—was using a glamour on her any safer? Perhaps it would be enough for Math to change his own appearance, plus mine and Yestin's. It was not uncommon to see women beyond Gwynedd's borders go veiled in the Roman fashion. With her hair coiled up and covered, wearing the drab garb of a common farmer's wife instead of the clear, bright colours she was used to as one of Blodeuedd's ladies, I thought no one would recognise Modwenna.

After a farewell feast, which I would have liked to decline but couldn't without seeming ungracious, we said our goodbyes and set off east through Merionydd and Powys. Math had given himself and me iron-grey hair and a few extra pounds, as well as too many wrinkles. To all outward appearances we comprised a small family group of an older couple and their young married children, riding a quartet of unexceptional ponies.

"It's as well I'm not vain," I said the first morning as we set out, stroking the sagging skin of my cheeks. The illusion was tactile as well as visual, to ensure it would hold up under scrutiny.

"You still look lovely, my lady," Modwenna assured me. "You have a kind face, and that's worth more than beauty."

I laughed. "And you're a sweet child. We don't want the world to see how pretty you are, though. Pull your veil forward and throw the ends over your shoulders to shroud not just your hair but part of your face, too. Like so."

She watched me mime the action and did as I suggested. I nodded, satisfied. The loose Roman robes also helped to conceal her pregnancy, and Yestin's distinctive blond thatch and fair skin had been replaced by lank brown hair and a swarthy complexion. No one would recognise us. Math had also glamoured our horses. The two greys, Cant and Blawr, were now a pair of black ponies; beautiful chestnut Rhosyn and Math's favourite bay gelding, Eilio, had faded to a dirty cream. They too, appeared to be ponies.

Nevertheless, I kept an eye out for red kites, but only small birds and the occasional crow or raven were visible in the skies overhead. A pair of owls appeared at regular intervals whenever we stopped for the night, although I couldn't tell if they were the same pair. Owls didn't venture far from their nesting site. I smiled to myself and said nothing of it.

As promised, whenever we were away from prying eyes, Math changed into raven form and returned to the Otherworld, searching for any sign of Meghan or Blei. From the uplands to the deepest valleys he flew, from the icy heights of Yr Wyddfa to the shores of Ynys Môn.

He covered the rocky southern coast of Kernow to the rugged shores of Alba, and everywhere in between. East to west, south to north he searched, but of Blei and Meg he found no trace. They weren't in the Otherworld.

That left the mortal realm. I couldn't understand it. Why would Gwydion bring them here? Neither had much experience of the world of men. Blei might have ventured through the veil a few times, but Meg, as far as I knew, not at all. How could they cope with it? How would they survive?

We each reacted differently to threats to our loved ones. With each unsuccessful foray, Math got more and more frazzled, as I became more and more calm.

Three days later we crossed the border into Prydain and turned north towards Devau, where we planned to spend several nights at an inn and replenish our supplies. That done, we'd continue our northward trek, which would take the better part of a week. Math chafed against the necessity of travelling so slowly, which made Yestin and Modwenna feel guilty, I could tell.

"Take no notice of him," I said, as the solid new walls of Devau township came into view. "He's frustrated, which in turn makes him angry, because he encounters setbacks so seldom. Once we're sure you're safe, I can also help, and I'm sure we'll find our children in no time."

We dismounted at the city gates and had to jostle our way through a tight-packed throng of people. Every soul in Devau must have been out in the streets that day, and a palpable air of excitement was evident. A festival, perhaps? We were well past Gwyl Forwyn by now, and some weeks away from Alban Hyfed, but perhaps they honoured some local deity or occasion.

"What's going on?" Math asked a slight youth pushing a barrow piled high with wood.

"There's a mummer in town, and everybody wants to see him. Word is his act's right amazin'. I better not linger, though. Master'll have the hide off me if I'm late with this lot." He jerked his chin at his burden and trundled off down a side street.

"More than amazin'," breathed a portly woman behind us, overhearing. "It's like magic, it is. I've never seen nothing like it. He says he's performed for kings, and I got no trouble believing that, none at all."

Math and I exchanged glances, and uneasiness stirred in me. Mummers, a type of travelling jester, weren't commonly found at the courts of kings. Country folk were, on the whole, easily impressed with tricks and sleight of hand, but the press of crowds clamouring to witness a single performer lent weight to her words. Perhaps there was genuine magic at work here.

"What's his act like?" I asked, turning to face her. "You said you've seen it?"

She gave me a gap-toothed grin, delighted to have her own audience. "Well, he starts with the usual, you know, juggling and suchlike. Then he tells stories—right wondrous stories, they are—and he sings. Beautiful voice he has, just beautiful. But the best bit, well, you just won't believe it."

A trained bard, by the sound of it. Which might not necessarily mean Gwydion, or even another magician, but the premonition of disaster that had trickled down my spine at the first mention of magic wrapped itself around my chest and squeezed.

Modwenna must have had the same thought. She gasped in dismay, and Yestin moved closer to lay a protective arm around her shoulders. "Why don't you tell us about it?" he said. "We'd love to see him perform. My wife's partial to storytellers."

The old dame shook her head. "You've never heard one like this 'un, I'll warrant. Why, you can just about see the pictures he paints with his words. It's a marvel, it is."

"I'm sure it is." Yestin continued to draw her out, showing more patience that I had. "What's his name?"

"Bevan the Bard, he calls himself, and like I said, he's right good at it, too. But the best part of his act is the bears."

I hissed in a breath. Gwydion had used that pseudonym in the past. He had brought Meg and Blei to the mortal world with him. As bears! I'd seen the appalling conditions trained bears lived in, and the thought of my girl being subjected to that made me want to throw up. The band around my heart tightened, constricting my diaphragm, and making it hard to breathe.

"Got 'em trained real good, he has," said the dame, rubbing her hands together in glee. Then her smile faded, and she peered more closely at me. "You all right, love?"

"I..." Searching for a reason that would make sense to her, I fell back on religion. "I follow the bear goddess, Artio, and it pains me to see her kindred mistreated. For me, that is sacrilege. I think I need to have words with this mummer."

"Oh, no," she hastened to assure me, looking shocked. "He don't use chains or anything like that. It's all done real humanely, from what I could see."

Humanely, my witchy arse. Humanity had nothing to do with it. Of course, Gwydion would eschew the use of such clumsy methods when he could rely on magic.

I thanked her, and when she'd left, turned to Yestin. "Math and I would feel much better knowing you two were safe. Find an inn and book two rooms, one for you and one for us." Ignoring Math's raised brows, I pressed several silver coins into Yestin's hand. "This will be more than enough to cover accommodation and stabling. Devau's not that big; we'll find you later. Now, go."

He nodded, and the pair of them left, leading our horses. "So good of you to speak for me, my queen," said my husband, then mock-shied away from my answering glare. "Of course, I'm not saying you're wrong. If it comes to a magical battle, they'd only be in the way."

"It had better not," I replied grimly. "Because then Meg and Blei are also potential casualties. Even though they have powers of their own, they'll be hobbled by Gwydion."

"I agree. We should hurry."

Winding through the back streets of Devau in a vain effort to avoid as many of the crowds as possible, we finally tracked Gwydion down in the town square. Comments about the lovability and obvious intelligence of his two performing bears reached us from all sides. It would have served them all right if Artio had appeared in their midst. She was a force to be reckoned with, according to Math.

Unfortunately, the popularity of 'Bevan's' act meant we had no chance of getting close to him without paying the ruffians he'd employed as his crew. They had set up temporary screens around a square in the centre of town to ensure any who hadn't paid couldn't view his performance for free. Although the square was a reasonable size and permitted standing room only, audience numbers were limited. This resulted in a continuing stream of impatient patrons waiting outside the screens, all eager for their turn.

At last, Math's patience evaporated. After three sessions brought us no closer to being admitted, he brought out his hazel wand. A single tap, and the first screen toppled, bringing the others down in its wake.

I'd expected some sort of stage, but 'Bevan's' performance apparently required no more than a clear area at the front, divided from the audience by a series of portable posts, strung together with rope. And flanking him... My heart juddered and tried to punch through my ribs, before settling into its accustomed rhythm. To either side stood a pair of brown bears, one a glossy brown, the other, slightly smaller, the colour of a fox's fur. Neither appeared to wear any restraints, other than black leather collars embedded with silver studs. Relief flooded through me at the sight of them, sweeter than honey wine. The crowd inside the screens roared its disapproval, and those outside cheered, thinking they could now jump the queue. Gwydion's ruffians beat them back.

"I'm King Math's courier," announced Math, demoting himself. "And I have an important message for the king's bard." He strode forward, his voice and his stature proclaiming authority. Enhanced by magic, of course, but no one recognised it as such.

The audience took one look at him and scurried off, and even Gwydion's men hesitated. Math smiled at them, nastily, and they too departed.

Not noticeably concerned, 'Bevan the Bard' sauntered up to us. A persona less like Gwydion's own would be hard to imagine. A thumb-width or so shorter than me, with a weathered, freckled face and a mole on his chin, he looked like a man who'd spent a hard life outdoors. Straight, grey-streaked brown hair all but obscured his eyes, and his coarse dun-coloured clothing hung loose on his frame. A bright scarlet scarf knotted around his neck and a bronze pendant set with a gaudy red stone dangling against his chest were the only outward trappings of his profession that I could see.

"Hello, Uncle," said Gwydion. "I seem to have lost the bulk of my audience, but I'm sure you don't want to air our business in public. Let's go somewhere more secluded, shall we?"

Unhurriedly, he turned down an alley and entered the ground floor of a modest stone building, the two bears at his heels. The back door, I assumed. Even a second-rate establishment such as this appeared to be wouldn't allow bears in the front door.

We trailed down a long hallway to a square room with whitewashed walls and sweet rushes on the floor, where the only furniture was a simple table and a couple of plain pine benches. A kitchen, I assumed.

"Ha!" I said, closing the door behind me and leaning against it. "Found you at last."

Gwydion smirked. "I think you have that the wrong way round, Aunty Wynne. I've been trailing you through the countryside for the past few days, and very boring it's been, I might add. But I'm forgetting my manners. Please, all of you, have a seat."

I remained standing. So did Math. The bears lolled at ease in front of the dead fireplace, and with an off-handed gesture, Gwydion brought it to blazing life. Neither Meg nor Blei took any notice of the newcomers.

Fighting the impulse to pet my children as if they were oversized cats, I glared at their jailor. "Trailing us? How?"

He moved across to the window facing the back of the room and pointed. Triumph glowed on his borrowed features, and apprehension clawed at my throat. Math pushed him aside, and peering through the warped, uneven shutters, let fly a string of curses.

I saw why, as the now-familiar sinking sensation swept from my throat to my knees. Four horses stood tethered in the lean-to shack that served the inn as a stable, recognisably ours. I groaned aloud. What ill fortune had prompted Yestin and Modwenna to choose the same inn as Gwydion?

Gwydion pointed again, indicating the basket tied to Modwenna's horse. "You should have checked that. Don't you know how things can get stuck between wicker?"

I raced for the door, but Gwydion beat me to it, slamming it in my face and wedging it shut with magic. Why, I had no idea. Just to be difficult, probably. By the time Math found a counterspell to open it, Gwydion had reached the horses and removed the basket. Laughing, he danced away from me, holding it tantalisingly just out of my reach.

He might have led me in a convoluted set several times around the yard if Math's fist hadn't slammed into his jaw. I delighted in the sound, the crack of bone against bone. Gwydion stumbled back and dropped the basket, which skidded across the cobblestones.

Before he could move again, I grabbed and upended it, scanned the bottom. Nothing. What was he talking about? Turning it over again, I shook it vigorously, and was rewarded by a glimpse of rufus red. I changed the angle, and the colour disappeared. Another twist, and there it was again. A cursed feather lay threaded between the canes on the bottom of the basket.

"But the only spells set on the feathers were useless," I protested, as Gwydion rubbed his chin and glared at Math. "I checked them when Blodeuedd showed them to me."

Math ignored him. Taking the basket from me, he extended a finger to coax the feather out. "Why didn't either of you show this to me?" Stern-voiced, stony-faced. Uh-oh. "Wynne, you at least ought to have known better. Of course, he's been able to track you. This would be how he kept in contact with Cara, too. A shapeshifter mage always retains a connection to any fur or feathers they shed. How could you have overlooked that?"

How, indeed? Because I wasn't godborn, and all the esoteric knowledge I'd gained over the years had had to be pounded into my skull through long, arduous hours of study. Trial and error. Rituals gone awry. And a human brain could only retain so much information at a time. Some was bound to get lost occasionally.

I couldn't recall if I'd even been aware of the connection Math referred to, but it did make sense. Witches such as I used hair, nail clippings, skin scrapings and even blood in spellwork, for good or for ill, because they provided a direct link to the donor.

"You were away when Blodeuedd first found them," I said, answering the first part of his question. "Gathering wand woods, as I recall. And then you kept her so busy with testing them I suppose she didn't think of it until much later. So, she asked me to look at them, and I did. The error was entirely mine; no blame lies with Blodeuedd."

A cackle of laughter snapped my attention back to Gwydion, who'd been listening to our exchange with mockery etched on his face. The bruise on his jaw had already faded. I glanced from him to the basket. "Chance played a part in this," I said. "Unless Cara knew there was a feather lodged in there?"

"Probably not," said Modwenna, appearing suddenly at my elbow. Focused wholly on Gwydion and his feather, we hadn't noticed her approach.

This day just kept getting worse. I spun to face her. "What are you doing here? Get back inside, now."

"Modwenna," called Yestin, clattering down the stairs opposite. "Is everything..." His voice trailed away as he caught sight of me and Math.

"Everything's fine," his wife assured him, smiling too brightly. A pulse beat in her throat, and the knuckles clutching the edge of her shawl showed bone-white. "I saw a strange man approach our horses and came down to investigate. If he was a thief, I hoped to scare him away. But he's no thief at all, is he? Just a charlatan. 'Bevan the Bard', I presume."

Gwydion swept her a bow, and as he straightened, assumed his own stance and face. Yestin drew in a startled breath, but Modwenna didn't react, other than to shiver.

"Cara still had her 'love charm'," she said, making it plain her reaction wasn't occasioned by Gwydion. "She wouldn't have needed the feather. Blodeuedd told me Mabli didn't want the basket, so she took it to carry tools on our gardening expeditions. That's how it ended up in my rooms. It was sheer ill-chance that led me to use it on our journey."

"No," Gwydion corrected her. "Not ill-luck but blessed fortune. For it led me to you, and you and your brat will be the lodestone that draws Lleu back to me."

Anxiety fluttered against my ribcage. I fought not to show it. "It's cold out here. Let's go in and discuss it by the fire. Modwenna, Yestin, you should go upstairs and wait for us. We won't be long."

"No," said Gwydion. "I insist we all stay together."

Unable to think of a response which wouldn't risk provoking him, I led them all back inside. Keeping a wary eye on Gwydion, and a conciliatory one on Math, I approached the bears. Neither reacted; I couldn't tell whether they recognised me or were simply, as the old dame had told us, well-trained.

"I can tell you where to find Lleu," I said, turning back to Gwydion and ignoring Math's frantic signals. "But first, you have to change Meg and Blei back into their natural forms. Properly, without any tricks or cheating. I want to see them stand before me as they did at our last meeting back in Caer Dathyl, before you and Lleu desecrated the place and almost burnt my beloved home to the ground."

I expected a fight, or at the very least a long, drawn-out negotiation. Instead, he shrugged. "Sounds like a fair bargain. I agree."

"Just like that?" Was there a quaver in my voice? I cleared my throat and folded my hands to still their trembling.

He smirked in a way I'd learned to distrust over the centuries. Face still expressionless, Math reached out and caught my hand in his, squeezing it tightly. Forgiveness and support, combined with shared anxiety. He didn't trust Gwydion any more than I did.

But, unbelievably Gwydion knelt before the two by the fire, and laid a hand on each of their heads. The air blurred around them, and their fur disappeared, to be replaced by pale skin and red hair in one case, and brown skin and brown hair in the other.

Meg blinked and looked wonderingly around her, before getting unsteadily to her feet. "Couldn't you have at least given us clothes?" she asked, looking down at her nakedness.

Blei shook his head groggily then started to swear, fluently and with fervour.

Modwenna laughed. "Don't worry, we can lend you clothes. Let my husband fetch our packs and you can have our second spare set." She prodded the blushing Yestin with her elbow.

I didn't care that they were naked. I didn't care about anything except having them back at last. We fell into each other's arms, laughing and crying at once.

"Enough of that," snapped Gwydion. "I did as you asked and changed them back. Now it's your turn. What happened to my son?"

31

RHEGED

Gwydion always expected people to jump when he spoke, to fawn at his feet and pander to his wishes. I never had and was not about to start. Instead, I turned to Yestin, who'd returned to the horses and was now hauling a bulging leather bag through the door.

"Thank you, both," I said, as he set it down. Modwenna withdrew a gown, a pair of trews and a shirt and handed them to Meg. Blei turned his back as soon as Math and I let him go and stood by the fireplace, staring into the flames.

"I said, where is Lleu?" Gwydion reached out, gripped me by the arm and spun me around.

Three rumbling growls made him slacken his hold, as Math and a still-unclothed Blei advanced on him. Meg voiced her displeasure in the same fashion but was occupied with donning the clothing Modwenna had given her. She moved awkwardly, almost as if she had trouble remembering what to do and what limb went where.

"Huh," I said, stepping away. "You only acknowledged him as your nephew the last time we spoke."

"The two aren't exclusive, as you very well know. Out with it. Where is he?"

Was there an edge of anxiety beneath his anger? The only thing likely to make Gwydion nervous was genuine concern about Lleu.

Math picked up on it, too. "Lleu's disappearance put a crimp in your plans, didn't it? You expected him to murder us all, including the Lord of Annwfyn, and then immediately join you." He laughed shortly. "As if that would be possible."

Gwydion bunched his fists, his eyes glittering like sapphires. "It looked likely enough from where I stood. I ask you again, where is he?"

His tone was too similar to Lleu's when he'd demanded to know the whereabouts of his Caron: strident, harsh and cruel. Gone were the honeyed tones of the bard. For once, his voice matched his intent. By the fire, Meg had finally struggled into the gown, and Blei stood beside her, clad only in the trews.

"I'm not absolutely sure," I admitted, angling away so that Math stood between us. "How much do you know about what happened in Emania between Lleu and Arawn?"

I was playing for time, and the narrowing of Gwydion's eyes told me he knew it. But while many people would condemn me for facilitating his reunion with Lleu, I was prepared to pay that price and trust Math, Arawn and others to bring them both to justice later. First, however, I needed to ensure the safety of Modwenna, Yestin and my two children. Which meant distracting Gwydion.

"Enough," he snarled. "I know Arawn and Lleu fought, before vanishing together. I've questioned all my Underworld contacts and come up with a blank. And if you're trying to tell me that's where you were going, don't bother. Living mortals can't enter Annwfyn or Emania, unless they're married to an Otherworld king. Where were you off to, by the way?"

"We were travelling to Rheged to visit your younger brother, to, to..." My voice trailed away as invention failed me. There was no point in trying to hide Modwenna there now, when Gwydion had already discovered her. But I had to persuade him to let us leave. If I couldn't get her out of that abandoned kitchen—presumably it had once been a kitchen—Gwydion would kidnap her and her baby and hold them in one of his many fortresses awaiting Lleu's pleasure.

"To beg his aid against you and Lleu," supplied Modwenna, earning a nod of approval from Math and a look of blank-faced surprise from her husband. "He's expecting us, and unless you want to add another godling to the ranks of those already hunting you, I'd advise you to let us continue our journey."

Perhaps Gwydion recognised she was spinning a tale, and the bard in him appreciated her effort. His lips twitched, and his stance relaxed. "I haven't seen Euyd in an age. By all means, let us travel together."

Not ideal, but at least out on the open road we might have a chance to do... something. The question remained, what was Gwydion up to? Despite his barrage of questions about Lleu's whereabouts, he seemed to be acquiescing to our suggestions too readily. Perhaps he planned to divert our route by arcane means and capture Modwenna that way.

Would he dare? Just as Lleu and Arawan were evenly matched, so were he and Math. He was presently outnumbered, but that could be as much a handicap for Math as an advantage. If Meg and Blei barely recalled how to behave as humans, they might not be easily able to access their magic. Even if they could, there was a chance they couldn't control it. I could defend myself and fight back against him, but Yestin and Modwenna were defenceless in a magical conflict. Finally, to do battle in this confined space would present Gwydion with too many potential weapons—the fire, the timber table and benches, the window shutters. Even the bricks of the fireplace could become missiles launched by magic.

"Only you," I said, to be clear. "No one else."

He nodded. "Wait here. I'll organise an extra couple of horses." With a savage grin, he jerked his head towards Meg and Blei. "Better not make them travel in the cart anymore—I don't want to upset their fond mama."

I refrained from pointing out that one was his son. It seemed only Lleu mattered to him now.

When the packs had been restowed and I'd made Blei don Yestin's shirt, we set off once again in our own guises once more. Yestin seemed relieved to look like himself again, and Modwenna expressed herself glad to be rid of the veil. The horses seemed happier, too.

The road north to Caer Luil carried more traffic than that leading to Gwynedd, although it thinned when we reached Llifpwll.

On the second morning, after we'd broken our fast and were preparing to mount, Gwydion crooked a finger at Meg. She went to him, pouting, patently unhappy but without protest.

"I've a search to undertake in the Otherworld," he said, pinching her chin between finger and thumb and gazing into her eyes. "And I need you to keep an eye on this lot until I return. Make sure nobody deviates from the route and tries to hide from me. Am I clear?"

I started forwards, pacific intentions forgotten. "Get your hands off her!"

Gwydion smirked. Lady Mother, I wanted to rip it off his face, along with his skin. "Sweet Meg doesn't mind at all," he said. "Do you, sweetness?"

Meg looked down and shook her head, while Blei glowered in the background. "That goes for you too," added Gwydion, raising a finger, and Blei also studied the ground.

Seething, I clamped my lips shut, aware of Math's contained anger beside me. But if he could bide his time, so could I.

Gwydion then transformed into his kite form, lifted into the air, and vanished through an Otherworld veil, carrying the red feather with him. Why?

Standing beside the horse, considering possible scenarios, I said to Meg, "You can't disobey him, can you?"

She shook her head, looking miserable. I should have known Gwydion would retain a hold over them, or he wouldn't have changed them back so readily.

Math put a comforting arm around her shoulders. "You were more susceptible to being controlled by Gwydion's magic in beast form," he said. "When he transformed you, he obviously left that control in place." He hugged her tightly. "I'm sorry, cariad, little love. I'd free you if I could."

"Why can't you?" asked Yestin, pushing his questing horse away. He'd been in the habit of bribing her with an apple or carrot before we rode out every day. "Dylan told me once that only the mage who cast a spell can lift it, but surely you can override Gwydion? You're the king!"

Math shrugged. "Your confidence in me is warming, but unfortunately, I'm as bound by the rules as everyone else. Only Gwydion and Lleu are foolhardy enough to think they can break them, and that hubris will be their undoing. Eventually."

He released Meg and swung into the saddle. "We may as well do as Gwydion suggested, and ride. Lingering here will achieve nothing."

"But what's his aim?" I asked when I'd also mounted and brought my horse alongside his. "He said he'd scoured the Underworld already and found no trace of Lleu. Whatever inducements Arawn used to stop everybody's tongues must have been persuasive. Unsurprising, really. Gwydion is universally disliked, and there were many who'd delight in misleading him. They were probably laughing at him behind their hands."

"It's the feather," replied Math, his expression pensive. "He's tied its essence to Modwenna, and Modwenna is of Dafona's bloodline. That will call to Lleu and lure him out from wherever he's hiding. Because, as Gwydion has no doubt realised, it's possible that Lleu disappeared so thoroughly not because Arawn has him stashed somewhere, but because he's hiding from Arawn. He doesn't want to be found. But if anything can change his mind, the lure of reuniting with Caron will."

"I don't understand," said Modwenna, overhearing. Raw fear edged her voice. "Even if the prospect of kidnapping me and my daughter is enough to draw him here, won't Arawn find him as soon as he does? Why would he risk that? He'd have to be completely insane."

Behind her, Blei snorted. "I'll agree with that."

Mirthless laughter shook Math. "So would I, but I'm certain Gwydion has a plot to overcome all those objections. I just wish I knew what it was."

We rode in morose silence for a while, until the paved roads became a rarity and degenerated into muddy tracks across sometimes spectacular but treacherous terrain. Rocky crags towered above bleak moorlands, and an occasional fox darted across our path. Thick-coated, spindle-legged sheep and shaggy ponies could sometimes be glimpsed in the valleys below, among squat stone village buildings. Rivers and streams silvered the valley floor, and at stages along our route smoke rose from the blacksmiths' forges.

At dusk Gwydion returned, grim-visaged. I presumed his search had been unsuccessful, which made me feel a lot better. Better still, I heard the owls hooting above us as we made camp and settled down for the night. Only Modwenna glanced up quickly, then looked hurriedly away again. Nobody else paid them any attention, including Gwydion.

This pattern continued for almost a week. We passed the borders of Rheged, winding slowly through the uplands in the face of a biting wind. At least it didn't snow heavily. Misting rain might have made riding miserable, but there were advantages to journeying with a magician. Our clothes, hair, skin, and mounts remained dry, as did our belongings. Math's doing, of course, not Gwydion's. He showed no concern for anyone's comfort but his own.

I took advantage of his daily absences to quiz Meg and Blei about their experience. Had he harmed them? Was he cruel? At first Meg looked away and refused to answer, but Blei was less reticent.

"When is my father ever less than cruel? No, he didn't use the whips or prods or chains that form the repertoire of most bear tamers. He used magic—bespelled us to bend us to his will, so we'd dance and prance and juggle for him in front of all the crowds. And for what? The accolades. He thrives on attention; he can't live without it. He treated us like tools, or toys. I've met performing dogs who received more tenderness from their masters." He gave a short, bitter laugh. "My own father."

That was all he'd say to begin with, but each day I teased a little more information from him. From them both.

"It was because of Artio," Meg burst out a few days later, on a rare, bright day which held the first promise of spring. We'd stopped for lunch beneath an ancient ash tree, supping on a hare Math had caught in one of his magical traps, washed down with clear water from the neighbouring spring.

I glanced across at Blei. With all that had happened, we'd never got around to finishing that conversation. "What about her?" I asked.

He spread his hands and lifted one shoulder in a half-shrug. "I belong to her now. Or I did, before Father co-opted me for his travelling mummer's show." He looked at Math. "That's what I wanted to tell you, before everything turned to dragon dung. I was accepted into the junior ranks of her priesthood, and when I'd paid my prior debt to you, I was to leave Caer Dathyl." He grimaced. "Don't know how I'm going to accomplish that, now, though."

"But I thought she tried to kill you," I said, frowning. "It certainly looked like it."

A distant look stole over his face, like that of a man recalling a lover, and he smiled. "That's how her initiations work. She thrashes you, and if you survive, you're given the choice to stay, or to go. I chose to stay, but she knew what I'd done, how I'd betrayed Uncle Math in the forest. So before I could enter her service, I had to return to Caer

Dathyl and make my apologies and reparation. After all, Artio's in no hurry."

"And Gwydion absolutely hated that." Meg gathered the remains of our meal together and scraped a hole in the ground to bury the bones. "He viewed it as a personal insult that anyone, much less someone of his own blood, could prefer Artio over him. That's why he turned you into a bear rather than a wolf or a bird. He viewed it as punishment, and I suppose I just happened to be in the way."

I nodded. Ari had told me that Gwydion saw what he'd done to Blodeuedd the same way.

Math said, "You'll always be welcome at Caer Dathyl, whatever path you follow. And you'll always be one of Don's children, whether Gwydion repudiates you or not."

Blei sketched him a bow in acknowledgement. "Thank you, Uncle. I really appreciate that."

No more was said on that matter, and from then on, he and Meg contrived to ignore Gwydion as much as possible. Not difficult, when he seemed oblivious to their existence. To everyone, really. It seemed his search for his favourite son wasn't yielding results. Every night he returned more morose and ill-tempered, and every night the owls guarded our rest.

Until one dark evening, in drizzling rain under dark, clouded skies, Gwydion returned triumphant. As the kite glided to the ground and assumed the bright white glow that preceded his transformation back into a man, another bird followed—an eagle. He too morphed from avian to human shape, and straightening, stood beside Gwydion.

Brown-skinned, brown-haired, brown-eyed and of no more than average human height, the newcomer looked a little like Blei. I didn't remark on the resemblance, knowing neither would appreciate it.

The glamour held until he caught sight of Modwenna.

"Caron." He made the word a caress, and as the air around him brightened, the false visage disintegrated. If the eagle persona hadn't been enough to identify him, the wild golden hair, deep blue eyes and tawny skin removed any shred of doubt. Dropping to his knees before Modwenna, he placed his hands, gently, on either side of her protruding stomach and smiled up at her beatifically.

"No. Yseult. Her name is Yseult!" Modwenna flushed and pushed him away, then balled her fist and struck him, hard, against the side of his head.

Lleu dropped his hands and rocked back on his heels. I'd never seen anybody look quite so shocked.

"Get your filthy hands off my wife!" Barrelling forward, Yestin drove his knee, equally hard, into Lleu's back and hurled him to the ground. Surprise is often an underrated weapon. Before either Gwydion or Lleu could recover, I threw Modwenna's ill-fated basket at Gwydion, who was still standing, and pulled a pin from my hair to drive it into Lleu's earlobe. Blood pouring down the side of his neck, Lleu howled and rolled away from me.

"Modwenna, run!" I screamed, then ran toward the restive horses, calling over my shoulder, "Math!"

He didn't need my urging. He and Gwydion had already engaged, crimson mage balls shattering and shivering against violet, hissing, spitting, and sizzling as they met.

Unwisely, Yestin dived at Lleu, kicking and punching, and almost got a fireball in the gut for his pains. He survived only because Blei and Meg threw themselves in front of him, pushing him out of the way. Blei morphed into a wolf, while Meg muttered incantations in an attempt to douse Lleu's arcane fire.

We didn't bother with saddles. As soon as I'd bridled them, Modwenna and I flung ourselves onto our horses' backs and let them have their heads. They didn't need any encouragement, nor did the others. All six tore up the hill as if pursued by demons. Or battling gods.

"Blodeuedd, Lady Blodeuedd!" yelled Modwenna, her long brown hair flying behind her. With an almighty roar, Lleu threw Blei and Meg away from him and came after us. Could he run as fast as a terrified horse?

Thankfully, I never found out. No sooner had the second plea left Modwenna's lips than the owls descended. Soundless, deadly, their talons extended, they landed on Lleu, one on each shoulder. Beaks ripping, claws shredding, they tore into him as if he were their prey.

32

ARAWN

We learned of Wynne and Math's planned journey with Modwenna and Yestin as soon as we returned from Caer Sidi. Hearing that Math intended to transform the appearances of everyone in the travelling party reassured me. I worried about their safety, even with Math's protection, and decided to add my own protection—or at least, surveillance—to his.

Secure in the hollow of my oak tree, with Goronwy's comforting presence by my side, I viewed the change with fascination. I'd often seen him and Gwydion change their shapes, and had watched with horror as the spell I'd wrought did the same thing, less kindly, to Lleu. Even to one godborn, as I was, the process appeared mystical. To humankind, it must have been a thing of wonder.

Owlsight, however, allowed me to see deeper. Beyond the blurring I'd witnessed before, threads of colour lurked. They unwound from a tiny central crux of white light—the person's or creature's soul, the core of their being—and rewound into a different shape. No wonder a large man like Math could become a raven. We were all little more than thought.

A similar process took place for the horses, making them look like tough little Cymric ponies instead of steeds trained for battle.

Because tawny owls rarely flew during daylight hours, Goronwy and I thought it wisest to follow them at night so as not to raise suspicion, beginning at dusk and resting at dawn. I had no fear that we might lose track of them; we knew the road they intended to travel, and like all owls could see a great distance ahead.

Several times, when setting up or dismantling their campsite, Wynne looked up at us with a knowing smile but didn't make contact. Modwenna was less circumspect. Early one morning we were both out searching: she for a secluded spot to relieve herself, me for a comfortable resting hollow in which Goronwy and I could spend our day. She glanced up and saw me.

The walls of Devau township weren't too far distant; they'd reach it within a couple of days. Altogether, they had covered about fifty miles as the owl flies, although it was further on horseback. Being able to glide about the sky without negotiating around hills, rocks, trees, or rivers was a great boon. I understood why Math and his kin were so fond of avian avatars.

"Lady Blodeuedd!" exclaimed Modwenna as she dropped her skirts and rose hastily to her feet. She used the old pronunciation, I noted with approval, but she did so far too loudly.

"Hush," I sent, fluttering to a lower branch. Goronwy waited patiently above me. *"Do you want everybody else to know I'm here? Try just thinking the words to me."* It worked for me and the godborn; perhaps it would for her too.

She closed her eyes and scrunched her face into a forbidding frown, clasping her hands before her. After several heartbeats, her face cleared. Looking up at me hopefully, she asked, aloud, "Did it work?"

"No, you just looked constipated." She spluttered in annoyance, and I wished I could convey laughter. *"I'm joking! You're always beautiful. But if we're to talk regularly—which I would very much like to do—you'll need to wait until you're alone. And speak as softly as you can. Barely a murmur will be enough. I have phenomenal hearing."*

"All right. Like this?" Her voice was so low that somebody standing directly beside her would have had to strain to hear. That would have kept my presence a secret from Yestin, but I wasn't certain about Math or Wynne.

I uttered a soft hoot of approval. *"Exactly like that."*

"But why don't you want anyone else to know you're here?" murmured Modwenna, smoothing her skirts and looking around.

"I suspect Wynne—that is, Queen Goewin—already does, and so far, has said nothing to her husband. It's him I'm worried about. He'd order

me to go back, I'm sure, saying that looking for Gwydion's too dangerous for me. I couldn't obey, and I don't want to offend him by refusing."

Because offending him would probably result in me and Goronwy being removed by force. I didn't say that, however. Pretending concern for his feelings presented me in a much better light. Modwenna looked unconvinced but shrugged and agreed to my terms.

So, the pattern continued, uninterrupted, until we reached Devau. Huddled in the poor shelter offered by a pair of chimneys, I watched Gwydion lead the travellers into the adjoining building. Sound travels well through chimneys. I heard everything that was said, and it filled me with misgiving. When I joined Goronwy in the tree he'd selected for our rest and filled him in, he suggested we quit our surveillance.

Of course, I refused. Beyond a single "twoo" of dissent, he made no further comment, but hid his face under his wing and slept for the rest of the day.

The following night, when the company struck out again for Rheged, I voiced my concerns to Modwenna, whom I found in a small copse of trees.

"You're lucky I'm pregnant." She leaned against the trunk of a straggly birch tree. "Otherwise, everyone might wonder why I need to pee so often."

"We wouldn't be here to begin with, if you weren't." I shuffled sideways along my branch and ruffled my feathers. *"And you'll have to be extra careful from now on. Gwydion's presence alarms me, and I don't trust either of those young ones."*

She folded her arms and pursed her lips. "I agree about Gwydion, but the others seem nice. I think they're afraid of him."

"Everybody's afraid of him," I snapped, or tried to. It sounded that way in my head, but I was uncertain how she heard it. I knew too little about the process. *"As for the other two, appearances can be misleading. I've met Bleiddwn before, when he and his brothers tried to kill me. They murdered two of my people and crippled Cynar. I don't know how Math can trust him. I can't fathom why he's so lenient towards Gwydion, either."*

Modwenna made soothing noises and promised to keep me updated. Hearing that Gwydion had only to snap his fingers for those two to revert to his playthings did nothing to relieve my anxiety. When I heard about his daily forays into the unknown, searching for Lleu, I decided to follow.

At first I slunk through the tree branches instead of soaring across the heavens, trying to avoid his notice. It soon became apparent that my precautions weren't needed. Gwydion thought he owned the sky. The only time he paid any attention to other birds was when, faced with a lack of carrion left by other predators, he was forced to hunt. Even then, he fed on mice, voles, or insects rather than small birds. They seemed to be a last resort, probably because catching them took effort.

Things did not go as I'd planned. Again, my experience was too limited. I'd only ever visited Otherworld strongholds the same way mortals did—through the stone circles. My foray through the portal in the Sun Temple had been quite accidental. So, when Gwydion opened a slit in the veil by crying a Word of power, I was a little shocked that I not only heard but understood it.

Once both he and the portal had vanished and I faced empty sky, I considered. How was I to utter the Word, without a human voice? Gwydion had done so while in kite form. I'd still heard the Word. So must have the Elder Gods, or who or whatever was in charge of such things. I circled the area once, twice, and hooted, long and loud, projecting the Word in my mind.

Ahead and a little to the left, a rent appeared in reality. The void had opened for me. Before it could close again, before somebody out there realised there'd been a mistake, I darted through.

That was when things began falling apart.

Before it closed, another feathered form swept up from the trees below and followed, nipping at my tail feathers. He only just made it; the portal narrowly missed amputating his own tail when it snapped shut in his wake.

I alighted on a—rock?—column?—black obsidian spire of—something, folded my wings and glared at him. "*Goronwy! You shouldn't be here. Why did you come?*"

Head twisting from side to side, he settled above me. "*You can't expect me to watch you go flitting off into the blue after that maniac and do nothing. Of course I followed.*" His head rotated further, taking in our surroundings. "*Where are we, and what are we sitting on?*"

"*I don't know. We're somewhere in the Otherworld, obviously.*"

"A brilliant deduction. I was hoping for something more specific."

"Don't be snide, it doesn't suit you." He hooted derisively, and I softened my tone. *"I appreciate your concern, cariad, but I didn't want to put you in danger. That's why I didn't tell you what I was planning."*

Anxiety flooded through the link between us. *"What about putting yourself in danger? Immortality doesn't bestow invulnerability. You realise that, don't you? Gwydion could rip you apart and condemn you to live a half-life forever, crippled, in pain. Or transform you into a frog."*

"Sorry, cariad. I promise not to do it again." Contrite, I sent him love and reassurance along with my pledge. I had no qualms about making it, because I knew the events which had brought me here, wherever here was, would likely never recur.

Rotating my neck to its fullest extent, I looked around, hoping for clues to our whereabouts. Before Arianrhod had taken me to Emania, my only contact with the Otherworld had been a brief sojourn in Caer Dathyl when I was newly made, and my trips to her two castles. I understood it was enormous—vaster than I could comprehend—but that was all I knew.

The landscape looked similar to Cymry, except for the brilliant sunshine replacing cloudy skies, and pleasantly warm air. A patchwork of green fields surrounded us; beyond them, shrouded forests and glittering silver streams faded to misty blue hills. The buildings were different, too—more elaborate than anything I'd ever seen. To the left sprawled a castle built of warm golden stone, and to the right the blue roofs and brightly painted columns of a temple nestled among flowering trees and colourful plants. White-capped mountains crowded the horizon, majestic and serene.

"Hello, Blodeuwedd."

The voice came from everywhere and nowhere, and the rock beneath my claws leaked away into smoke. I squawked in dismay, flapping wildly. Goronwy, burn him, retained enough presence of mind to glide gracefully to the ground.

The voice gathered substance, revealing the black-clad, imposing figure of Arawn, whom I'd last seen in the Moonlands of Emania. Which meant that this must be Annwfyn, the realm of the dead.

Many cultures called it the Underworld. Some saw it as a gloomy place, a lightless underground cavern where the dead ate only dust.

Others portrayed a hazardous, unpredictable seat of judgement, or, at the opposite end of the scale, a land of never-ending pleasure.

Of these, Gwydion's memories informed me, Arawn's realm most closely resembled the last. A world of eternal summer, it lay beneath a brilliant moon or clear blue skies, where the feasts were never-ending, and the dead were free of fear. But only the godborn dwelt there permanently. For most humankind, it was a waystation, a place to decipher the lessons of their last life and make plans for the next one.

Goronwy ducked his head, spreading his wings along the ground in a fair approximation of a bow. *"My lord."*

I offered a perfunctory nod. *"I don't understand. Why would Gwydion come here? I thought he was avoiding you."*

The Underworld Lord chuckled, a surprisingly friendly sound. Colour bled into his raiment, changing it from lightless black to dark grey to slate blue. "You don't understand how any of this works, do you, Flowerbride? Or should it be Owlbride, now? Only those with innate abilities can forge a portal between Otherworld and mortal realms, which describes Gwydion, but not you. The portal he opened led elsewhere, most likely to somewhere in the mortal world. But your willingness to speak the key impressed me, so I intervened to let you into mine."

"You mean Gwydion's not here?"

"I'm afraid not."

I wasn't sure if I wanted to know but had to ask anyway. *"Then why am I?"*

"I need your help, little owl. Come along."

He clapped his hands sharply, and the black smoke swirled around us. When it cleared, we stood in an echoing chamber lined with mirrors and lit by floating balls of coloured light: gold, carmine, and pale rose. Twisting patterns in gold and silver covered the walls, and the floor was polished black marble.

Arawn gestured to a group of black leather couches in the centre of the room, around a circular table of heavy, aged oak. His décor fitted the Underworld theme. "Please, take a seat."

As if we still walked as humans and could sit at the table with him. Cautiously, we complied as best we could, settling on the chair backs.

I fluffed my feathers. *"What sort of help are you after? And where's Lleu? Have you locked him up somewhere?"*

Arawn's lopsided grin was wry. "No. He's currently sliding down sunbeams and hiding in cloudbursts, as far as I can tell. We have sunshine here too, as you'll have noticed. This is the land of promise."

Aware of a burst of curiosity from Goronwy, I swivelled my head to glare him into silence. He pecked at a foot, avoiding my gaze and closing his mind to me.

Huffing, I turned back to Arawn. *"Do you mean you don't know where Lleu is, even though you brought him back here with you? Surely someone as powerful as you knows what's going on in his own realm."*

"I'm aware of the movements of all my subjects, but Lleu isn't one of them, and isn't bound by Annwfyn's rules. He's a fellow god, albeit of a younger generation. I blush to admit it, but he outfoxed me. Once we'd reached my palace, I had to relax my shadow bindings in order to craft a prison for him. I assumed the weight of Annwfyn would limit his power. That was a mistake. As soon as the bonds fell away, he seized his opportunity and vanished in a dazzle of sunlight."

Weight of Annwfyn? Did that mean the entire realm was cloaked in a uniform power? A frightening thought. Goronwy's curiosity spiked higher, but I refused to look at him.

"Can't you track Lleu down, somehow?" I asked.

Half-seen shadows slid and shifted as Arawn lifted one shoulder. "I could set my hounds on him, but I don't want him damaged. Don't want to upset Lady Don. If it were Gwydion, on the other hand..."

I wouldn't object to seeing either of them bitten. *"Well, I don't know what you expect from me, if the great Afterworld lord himself can't find Lleu. He could be anywhere by now. His whereabouts have even confounded Gwydion, who knows him better than anyone."*

"But Gwydion doesn't truly understand love, only obsession." Stretched at ease on the opposite side of the table, Arawn laid his arm along the back of the chair beside him and fixed me with a fathomless dark gaze. "Whereas you once told Math that you repudiated all his plans for you and instead chose love. For your mate, who now sits beside you. For your friends, for your people, for the unborn child of your friend. And it's his love for Caron that now drives Lleu into madness. A warped, unsound love, perhaps, but still purer than anything ever felt by Gwydion, I suspect."

Unable to shrug, I bobbed my head and lifted one wing. *"I still don't know what to suggest that both of you wouldn't have already considered.*

Lleu and his lover never ventured outside Ardudwy, so if you've searched every inch of the cantref, that line of enquiry yields nothing. I don't know anywhere else that connects Lleu with Caron."

Arawn sighed. "My wife insists Caron's the link, and you can offer me insight. She thought the Cynfal might be the answer, as that's where they used to meet. But I've visited Caron's memorial stone and placed markers which would alert me if Lleu turned up there. He never has."

"Twoo," I said doubtfully. *"He'd be more likely to look for her at the waterfall, the place where she made her vow. My handmaids told me the story."*

"I agree." Goronwy looked up and stretched his neck sideways. *"My first, indelible memories of Blodeuedd are of a rooftop garden in winter, and violets at our feet. If I were to seek her in the afterlife, hoping she'd find me, that's where I would go. Not her grave, or her memorial. Somewhere that connected us in life, not in death."*

"Ah, perhaps you have something there." Arawn nodded slowly in acknowledgement, steepled his fingers, and pressed them under his chin. "Do you know where to find this waterfall?"

I nodded, then realised that could signify any number of responses and added, *"Yes."*

Arawn didn't waste words. A negligent wave of his hand, and the scene wavered around me again. No visible portal appeared to signal our movement from Annwfyn back to mortal Ardudwy, but when the world steadied, blue skies had ceded to grey. The air was also noticeably cooler and filled with the sounds of life. Small animals scuttling, insects humming, birds chirping, water splashing. I hadn't realised until then that all those things had been absent in Annwfyn.

We hovered in the air above a dark, rock-strewn ravine. The River Cynfal, swollen by recent rains, thundered over the mossy walls of the gorge, wreathing them in spray. I flapped vigorously, climbing through the air to the head of the falls. Alighting on a rock, I looked down. Apart from the rabbits and foxes, the beetles and dragonflies, the wrens, thrushes, waxwings and other small birds, nothing stirred. Only the ever-moving water, forming and reforming in lacework patterns as it crashed and tumbled over the rocks.

"There's nobody here." I fluttered down to perch on an overhanging tree branch and peered into the gorge.

Arawn hung in the air, garlanded with mist. *"Indeed. It was an excellent theory, but I fear you were incorrect."*

"No," Goronwy insisted, *"look. What's down there, beside that yellow creeper?"* He dived, coming to rest on a cluster of Trailing Tormentil flowers, which coated the rocks in a thick mesh of fleshy leaves and winding roots. Probing with his beak, he withdrew a tiny curl of creamy white fluff.

None but an owl or a god would have found it—or recognised the species of bird it had come from. These were the downy barbs from a red kite's tail-feather.

Gwydion's feather. Cara's feather: the plume at the root of so much of the trickster's latest mischief.

"We're too late," I exclaimed. *"Gwydion's been here, found Lleu, and given him the feather which will lead him to Modwenna!"*

"Go! Fly," said Arawn. "My power in this realm is diminished; I can't transport you there. But if you wish to save your friend's child from Lleu's twisted designs, you must return to Rheged with all speed. I'll follow as soon as I can."

He wrapped himself in shadow and vanished.

33

EXILE

F ar below, Modwenna screamed my name.

She and Wynne threw themselves onto the backs of their horses and followed the other panicked beasts now streaming up the hill. Behind them rode Yestin, without reins or saddle. Multicoloured lights flared in the background, accompanied by reverberating thunder, thrown by a pair of battling mages.

In concert, Goronwy and I dived, skimming past Modwenna. Together we attacked the man of fire who advanced towards the two fugitives—the glowing figure of Lleu.

He threw up his hands, trying to fend us off. I struck harder, deeper, rending him with beak and claws. In my mind I held an image of Lleu being struck by the spear, screaming, bleeding, changing into an eagle. Goronwy and I had hurt him then; surely, we could do so again. But on that long-ago day, the very stars had been aligned against him. The present season wasn't summer, and there were no arrows of the sun god shooting through the night sky. Every wound we made in Lleu's flesh healed between one breath and the next.

He ducked, twisting away from me, and reaching up one brawny hand, closed it tight around my neck. "I wonder what roasted owl tastes like?" His laughter held venom and a trace of insanity. "Let's find out."

"Nooo!" With a screech of anguish, Goronwy ceased raking his talons down Lleu's back and drew away, wings flapping wildly. Turning, he dived straight into my tormentor's face.

Unlike the dragons of legend, Lleu was no fire-breather. Although he could channel heat and flame through his entire body, he used his hands to direct the flow. He also needed to see what he was doing.

Perhaps Goronwy realised this; perhaps he was driven solely by the owl's instinct to stab and crush. He drove his wicked, hooked bill into Lleu's right eye.

With a roar of mingled pain and anger, Lleu released me. Blood flowed freely down his cheek, mixed with glistening tears, before the cauterising fire did its healing work.

The riderless horses had vanished over the crest of the hill. So had Modwenna and Yestin, but Wynne had turned around and back-tracked, heading towards us. To aid Math, I presumed. Unlike in a sword fight, neither combatant moved a great deal, but stood with legs planted apart and their hands describing arcs and slashes, alternating between balled fists and open palms. The two young ones, Meghan and Bleiddwn, stood ineffectually on the side lines, helping neither side. That Gwydion's son should prove a coward didn't surprise me, but I'd expected better of Math and Wynne's daughter.

Before she reached either of them, or before Lleu could recover enough to retaliate, a rent appeared in the sky just above the clashing magicians. From a bright white slit, it widened enough to allow a man to pass through. Instead, black smoke poured from it. Darkness covered the land. Between one breath and the next, it had blocked the daylight and dimmed Lleu's fire.

Dimmed, but not extinguished. He heeled away from Goronwy and threw pulses of flame towards us both.

"Blodeuwedd, get down." Wynne bypassed her husband and bar-relled straight towards me, swiping me to the earth and tangling my claws in her hair. We both crashed into the grass, shedding wisps of hair and feathers, as flame curvetted above us. Goronwy swerved the other way, but not before Lleu's fist hit him on the side of the head. He crumpled to the ground.

"Goronwy!" I flapped to his side, dancing from one foot to the other. Wynne knelt where she'd landed, panting.

"I'm alright, I think. Just stunned. Watch out!" Another fireball streaked by us, narrowly missing my head.

"Enough!" The voice, deep and resonant, issued from within the smoke. I recognised it instantly as Arawn's—a voice that could only belong to a god. Caught in his web of dark magic, everybody except Math and Gwydion became very still.

A form moved slowly out of the shadows, too slight to be Arawn. At first wraithlike and insubstantial, it solidified as it advanced towards Lleu.

"Lleu, my darling, stop. Please, stop." The sound was soft and hesitant, barely audible. With a lighter register than the first, it was unmistakably a woman's voice, and Lleu turned towards it, his eyes wide and his lips slightly parted.

I knew that voice, too. This was a woman I'd once called my friend, who had betrayed me in my husband's bed. She'd forsaken everyone who'd once loved her and ended her life by swallowing poison.

"Caron! Is it really you?" The glow around Lleu flared again into brilliant life. He stepped towards the swirling darkness, his arms outstretched in welcome.

"Caron," said the apparition, her voice gaining in strength and volume. "Gwenavala. Arlais. You know the names don't really matter. I'll be someone else next time, my love."

The shadows fused to form a human outline, faceless still, but recognisably female. Tall and curvaceous, her long black hair writhed and fanned around her, lifted by an unseen breeze. Lleu halted as if gripped by uncertainty, and the woman-shape closed the gap between them.

His hands reached for hers. As they linked, the smoky gloom around her cleared, revealing clear, tanned skin and grey eyes as soft as a dove's wing. Her hair remained inky black.

"Arawn, what are you doing?" Gwydion moved at last, although he didn't turn his back on Math.

Both Wynne and I leapt towards him, but before either could engage, Gwydion flipped his hand. The girl called Meghan careened into her mother. Bleiddwn, the one I called wolf-boy, grabbed me by the legs. An owl's best weapons are her legs and talons. I shrieked, effectively hobbled, and Bleiddwn swung me around several times before letting go.

I tumbled through the air, disoriented and unable to right myself. Green earth rose up to greet me and I ploughed, beak-first, through the grass and into the loam. Stunned, I rolled over, tucked my feet under me and remained where I was.

So did Wynne, folding her legs more comfortably beneath her and gazing, round-eyed, at Arawn. Her daughter cast a rancorous glance at Gwydion and stomped back to Bleiddwn's side. Something about her evident reluctance moved me once more to pity. I'd been wrong about those two. They were also Gwydion's victims.

"I said, enough!" No longer smooth and controlled, Arawn's voice boomed through the valleys and bounced from one hill to the next like a clarion of doom. Even Math and Gwydion took notice, dropping their hands to their sides.

The Underworld Lord shed his shadows and manifested fully into the mortal realm. Perhaps he'd been right when he said his powers weren't at their peak in our world, but he still put on an impressive performance. Twice man-height or more, he hovered in the air above the hill's summit, arms crossed on his chest and swathed all in black.

"Good. Now that I have your attention, I've an edict to enforce." Without unfolding his arms, he lifted one hand. A red kite's feather twirled between his fingers, dwarfed by his immensity. It looked no larger than a fine plume of down.

Gwydion snarled and bunched his fists, and Lleu pulsed with light. He stopped short of bursting into flame, however, perhaps because of the woman, or the woman's spirit, whose hand still rested in his.

"An interesting little spell," continued Arawn, shrinking to normal dimensions before releasing the feather. He pursed his lips and blew, sending it spiralling into the air. "Took me a while to untangle it, but in the end I did. Naturally." He descended to ground level and strolled casually towards me. "Your friend Modwenna ferch Dea and her husband are safe in the care of Math's nephew by now. The one most favoured by Don. Euyd, I believe he's called."

Reaching the spot where I lay, he reached a hand down and lifted me onto his shoulder. Next, he did the same for Goronwy. Wynne told me later that we looked like some bizarre coat of arms, a pair of tawny owls facing each other with the lord of darkness between us.

"Binding someone's essence to an object is a lot easier than you might think," continued Arawn, advancing relentlessly towards Lleu. "It's certainly within Gwydion's capabilities. A strand of hair, a fingernail, a drop of saliva from a glass's rim; any of those would work, but the first would have been the most likely.

"Cara was his agent, communicating with him through the feathers. He knew exactly how many there were, and he knew where the last one was hidden. So did she, and at his direction bound something of Modwenna's to it when she stole the basket from Modwenna's room. Thus ensuring Gwydion would be able to find her whenever he needed to. Why did he need to? To form a connection with the soul of Caron and introduce her to her new host."

"That's why she calmed so quickly when most of the feathers were ruined," I said, as enlightenment dawned. *"She knew Gwydion only needed one, by then. She mustn't have known about that at the beginning—she became almost hysterical when I threatened to destroy them."*

Nobody paid me any attention. "You've returned my love to me." Lleu's voice held wonder, a blend of astonishment and golden delight. "You swore you wouldn't, but you did."

Arawn shook his head, ruffling my feathers.

The ghost of Arlais, smiling sadly, touched a finger to Lleu's cheek. "No, my love. I'm sorry, but I can't stay. The Lord of Death spoke truly when he told you my suicide destroyed my vow. I can't return to you, at least not yet. He won't allow it."

Arawn's answering chuckle reverberated through the hills, bouncing from rock to rock and sweeping across the valleys. "Very true. Not for a couple of millennia or so."

"Two?" I bent forward and twisted to look into his eyes. *"You said one, before."*

"That was before your benighted ex-spouse spat in my face and led me on a merry dance through kingdom after kingdom. I can't let that pass. Where would we be if gods and spirits thought they could defy and insult the Underworld Lord with impunity?" He lifted his eyebrows, first at Lleu, then at Caron-Arlais. "But, if you're both good—and I mean very, very good—while serving your penance, I'll allow you to reunite when your time is done. Agreed?"

"No!" Lleu let go of his lover's hand and clasped her to him, resting his chin on her head. She wound her arms around his waist, her face buried against his chest. "That's horse dung. You can't just keep doubling the sentence whenever anyone disagrees with you."

More booming laughter, without any hint of mirth. "Foolish, foolish little godling. Yes, I can. For one thing, Arlais, or Caron, or whatever you want to call her, is dead. I rule the dead, therefore I rule her.

And as for you, I outrank you in terms of godhood. I'm one of the Elder Gods, who created the universe and all its dimensions."

Lleu lifted his chin, the movement stirring Arlais's hair. "So? I might belong to a younger generation, but my power's just as great as yours. I'm not afraid to dance with you again."

Arawn began circling, walking in decreasing circles around Lleu before coming to a stop. They now stood face to face, each the antithesis of the other. Light and shadow, bright sunshine, and the dark depths of night.

"Gods, Lleu. Plural. You've alienated most of your kin, even your brothers. Your only ally is Gwydion. Whereas I can call upon any number of my brethren for assistance if I choose to, including your grandparents."

He lifted both hands to a level with his shoulders, and taking his meaning, Goronwy and I stepped onto them. As Arawn flung wide his hands, we launched into the air.

"You couldn't. You wouldn't. Calling the Elder Gods to battle would shake the foundations of the world," Math protested.

I circled around him, before gliding down to land on a rock a few feet away. Buoyed by the updrafts, Goronwy continued in flight.

Arawn nodded. "Indeed, and even a nihilist like Gwydion doesn't want that to happen. Do you, Trickster?"

Gwydion rubbed his hands together and snuffed out the crimson nimbus around them, before shoving one into a pocket in his vest. "I just want my son to be happy," he grated. "This woman makes him happy, therefore I'll do everything I can to keep them together. Two thousand years is too long to wait, I'm afraid. I wonder if this might speed things up?"

Withdrawing his hand from his pocket, he held up a small, cloudy-green glass bottle. Popping the glass stopper free, he shook the container, and a small quantity of fine ivory powder drifted upward.

With a hum of astonishment, Wynne drew in a ragged breath. She shot to her feet and ran towards them. Math growled, deep in his throat, and spun around to grab at the bottle.

Instead of trying to keep it from him, Gwydion threw up his hand, sending half the contents flying upward. Golden motes of dust floated around us before settling on Math, light as thistledown and yet somehow weighty. Dangerous.

Squawking in fright, I lifted into the air to join Goronwy, high above the unnatural, settling dust.

"Give me that!" Below me, Wynne tried to snatch it from Gwydion, and stopped, choking, as he tilted the bottle. More of the glittering stuff drifted over her head and shoulders. Her face went blank, and she blinked at him, slowly. So, so slowly.

"No, don't. I know what..." Her voice faded and trailed away, before she closed her eyes and crumpled slowly to the ground. Oddly unnatural, her movement also seemed slow, as if she were consciously controlling her fall. I doubted that was the case, though.

"Wynne!" Math caught her and tried to lever her upright, but his motions, too, looked as if he was wading through molasses. Eventually, he lowered her to the ground and knelt at her side.

"Dragon dust?" roared Arawn, expanding again.

I veered away, afraid he'd bump into me, although that would have been ridiculous. Despite being twice as tall as the grandfather oaks, we owls still soared far above him. Such was his presence, though, that he made it feel possible.

"Dragon dust?" he repeated, even louder. I wished he wouldn't shout. Owls could hear a mouse miles away and see almost as acutely, especially in dim light. "You frivolous bloody bard, where in Annwfyn did you get dragon bone dust from?" His outline shimmered, and his shadows wisped from smoke into fine mist.

A delighted smile spread across Gwydion's face. "That would be telling. I can get more of it, too."

"The...cave." Math's speech dragged, as if each word was an effort.

Gwydion laughed. "That's right. When you and Lleu fought, the reverberations unsettled the stones you'd laid across the entrance. I felt them shift. When I went back, I was somewhat perturbed to find not much remained. That was unkind of you, Uncle, if clever. But I still felt—something. An echo of dragon essence. After a bit of a search, I discovered some dust had drifted above the tide line, and was sitting there, waiting for me. Not a huge quantity, but enough."

All eyes fastened on him as he waved the bottle, swirling the remainder of the dust. "The thing is, although I can feel the strength of its magic, I have no idea what it does. But I think Arawn can tell me. Am I right?"

The gigantic form of the Underworld Lord began to disintegrate.

"Perhaps, but I'm not about to enlighten you, Trickster." He reached down, lifted both Lleu and Arlais in one huge fist, and all three disappeared.

Gwydion swore, re-stoppered the bottle, and created a portal to fling himself after them.

34

HOUNDS

Silence fell following Gwydion's departure. Several long moments passed, followed by several more. Still, no one moved.

"You don't suppose they've all been turned into statues, do you?" asked Goronwy, sliding past me on a cushion of air.

Mother Goddess, perhaps they had. I dived, coming to rest on Math's shoulder. He didn't move, didn't respond to my presence.

"He's still breathing. They all are," said Goronwy, alighting on the same rock I'd used before.

"It's the dust. I—I think it slows time, somehow."

I looked around to see Meghan coming towards us, Bleiddwn at her side. Unlike Modwenna, these two could obviously understand mental speech.

Wolf-boy nodded. "It affected us, too, but not nearly as much. We only caught a little of it, but Father practically coated Uncle Math and Aunt Wynne in the stuff. Perhaps it will wear off if we can just get them home. That is, if there's anything left of it."

I hooted, bobbing my head. *"Arianrhod mentioned that. Lleu attacked Math's castle, didn't he?"*

Meghan nodded and gave a brief synopsis of recent events in Caer Dathyl. "There were no lives lost, but Caer Dathyl now lies in ruins."

"And then," Bleiddwn added bitterly, "Gwydion turned us both into bears."

"What will you do now?" I asked.

Meghan shrugged. "First, take Mam and Da back to Caer Dathyl, and see if the healers can restore them. Then help with the clean-up, and hope Gwydion doesn't come looking for us. Because if he does, we'll have no choice but to obey him. I hate, hate, hate to admit it, but in essence, Blei and I are still his trained bears. His slaves."

In all the turmoil which followed Lleu's forced departure from this earth, one thing at least brought me comfort. Arawn had spoken truly: Euyd ap Don had welcomed Modwenna and Yestin and offered them sanctuary in his castle in Rheged. Declaring herself to be heartily sick of travelling, Modwenna wanted to turn around and return home to Ardudwy immediately, but Euyd counselled caution.

As Math had pointed out, Lleu was not the only god to represent the sun. Others kept the heavenly fire burning, from Lugh Lamfada in the west to Xu Kai far in the east. There were hundreds of them, said Euyd, and he knew all their names. I couldn't even pronounce most of them. Some scorned interaction with mortals and applauded Arawn's decision to exile Lleu. They viewed the affair with Caron, in all her incarnations, as heresy.

But others disagreed with that judgement, and the heavens boiled with their fury.

"More rain coming." High on the ramparts, Yestin scanned the heavy grey skies of early morning and looked back over his shoulder at Euyd. "I'm sorry to presume on your kindness, my lord, but it's terrible weather for travelling. The roads deteriorate daily, so I'm told."

"I'm happy to have you stay here for as long as you need to," Euyd replied, and glanced up at me on my rooftop perch. "Come down, Lady Blodeuewedd. You have a visitor."

Although choosing to live in the mortal realm most of the time, Euyd had harked back to the Otherworld when building his fortress. The stone and earthen walls set hard against the hillside appeared outwardly little different from the caers of other local lords. But the interior ran deep within the hill, leading to palatial rooms and winding ways reminiscent of Caer Dathyl. So Modwenna had told me. I preferred the open spaces, and the many trees which lined the banks of the river flowing to the western sea.

"Thank you, but they can't stay forever." I bobbed my head for emphasis. *"Cynar and the others will have heard about the fight between Arawn and Lleu; the whole countryside's buzzing with it. We need to let them know these two are unharmed, but I can't fly that far in this weather to deliver the news. Owls get waterlogged too quickly. Besides, unlike Gwenhwyfar, I'm not an oversized courier pigeon."*

Euyd, who looked like a dark-eyed, less haughty version of Gwydion, smiled, and translated the first part of my comment for Yestin. He left out my complaint. "We will endeavour to let them know and help the young couple return. But I mentioned a visitor. Dylan's here to offer a solution. "He walked out of the sea this morning, not long after Yestin and Modwenna arrived."

Dylan! I swooped down, chirping excitedly. *"Where?"*

"Here I am." He stepped from a shadowed doorway, his wild, bright hair forming an aureole around his head, and a foam of white lace spilling over the collar of his green leather jerkin. "Hello, Blodeuwedd. You don't mind if I use that name, do you? You are indisputably an owl, now. Still beautiful, though."

"No, I don't mind." My only possible objection, that the name had been given me by Gwydion, didn't really hold weight, because so had the original. I settled on Dylan's shoulder, hopping from foot to foot and cooing. *"It's good to see you again. What's this solution you've found?"*

"I'll take them home by ship," he said, stroking my head feathers. *"Sea Wolf* can withstand conditions which would sink other vessels. We'll leave as soon as the rain eases and the wind drops." He held out a hand to catch the first raindrops as they spattered down. "Which might not be today. We should go back inside. Are you coming, Blodeuwedd?"

"I prefer the forest. Goronwy found a cosy hollow for us. I'll join him."

"Do that," said Euyd as he turned toward the stairs, "but you should both return here at sunset. I plan to go to Caer Dathyl to find out what happened to Uncle Math and Aunt Wynne and thought you might wish to join me."

I'd like nothing more. "*Of course. But how? I haven't noticed any stone circles hereabouts.*"

He paused in the doorway, a crooked grin splitting his face. "Caer Gwarchodwr is more than it seems, as I believe Modwenna has told you. There are passages within the hills leading straight to the Otherworld. We'll be there in no time. Unfortunately, she can't take those paths at present, but I believe you know that."

I nodded—one of the few human expressions left to me—and took wing before the downpour began. To my surprise, Goronwy didn't offer any objection to Euyd's proposal. Even as a man, he'd preferred to be outdoors, and since living in feathered form he'd developed a strong dislike of entering houses or other structures. But he hated rain, and flying over bodies of water, just as much as I did.

"*Something bothers me,*" he said as we cuddled together, waiting for the rain to clear or at least decrease to a drizzle. "*If the foreign gods are so bothered by Lleu's banishment, why didn't they react the same way when I speared him? Did they not notice he'd become an eagle?*"

I'd discussed this with Euyd earlier. "*He remained on the earth plane and could still fulfil his function, apparently. Also, Euyd thinks some might be jealous, more than angry. They'd love to spend a few centuries swimming in fire instead of attending to the needs of humanity. And then there's the part played by Arawn. Having one of their own defeated by an Underworld god doesn't sit well with them either, it seems.*"

Goronwy gave a low hoot of derision and settled to sleep with his head under his wing. I followed his example. The events of the last couple of days had disturbed my sleep patterns, and I needed to catch up on my rest.

Luckily, our trek through the hidden ways hollowed into the hills was of short duration, because I did not enjoy it. Faced with stone, narrow and winding, they felt small and tight. The eerie darkness didn't bother me greatly, but the oppressiveness did. Goronwy seemed content to remain perched on Euyd's shoulder, but I needed to spread my wings now and then. Unfortunately, I couldn't go too far each time, because I couldn't tell where I was.

Not due to the lack of light—Arianrhod's gift of colour vision hadn't diminished my ability to see well in the dark. But although these ways shared none of Caer Dathyl's beauty, they were alike in that their contours changed randomly between one breath and the next. Without Euyd to guide us, we might have been lost in there for eternity. I kept scanning the paved floor, fully expecting to see the bones of other unfortunate travellers. None appeared.

After several spiralling turns which I was convinced must send us back to our point of origin, we emerged into the stableyard of Caer Dathyl. It was just as I remembered: a large rectangular space overlooked by a tall wooden barn, immaculately clean. The creak of floorboards as booted feet moved across them; the rustle and crackle of hay being disturbed by mice and other small creatures, which I had to work to ignore; and the soft pad of innumerable cat's feet. Barn cats usually outnumbered the horses by at least two to one, even in Caer Dathyl.

"Why the stables?" I asked, lifting into the air, and soaring above the trees in delight. Clean, fresh air beneath my wings, sharp colours and the distant sound of trilling bells proclaimed that we'd at last reached freedom. Goronwy spread his wings but didn't leave Euyd's shoulder.

"Because having walked this far, I might not always feel the need to continue on foot. This time, however, I don't need a steed." He stopped and took a step towards the stable door, frowning.

"There are none. Where are the horses?" Goronwy's question was sharp.

He was right. No snorting, snuffling, whinnying, as would normally greet the arrival of strangers, issued from the building. Instead, I heard the whines and howls of a number of dogs in the distance. The clatter of running boots grew louder, and moments later a tall woman with a wealth of elaborately braided fair hair and a smooth, ageless face burst into the yard.

"Ianaura." Euyd gripped her by the arm as she tried to rush past him. "What's going on?"

"The Underworld and the Otherworld are colliding, and it's about to put my patients at risk." She pushed a stray strand of hair away from her face, picked up her trailing skirts and took off again, throwing over her shoulder, "Well, come on! Are you planning to help, or not?"

"What patients?" Euyd fell into a jog beside her, and Goronwy lifted into the air. "Do you mean the king and queen? And what are you doing out here?"

"Delivering a message from Lady Meg to Heilyn, the arms master. And yes, I do mean our royals. It took them some time to recover, but although they've finally revived, I want to keep them under observation for a while. Lady Meghan and Lord Blei are watching over them at the moment. And now Gwydion's turned up with a pack of the Cwu Annwfyn on his tail. I need to get back to them before he can."

More spine-chilling barks and growls punctuated her speech, lending weight to her words. I shuddered. The hounds of Annwfyn, like the other guardians of that realm, were employed by their lord to ensure that none left without his approval. I hadn't considered, until then, how greatly Goronwy and I had been honoured. Arawn himself had overseen our arrival and our departure.

Euyd cocked his head, listening. "It sounds as if he has other things to worry about right now."

"Maybe, but after hearing Meg's story, I'd prefer not to take any chances." Ianaura skidded around a corner, pounded across a stretch of open ground and through an open archway, and halted in her tracks. A writhing crimson mist enveloped her, thick as the fog of an Ardudwy winter. "Beli's balls and Mother's tits. I can't see!"

I could.

Ahead, in a natural corridor between a row of conifers, I beheld a nightmarish vision. Backed against a weeping cypress, Gwydion held a pulsing globe of red light in each hand, weighing them as if about to throw. Facing him stood four of Arawn's red-eared hounds, their satin-white coats spectrally glowing. On all fours, each one stood as high as Gwydion's shoulder; on their hind legs they'd tower above him. Several leather-clad warriors lay on the surrounding ground, lax-limbed and with their eyes closed.

"Turn back," I sent to Euyd. *"Get the healer out of here. Gwydion's using magic to fight off the hounds, and the only guardsmen I can see—Math's, I imagine—are unconscious. I can hear their heartbeats, so none are dead. Yet."*

Goronwy hadn't wasted time talking, but swept through the haze, long legs and talons extended as if seeking prey—namely Gwydion. He might have connected, too, if one of the hounds, unable to distinguish friend from foe and acting on canine instinct, hadn't seen him. The massive dog pivoted on its haunches and leapt into the air, its gnashing teeth slicing through the tip of his tail. A couple of tail feathers floated downward, dyed by the light from tawny to red.

My screech of alarm drowned out Goronwy's pip of surprise, competing with the dog's snarls and Gwydion's curses.

"I'm all right," he sent, *"just a bit off balance. Keep away from the hounds—they're primed to attack anything that gets between them and their quarry. And don't you dare take Gwydion on by yourself. I'll see if I can fetch Euyd back."* He tilted unsteadily and fluttered upwards to a branch of the tree directly above Gwydion.

The other three hounds milled aimlessly for a moment, allowing Gwydion time to regroup. Piping, high and shrill, I dived at him with talons extended.

"Blodeuedd, no! I told you not to." Goronwy dived toward me, the lead hound leaped at Gwydion, and Euyd reappeared with a wolf on one side and a bear on the other.

I swerved to avoid the hound, which sank its teeth into Gwydion's thigh with a satisfying crunch. The wolf, whom I presumed to be Bleiddwn, confronted the other three dogs, stiff-legged and snarling. The bear rose to its—her?—full height and roared, lips drawn back and teeth bared, but made no move to attack.

Unsure what to do and unwilling to risk getting in their way, I joined Goronwy in the cypress.

"Enough!" Euyd clapped his hands together, producing a gust of icy wind which dispersed the red haze and ruffled the pelts of both the bear and the wolf. The sleek-coated, red-eared hounds narrowed their eyes against the blast and lowered their ears. The one with Gwydion's leg in its mouth released him. Shuddering, he collapsed onto his side.

Taut with tension, I almost fell off my perch when the harsh, reverberating note of the war-horn sounded. It pealed through the trees, bouncing from one to another and levelling the Cwu Annwfyn as thoroughly as a pack coming face-to-face with a lion. Then the lion himself strode into view.

King Math had fully recovered. Behind him swept his queen, followed by Ianaura.

"You need a healer—let me see that." She bustled forward and bent to inspect Gwydion's wound, before nodding brusquely to Euyd. "See to them, will you? I assume you know how to assess for injuries?"

"Of course." He crooked a finger at Meghan and Wolf-boy, both half-changed back to human, and knelt by the nearest of the fallen guard. "First check for a pulse, then for obvious wounds and broken bones, but don't move them until the healer agrees. Got that?"

Meg nodded and competently set to work, following his instructions. Bleiddwn glared at him before joining her. "I have done this kind of thing before, you know."

It became plain that the warriors felled by Gwydion's magic had suffered no permanent harm. The same could not be said of Gwydion. Uncharacteristically silent, he made no protest as Ianaura cleaned and bound his injury. I wondered if she always carried bandages and salves with her, or if she could summon them as needed.

"You can come down now, my warrior owls," said Queen Wynne, in my head. Heart pounding against my ribs, I swooped to perch on her outstretched, gloved arm. My mate followed to alight on her shoulder, his flight still somewhat erratic.

"What's wrong with Gwydion?" I asked. *"Is the hound's bite venomous, enough to affect even one of Don's children?"*

"Not as such," replied Math, overhearing. "But just as a dog's bite can poison a human, so the hounds of Annwn can infect us. He'll recover under Ianaura's care, but just to be sure he doesn't do so too quickly and disappear..." A twist of his hand manifested a coil of bright purple rope, which he knotted around Gwydion's wrists, tying his hands together.

I wondered why he hadn't used that on Lleu, then realised Lleu would have burnt through it, as he'd eventually destroyed the raven-feather cloak. Math nodded to the others and continued aloud. "Heilyn's coming around. I'll let him take care of his men; the rest of you, follow me."

He snapped his fingers at the cringing hounds, and I gave a short hoot of surprise. Surely, he couldn't mean them, too.

But he did. One after the other they slunk to him, then rolled over, presenting their undersides in submission. Math squatted down and rubbed each canine belly in turn, before fondling their ruby-red ears. He rose, and so did the hounds, tongues lolling and as docile as any noble lady's spoilt lapdogs.

Caer Dathyl being what it was, we didn't have to go far. Unfortunate, in a way; I could have done with more time to collect my thoughts and get my disordered breathing under control. Not to mention my stampeding heart.

Math halted outside a large pair of carved, double oak doors, black with age. Wynne rapped a tune on the raven-shaped brass knocker with her free hand, paused for a second, and added several more staccato beats. We waited for several moments, while the dogs whined and danced. At last the doors fanned open, and we entered King Math's Audience Chamber.

Otherworldly kings obviously aimed to impress when conducting their royal business. The room was huge, in breadth as well as height, and tastefully decorated in shades of deep blue and gold, accented in places with ivory. Shell-shaped lamps set at intervals along every wall made the place as bright as day. Overhead it boasted a fretted, painted ceiling, and fine woven rugs complemented the colour scheme. A couple of upholstered couches and an array of fringed and padded cross-legged stools on either side of the hall.

An impressive throne, currently unoccupied, dominated the far end of the room. The image of a dragon curved along its back, its wings and claws forming the armrests. Gold, or well-polished bronze, glinted in its scales, and ivory formed its teeth, claws, and bone ridges.

Ianaura guided the unresisting Gwydion to the couch and bade him sit. He complied, still looking dazed. She then turned her attention to Math and Wynne.

"My lord, my lady, I'm so relieved you're fully recovered." She exhaled a noisy breath and crossed both hands over her collar before becoming businesslike again. Stepping up to Math, she waved a hand in front of his face, index finger curled over her thumb. "I'm not sure all this frantic activity's good for you, though. How many fingers am I holding up? Do you have a headache, nausea, ringing in the ears, anything like that?"

He pushed her away. "Three, and I'm fine. We're both fine. No thanks to Gwydion, I suspect."

"Dragon dust," murmured Gwydion groggily. "Knocked you out for a while. Should have kept some with me... it might have proved useful against this lot, magnificent beasts though they are." He jerked his chin at his bandaged thigh, through which a faint red line showed. "A bit inclined to nip, I fear, but you can never blame the dog, can you? The fault always lies with the master."

Wynne gave a snort of disgust or derision, and Math smiled wryly. "The hounds are tasked with ensuring nobody leaves their master's domain without his permission, which is rarely given. They were trying to herd you back to Annwyfn, where Arawn would no doubt imprison you. Perhaps I should let them. What were you doing there? Looking for Lleu, I suppose."

"I found no trace of Lleu," said Gwydion. "It appears Arawn acted quickly."

"And pleased I am to hear it." His pace deliberate, Math approached the throne and sat down, facing the room. Fingers drumming on the right-hand paw of the dragon-chair, he surveyed us, his expression stern. "Take a seat, everyone. This could take a while."

Gwydion's face tightened and his eyes narrowed, but he made no reply.

"In some respects," continued Math, "my family and mortal men are alike. Some are born with more power, more potential for greatness than others. Not all fulfil that potential. The nephew you see before me is one such." His flat gaze bored into Gwydion. "All your life you've tested the boundaries, making mischief, causing harm. And always, I forgave you, because I sensed the seeds of greatness within. Teilo said once that he couldn't but acknowledge your gift, and I, perhaps foolishly, agreed with him. So did many others. The world's greatest storyteller, men call you. The poet's god."

His fingers ceased their drumming, and he pointed an accusing finger at Gwydion. "I allowed you to raise Lleu because your actions left his mother too fragile to do so. I thought, also, that caring for a child might temper your recklessness. Perhaps it did, for a while, but lately I think that trait has increased.

"You no longer have a place here, nor do you belong in the realm of the dead. I won't send you back to Arawn, but neither can you remain in the Otherworld. You must take up the mantle of godhood and return to mortal lands as the lord of poets and songsmiths. Use your gifts for the benefit of others, instead of their detriment."

"What!" I squawked from my perch on Wynne' wrist. *"That's not fair—you'll put people at risk. They have no defences against him. Can't you imprison him here?"*

The queen shook her head. "You had to commission your architect to build such a place to house Cara, remember. If Ardudwy lacked such a system, that holds doubly true for Caer Dathyl. Besides, the source of his power lies here. It will steadily decrease in exile, making him less and less dangerous over time. And don't think he can ignore this edict as he's done all the others. I can and will seal all entrances against him. I've been too lenient in the past, respecting my sister's wishes. But now, even Don's had enough."

A malicious smile playing about his mouth, Gwydion struggled to his feet. "Very well, but I'd prefer to choose the time and place of my exit, if it's all the same to you. That is, here and now." He lifted his bound hands. "Do you mind doing the honours? I'm afraid I'm a little tied up."

Math nodded and clapped. A portal appeared less than three feet in front of Gwydion, who stepped towards it.

He turned on the threshold and raised his hands, still tied together, then crooked a finger at the two young ones, standing closest to him. "All right, children. Let's go."

"No, you don't." Another clap from Math, and a blaze of violet light cut Gwydion off from the rest of the room. "Where you go, my lad, you go alone."

With a roar of frustrated fury, Gwydion spun away and dived towards the portal. Before anyone realised what was happening, the leader of the Cwu Annwfyn lunged after him. Several hundred pounds of solid muscle punched through Math's shield as if it were paper and barrelled into its fleeing prey.

Gwydion's injured leg gave way, and as he twisted and fell, a glass vial tumbled out of his vest pocket. Its glittering, powdery contents floated free, coating those closest to him—the youngsters and the dog, as well as the portal—in the last of his dragon dust.

A wail of anguish cut through the collective gasp of dismay. Wynne flung out her hands, sending me squawking and flying, and stumbled toward Meghan and Bleiddwn.

Tiny spheres of light, like glittering grains of multi-hued sand, circled around them, and with each revolution, they dissolved into the light. In vain, Math, whom the dust hadn't touched, reached for his daughter and nephew, weaving desperate sigils and shouting spell after spell.

It had no effect. Spiralling forward, their essence flowed after Gwydion. A stunned silence encased the room, and the portal snapped shut behind them.

35

DRAGONS

M ath's second portal blazed into existence and snarled at the heels of the first, but the laws governing such things decreed that one could not follow too closely upon another.

"You just had to pontificate, didn't you?" Wynne's voice could have skinned an afanc. "Giving him time to plot, and to plan. Now he's stolen our children!"

Math stroked her hand. "We'll discuss this later, cariad."

"I don't have time for later! What happened to them? How could they just—flicker away like that? Are they dead? Oh," her voice broke, "Lady Mother, Mother of All, please tell me they're not dead. Please, please, don't let them die."

Grim-faced, Math clasped her to him, his gaze trained on the rent forming in the veil in front of us. Portals usually took a couple of heartbeats to form, but I counted at least eight before this one took shape. Perhaps because Math made it large enough and tall enough for all ten of us to exit together—four people, four hounds, and two owls soaring above.

The outline of another portal glinted directly in front as I swooped through. A shout from Euyd halted my dive towards it, while the remaining Cwu Annwfyn kept bounding forwards.

"Uncle! Oh, no, please no. Not again." The baying hounds almost drowned out his voice.

"My lord—my lady!" Ianaura's voice echoed Euyd's, with the same note of dismay.

I swivelled back to see first Math, then Wynne freeze in mid-step.

"He's getting away!" Goronwy sped toward Gwydion's portal, but the remaining hounds of the Underworld reached it before him.

The resulting roar and blaze of light fractured the air beneath me and sent Goronwy somersaulting across the sky. A glimmer passed over the coats of the dogs, and with a yowl worthy of their master himself, they one by one flickered and disappeared. The portal collapsed in on itself until it too faded from view.

Terror ripped through me. *Goronwy!*

My fright eased as he levelled out, and by the time I reached him he'd landed, a little shaken but unharmed.

"You have the gods' own luck," I said, chiding. I'd never felt my lack of arms so keenly; I wanted to wrap them around him and hug him tight.

He chuckled. *"No more than you."*

We sat there for long moments, trembling, before Goronwy rose into the air again. Without saying anything more, he swept upwards, high above the sparkling, crackling rent left by the vanished portal. I left him to it and turned back towards Math and Wynne.

"Arawn!" Euyd clapped sharply and added a string of syllables which had the cadence of poetry but belonged to no language I knew. He finished with, "Lord of Annwyfn, I summon thee."

Another rent appeared in the fabric of reality, as dark as the smoke from a campfire. Arawn stepped through, darkness personified, wrapped in endlessly shifting shadows. Darkness scowled, exuding annoyance. "What have you done to my dogs, pup? And where's the excrescence I sent them to fetch?"

"Gwydion's gone, and I don't know what became of your dogs." Euyd's voice shook, but his flaring nostrils and clenched fists signalled anger, not fear.

"Oh, they're fine," said Arawn, with a wave of his hand. "A little shinier than usual, but that's naught to worry about. I'd like to know how they came tumbling back into my realm in such a state, though."

Wrath emanated from Euyd in waves. He gave a synopsis of recent events, and finished by stabbing a finger towards Math. "This is because of that damn dust—it has to be. Modwenna said you know more about what this means, and I demand you tell me. Now."

Head tilted to one side, shadows and smoke writhing around him, Arawn approached Math and peered into the king's eyes. I circled, looking for a place to land, and finally selected a tree about six feet away. Goronwy continued to fly, around and around the site of Gwydion's vanished portal.

"The Old Ones were rumoured to move through time as well as space," Arawn said, waving a finger in front of Math's face, much as Ianaura had done earlier. "That's partly why they were so feared. They came and went without warning. One moment the skies would be clear, the next, full of ravening, flame-breathing beasts."

"What does that have to do with King Math's predicament?" I asked.

Arawn looked up. "Ah, little owl, come closer." He held up a wrist, ungloved. "Gather round," he continued, as I glided down to him, "and let me tell you a story."

"We don't have time for bardic nonsense," Euyd sputtered. "Gwydion's gone, and so have my nephew and cousin. We need to find Gwydion and the two youngsters he's kidnapped and restore the king and queen. Just tell us whatever you know."

Like a man inspecting a statue he was considering purchasing, Arawn described a slow, smooth circuit around first Math, and then Wynne.

"Long and long ago," he continued, indifferent to Euyd's protest, "there was a tale often told, of two brothers. Their names were Lludd and Llefelys, and the bards called them kings. In truth, they were dragonwatchers, gatekeepers for the great beasts, an office far above that of mere kingship."

Ianaura sucked in a breath. "I know this one. It's about a conflict between a couple of dragons, one red and one white. So, which did the bones belong to, that formed Gwydion's dragon dust?"

If Arawn had glared at me the way he did her, I swear I'd have shed all my feathers in fright.

Ianaura paled a little but held her ground. "It's the dust that concerns us, my lord, not ancient fables."

"Not fables. History. I speak only truth." The shadows peeled away from Arawn and formed into the likeness of a dragon. "A lot of nonsense accumulated around their exploits, as it always does in the tales told by men. For instance, it was said a race called the Coranieid became great enemies of Lludd, which is untrue. If I tell you that the greatest of the dragons was called Coraniei, I'm sure you can work out the rest."

The shadows separated and reformed into several winged beasts of smaller size. "The entire sky was their domain, not any one section of earth, but these lands were their breeding grounds. These, and no others." Arawn turned to point a finger at Euyd. "Tell me, son of Beli, what colour were they?"

Euyd shrugged. "Red or white, I assume. So your tale tells, anyway."

"No." The shadows regrouped again and became two dragons. A wave of Arawn's hand, and red bled into the grey. "Dragons are distant kin to the wyrms and the serpents, who are rarely, if ever, born white. The majority were shades of red—plum, russet, ruby, rust, sometimes edged with bronze or very rarely gold, but never white."

A snap of the Underworld Lord's fingers, and a bright white, vertical line appeared in the air. "Pray tell me, what is that?"

"A portal," snapped Euyd. "A rent in the veil. Is there a point to all this?"

Arawn chuckled. "And I thought mortals were impatient. Bear with me, son of Beli. I'm explaining your uncle's dilemma. You see, dragons are magical beasts, but must learn how to use their gifts through trial and error, just as humans do. They early learned how to move through the veils which separate the mortal world from other realms, but being insatiably curious creatures, they pushed even further.

"As I mentioned, they discovered they could manipulate the portals to shift through time. Not a lot: usually only a few dozen heartbeats, which for a dragon is ten times that of a man. So they'd lift into the sky, shift back in time and steal sheep, pigs, or cattle, and no one would know they were coming. Such raids didn't happen often, because on the whole they preferred fish. But it was enough to strike fear into the populace and embolden them to take their concerns to Lludd."

His audience had fallen silent. Both Euyd and Ianaura seemed as enthralled with the story as I was. I wished Goronwy would return to hear it, sure that I'd leave out something vital if I had to retell it for him later. I tried to relay Arawn's words to him as I listened but found it too hard to concentrate. He was now just a speck in the distance, soaring below the clouds.

"Lludd sought help from his brother Llefelys," said Arawn, "who facetiously advised him to introduce the dragons to mead to replace their taste for fresh meat with that of honey. Lludd wasn't foolish enough to try that, and I could have told him it wouldn't have worked. Dragons have a prodigious capacity for liquor.

"But on to the white dragon." Arawn waved his hand again, and the red smoke dragons coiled around the white line. That it had remained undisturbed during the story's telling proved how different it was from the norm. I'd heard it took effort to hold the veils open; left to themselves they'd either dissipate or snap closed.

"Have I mentioned that dragons are not only highly intelligent, but also revel in novelty?" asked Arawn, as the smoke faded to nothingness. "They agreed to Lludd's request, but being deprived of one form of entertainment, they sought another—experimenting with the time portals. They gradually increased their range from moments to days, weeks and finally months. But extended travel took a toll on them, one they hadn't foreseen."

Ianaura's brows furrowed. "They turned white? I don't see how…"

"Not exactly." He gestured to the stationary portal, which had defied every natural law I knew to remain visible throughout this long speech. "It detached them from reality, made them briefly transparent. When people saw them silhouetted against a portal such as that one, rumours began of a white dragon. Still they continued to experiment, and many died trying to leap years or even longer, leading to more stories of unearthly screams." His face clouded. "Lludd laid those who perished to rest in Dinas Emrys, in the shadow of Yr Wyddfa.

"There the story ends. The next part is conjecture on my part but would account for what happened to King Math and his queen. Even reduced to dust, the dragon's bones still have the power to move through time. Perhaps Math's initial exposure in the cave made him susceptible to it, leaving him vulnerable to whatever spell Gwydion used. I hear Goewin had been fooling about with time, and that would have put her at risk too. Her being mortal wouldn't help, either."

"Then why did they revive when they returned to Caer Dathyl?" I asked.

Arawn sighed. "Dragons and their magic arose in this realm; it holds no sway in the Other or Underworlds. Take these two back home and they'll be perfectly fine. But whenever they try to step into the mortal realms, I suspect the same thing will happen. They'll be trapped in a time bubble, making the world appear to whirl around them at dizzying speed."

"So how do we free them?" I persisted.

"That I can't tell you, little owl. Perhaps it will wear off," a smile twisted his mouth, "with time. The other option would be to confront Gwydion and persuade him to reverse whatever he did." He shrugged. "Good luck with that one. And now that I've answered your questions, I'll bid you farewell. I wish Gwynedd's king and queen a speedy recovery, and I do mean that sincerely."

"Wait!" I hooted for emphasis, and the Lord of the Underworld lifted his dark brows and bent on me a look of patient enquiry. *"Is Lleu truly gone? Have removed him from this plane, as you threatened?"*

"No, little owl. As I promised. You have nothing to fear from Lleu Llaw Gyffes for a good long while." He wrapped his shadows around himself and vanished.

Deprived without warning of my perch, I flapped like a fool before drifting to the ground. A speck in the distance got larger.

"What happened? What did I miss?" asked Goronwy, gliding to a stop beside me.

I fluffed my feathers. *"Arawn gave us a history lesson, and now we're taking Math and Wynne home. Did you find out anything?"*

"No," he said, as Euyd and Ianaura parted the veil and guided the royal couple back to Caer Dathyl. *"All trace of the explosion, or whatever it was, had gone completely by the time I reached it, but it left an odd sound behind. A kind of vibrating hum I've never heard before around portals. Not that I'm an expert, I suppose."*

"I've never heard of anything like that," said Euyd when we arrived back in Math's Audience Chamber. He settled his aunt and uncle on a couch and knelt beside them, waiting for signs of movement. It wasn't long coming.

Wynne was the first to stir, jerking upright and looking around her with wide eyes. "What happened? How did we get back here so quickly when we'd just arrived in the mortal world?"

"Time slowed for us," said Math, shaking himself like a dog and rising to his feet. "I have a vague recollection of a portal blowing up before Arawn appeared. He sketched dragons in the air and rattled on for a while—about what, I don't know. I couldn't understand him; his speech was too fast for me to follow. What did he say?"

Tersely, Euyd related the story, stripping it back to bare bones and eliminating the embellishments. "The dust Gwydion used on you distorts time for you in the mortal world, although it has no effect here. But if you can't search for him, Uncle, rest assured there are others who will. Myself, Dylan, Ari...I promise we'll find them and bring Meg and Blei home. If...that is, if we can."

I knew what he meant. We all did. If any of them survive.

36

REGRETS

The birth of Modwenna's daughter Yseult marked a turning point in my life as an owl—the first of many. There were, after all, limited opportunities for men and women to interact with owls. We hunted together, often. Modwenna and I continued to converse, and she taught her daughter how to optimise her gift and talk to me as well. But although we were close neighbours, we lived different lives in very different worlds.

Still, I kept tabs on them all—Cynar and Delith, Yestin and Modwenna, as well as Goronwy's numerous kin. They were my true family, of a different order to the ties I shared with Math and his relatives. Even when I wore feathers, the trees surrounding Mur Y Castell welcomed me more than in any Otherworldly fortress.

But nothing stayed the same forever, and over time, our paths diverged even further. Cynar eventually entered the priesthood of Arianrhod and moved to Ynys Môn to join his brother's household. His sons grew to manhood there, and both Garth and Pyrs married women from Eriu, across the Irish Sea. The Erinnish had always encouraged Otherworldly connections, and whether Cynar's new calling was the catalyst or whether it came as a gift from Garth's wife, his descendants shared the ability Modwenna and Yseult had inherited from Dafona of the birds.

Free of Lleu's threatening presence, Yseult also grew up, married, and had sons and daughters of her own.

She became great friends with Oonagh, who, with Dylan, continued to pay regular visits to Mur Y Castell. Unlike the other friends of my heart, those two never aged. And they never ceased searching for Gwydion, Meghan, and Bleiddwn.

"I don't understand how they could have vanished so thoroughly," said Oonagh, at Yseult's youngest daughter's nuptials. Yestin and Modwenna were known to be very attached to their pair of trained hunting owls, and nobody raised an eyebrow to see one at their granddaughter's wedding. "I know the world is wide, but my people inhabit all the world's oceans, and we've asked among all the clans. Surely somebody, somewhere, would have heard something after all these years."

Modwenna shook her head, her expression solemn. "Dylan says the same thing about his enquiries in the Otherworld. It would be unlike Gwydion to be discreet, especially for so many years. He creates drama wherever he goes. You don't suppose..."

She hesitated, and I filled in the thought for her. We'd both had it several times throughout the years, but never voiced it to others. *"That he's dead? I'd welcome that news, providing the same isn't true of Meghan and Bleiddwn. I might not be especially fond of Wolf-Boy, but I don't wish him harm. I know how much that news would sadden Math and Wynne."*

No one responded, because we all knew sadness fell far short of the storm of emotions which swept over Wynne whenever those two names were mentioned. Math wasn't immune either, although he concealed it better.

When all the marriage rites were completed, the toasts drunk, and the feasting finished, I left the humans to their revelry and flew back to the nest where Goronwy waited. There, I took out the small strip of iridescent snakeskin which Math had given me so long ago. Modwenna had removed it from the locket for me, and it was all I ever used now to visit Caer Dathyl.

"Do you suppose Math foresaw his gift being put to this use?" asked Goronwy as the rainbow scales began to glow.

I hooted softly. "I *don't know. I'll have to ask him when I see him."* Snakeskin gripped tightly in my talons, I transitioned smoothly into the Otherworld.

Enfys always greeted me on these visits, but as she was either attached in shrunken form to Math's wrist or, as now, coiled full-size close to Wynne, I had no cause for complaint. She'd never made a move to attack me, and sometimes even failed to notice my arrival. I settled beside the queen on the arm of her stone bench.

"How long has it been for you?" she asked, glancing up from petting the serpent.

The surrounding glade fluctuated between autumn gold and glinting frost as I watched, finally settling on a palette of russet, beige, and mahogany. A panorama of low hills in the distance echoed the same colours, interleaved with faded berry and sharp green. Spring seldom visited Caer Dathyl anymore, and summer never.

"A little over fifty years. And for you?" We had the same conversation every time I visited, and while my answers varied, hers never did.

Wynne shrugged. "Weeks, months, years maybe. I can't tell anymore. The days slide into one another and all look the same. Tell me, how are Cynar and Delith, and all the rest of our friends?"

She listened, smiling and nodding occasionally, as I caught her up on all the news. Our talk then moved on to the wider world, to the doings of other nations far beyond the borders of Cymru. Eventually, as always happened, the talk circled back to Gwydion.

"There's been no word, of course." She made it a statement, not a question. If I had news to tell her, good or ill, I'd have arrived with trumpets blaring. Or as close to them as owlsong would allow.

"No. But even though I wish it was true, I don't think it can be. Because if he were truly gone, wouldn't the tynged he put upon me have lifted? I'd expect to become a woman again, and as you can see, that hasn't happened."

Wynne shrugged. "Perhaps. Perhaps not. A tynged is as much a vow, a destined outcome, as it is a curse. It may be that there's some other condition which must be fulfilled to release you from this fate. And if they did survive, we surely would have had some word by now. Sometimes I think it's better not to hope. Hope only keeps the pain alive."

I ducked my head. *"I'm... I'm so sorry."*

"Don't be. None of this is your fault."

"Something's always puzzled me," I said, hoping to lead the conversation into less painful channels. *"Perhaps you could explain it. Why did the dust affect you and Math, but not Gwydion or anyone else?"*

Wynne shook her head. "Whatever else Gwydion is, he's certainly no fool. He may not have known exactly what effect the dust would have, but he'd have been sure to safeguard himself against it. A form of invisible armour, if you like. Everyone else was too far away, and Arawn would be immune to dragon magic."

Giving Enfys a final pat, she rose and attempted to smile. The corners of her lovely mouth lifted, but her eyes remained dark pools of sorrow. "Do continue to fly in now and then, Blodeuwedd. I enjoy your visits; they serve as a link to another, happier time. Before Lleu's exile and all the drama that followed." She reached out to stroke my head, much as she'd done with the snake. "I'd ask that you keep me informed, but of course I know you will. Goodbye, Blodeuwedd."

I recognised a dismissal when I heard it. Our discussions always ended thus, with Wynne retreating into her cocoon of sorrow. I bade her farewell and used the skin to return to Ardudwy.

The same pattern repeated, over and over, throughout the long years. Wherever Gwydion and his two hostages had gone, no trace of them remained in either of our worlds.

Time passed, and all those I knew and loved quit the mortal realms for the Moonlands of Emania. I did not mourn them, for I knew their souls endured and would be reborn again. Some maintained that friend and family ties remained intact through different lifetimes, but if that were so, none ever recognised me, or I them.

My islands changed immensely throughout the centuries, as light flickered in the darkness. From hubris to humility, from insignificance to greatness, and back to irrelevance again. New kings and princes took power, wrested it from each other, gained it back and went to war. Again and again, they fought incessant, bloody wars. From time to time they'd take their bloodshed and their power struggles far from these shores, to the distant corners of the earth, but neither Goronwy nor I paid attention to that. Gwydion's magic bound us to Cymru, in what had once been considered the far western corner of the world.

I saw the last of the legions depart and the Saxon hordes overtake our green isles, followed by the Norsemen, the Angles, the Jutes and the Danes. Unlike the Romans, these people never retreated, but intermingled and interbred with my own folk, the British. And always, always, I quizzed the newcomers for news of Gwydion. He was out there somewhere, I knew it.

I had known great happiness, and thanks to Gwydion ap Don I was well acquainted with misery. Since that day by the Cynval, when he'd turned me into an owl, I'd developed a gift for patience and a keen appetite for vengeance.

I'd continue to fly through the moonlit forests at the side of my reborn love, and one day I and my allies would rescue Wynne's missing loved ones. Then, when they were safe, I'd make Gwydion regret he had ever made me.

I was the huntress of the night, and I was still immortal.

THE DRAGON'S CURSE

O ddly, being dematerialised and subsequently reassembled caused Blei no pain. It felt little different from transforming from human to beast form and back again, apart from happening more slowly. It was the indignity of being forcibly sucked through a portal in Gwydion's wake that ripped like a hook through Bleiddwn's gut. If he hadn't hated his father before the day of Math's judgement, when Gwydion had turned and run like a coward, he did now.

Although in incorporeal form, he was still aware of a second portal opening behind them. It disgorged his relatives and the healer, followed by a slavering trio of Arawn's deadly hounds. At first, they appeared as glittering motes of light, wavering and insubstantial, but they solidified in his sight as he too regained solid form. Undergoing the same process, Meg stumbled against him, and he put his hand out to steady her.

"Are you all right?"

Stupid, stupid question. They'd both been unmade and put back together again, courtesy of Gwydion's damnable dragon dust.

Meg shook her head, but the belling hounds of Annwfyn drowned out her answer. Blei barely had time to register the clash between the energies of the Underworld and those of his father's unnatural portal, when amid a shimmering cloud of dragon dust, the universe ruptured around them.

Deafening sound merged with a fury of eye-searing light. The world tilted and lurched. His stomach did the same, and a thousand war drums beat in his head. Dazed, nauseous, he tried to scream. All that emerged was a weak, strangled gasp.

Blackness closed in, and the world disappeared.

"Blei?" Sometime later—exactly how long, he couldn't tell—a soft hand touched his cheek. Meg said, "Blei, please wake up. I'm... I'm frightened."

He groaned, and the contents of his stomach rose, hot and vile, into his throat. "It's all right," he lied. "I won't let him hurt you."

"Believe it or not, for once Gwydion isn't the problem." Meg's voice shook, and Blei forced his gritty eyes open. A trace of tears marked her too-pale cheeks.

Blei pushed himself to sit up, registering an odd smell in the air and a dreadful, raucous noise, like a hundred squabbling seagulls competing with an angry owl.

"Where in Arawn's name are we?"

"Somewhere neither he nor Math will ever find us." Gwydion spoke from behind Meg, more self-satisfied than Blei had ever heard him. He jerked his chin at Blei. "Untie me."

Fists balled, he fought to oppose his father's orders. "What if I won't?"

"You can't help yourself. Hurry up and stop resisting, or I'll order you to punch sweet Meg in the face. Now, Bleiddwn."

Gwydion spoke truly. Against his will, Blei's hands uncurled and inched towards the rope. Rising unsteadily to his feet, he used mage-sight to tease the twisted knots apart, wishing he could instead wrap the cords around his cursed father's neck. He rubbed his temples to try to ease the ache in them and looked around.

They appeared to have arrived at their destination, wherever it was. It was still daylight but palls of smoke rolling across the horizon dimmed the blue of the sky. The landscape was almost completely de-void of trees, and odd, boxy buildings clustered around a long strip of even odder black paving. Along it trundled a peculiar-looking chariot, like an elaborate cart, drawn by a pair of large, heavy-set horses. Beyond that, winding through the hills like some monstrous serpent, shrieked the source of both the noise and the smoke.

Gwydion smiled, clasping his hands together, then threw his head back and laughed. "The dragon's dust performed just as I hoped, and the hound's interference didn't matter at all. The question you should be asking, my boy, isn't where, but when."

About the Author

Christiana Matthews is the author of the fantasy trilogy, Flowerface and Owlfeather, now available on Amazon, and Soulflight, due out in October 2023. She's also working on the Heirs of Samandahl series of novels and novellas.

Four short stories appeared in the Independent Press anthologies Bound in Blood, Trials by Tides (both by Zasra Press) and Fractured Folktales in 2021/22, and a flash fiction fantasy story in SFS Stories in February 2022. Two more, The Bequest and A Frog Among Princes, are due out in Zasra Press's Rogues and Redeemers anthology in March 2023.

Christiana lives in south-east Queensland, Australia, with her cats, Lilah, Onyx and Ulysses, and a constant stream of foster cats and kittens.

https://www.christianamatthews.com
https://www.instagram.com/christianahmatthews
https://www.facebook.com/ChristianaHMatthews
https://www.facebook.com/groups/starlightandshadows

More Books!

THE BLODEUEDD TRILOGY
FLOWERFACE
If you haven't already, read how it all began.
https://books2read.com/FF3112022
To be followed by TRICKSTER'S BANE, a duo of short stories about Goewin and Arianrhod, out in April 2023, and SOULFLIGHT, the final of the trilogy, to be published at the end of the year.

THE HEIRS OF SAMANDAHL
The first book in this series, Witch Queen, began as a retelling of Snow White, narrated by the (slightly) wicked stepmother, Grizel. The author's original intention was to continue with sequels based on other fairy tales, such as Rapunzel and Snow White and Rose Red, but the characters took over and outgrew their origin stories. The seeds are still there if you look closely, but the world which evolved is multi-layered and complex, owing more to the historical novels of Dorothy Dunnett, Georgette Heyer and Mary Stewart than the Brothers Grimm.

WITCH QUEEN
https://books2read.com/WQ2542022
and set in the same universe, one thousand years earlier:
THE KNIFE OF TRUTH
https://books2read.com/KoT172022

PURRANORMAL TAILS
A Fantastical Cat Anthology
Love cats? Love fantasy? This book contains both!
Twenty-one authors from all over the globe bring you a collection of stories and poems celebrating our feline friends.

All proceeds support cat charities in Australia and the USA.
https://mybooks.to/Purranormaltails

Future Titles

TRICKSTER'S BANE

If you'd like to know more about the backstory behind this trilogy, check out the novella Trickster's Bane, coming in late July. Comprising two short stories, The King's Footholder and Silver Wheel, it presents the stories of two of the three women who prove to be a thorn in the side of our Trickster, Gwydion. The first is the tale of Queen Goewin of the Raven Hair, the second is his sister, Arianrhod of the Silver Wheel. The third, of course, is Flowerface herself, whose story concludes in—

SOULFLIGHT

Journey with Blodeuwedd and Goronwy through the years, visiting the court of King Arthur, and finally arriving in now, the 21st century. Others have made the trip as well, notably a pair of dragons who are somewhat miffed to find Gwydion has stolen the remains of one of their brethren and used the dust for his own gain. Old friends and new must come together to try to defeat the Trickster once and for all, and restore the owl lovers to their former selves. Available October/November 2023.

OWLFEATHER
GLOSSARY OF WELSH GODS, PLACENAMES
AND OTHER TERMS

Alba	Scotland	Al-buh
Annwfyn	The Welsh land of the dead	ANooven
Ardudwy	Cantref (region) ruled by Blodeuedd	ArDUDwy
Arfon	A northern principality within Gwynedd	Arvon
Bara Brith	Tea cake made with dried fruit and spice	Bara Breeth
Caer	A fortress, citadel or castle	Ka-ir
Caer Arianrhod	Arianrhod's castle on Ynys Mon	Ka-ir AriAHNrod
Caer Dathyl	Math's Otherworldly castle	Ka-ir Dar-THILL
Caer Sidi	Ariahrhod's castle in the Arctic	Ka-ir See-dee
Calan Gaeaf	1 November, Irish Lughnasadh	Kallan Gay-av
Cantref	District	Kantrev
Cariad	Darling	KA-ree-ad
Cariad aur	Precious darling	KA-ree-ad Or
Cymru	The land of Wales	Kumry
Cymry	The Welsh people	Kumry
Cymric	of Wales	Kumric
Dyfed	Kingdom of southern Cymru	Duh-ved
Eiru	Ireland	Ay-roo
Emania	The Moonlands	Emaynia
Gwarch	Witch	GWARc
Gwarchod	Male witch, warlock	GWARcod
Gwynedd	A kingdom of North Wales	Gweneth
Hamartia	Achille's heel, fatal flaw .In Blodeuedd's world, a god meeting their hamartia is transformed into animal, sea creature or bird	Ha-mar-TIA
Iechyd da	Drinking salutation, cheers	Yacky-DAR
Llogyr	England	Hlo-GRES
Mur Y Castell	Blodeuedd's home, lit. walled castle	MEE-ver-Castesh
Prydain	The British Isles	Pre-DANE
Rheged	Cumbria and south-west Scotland	Rheg'D
Ynys Môn	An island kingdom of North Wales	Innis Mon
Yr Wyddfa	Mount Snowdon, in the north-west	Uhr Withva

Note: dd is pronounced as th, ff as f, f as v, ll as an aspirated l (sounds almost like sh or k), c as k, g is always hard, and ch is soft, more like sh.

CAST OF CHARACTERS (In order of appearance)
and
PRONUNCIATION GUIDE

Math ap Mathonwy	Magician god and King of Gwynedd	Math ap MaTHONwy
Gwydion ap Don	Ariahrhod's brother, Math's nephew	GWIdion ap Don
Blodeuedd	Flowerface. Created out of flowers as	BlODweth
(later Blodeuwedd)	a bride for Lleu Llaw Gyffes	BlodEYeth
Cynar ap Garnoc	Delith's husband, Blodeuedd's guardsman	Kynar ap Garnok
Delith ferch Yseult	Blodeuedd's handmaid and best friend	Delith verch Eesolt
Garth ap Cynar	Cynar and Delith's son	Garth ap Kynar
Modwenna ferch Dea	Another of Blodeuedd's ladies	ModWENna verch Dee
Goronwy Pebyr	Blodeuedd's mortal 2nd husband	GorONwy Pebeer
Yestin ap Dafydd	Modwenna's husband	Yestin ap Davith
Dylan Ail Don	Lleu's brother, Math's nephew	Dillon Ail Don
Cara ferch Mabli	Ex kitchenmaid, Gwydion's lover	Kara verch MabLEE
Goewin (also called Wynne)	Math's wife	Go-WIn Win
Mabli ferch Elen	Cara's mother	MabLEE verch Ellen
Heilyn	Math's Master of Arms	HYlin
Lleu Llaw Gyffes	Avatar of the sun god, son of Arianrhod, son and nephew of Gwydion	Lhai Lhau Gefes
Meghan	Math and Wynne's daughter	MegAN
Bleiddwn	Wolf shifter, one of Gwydion's sons	BliTHIN
Arianrhod - Gwydion's sister	Goddess of the Silver Wheel,	AriAHNrhod
Arawn	God of the Underworld	AR-own
Pyrs ap Cynar	Second son of Delith and Cynar	Peers ap Kynar
Rhun Pebyr	Goronwy's youngest brother	Rheen Pebeer
Euyd ap Don	Gwydion's younger brother	Ay-EE-d
Ianaura	Chief healer at King Math's court	Yan-OUR-ah

GODS AND GODDESSES
Mentioned but not appearing

Beli, Beli Mawr	Don's consort	Belly Mour-er
Dôn	The Mother Goddess, mother of Gwydion, Sister of Math	Don
Artio	The bear goddess, one of the Elder Gods	AR-tee-o
Manawydan	Welsh god of the sea	Man-ow-a-DUN

ANIMALS

Taran	Blodeuedd's deerhound	Tahren
Glas	Goronwy's dogs	Glass
Dawelo	" "	Daywello
Cochach	" "	Kokach
	" "	
Chynwyrn	Arianrhod's wolf	Chin-WIRN
Sipsi	Arianrhod's wolf	Sip-SEE
Enfys	Math's serpent	EN-viss
Gwenhwyfar	Arianrhod's snowy owl	Gwen-HUI-var
Taffy	Horses	Taffee
Gyso	"	Gyso
Cant	"	Cant
Rhosyn	"	RoSIN
Manon	Faerie steed	Man-NON

Acknowledgments

Thanks to my critique teams, my alpha and beta readers, and friends both online and in person, who offered me advice and encouragement on this journey. I couldn't have done it without you.

As listed earlier, I owe my stunning cover to Uwe Jarling from Joolz and Jarling, and the type to Julie Nicholls.

My deepest gratitude goes to my editor, Emma from Emma's Edit, who polished the chunk of manuscript I gave her into a shining gem.

And although we're now scattered across the country, I can't finish without mentioned the bards of Caer Witrin. The ancient myths collected in The Mabinogion still resonate today, and find an echo in my writing.

Y Gwir yn erbyn y byd

The truth against the world.